PENGUIN BOOKS

THE SLEEP OF LIFE

Richard Gordon was born in 1921. He has been an anaesthetist at St Bartholomew's Hospital, a ship's surgeon and an assistant editor of the *British Medical Journal*. He left medical practice in 1952 and started writing his 'Doctor' series. He is married to a doctor; they have four children and live in a Victorian house in South London.

Richard Gordon's twelve 'Doctor' books have been made into seven popular films and have more recently inspired a long-running television series which enjoys worldwide success. He has published five other novels on medical themes and *Good Neighbours* – a witty observation of suburbia.

D0904443

Richard Gordon

THE SLEEP OF LIFE

PENGUIN BOOKS

Penguin Books Ltd, Harmondsworth, Middlesex, England
Penguin Books, 625 Madison Avenue, New York, New York 10022, U.S.A.
Penguin Books Australia Ltd, Ringwood, Victoria, Australia
Penguin Books Canada Ltd, 41 Steelcase Road West, Markham, Ontario, Canada
Penguin Books (N.Z.) Ltd, 182–190 Wairau Road, Auckland 10, New Zealand

—

First published by William Heinemann Ltd 1975
Published in Penguin Books 1976

—

Copyright © Richard Gordon, 1975

—

Made and printed in Great Britain by
Richard Clay (The Chaucer Press) Ltd, Bungay, Suffolk
Set in Monotype Baskerville

The novelist Guy Romilly was born at Purbeck Castle, Dorset, in 1825, and died at Putney, near London, in 1905. His reminiscences of the discovery of anaesthesia, and of medicine and medical men during the mid-1840s in London, Edinburgh and Boston, were written in 1900. They remained unpublished, at the author's wish, until the present day.

ROBERT LISTON WAS professor of clinical surgery at the North
London Hospital, a plain, four-storey, agreeably proportioned
building in sight of the new Doric arch of Euston Square
Station. The hospital had been founded some dozen years
before, less through charity towards the local sick than to
congregate them conveniently for medical students at University College opposite. That was the 'godless institution in
Gower Street' – Henry Brougham's 'Cockney College', open
to unbelievers in either God or even the Church of England,
and thus banished from the smiling banks of Cam and Isis. I
write now in the early days of 1900. But then, in the year
1846, both railways and atheistic education were startling
novelties.

The operating theatre at the new North London was built
next to the *post mortem* room for ease in teaching. The students
wandered freely from one to the other. The theatre was a filthy
place, no more thought in need of a scrub than a slaughter-
house. It was opposite the hospital's back door, which gave on
to an L-shaped yard always busy with doctors' carriages, carts,
drays, horses and dogs, the cobbles of one corner for ever
glistening under the pump. When Liston operated, the room
was always crammed. He was a Caesar, who bestrode the
narrow world of mid-nineteenth-century surgery like a
Colossus.

The theatre was a dozen yards across, the students entering
from a door at the top and filling up, as sand in the glass, the
four tiers of narrow benches which rose in a half-circle. Iron
bars provided an uncomfortable rest for the elbows, and a

decorative railing with a design of linked circles fenced the nearest spectators from the operating area, another two feet below the soles of their boots. By custom, the lowest tier was allotted to junior hospital staff and students taking the day's surgical cases – the 'dressers'. Inside the railing was an ordinary wooden bench, to afford senior doctors and visitors a better view. The audience faced a pair of sliding doors, to the right of which stood a tall, narrow mahogany cabinet, its seven drawers filled with Liston's instruments. A row of pegs alongside held the operating garb, discarded frock coats stiff with blood and stinking with pus, with a bibbed grocer's apron for the more progressive surgeons. To the left was a water-jug in a basin the size of a soup plate, for the operator to wash his hands afterwards.

The operating table itself was of plain polished deal, four and a half feet long with the flap let down at its foot. It stood two and a half feet from the floor on sturdy legs, bolted to the bare boards with angle irons. Its flat top was waisted to afford the surgeon better access, and under the thin straw mattress eight slots like keyholes ran along each edge. These were for straps to hold the patients down.

In those days when our Queen was twenty-six years old, and married for six of them, her Realm went back to work on the Monday after Easter. Lubbock's kindly Act, which gave us four extra mornings a year to lie abed, was a quarter-century in the future. It was the 13th, another cold and wet day in that cheerless April of 1846. It was the one I first met Robert Liston. Though our paths did not cross – very much at right angles – until that evening. I was later privileged to know both the surgeon and his workshop so well, that I may present him as he deserves, dominant in so formidable and forbidding a *milieu*.

By midday a watery sun had appeared, to dispel notions of the appointed surgery again being postponed through poor light. That afternoon held an attraction for the students of two 'capital' operations – as the more difficult ones were called. By one o'clock the theatre was already near full. As two passed, the lively chattering became hushed, as a theatre anticipates the curtain rising on some artificial and unhurtful drama. At a quarter past the hour, a purposeful click of heels came down the stone-flagged corridor outside. Liston entered at the head of four assistants.

'Good afternoon, gentlemen.'

The reply was barely more than a deferential murmur. Robert Liston was of that notably small company of men whose heroic mind and spirit is matched with an heroic frame. He stood six foot two, built like a prizefighter, going bald but his hair and side-whiskers hardly tinted by fifty-one years. His nose was long and bulbous-tipped, his chin clean-shaven, narrow and pointed. From his portrait in Edinburgh, which I have seen there in Surgeons' Hall, the mouth of his youth was as soft and sensuous as a woman's. Now it had grown into a line of no compromise. Under heavy brows his blue eyes raked the packed benches with the excusable arrogance of the superbly self-confident expert.

He wore his customary bottle-green coat with velvet collar, grey worsted trousers and the Wellington boots for which he had a celebrated fondness. His left thumb found through long habit the armhole of his double-breasted shawl waistcoat. Liston's hands were the feature which arrested the glance. They were huge, and claimed by his students to combine the controlled power of the pugilist 'Gentleman' Jackson with the delicate dexterity of the violinist Nicolo Paganini. He could amputate a leg under thirty seconds.

'The first capital operation, gentlemen, is excision of a tumour of the mamma.' His voice was Scots. He was from Ecclesmachan in West Lothian, son of the manse, his grandfather and great-grandfather, too, ministers of the Church.

Shoulder to shoulder, the students leant across the rails, eager to miss nothing with eye or ear. As Liston sometimes fired a question or two on the broad principles of surgery, each wondered if the professor's glance might fix on himself – with varying proportions of excitement or fright, depending how much he expected to shine or feared to fail.

'Bush, pray don't hide yourself.'

Liston picked on a yellow-haired, ruddy-faced student

3

in light trousers, with bright buttons on his sky-blue waistcoat. He was sitting in the furthermost row, and now seemed inclined to withdraw himself further.

'Bush, are you familiar with the name of Pierre-Joseph Desault?'

A silence. 'He is a Frenchman, sir.'

'I congratulate you on your skill in diagnosis.'

Bush's face turned redder, as the class roared. They wished to leave no doubt in the professor's mind whose side *they* were on.

'Even so, you have failed to disclose one important point. The unfortunate monsieur is dead.'

There was more laughter. Liston began slowly to cross the confined operating space, thumb still in armhole, his walk an easygoing amble, like a captain pacing his quarter-deck. 'But Monsieur Desault, whom we remember for his improvements in the treatment of fractures, bequeathed us an important surgical precept. *The simplicity of an operation is the measure of its perfection*. That saying has ever been my guide. Let it be yours.' He turned to business. 'Clover, the case history, if you please.'

Joseph Clover was the dresser, pale, serious, like most of the students in a black frock-coat. He stepped from his place behind the surgeon, opening Liston's long, leather-bound casebook with the air of an inexperienced curate about to read the lesson. The patient was Anne James, *aetat* twenty-nine, he related, in service as kitchenmaid in a gentleman's household. She was contented in her work. She slept in an attic room with four others. Her appetite was strong. Her food was of good quality. She was of regular habits, and temperate. The female health was good.

Clover turned a page. Six months ago she felt a lump in the right breast, while washing. Through the ignorance of her class, she had sought no consultation with a medical man until the present. On examination, the nipple was now retracted and fixed. The lump was the size of an orange, irregular and hard. The condition having been diagnosed as malignant, it was decided to operate.

4

The customary preparations were meanwhile progressing, so familiar as to go almost unnoticed by the onlookers. Liston's house surgeon Ransome, a burly man about thirty, had selected from the tall mahogany cabinet the necessary instruments – a scalpel, the long narrow bistoury curved at its tip, a a pair of hooklike tenacula, a handful of the bulldog artery forceps invented by Liston himself and bearing his name. There was a low, heavy chair beside the operating table, used by the surgeons performing lithotomy or the excision of piles, on which Ransome set these implements and covered them with a towel.

Young Clover finished the case-notes. 'Ready, Mr Ransome?' demanded Liston.

The house surgeon nodded, threading through his buttonhole a sheaf of ligatures cut from well-waxed hemp. Sheldrake the porter, a man as large as Liston himself, took the bottle-green coat from the surgeon's shoulders. Liston rolled up his shirt sleeves. His forearms were declared by his students to resemble legs of mutton hanging in the butcher's. 'Then have her brought in,' Liston ordered.

Ransome nodded in turn to the dresser, 'Run along, Clover.'

Clover disappeared through the sliding doors, making across the stone corridor and down a shorter one towards the front door leading into Gower Street. The North London had two large wards on the ground floor, approached through a cluster of anterooms from a cruciform lobby (where eight months later I was to make my acquaintance of both the hospital and Joseph Clover himself). He turned left towards Ward Two, allocated to females. Just outside the door, a pair of porters were waiting to scoop the woman from her bed and hasten her away on a stretcher. Once the sequence of an operation had been started, delay was as gratuitously cruel as before an execution. In those early months of 1846 there were no anaesthetics. Every stroke of the knife cut the consciousness with pain. Surgery was the alternative only of death, which was often the one preferred.

Clover told the porters, 'She'll walk.'

The woman was sitting on a bed beside the door. She was thin, chalk-white and large-eyed, her dark hair crammed into a mob cap. She wore the same gown of brown Holland in which she did her day's work.

'They are ready,' said Clover.

She stared at him, seeming not to understand who 'they' were, nor what they were about to do

'Did you take the laudanum?'

'It made me sick, sir,' she answered in a meek voice.

That always seemed the case, Clover thought impatiently. They prescribed a hundred, two hundred, even five hundred drops of laudanum to dull the pain of the knife, and the patients vomited it uselessly into the pail. The doctors were beginning to suspect this was not from simple irritation of the stomach, but an effect of the opiate itself on the brain.

'We must make haste,' Clover directed, trying to sound more than perfunctorily sympathetic.

He took the woman's arm, hurrying her along the flagstones to the theatre. As she came through the sliding door she stopped short, gasping, startled by the audience. Clover gripped her harder. 'It'll soon be over.'

As the patient appeared the benches became silent, the atmosphere solemn. Ransome and Clover laid the woman on the operating table, feet dangling over the end. Even in such adversity she made a pathetic automatic gesture, brushing down her skirt over her ankles. Two more students approached, positioned to hold her down. She started to whimper, her jaw quivering.

Ransome felt under her back, loosening the buttons of her gown, drawing it off her right shoulder to expose the diseased breast. The leather straps were secured, one across the lower part of her chest, the other tightly across her hips. Her right fist was now crammed in her mouth, her left hand pinioned by the strap, gripping the mattress hard enough to tear it. Clover tugged away the right arm, firmly crooking it over her head. She began to moan, writhing in her bonds.

To Liston, her eyes had an expression he knew well. They were no longer a human being's. When the sickly clutch of

6

overpowering fear holds the soul, its mirrors reflect nothing but the atavistic stare of a trapped animal. He leant over her. 'I shall be quick.'

The brusqueness of his voice had gone. The tyrant king at court had become the tender suitor. The tongue which served his students as a lash turned as ever into a silken cord which bound his patients to him. Liston's awareness of the knife's terror was sensitive and precise. Hidden under the enamel of his manner, this had driven him to perfect over a lifetime a skill which enabled him to operate twice as fast, and so inflict half as much pain, as any surgeon in the world.

The bistoury was held out to him, its curved point in Ransome's fingers. Liston took the ebony handle, milled for surer grip, testing the blade's keenness against his thumbnail, a gesture half automatic, fondly familiar to his students. He looked up. 'Now, gentlemen – time me, time me.'

He was vain. This famous speed must be proclaimed by a dozen applauding voices. The *claqueurs* were eager. Watches were drawn from every pocket as Liston leant over his patient. His huge thumb and index finger stretched the flesh across the malignant lump – a cut through taut skin was less painful. A flick with the bistoury, there was a slit four inches long beside the nipple. She did not start to scream until he swept a matching cut on its other side. But the audience were no more concerned than were the iron bars they leant on. Screams were as normal an accompaniment of an operation as the bleeding, and they fell upon ears and eyes numb to emotion. Those students had as much pity as ordinary men – more, or they would not have been impelled towards the sick. But their pity was practical. Where others sighed, or wept, or wrung their hands, they thought and ransacked their knowledge and acted.

Liston's knife, flicking and burrowing, dissected a tumour like the hard flesh of an unripe pear away from the fatty material of the breast. The toe of his beautifully-lacquered Wellington boot sought the box of sawdust, kicking it into position to soak the gathering shower of blood. He deepened his cut, to the chest wall itself. As the woman screamed

7

louder Ransome remarked to Clover, 'Give her the cordial. She's a bad patient.'

The cordial was a medicament which Liston had introduced from Scotland, a pint of strong whisky. But even as Clover reached for the bottle, the surgeon finished. Massive man drew away from frail woman. A bloody lump, one surface attached to an ellipse of skin with the deformed nipple at its centre, the other to beads of yellow fat, was dropped into the reddening sawdust.

'Two minutes twenty seconds, sir!' several voices cried at once.

'Two minutes sixteen!' shouted another.

'Two minutes and a quarter, sir!'

Liston smiled at this strange auction of his skill. He knew well enough that some students always declared him quicker than others, in the hope of drawing favourable attention. The cutting was over, but there was still work to do. He never prolonged the stage of dissecting away every fragment of the malignant tumour, which demanded caution and deliberation in the face of his urge for speed. Now the bleeding must be staunched. Liston took from Ransome's attentive finger-tips the bulldog forceps and strand after strand of waxed hemp, tying off bleeding arteries and veins, as a miller seals holes in a leaking sack of grain. Clover felt the arm go limp. 'She's fainted,' he observed.

Cold water was dashed on the wound. Strips of Liston's special isinglass plaster drew the oozing edges together. As the right arm was placed in a sling the woman's eyes opened. She stared round dumbfounded, unable to believe what had happened to her. The porters appeared with the stretcher. Liston wiped his hands on a towel. As she was borne away, she could escape from his thoughts. She became the responsibility of Clover. The surgeon's white shawl waistcoat was contaminated with a spot of blood, which Sheldrake busily removed with one of the sponges used, operation after operation, to dam the blood.

'That procedure, gentlemen, can also be performed in the sitting posture. A nurse or assistant supports the patient, a

8

jack-towel securing the pelvis, the surgeon standing behind. As he looks *down* at the wound, his view is less impeded by the bleeding.' The surgeon's eye travelled the benches. 'Lister —'

'Sir?' In the second row sat a handsome, square-jawed, dark youth just turned nineteen, humorously considered by his fellows to enjoy something of an honour in approximating the namesake of their professor.

'The differential diagnosis, if you please?'

Lister replied without hesitation, 'A cystic sarcoma, sir.'

'Had *that* been the unfortunate woman's condition, should we have had recourse to the last remedy? To an operation?'

'No, sir. A cystic sarcoma not being a malignant condition, we could leave it *in situ*.'

Liston's nod was the highest of praise. 'Had the lymphatic glands of the axilla been involved —' His thumb indicated his own armpit. 'Should I have operated?'

'No, sir.'

Another nod. 'Correct, Lister. To dissect away those glands in the axilla, to clear every scrap of malignancy, would take far too long. No surgeon in Europe would be rash enough to attempt it. Or cruel enough.' He threw the towel to the floor-boards, which were dirty, greasy, blood-soaked and sawdust-crusted. 'Simplicity, gentlemen.' He returned to his earlier, cherished theme. 'Apply it to your operations, to your dressings. Filthy unguents, greasy poultices, stimulating plasters, hot dressings, complicated bandages – eschew them as you would the breath of a leper. Substitute instead an unirritating isinglass poultice, and combine it with careful positioning of the injured part. Likewise with your armamentaria. Use *simple* instruments. Springs and grooves, sliding blades and notches, are only dodges which certain surgeons invent to compensate for their own want of manual dexterity, their own lack of *tact*.'

He used the word in its stricter meaning, sense of touch.

'But keep your tools in good order,' Liston continued the admonishment. 'Clean, bright and sharp. Heed the advice of Rionalaus, *Et prompta semper habeat instrumenta; nam in iis, penura detrimentosa est et artem inopem facit.*'

9

Liston was of an academic family, the eldest of two girls and two boys, his brother professor of Hebrew at the University of Edinburgh. A surgeon could afford the time and taste to be a classicist, in a period when his profession had not fled far along the distance from witchcraft to science. In the middle of the century just quit, he was a singular mixture of learned man and master butcher.

The next operation that afternoon of pallid sunshine was evisceration of the eye socket. The patient was laid on the table, Ransome grabbed his head, a dresser held open the blind and bulging eye. Liston took the eyeball in a pair of hooked forceps, drew it towards him, slit the outer angles of the lids, then with a narrow sharp-pointed knife scooped the bony walls to the depths of the socket, as though cleaning out his breakfast egg, pulled out the eye and dropped it with the breast tumour, now chilling and congealing in the box of sawdust.

'MR GUY ROMILLY, IS IT?'

I inclined my head submissively. 'Your servant, sir.'

'That's an uncommon name – Guy.'

Robert Liston was staring down at me from the doorway of his drawing-room in Mayfair. His left hand was tucked into the armhole of his shawl waistcoat, his right played with an orangewood toothpick, which he had the habit of chewing to aid his thoughts or his repose.

'It is not uncommon in my family, sir.'

I wondered, with a moment's alarm, if this sounded pert. But Liston observed in an easygoing way, 'I fancy the activities of Mr Fawkes threw it out of favour for a century or two. Are your family Papists?'

'Oh, no, sir!'

'Why do you assure me so ardently?' He looked at me quizzically. 'May I be flattered that you have taken the trouble to discover that I am a died-in-the-wool Low Church Scot?'

I knew that Liston's reputation – or his several reputations, some of them uncomfortable and even unsavoury – had been made in Edinburgh. He was 'The Great Northern Anatomist' of *Noctes Ambrosianae*, the boisterously convivial conversations, wit flashing like his own bistoury, which *Blackwood's Magazine* set at Ambrose's Tavern in West Register Street.

As I did not venture a reply, he continued, 'I must confess, I had completely forgotten your existence since I wrote in reply to Lady Aubery's letter.'

'Lady Aubery presents her respects, sir.'

'Oh, I'm sure.'

That April Monday evening in 1846 I had never set eyes on Liston before. I had heard much of him. London was smaller in those days, and he was a celebrity set in the same frame as Tennyson, or Landseer, or the actor William Macready. Nowadays our society has become so compartmentalized that even Liston's famous pupil Lord Lister is a stranger to most men's tongues. But when the Town thought of surgeons then – and it much preferred never to think of such personages at all – Liston was instantly recalled as the amazing practitioner who operated as gentlemen once duelled, whose flash of knife was followed by rasp of saw so rapidly the two seemed simultaneous. The imagination of all London was touched with the potent spell of his unerring bistoury.

I had arrived at the house terrified of him. His reputation, his intimacy with the operating theatre and charnel house, and the delicacy and importance of my errand, had all conspired towards this. I had buttressed myself that, once in his company, I should not be overwhelmed and perhaps even at ease. Facing his six-foot-two frame and piercing eye, I discovered such hopes to be misplaced.

'Her Ladyship made me aware that an invitation to dine at your table, sir, is an honour and pleasure much sought in society.'

His grunt indicated that the wine of flattery was, from me, small beer. But he said politely enough, 'Well, Mr Romilly, you are due my apologies for not receiving you in person. But my patients claim my attention before my guests. I've no doubt that you've been adequately entertained by the ladies,' he added, nodding towards the demure trio of wife and daughters.

He advanced into the drawing-room, ambling, thumb still in armhole, chewing his orangewood stick. A young Irish footman, in scarlet livery edged with gold lace and white cotton stockings, shut the door with a clumsy slam behind him. The room was large but plain, occupying the whole front of the first floor. It was dusk, the lamplighters busy along the pavements outside, white-painted interior shutters screening three tall windows facing across the area railings into Clifford Street. This was a short thoroughfare, a slight slope up from New Bond Street, in which two rows of well-to-do houses a century old addressed each other with dignity, presided over by No 18, the old home of General Sir John Moore, whose burial at Corunna was depicted by the Irish versifier Charles Wolfe. I could hear from the street carriages clattering and rumbling their way towards the myriad sparkling delights of the evening.

'We are *en famille* tonight, more or less,' Liston continued, taking stand with his back to a grate heaped with coals. He had renounced Scots economy to follow smart society, by moving his dinner-time from sunlit five to candlelit seven o'clock. I had gathered from Lady Aubery that the Listons scented the fox of fashion with alacrity. 'I'm afraid a young fellow like you may discover it deadly dull.'

'I assure you, sir, I have already found the company utterly charming.'

Mrs Liston sat by the firescreen, a gingery-haired freckled Scotswoman, a deal younger than him, perhaps in her late thirties. She wore a modish gown of printed silk, with best Honiton lace at the cuffs and a Brussels shawl across her spiky shoulders. I gathered also from Lady Aubery that she strove to transform herself in London into a fitting decoration to her husband, with quite disastrous enthusiasm.

'I may, of course, have already wearied the ladies,' I added politely.

'I doubt it,' returned Liston shortly. 'You look to me as smart as a carrot new scraped.'

I coloured, as his two daughters suppressed laughter on a sofa against the wall. They were about seventeen or eighteen, sandy and freckled like their mother. She was blessed with two other girls and two sons, but of an age when we may thankfully be untroubled by our offspring's existence, beyond a ceremonial visit under command of the nurserymaid once a day, and the nursery bell had already rung them to bed. I liked the look of the elder girl, particularly as my father had

13

once vouchsafed that under their flinty exterior Scotswomen are as warmly sensuous as any *signorina*.

'Lady Aubery wrote of some information you were anxious to pass on,' Liston continued.

I assumed a grave look, though my confidence – my *morale*, as the generals call it – was oozing out of me like sweat on a summer's noon. 'I have certain information from America.'

I felt in the pocket of my dark coat, tailored in the latest cutaway fashion, but Liston cut my gesture short with, 'Not now. All that can wait until we have dined.'

He continued to stare at me, toothpick in corner of mouth. My abashed glance wandered, encountering with pleasure the elder girl's ankle, neat above a shoe of Dutch satin. Even Liston could not budge me from the assurance that I cut a good figure in the room. Though overtopped by my host, I was tall enough. I had a trim form, dark hair brushed back, good looks with a pale complexion, and large brown eyes furnished with generous lashes – eyes which, I knew, could hold a feminine glance for longer than its bestower cared, or dared. My linen was best Irish, and spotless, my black silk cravat well tied. My deportment was supple, my hands constrained a little self-consciously. My intimates sometimes accused me of mannerisms, and I suspected that many others noticed something of the Frenchified air which I had inherited from my mother.

'I don't believe I am aware of your station in life, Mr Romilly?' remarked Liston.

'I come of good family, sir.'

'Oh, doubtless. How did you become acquainted with Lady Aubery?'

'Her Ladyship was related to my late father. I imagined this fact to have been mentioned in her correspondence.'

'If it were, I've forgotten it. Your father – has he long been with God?'

'He departed life last June, sir. It occasioned my withdrawing from my studies at Trinity Hall, at the end of my first Easter Term at the University. My father was an exponent of

14

natural and physical science. Amateur,' I added, recalling Liston to be a Fellow of the Royal Society, a body to which my father keenly aspired, and even referred with affable familiarity, yet could have become no more intimate with than strolling past its apartments in Somerset House. 'He was acquainted with Sir Humphry Davy,' I enlarged. 'Inventor of the miner's lamp.'

'Thank you. I was aware of the connexion.' He seemed to find me mystifying. 'How *old* are you, Mr Romilly?'

'Twenty-one, sir.'

'Lady Aubery told me little about you, my relationship with her Ladyship being confined to the professional. As you are no longer a Cambridge undergraduate, do you follow a profession yourself?'

'Yes, sir. I am a journalist.'

'*A journalist!*'

His back straightened with contempt. I knew but one item of Liston's personal qualities – a reputation for unlimited rudeness. I expected that, like most reputations, this would prove exaggerated. For the second time that evening I recognized my hopes to be misplaced.

'And what journals, pray, have the benefit of your pen?'

I hesitated. 'I have had articles published by . . . by *Lloyd's Penny Weekly Miscellany*.'

For a moment the surgeon stared as though trying to digest such unpalatable information. Then he startled me by smiling. Perhaps he had overrun the limits of horror at the young sprig he had so rashly invited to dinner.

'My dear —' He turned towards the elder daughter. Apart from the zephyr of mirth, all three ladies had sat through our exchanges in the respectful silence which had fallen upon them at Liston's entry. '*Lloyd's Penny Weekly Miscellany*. You know of such things? I assume it is hardly a rival to *The Times*?'

'It is the same Mr Lloyd who publishes the *Penny Dreadfuls*, Papa.'

My spirits contrived to fall further. 'Those are stories, sir . . . novels . . . issued in ten penny parts,' I enlightened him painfully. 'You have perhaps heard people about Town talk of

"Salisbury Square fiction"? Such popular works are named after Mr Lloyd's office there, just off Fleet Street.'

'I am grateful that Lady Aubery recommended you to my attention, Mr Romilly. I learn something new every minute.'

In my literary life, *Lloyd's Penny Weekly* was my thin-papped wet-nurse. Edward Lloyd sold not periodicals, but escape for the poor into the wider ambits of aristocracy, crime, fashion and general depravity, each world peopled with creatures of action which was always violent, vice which was always base, love ever shining and suffering unfailingly lachrymose. With his steam presses and starvation wages, I knew him to be making a fortune.

Mrs Liston addressed her husband for the first time. 'The stories have a large following among the lower orders. Those of them who have taken the trouble of learning to read.'

'I've no doubt, the only other literature of grooms and housemaids being tracts pressed upon them by the perennially hopeful improvers of the human mind. Well, Mr Romilly, you would seem to have adopted an enterprising life's work. Your father, the amateur man of science. In which fields did he choose to divert himself?'

'Chemistry and pneumatics, sir.'

My poor father had in truth known little of either. He loved recalling that Francis Bacon was a cultivator of science, and that Dr Johnson was fond of performing with scientific apparatus in the garret library over his chambers in the Temple. My father saw science as an occupation for the serious-minded aristocrat as appropriate as agriculture or racehorses. I had the terrifying prospect of being sucked into a whirlpool of disputation on these two subjects with Liston, and swiftly drowned. But this was luckily erased by the abrupt reappearance of the young footman – very much 'Mick' and not within measure of earning the 'Alphonse', or similar name, with which some genteel households aggrandize their hobbledehoys. He had shown plain contempt towards me at the front door through my lack of card-case, and even of cards.

'Dr Thompson and Dr Wilson,' he announced raucously.

I was immediately treated as though dematerialized into the drawing-room air. Wilson was a peaky, grizzled Scotsman in an ill-cut grey frock-coat, who walked with a limp. He appeared to be a country doctor, and like myself a stranger to both the house and its master. The other was elderly, seemingly a professor from the North London Hospital, and close enough a friend of the family to be kissed by the girls, somewhat to my envy.

'You've established a fine practice in London, I hear, Liston,' Wilson complimented him.

'They say we Scots come here only to fill our pooches,' Thompson remarked humorously.

'The North London Hospital, being brand-new,' Liston told Wilson, 'is free of the traditions – by which they mean the prejudices and nepotism – that encrust the established metropolitan hospitals. It was therefore free to seek its brains from anywhere. Even Scotland.'

The conversation fell genially and heartily upon the fashionable custom of taking a whet-cup, or *coup d'avant*, before meals. (I know this, or I learn it afresh, fifty-four years after the words flew about my ears, because I have been always as busy as a Boswell noting down talk which might be of use to my pen.)

'Rum before I dine?' protested Liston loudly. 'The Devil! It crisps the stomach.'

'The Russian bear downs a glass of vodka or *aqua vitæ* before he feeds,' argued Wilson.

'And what *does* he eat?' Liston rounded on him. 'A diet of salt, fatty fish. What matters the condition of your digestive organs, to receive a dinner like that?'

'If I may speak as some authority on *materia medica*,' interposed Thompson fussily, 'a cold infusion of camomile, or of quassia, or of any other good bitter will serve far the best as a stimulant to the appetite.'

'Hunger is the best sauce,' concluded Liston. 'It's the blessing of the poor, who suffer from neither corpulence, dyspepsia nor gout. I see gentry every day who'd be cured in a week

17

with a pauper's bread, a milkmaid's dram and a child's skipping-rope.'

The hour was struck from the mantelpiece by an ormolu clock – doubtless from Howell and James's, the furnishings being sparse but in tip-top fashion. The door reopened, a butler in blue coat with bright buttons announcing dinner. I was invited to take down the elder daughter. I managed to imply to her father my sense of honour at this arrangement, more skilfully than she managed to conceal from him her delight at it.

FROM CHIMNEY-POTS to front-door scraper, No 5 Clifford
Street was a rich man's house. But its ornamentation had a
simplicity which I assumed to be admirable in the eyes of a
Scots academic like Liston. We descended to dinner by a
plain oak staircase with delicate banisters, which spiralled
through three storeys like the steps of some well-appointed
lighthouse. The inner front hall was hardly palatial, panelled
in plain oak, a huge square gas-lamp jutting into it by a cast-
iron bracket. The bare, yellow flame flickered and smoked
from a batswing burner – the familiar, steady incandescent
glow of the Welsbach mantle illuminated only the later years
of the past century.

From this small hallway, a narrow flagged passage with an
elaborate cross-vaulted stone ceiling ran a yard or two towards the front door, surmounted by an elegant, louvred
transom. The lock was huge, the chain fit for some small
craft's anchor, and outside a massive knocker invited each
visitor to deliver an involuntarily imperious introduction.
The other side of the house gave on a narrow cobbled mews
leading into Coach and Horses Yard, where Liston had his
stables. He always went to the hospital and about his surgical
business on horseback. He could not abide travelling passively
in a carriage. To Robert Liston, to be alive meant to be
physically active.

We dined at a long table set in a long room occupying one
side of the house, immediately over the kitchens in the cellar.
The tablewear was solid rather than stylish, having been
bought in Edinburgh. The food was solid, too, though well

enough done to suggest the hand of a Frenchman below stairs. We started with a fine turbot and a handsome salmon, which our host declared to have been caught in the Thames that very morning, at which Thompson sharply disagreed.

'A salmon just now, at Eastertime, is indeed the king of fish,' he declared. 'But one from the Thames a rarity of rarities, surely? Why, hardly a single salmon has been taken from London river for ten years! The lock-weirs, and the filthy dregs of our civilized life, have so ruined the fishery that even the poachers have turned elsewhere.'

'But where else could the fish have originated?' demanded Liston. I noticed that he had coloured. My friend George Meredith once declared to me that when people discuss politics at dinner they become as red as the roast and as white as the boiled. Robert Liston seemed as powerfully affected by contradiction on any subject whatever. 'See how fresh it is. It *must* have been caught today. Isn't that so, Mrs Liston?'

She adjudged it as fresh as a Tweed salmon at Kelso, but Liston amputated the argument by raising his glass towards Wilson with, 'Sir, I will take wine with you.'

I chose the humbler turbot, as tactful. Afterwards there was roast saddle of lamb, which I fell upon, it being well beyond my own pocket at one-and-six a pound. Next came rabbit done on the spit and some roast chickens, then a ragout with truffles was produced to my host's eye-gleaming satisfaction. With the fish we drank Rhenish, one of the trickles of Germanism starting to seep through English society, their source the Prince Consort. Afterwards, decanters of claret – a good Médoc, I judged, the only knowledge I retained from Cambridge being of wines. Trinity Hall stood on a cellarful of good drink, a most attractive incidental in any college, which I was forced to abandon through impecuniosity, exactly as Samuel Johnson had prematurely to leave Pembroke College, Oxford.

The three medical men dominated the conversation, and Liston dominated the medical men. Like every fashionable table in Mayfair or St James's that evening, talk turned to the

20

chances of Peel's Government surviving, some inevitable
change in the Corn Laws, the public mania for railway
shares, the surly mood of Ireland. Liston seemed surprisingly
unmoved by such topics. He asserted that so long as the old
Duke remained Commander-in-Chief little harm could befall
the country, and if every Irishman was arming himself with a
gun – well, it meant prosperity for Birmingham. I calculated
that my host had little interest in public affairs, or in money. I
myself did not join the discussion, having no encouragement
to do so. Indeed, it proceeded without any recognition of my
sitting there at all. Liston became more animated when
the trio slipped into medical talk, which I found fascinating,
though baffling, like exercising an ear for a half-learned foreign
language the first day abroad.

'Did you see that mysterious case earlier this year?' Liston
asked, leaning across the table. 'It was revealed in the public
press in January. A woman had four young boys who bled to
death, one after the other. Not from gross injury, just trivial
scratches and cuts. Now, the strange occurrence is this – it
happened in exactly the same way to a dozen males in her
family, though the woman is as robust as a Grenadier.'

'Perhaps she poisoned them all in sequence,' suggested
Thompson waggishly.

'It's remarkably curious.' Liston seemed puzzled. 'If the
mother were well, any hereditary peculiarity is ruled out. Yet
the progeny all died.'

He stopped the topic abruptly, I supposed because it had
brought to his tongue some indelicacy, and ladies were
present. Now I read that scrap of conversation in my notes,
my mind is illuminated by the later-discovered principles
governing transmission of the bleeding disease, haemophilia –
which is passed exclusively to males by healthy females. Such
perceptions were beyond Liston's mind. He was a magnificent
surgical practitioner, as I later discovered with my own eyes.
Had he not lacked an instinct to draw true conclusions from
the irritatingly unusual, he would have been a genius.

His three ladies stayed quiet until Liston threw them a
word, like scraps to the dogs. I spoke to the elder daughter at

my side about shipwrecks. I always conversed to young ladies about shipwrecks. They aroused simultaneously excitement and melting sympathy, and every winter was generous in providing instances. The SS *Caratacus* had just drowned four hundred emigrants to Australia, but Miss Liston was disappointingly unmoved by even a single one of them. I wondered whether she, or I that trying evening, were unduly dull.

With the pies and puddings we drank champagne. Liston grew even redder. I hoped it was the glow of conviviality replacing that of irascibility. 'I catch my lady's eye,' he said abruptly.

We four gentlemen stood. Liston opened the door. The ladies filed out, mother last. We resumed our seats. The butler removed the cloth and set the decanter of port at Liston's left elbow. As it circulated, Liston raised his glass to Thompson with, 'Take wine with me, sir,' smacking his lips and pronouncing it a magnum of double-diamond.

My heart had started beating faster, partly through fear and partly through the wine I had taken to douse it. The future of my life was to be decided within the next few minutes.

'But weren't you sorry to leave Edinburgh, Liston?' suggested Wilson, returning to his original theme.

'Any man with a sense of values in this life is sorry to quit Edinburgh.'

'But I understood your colleagues there to be difficult?'

'Oh, damnably! How simple our profession would be, had we to deal only with our patients and not with our brothers! For five years the Royal Infirmary was barred to me, the current of my career dammed. Five years! Why? They said I was impudent and presumptuous. They said I quarrelled with everyone. With John Barclay, when I left off teaching his anatomy classes, and set up a class of my own. Which was much better, it gathered students as a corpse gathers maggots,' he boasted.

'A strange fellow, John Barclay,' reflected Thompson. 'He was so interested in the subject of anatomy that he would sometimes continue to flood empty lecture-benches with his erudition, after the porter's bell had released his students for their dinners. I suppose, as he set out in life to be a clergy-man, he had the preaching instinct.'

'They said I quarrelled with the Managers of the Infirmary even while still a student,' Liston continued. 'Well, I did. I diagnosed incompetence, but unlike everyone else in the place I applied the remedy. They said I operated outside, inde-pendently of the Infirmary, on patients the Infirmary had already discharged as incurable. I confess to that, too. The point of *my* operation was that it cured them.'

I held my tongue. I realized that I was hearing the gossip, indeed the secrets, of their dreadful profession, through the simple fact of my being too inconsequential to merit notice.

'The surgeons should have been grateful for your doing their work,' murmured Thompson, pouring himself a second glass of port.

'Gratitude! You'd as like get a fart from a dead man,' Liston said roughly. 'The Managers of the Infirmary, in their wisdom and magnificence, on the 14th of March, 1822 – I wear the date like a vicious cicatrix – resolved that I was inter-fering improperly in the surgical department of the House. And considering it their bounden duty to prevent and deter others from doing the same, prohibited and discharged me from the wards and operation-room. Which information they dispatched with commendable thoroughness to all the phy-sicians and surgeons, the apothecary, the matron, the clerks and even the porters.'

As Liston recited this proscription his voice trailed into a bitter whisper and he slumped back dejectedly in his chair. The silence was broken by Wilson asking wonderingly, 'But Liston! How did a man of your vigour contrive to fill those five vacant years?'

'I operated, like a whirling and howling dervish!' Liston laughed, recovering his spirits and sitting up. 'In garrets and hovels, in reeking and ill-lit rooms, in Grassmarket, Lawn-market, the Wynds, all over Edinburgh. I operated on five cases of aneurism in five weeks,' he declaimed in triumph. 'I was the first man in the world to remove the entire scapula – the whole shoulder-blade plucked from the chest! Oh, I remember the case well, it was a boy of sixteen, a Robert McNair from Kinross. He'd an ossified aneurism under the bone.'

'Did he survive?' I did not need Wilson's admiring glance at the surgeon to tell me the magnitude of this mutilation.

'Four months. He died at home.' Liston seemed satisfied with this, though I had at once a vision of the poor lad spread across our very dinner-table, like a juvenile gory-locked Banquo.

'I operated on an elephantiasis of the scrotum,' Liston continued with relish. 'The surgeons at the Infirmary wouldn't touch him. The man had a tumour of forty-four and a half pounds – imagine, Wilson, the poor fellow needed a wheel-barrow to get about. The blood came like a showerbath.' I felt my stomach turn, little knowing that within the year my eyes and ears would be hardened against such ghastliness. 'And guess who assisted me at that operation?' Liston ended contemptuously. 'James Syme.'

From the silence, an unpleasant subject would seem to have been raised. 'Am I right in understanding that Professor Syme is your own fourth cousin?' asked Wilson, by way of restoring equanimity with small talk.

But Liston sneered, '*Professor* Syme. *I* should have been professor at Edinburgh these thirteen years, not Syme. Cousin or no, he's a rascal. Do you know how he got his pro-fessorship, Wilson? He bought it. You think that incredible, I see from your face. But it's as stark and simple as a man's buying himself a commission in the Dragoons, or a pocket borough for Parliament. Syme swayed the votes by offering to pension off old Professor Russell. Three hundred pounds a year, that cost him. It shows the cash value he set on the dignity of his Chair. Particularly as James Russell was past eighty at the time, and not likely to impose for too many years on such generosity. Syme and his hangers-on are wretched and malignant ninnies, and my temper has im-proved amazingly since I got away from them.' Suddenly Liston's eye was fixed on me. 'Well, sir? What's your business here tonight?'

Badly off balance, ears dinned by the surgeon's vituperation, the showerbath of blood still in my mind, I faltered. 'Lady Aubery indicated you would have the kindness —'

'Yes, yes, I know all that.' I noticed the other two staring at me with amused interest, as though I had just intruded into the room. 'What I did *not* gather from Lady Aubery was exactly why you should put yourself to the trouble of this visit. You're not sick, are you? You don't want me to attend you professionally?'

I shook my head violently at this chilling suggestion. 'I have some information —'

'As you said. Well? What is it?'

'Information discovered in the course of my profession —'

'Mr Romilly is a journalist.' Liston gave a quick, bleak smile to the others, asking them, 'I suppose you can call it a profession?'

'Some information of a method, sir, for performing surgical operations without the infliction of pain.'

My visit had been so carefully engineered, its course so anxiously conjectured, I had planned a hundred ways of reaching my point with diplomacy. It had somehow emerged with brutal abruptness. But this seemed an advantage. Liston only started chewing his orangewood stick, in silence. I supposed that such effrontery had stunned him.

'You have come to enlighten me about mesmerism, I take it?' He spoke resignedly. 'Or you're a mesmerist yourself? A disciple of Franz Mesmer, versed in all the Viennese mysteries of animal magnetism?'

'I have never heard of the gentleman, sir,' I confessed nervously.

'You must be the only one in Europe,' said Liston. 'The Swabian Mesmer, who would have us believe the nerves of men run with some subtle and mobile fluid, connecting us to one another and to the sun and the moon and the stars . . . he cured a *mädchen* and a *mademoiselle* or two of their hysterics, I suppose. His consulting rooms in Paris were pervaded with the dim light of stained glass, the scents of orange-blossom and incense, and the murmurs of Aeolian harps, while his ladies grasped iron rods from his vat of magnetized water, and pressed their knees together to facilitate the flow. Then handsome young magnetizers appeared to run finger-tips down their spines and massage their breasts. No wonder he enjoyed a *succès fou*,' he ended in disgust. 'Mesmer would magnetize anything in sight for a fee – people, pots and pans, dogs, even trees.'

'Or perhaps the young gentleman's a devotee of Dr Braid of Manchester?' suggested Thompson with amusement. 'Did you read Braid's *Neurypnology*, Robert? He dazzles his patients with his lancet-case, then attempts to extract their teeth without unduly attracting their attention thereby.'

'So that's your trade?' Liston insisted to me. 'Then like many other enthusiastic young parties, you've been badly misled. Mesmerism has one paramount disadvantage in surgery. It fails to work. It's quackery, practised on those in possession of minds too feeble to resist. King Louis of France, before he lost his head, established a commission of medical men who decided as much.'

'The commission included Dr Guillotin,' Thompson added cheerfully, 'whose device was so useful in the later event.'

'Had you taken pains to find out as much,' Liston continued abrasively, 'you would have saved yourself the trouble of a journey and a shilling to starch your linen. I am subjected to much importuning by persons like you. And why should you presume my ignorance of any practice whatever to relieve the pain of a capital operation? I assure you that I would try anything – *anything* – to that desirable end.'

Dr Wilson having sat silent through these hot exchanges, now intruded with a quiet voice. 'I have *had* an operation. The removal of a bony tumour of the femur, by the cold chisel.' He tapped his short left leg. 'Suffering so great as I underwent cannot be expressed in words – so fortunately it cannot be recalled,' he said soberly. 'The particular pangs are now forgotten, but that black whirlwind of emotion, the horror of a great darkness falling upon me, the sense of desertion by God and man, bordering close upon despair, which swept through my mind and overwhelmed my heart . . . that is

26

something I can never forget, however gladly I would do so.'

This came so gently, after the violence of Liston's language, that its effect was deep on all of us. There followed a silence. Liston slouched again in his chair, reaching his huge hand for his glass of port. 'I'm sure you were a good patient,' he commented.

'We talk of "good patients" and "bad patients", yet the bounds of human fortitude press close enough on us all,' Wilson continued in the same voice. 'When I learned of the decision to operate, at first I refused to think of the ordeal and refused to submit to my fears. This was followed by reflection, reflection by resignation, resignation by submission to the inevitable, and submission by a kind of holy courage, which lasted completely until the suffering began. Upon which there was a change of view, and insistence of the strongest kind that the operation be stopped at all risk to myself. But they held me, you know.' His eye caught mine, telling me more than his words. 'When my resistance was useless, I cried for them to finish as rapidly as possible, to make haste, to make haste . . . Don't you find, Liston, these successive pleadings – to stop, and then to hurry – become so familiar to your ears, that you may calculate the very stage of the operation from them?'

This evoked a sharp nod from Liston. The lame doctor continued, 'Afterwards there was great nervous shock, the shock not infrequently full of danger. Then deep depression for a long period of time. Had I known precisely of the suffering to come, and its subsequent effects, I think I should rather have died. Such fears must have hindered many people, not just the feeble or the excitable, from having their lives saved by an operation.'

'And hindered many of their surgeons, too,' said Liston dourly.

I broke in desperately, 'But sir! My system has no connexion with mesmerism. It is a means of obviating pain with a gas.'

Liston was disinclined even to notice this news, but Thompson looked at me kindly. He was perhaps sorry for yet another young man frizzled in the surgeon's scorn. I had gathered from the conversation that he was of American origin, his father Collector of Customs at Savannah, Georgia, a 'Tory' loyalist who had been obliged to exile himself in Edinburgh in '76. Like many Scots doctors, Thompson had achieved success in fashionable London. Of Wilson, I knew only that he was an acquaintance of Dr James Young Simpson of Edinburgh, a name which that evening meant no more to me than Herr Mesmer's.

'But we have already tried every possible drug in our armamentarium for this purpose, Mr Romilly,' Thompson explained pleasantly, leaning across the table. 'You must take my word for it, I fear, as professor of *materia medica* and author of the *London Dispensatory*. We have given opium, wine, brandy . . . but our soporific draughts are no better than that prepared in the *Decameron* by Maestro Mazzeo della Montagna of Salerno, *a leech most eminent in surgery*,' he quoted, with a sidelong glance at Liston.

'The draught was drunk by the leech's young wife's lover, as I recall,' grunted Liston. 'Who fell into a sleep so profound the lady could singe him with a candle-flame. On what part of his anatomy I would not speculate.'

'Such potions may bring the sleep from which there is no awakening,' Thompson continued to me patiently. 'And we medical men must exercise eternal caution in restricting their use. We have really got little farther than the medieval *spongia somnifera* which Nicolas of Salerno described in his *Antidotarium*, made by mixing in a copper kettle opium, hyoscine, unripened blackberries, lettuce seed, henbane, wild mulberries, sorrel, hemlock, poppy, mandrake and ivy,' he recited. 'Into which was plunged a sponge fresh from the sea, to be left in the sun during the dog-days for activation when needed by dipping in cold water. Though I should prepare the same this very night, if I thought it had any chance of success.'

'*Not poppy, nor mandragora, Nor all the drowsy syrups of the world, Shall ever medicine thee to that sweet sleep Which thou owedst yesterday*,' recited Wilson in barely more than a whisper.

'I assure you, my dear sir,' Thompson concluded, 'the dark

cave of pain has been well explored, and found to have no exit.'

'Yet every month, men come to me with some new ano-dyne.' Liston now spoke calmly, even despairingly, powerful fingers slowly turning the stem of his wineglass. 'Some are medical men, some are not. Some are charlatans, some plain scoundrels. Well, Professor Louis Velpeau said in Paris that the avoidance of pain in surgery is a dream we can no longer pursue. *Instrument tranchant et douleur, en médecine opératoire, sont deux mots qui ne se présentent point l'un sans l'autre à l'esprit des malades, et dont il faut nécessairement admettre l'association,*' he said in a fair accent. 'You speak French, Mr Romilly?'

'It is my mother's native tongue, sir.'

'You'd agree with Monsieur Velpeau, gentlemen?' He eyed the other two doctors. 'We must turn our imagination to more fruitful things, and our patients must simply screw up their courage.'

Suddenly, that powerful arm darted across the table to take me by the throat. I stared with fright into Liston's eyes, steady and expressionless while his huge hand encircled my neck, pressing alongside my windpipe. 'If I squeezed a little harder, Mr Romilly, do you know what would befall you?' His tone was perfectly cordial. 'I should compress your carotid artery, to drain your brain of blood and have you unconscious within a minute. It's a dodge tried in the sixteenth century, to tame the pain of the knife. But garrotting is useless for modern surgery. No better than deliberately bleeding a man through his veins nigh unto death, to set his dislocated shoulder without hurt. That's a dodge they try at Bartholomew's.'

He released me, gratified at my discomfiture. It had been an act of impetuousness, a flamboyance, both strong ingredients in a character mixed as subtly as any of Dr Thompson's physic. He pushed back his chair, and I saw with despair we were about to quit the table. I cried, 'But won't you even listen to my information?'

'I have listened enough.'

'I have a friend, a childhood friend, now living near Boston in Massachusetts.' I was determined to have my say.

I continued quickly, 'There are two dentists in that city, or thereabouts, not quacks in any way, who have a practice for removing teeth painlessly after the inhalation of a gas.'

'Who are you, sir? What are you?' Liston was angry again. 'A damned scribbler. I know men. You have the smell of seediness about you. You know nothing of scientific truths. If this gas . . . whatever it is . . . whether it really exists . . . is possessed of so magical an effect, do you suppose that *I* should not have learned the news before you?'

'I can vouch for my informant, sir,' I replied stoutly. 'So sincerely, that I am prepared to cross the Atlantic and witness the process with my own eyes.'

'Pray do. Go to New South Wales if you wish.'

'I should sail to Boston by the next steam-packet, had I . . .' I found myself stammering. 'Had I the resources.'

'Then I can only sympathize with your impecuniosity.'

I drew on my last reserves of audacity, rather than of courage. 'I had hoped, sir, that you might see your way to furnishing my fare and necessary expenses —'

'I am not a moneylender, Mr Romilly.' Liston's eyes seared me, as might the actual cautery in his hands. Even the amenable Thompson gave a half gasp, half laugh at my effrontery. 'It is ill-mannered and deceitful of you to have abused the privilege of Lady Aubery's acquaintance. You should have directed your footsteps instead to the pawn-broker's.'

Then a strange interruption occurred. Suddenly Liston grabbed the table-edge, mouth open, gasping, the two doctors instantly on their feet. 'It's nothing . . . nothing . . .' He dabbed spittle from his lips with his napkin. 'Some passing disorder of the deglutition, which comes on me now and again.'

'Shall I ring for water?' asked Thompson, alarmed.

'No, don't trouble. The seizure soon goes. You physicians fuss too much.'

'You should have a word with Watson about it, surely?'

'I shall, by and by.' Liston stood up, seemingly quickly recovered. 'Shall we join the ladies?' he asked formally, as I noticed how pale he had turned. 'Wilson, if you're in Town long, you must take a cruise on my boat. My man keeps her down at Rotherhithe, which is handy.'

'That sounds an adventure, to be sure.'

'It blows away the perpetual stink of pus,' Liston told him.

We filed out, myself last, neglected, hardly noticed at all. The dramatics of the last minute failed to overshadow the failure of a mission on which I had staked and hoped so much. I had won nothing, only ridicule and contempt in the eyes of the three doctors, and humiliation in my own. I took but one polite, hasty cup of tea upstairs in the drawing-room. When I excused myself, the company plainly welcomed their disencumbrance. As the insolent footman handed back my hat, stick and gloves in the hall, the drawing-room door above abruptly opened and shut to emit a loud burst of laughter. I left the house wondering if it were at my expense.

4

WAVING AWAY THE swooping link-boy, I strode down Clifford Street towards Bond Street, anger deepening with every step. I had been not humbled, but humiliated. I had expected the reception afforded a gentleman, even a young and inconsequential one. Liston had consigned me to the lower orders, as starkly as he bared living bones. My occupation as a journalist had gained me nothing in his eyes but a reputation for impudence.

From the corner came the jangling hurdy-gurdy of a street-organ, its hunchbacked, black-bearded grinder playing for the exclusive delight of his pair of white mice tumbling pathetically in their cage, plus a pair of solemn-faced butlers, their families dining out somewhere, standing at their front doors in the gaslight. I turned into Piccadilly, making towards the Circus, retracing the quickest route from my lodgings in the Borough. Allowing for the sharp elbow of the Thames against Somerset House, this lay over Westminster Bridge then along Lower Marsh and The New Cut in Lambeth. It was almost three miles, allowing for the easygoing aimlessness of London streets. I walked both ways because I could afford neither mount nor hackney-coach. And the omnibuses brought to London from Paris by Monsieur Georges Shillibeer – along with the Shillibeer patent funeral coach – though elegant and comfortable with their velvet-liveried drivers, and their magazines and newspapers inside, were neither cheap nor plentiful. Besides, in the 1840s of which I write, walking was the usual way of Londoners' getting about.

Only on reaching the building works for the new Houses of Parliament did I begin to slacken my pace and the angry grip on my cane. It was still early. I was not eager to be home. My walk had blown away the fumes of Liston's wine, and sobriety found me with a roaring thirst. I decided to broach the first reasonably respectable tavern for a pot of beer.

The Three Tuns looked passable, at the corner of Belvedere Road on the Surrey bank. I pushed open the door, to find naked, flaring gas competing in the parlour with tobacco smoke like a London fog. It was as noisy as an ape-house, a beef-faced man in the chimney corner roaring out *Drink To Me Only With Thine Eyes*, clearly no practice of his own. All fell silent as I entered. The importance of that evening had urged me to dress my best, better than my best, with Floy at home – who played my laundress and sempstress – working hard with sponge and flat-iron to starch my high collar and the modest frill on my shirt. Surprise at the manifestation among them of one of their betters gave way to grins, suppressed chuckling, laughing and mutual elbow-digging. But I was beyond the capability of embarrassment. I made for a small round table where a man in a glazed hat and dirty white muffler, smoking a foul clay, resentfully made room on the bench against the wall. I sat down, tipped back my new four-and-ninepenny silk hat, and asked the potboy for a pint of porter.

The customers soon bored of their new amusement. To occupy my eyes elsewhere, I drew from my side pocket the letter I had been hoping to quote to Robert Liston. I should anyway not have left it at home. I would not deny Floy the effrontery, the slyness and even the initiative to rifle my pockets, though she could not read very ably. I sipped my tankard, spreading the sheets of thick paper covered in a primly regular hand. Miss Charlotte Conybeare fancied her talent for the pen, while the slowness and irregularity of the mails between Boston and Liverpool demanded most advantage be taken of each.

It was headed,

33

Dearest Guy, it began.

I have done absolutely everything you asked in your dear letter last month! Who dare still say that I am an impractical female, a pampered parson's daughter? One unable to earn her own living as a governess in this rough country?

Neat-waisted, golden-haired, lively young Charlotte! No less adventurous than ten summers before, when I had first grown aware of her as the child climbing trees next door in the Vicar's garden. My father then lived near London at Kew, in a substantial house against the Botanical Gardens. It was the half-way period of that muddled, vigorous, kindly, befooled, quixotic gentleman's existence, which began in the same Dorsetshire castle as my own, and ended in loneliness in a labourer's cottage almost in sight of its walls.

My father took a liking to this bright-eyed girl. He paid her the extreme compliment of admission to his laboratory in the attic, an unforgettable room jammed to its sloping ceilings with chemical apparatus jumbled together like the stock-in-trade of a country chandler's, of glass, copper and cast iron in shapes always weird to my eyes, two or three vessels forever bubbling away over the flame of candle or spirit-lamp. Against the walls were glass-fronted cabinets of butterflies and moths, neatly arranged and meticulously labelled. A triangular corner-shelf presented the foetus of a monkey preserved in a jar of spirit, a bat pinned to a board under a rich patination of dust, and a human skull. The attic resembled less a scientist's laboratory than an alchemist's den. My father lacked but the decoration of a tall conical hat and a black cat. With his rheumy eyes behind small oval glasses and his brown calico smock, his long white beard and gaunt features, he could have shared unnoticeably any etching of wizards and witches in busy search of the alkahest or the panacea, which my childish eyes found in story-books. His own heavy volumes, covered with flaking leather, shared his table with the remains of a loaf, a half-empty jug of beer and the rind of a cheese. He was far too absorbed to stop for meals.

My father never conducted inconsequential experiments. Each was to change the thinking of the world. Though I doubt he had ever witnessed a genuine scientific experiment, nor shared the same building as one being conducted. At Cambridge, he had read mathematics and natural philosophy. He embraced the more dramatic disciplines of chemistry with his pet justification – that the wrangler Richard Watson had been made Professor of Chemistry to the University in 1764, after studying as an undergraduate exactly the same subjects as himself, and therefore in a comparable state of total ignorance. My father still did not know what he was looking for, how he should find it, and who should want it, when he blew himself up in his Dorset cottage the previous summer, and a week later slept the euthanasia from the effects of apoplexy and shock.

I turned back to the oft-read letter.

I talked to Sam Cooley again last week, as you wanted. He is a clerk (what you would call an assistant) in a drug store (which you might recognize as a chemist's). This shop is quite near our house. He is a young fellow, sandy-haired, with a face rather like a hog. He is not very clever, and clumsy at the best of times. But he seems to recall everything which occurred that night in the Union Hall, even so long ago as December the year before last. It was, I suppose, the most important event in his life. Which here in Hartford is inclined to be somewhat humdrum. To think! When it all happened I was still at home in Kew!

I smiled at dear, gossipy, wasp-waisted Charlotte, whom I had vowed one day to marry, when my father and I were driven to Dorset by impoverishment, at a canter. Had God blessed that evening with Liston, I should have already been on my way to such happiness.

The lecture in the Union Hall that night was given by Professor Quincy Colton, Charlotte's letter went on. *I'd better explain that*

35

he wasn't really a professor at all. People out here often call themselves 'professor' if they want to impress folk in some way. Well, I suppose a man may call himself a professor as readily as a farrier, if it helps him to make a living. 'Professor' Colton arrived in town to give his lecture on electricity and laughing gas, which he advertises all round New England, and says he has delivered at the Broadway Tabernacle in New York, before an audience of a thousand people. All Hartford society attended, even at 25 cents a ticket. Dr Wells the dentist was there, with Mrs Wells. Sam knew them well from the store, where they purchased oil of cloves and suchlike. Hartford is a charming community, but there is usually little to distract one apart from the doings of one's fellow-citizens, which are seldom exciting.

The laughing gas was in a rubber bag, which the 'professor' carried round the rows of seats calling for volunteers – among gentlemen only, and of the first respectability. Sam says he didn't inhale that night. Perhaps he wasn't sure of being respectable enough. Or he was scared of making an exhibition of himself. Under the gas, you are supposed to act out your leading trait of character, to sing, laugh, dance, orate – or fight! There were special strong men put in the front row to restrain folk who did. But it seems no one performed these antics. Perhaps such aren't among the leading traits of anybody's character in Hartford.

I looked up from the letter, interrupted by the greeting, 'Hello, my Lord.' A sallow, scrawny girl leant against my table, grinning tipsily, her pink gown low over her breasts, the material stained and crusted round her ankles with mud. She was using an affected accent, on the urging of my appearance. 'How about a-coming along with me? Coming for a bit of fun?'

I shook my head violently. I was having too much fun in that line already. That was the tap root of my flourishing troubles.

'Now's yer chance, lovey.' The girl's pressing voice resumed its normal Cockney, 'I'll be nice with you. I'll do you famous. Honest I will, strike me blind.'

'I've no time.'

'Step out, love, and I'll give you a penny flash,' she suggested as an alternative.

I shook my head again. Had I pennies to spare, I could spend them on a million things more attractive than a fleeting view of her well-rogered private parts. 'I've that waiting at home,' I said as discouragement.

'Oh, hoity toity!' she exclaimed. 'Go on with you! I bet you ain't never seen it. You're too young. Buy us a dram of Holland's.'

'Do me the favour to leave me alone,' I told her severely.

'What's the matter, love?' she demanded cheerfully. 'Got the clap?'

'Of the mind, yes.'

'Go on?' She stared, far from understanding. 'You don't fancy me?'

'Oh, stow it!' I said in ill-tempered desperation. At this she simpered and made abruptly across the sawdust on the floor to someone else. I brought my mind back to Hartford, Connecticut.

'Professor' Colton was persuaded by Dr Wells and a few others to give a private show the next morning, which was Tuesday, December 11, 1844, Charlotte continued. *Perhaps they hoped something more amazing would happen, and it did. This time, Sam Cooley inhaled. It seems he went off like a pony scared by a rifle-shot. He plunged through the settees left over from the last night's audience, knocking them in every direction. But all he remembered after taking the gas-bag to his lips was finding himself in the middle of the hall, wondering why everyone was asking if he was 'OK' (as President van Buren taught us to say), meaning was he not hurt? They told Sam he had been bellowing like a bull, sat him down, pulled up his inexpressibles, and Sam saw with amazement how his knees were bruised, his shins abraded, his skin broken all over. He still has the scars, which I think he was almost tempted into the indelicacy of displaying to me!* But he had not felt a thing!!

The beef-faced man by the tavern fire drew a glare of irritation from me as he started a loud rendering of *There Is a Lady Sweet and Kind*, an assertion in which he was joined by four or five equally unmusical companions.

Then Dr Wells jumped up and said to Sam 'Could a man have a tooth drawn with no pain under the gas?' To which Sam replied, that he guessed so, that a man could get in a fight with a dozen, and feel no pain under it! It was then, Sam told me, his legs began to recover their feeling, and his wounds to hurt. But Dr Wells wasted no time. He was suffering from a bad wisdom tooth of his own, and the next morning had the 'professor' and his gas-bag, and Sam and some others, back to his office, which is in his own house, across town from the Hall. Dr Wells inhaled while Dr Riggs – one of our most eminent dentists in Hartford – pulled out the bad tooth. And Dr Wells didn't feel a twinge, either!!! *'Not so much as the prick of a pin!' he exclaimed when he came back to earth, Sam says. And, 'This is the greatest discovery ever made!'*

And well it may be. Dr Wells now has a big practice here and in Boston, and everyone is talking about the 'New Era in Tooth-pulling'. It is hard to believe, though, that the agony of losing a tooth at the dentist's has gone for good. I think I should be quite happy to go for a painless extraction myself, but my teeth are all sound, through Papa dropping the first milk tooth I ever lost down a mouse-hole. Now I hear from Mr Tooms (who is a lawyer friend of my employer, and like all lawyers very highly thought of in America) that Dr Wells has become indisposed through so much work, and has had some trouble with the doctors in Boston, where he has been giving the gas for surgical operations at the hospital. Mr Tooms is a great friend of Dr Wells, and tells me the real name of the laughing gas is NITROUS OXID. There was a bit about it in the Boston papers early last year, but of course no one reads the Boston newspapers outside Boston.

Nitrous oxid, or oxide . . . I knew from my father that to be a gas discovered by Joseph Priestley, who also discovered oxygen – his 'dephlogisticated air', so strangely more beneficial to the flame of a candle, or the flame of life itself in the quivering little bosom of a mouse, both of which lasted longer than in normal air before snuffing themselves to extinction. My father enriched my boyhood with breathless tales of heroes in natural and physical science, as Pindar sang of the Argonauts.

I knew Priestley to be a Yorkshireman, the son of a poor

cloth-dresser, a scientist and a theologian in an age when one man's mind could achieve enduring distinction in both. He was genius misled by the phlogiston theory, the *Father of modern chemistry who never would acknowledge his daughter*, in the words of Baron Cuvier. His scriptural writings rejecting the Trinity were burned by the common hangman and had him proscribed by unthinking men – who sadly form the majority of God's creatures – as an atheist. His support for the French revolutionaries brought the mob to his doors, wrecking his house and destroying his papers and apparatus, that he became yet another Englishman to sail westwards under the full canvas of his opinions to the welcoming havens of America, to die in Pennsylvania.

My cherished correspondent ended, *It is growing dark now, dear Guy, and I must light the lamp. We have no luxuries like gas (not the laughing variety!), but Hartford becomes more prosperous every day, and I expect will soon have all that is the latest, like in Boston itself. I hope you will make the voyage, Guy. With all my heart, I do. You are always in my thoughts, and I long to see a fellow-countryman. Though to tell the truth, everyone is so friendly here, with none of the snobbing and snubbing a governess, even of good family, might be subjected to in the Old Country.*

> *Your affectionate,*
> *Charlotte.*

I knocked back my tankard of porter, rose, kissed the letter briefly, and made for the fire in its ill-blacked grate. I felt that I should never see its fair authoress again. Nor the fortune which I had promised myself, for proclaiming to the world this wonder of tooth-pulling and even surgery without pain, a secret so far locked within the bleak shores of New England. Robert Liston had slammed down a shutter on both visions. My hand was already over the glowing coals when I hesitated. The spring of hope trickles, but rarely dries. There *must* be other ways across the Atlantic than through Liston's dining-room, I told myself. I stuffed the pages back in my pocket, and eager to quit the reeking tavern turned to push aside the part-opened door with my stick. A man stumbled through, bumping against me, half-drunk, not ill-dressed, who I took for a clerk or counter-jumper.

'Are you off for the hanging, sir?' he asked jovially, silk hat over one eye. 'They're topping Mrs Arbuckle at Newgate in the morning. I'd be along now, to get a good perch.'

'I've seen enough executions,' I replied hastily, trying for the exit.

'You, sir? You don't look half old enough, that's a fact.' The man swayed against the doorpost. '*I*'ll be there, sure as the sun comes up. There's never hangings enough for me,' he continued with relish. 'Oh, I likes to see 'em kick their last dance at Newgate and Horsemonger Lane! A fine job Calcraft does on 'em, a fine job, sir. It's not often you see women topped, eh? Mrs Arbuckle will go down with a mighty crackfart, I wager.' He leered and laughed at the same time. 'I wonder what she'll wear?'

'Black would be decent.'

He received my cold remark with a moment's uncertainty, then gave a guffaw. 'Quaite *à la mode*,' he added mincingly. 'What a fashionable lady wears to her own funeral.'

Sickened, I pushed roughly past him into the street. I had got my bellyful of hangings. I had watched some half a dozen of them, with the prompting that they – and they alone – so regularly achieved diversion for London society at all its levels, they must surely make a worthy scene for one of Lloyd's Penny Dreadfuls. But they repelled me too much to turn a guinea from them. The last execution I had watched amid decent company, from a window specially hired at a tavern in sight of the scaffold, places rising to twenty-five shillings each. I was close to a young woman, pretty and well dressed, open mouthed in excitement, squealing and rubbing her soft hands, and when the man dropped she turned to face me, crimson-cheeked with heaving breast, as though just come from her lover.

But if executions appalled me, it was not in the sentimental, sensuous way they affected Charles John Huffam Dickens, who educated his public so regularly about such matters in print. I was a practical young man. Human suffering which could be avoided, on the scaffold, the triangles, or the operating table, simply irritated me as stupid.

Hands in pockets, stick under arm, I made briskly along The New Cut, past the warm, yellow-glowing, streaming windows of the gin-shops. Past the Victoria Theatre – which had been the Coburg, was to become our present temperance music hall, but was then haunted by gory-visaged melodrama. I strode among a crowd of idlers fashionable and otherwise, pickpockets, pimps and assorted criminals, eagerly prurient copying clerks from attorneys' offices and counting houses, a top-hatted peeler or two, the inevitable horde of street arabs, brightly glowing representatives from the whole spectrum of drunkenness, and young women obliged to hire their bodies for what labour or what pleasure men could wring out of them. The night was clear, an east wind blowing away the smoky fog which clings to London so affectionately all winter. It was growing colder, moon and stars shining like ice. The church clocks struck an irregular eleven as I hastened across Blackfriars Road to Union Street. Mrs Arbuckle would hear them in Newgate, and know too that she had only another nine hours on earth.

Promptly at eight she would die in the Press-yard, in much the same company as I moved among. The prayers of the Ordinary – the Newgate prison chaplain – would be swamped as she dropped by a shout of excitement to be heard almost across the river. Then Calcraft would cut her down, for the anatomical attentions of students at near-by Bartholomew's Hospital.

Indeed, the ceremony of Mrs Arbuckle's demise was already well begun. Her obligatory Sunday devotions in the Newgate chapel that Easter Day had been less preoccupied with the Resurrection of Christ than the permanent extinction of herself. She would have been moved from anonymity behind the heavy curtain of the women's gallery, to full minatory exposure before the felonious congregation in the condemned pew. I had seen this, a box of heavy black timber immediately under the pulpit, in which those to die the coming week heard prayers for their souls yet unreleased, were

41

expected to join the responses of their own burial services, and to attend diligently a sermon underlining their own utter wickedness while urging full repentance in the regrettably limited time available.

As always in London, a laggard clock somewhere tinnily attained its hour. I reflected as I walked that Mrs Arbuckle had been spared the company in chapel of her own coffin, the custom of setting them on the seats beside their forthcoming occupants having recently fallen into disuse.

5

WE LIVED IN King's Bench Walk. The name in this, our new twentieth century, brings to mind those generous, leafy squares of the Temple, with grave, gowned barristers strolling about airing their wigs. To the century just past, it signified something much different. The street lay within the Rules of the King's Bench, an area at the very kernel of the Borough, confined between Newington Butts and Marshalsea Road near the obelisk of St George's Fields. 'The Rules of the Bench' were convenient for the Sessions House in Newington Causeway, in which imprisoned King's Bench debtors were allowed to purchase the liberty to reside in their strict confines. King's Bench Walk itself was a short, sad cul-de-sac of monumental mediocrity, then unroofed by the railway which soars across the Thames, not far from Blackfriars Road. It backed hard on Hill Street, now called Glasshill Street, and the Drapers' Alms Houses, newly rebuilt, their enormous chiselled plaque affording perpetual glorification for the three churchwardens – the two Williams, William Giles and William Pugh, and Joseph Kesterton – responsible for the resurrection.

I was condemned to live in 'The Rules' by nothing but my own poverty. My fellow-colonists in such a shunned outpost were understandably seedy. Dock labourers, unshipped sailors, washerwomen and muffin men rubbed threadbare shoulders with a sprinkling of prison agents who went daily to oversee those debtors still confined. Round the corner in Lant Street had lodged that eminent literary gentleman, amateur actor and ringmaster of humanity's freak-shows, the aforesaid Charles John Huffam Dickens, when he had been like myself a pushful twenty-one, a scribbler for the penny papers, and as hotly ambitious for the acclaim and fortune which I *now* – nigh on seventy-five – have long reconciled myself to doing without. I have never contrived to care for Dickens's oozy works. But when we met briefly, he was kind to me. Now he has lain in Westminster Abbey these thirty years. And I await my ascension to the spectral host of England's neglected novelists.

In that April of 1846 I extravagantly enjoyed the best room in a cramped three-storey terrace house, the upstairs front. An icy bedroom the size of a cupboard jutted into the yard behind, where there was use of the privy. The house was shabby outside and in, the windows loose and rattling, the muslin curtains sagging and grey, the carpeting stained, the oil-cloth pockmarked. It smelt always of turpentine, which a brisk turnover of lodgers obliged the landlady to be generous with, to keep down the bedbugs.

A pale, wretched charity-girl in pattens scrubbed the floors, then got up the coals, and donned leather gloves to black the grate and much of the surrounding wallpaper. The landlady herself, with ever-running nose and ever-crumpled black stockings, was perseveringly disobliging. I knew I should find the street-door left for me on the latch, because she would never disturb herself by answering it. I kept a key on our mantelpiece, and when I had visitors sent it ringing on the cobbles outside.

I noticed the lamp glowing behind the curtain. Floy was not abed. I expected she would be waiting. Hearing my step on the stair she jumped to open our door, sewing still in her hand.

'Guy – lovey! You seed Mr Liston? Did you?'

I laid hat and gloves on the crimson chenille cloth of our table. 'I spoke to him. But our conversation was somewhat one-sided. I imagine that conversation with Mr Liston generally is.'

She caught my expression, and as always she mirrored it with her own. Floy was full of Cockney quicksilver, but she could only reflect her betters, never raise a gleam of her own. I had, at first, thought this an estimable feminine quality.

'Didn't he give you no money?' she asked, half-dejected, half-unbelieving.

I shook my head. 'He found no attraction in my schemes, nor in myself.'

'Guy, love, you're cold.' Her arms were round me, she was smiling, as usual obliterating instantly the unpleasant intangibles of life for the comforts and pains of the moment. 'Come to the fire, lovey, come and warm yourself.'

The embers were low, the kettle cold, and scuttle empty. But I crossed the little square room and obligingly spread my hands before the grate. I had been sharing life with Floy – Miss Florence Fuller, were it conceivable I should ever formally introduce her – for almost half the past winter. Floy was certainly a dazzler. She was a mantua-maker with the face of a Murillo virgin, whom I had found on wages of one-and-sixpence a day. A woman lying beside me at night then seemed as essential to my existence as pen and paper to write with. Though in truth, I had little but the youthful fancy of myself as a raffish *littérateur* ceding from conventionality, a gypsy of society, a flaunter of irregular and immoral living. And in the Borough! In the very Rules of the Bench! (My life since has been one of impeccable and almost intolerable respectability.)

'Was there a lot of smart people there? What did you get to eat and drink?' she asked eagerly, her greater interest in the form, rather than the purpose, of any gathering being an oddity common among women, even of far better station.

'There were three rich ladies in nice frocks. They had nothing else to recommend them. Did you eat any supper?'

'There was a crust left. I don't mind,' she replied uncomplainingly.

'Couldn't you have got some ham from the German sausage-shop?' I sounded resentful, though the annoyance was at myself.

She laughed. 'How can a gal? With nothing but a ha'penny tied in the corner of her handkerchief?'

45

I crouched down, trying to rattle warmth from the greying coals with the poker. 'I should have left you some money,' I apologized. I plodded across my arid life like a two-humped camel. One hump my debts, the other Floy. 'Tomorrow I'll order some pickles and cheese and oysters, and have a bottle of spirits sent round from the wine vaults in Borough High Street,' I promised.

'Have you got the ready money, Guy?' She spoke as though inquiring my state of health.

'Mr Lloyd may pay another advance.'

She was down beside me, arm round my neck. 'I'd starve, Guy, just to be with you. Honest to God I would.'

I found such enthusiasm for martyrdom dejecting. 'Go to bed, Floy,' I bade her.

She stayed where she was. 'Pr'aps one day we'll be married, Church of England fashion.'

It was a playful remark. But I knew that such a glorious union lay at the edge of her dreams, rather than beyond them. I made no comment.

'I dare say there ain't ten gals in a hundred what's living in the same beds as men in London, and *is* married regular.' She was eighteen, a child of the Borough, maturer in her shrewdness, philosophy and knowledge of life than any lady of fashion. 'I know plenty myself, that's a fact. Some is fools to be 'ticed away, but o' course they needn't go without they likes to.'

I drew her to her feet. 'They're always free to leave again,' I suggested.

'Be turned out, more like,' she returned with spirit. 'I've seen a gal or two with a dreadful swole face and black eyes, because her man's had a few words with her. Sometimes they swear they're going to take a warrant out, but they never appears against him. For fear of getting the same or worse, I s'pose.'

'You've at least no fear of such treatment from me,' I observed cordially.

'But you ain't obliged to keep me, like we *was* married.'

'What would you say if I went to America?'

'America?' she screeched, aghast. 'That's like going to the moon.'

'No, it isn't. People go there regularly. It's perfectly safe, these days.' I had confided to her my aim of extracting money from Robert Liston, but not its purpose. Could I but have escaped to America, I could have shaken off my debts, shaken off Floy, found employment on one of the country's blossoming newspapers, proclaimed to the world this new pain-destroying drug, married Charlotte . . .

'Don't leave me, Guy,' she implored. 'Don't make me seem a fool to have been 'ticed away by you.'

'I wish I could provide better for you, that's all.'

'You're very good to me,' she replied artlessly. 'If I was in the family way, you wouldn't send me to the workhouse, would you?'

'No, of course not!' I stood full of horror at the vision. The gallant's nights of our present age are illuminated by the comet-tails of Charles Bradlaugh and Annie Besant, who faced gaol for suggesting that love and its natural consequences might be separated. But I know not how such a state – such an assured triple-tragedy – was avoided between Floy and myself. I surmise that in my youth, a poor diet imposed upon girls of Floy's class a convenient barrenness. Now dressmakers eat better, and are as fertile as chickens.

'Lads who ain't married mostly sends their gals to the workhouse to làv in,' she informed me solemnly. 'They goes to see them with a bit of tea and sugar, then forgets them, and goes off with another, most likely.' She tossed her head. 'Men wouldn't behave in such likes to their poor wives.'

'Sleep easy. I shan't turn you into the streets.' My heart ached with guilt. This was precisely what I intended.

'If you did, what's a poor gal to do?' She spoke resignedly, many in her acquaintance having faced exactly that fate.

'Go to bed, Floy,' I repeated.

This time she took her candle. 'Was you going to the hanging in the morning?' I shook my head. 'But you always did,' she insisted.

47

'I've lost the taste for diverting my life with another's death.'
I took off my cutaway coat, replacing it with a loose jacket
from the wooden peg behind the door. 'It's the only, single
tragedy in life, that which ends it. All else we groan about is
trivial.'

'I'll be awake still, lovey, when you comes to bed.'

She stooped to light her candle in the dying fire. She
always undressed before I entered the bedroom, and blew out
the flame. I had never seen her naked. It was a strange
modesty, but one to be respected.

'I've a deal of work to do yet,' I told her.

I reached out, touching her soft cheek with the back of my
fingers. She clasped the hand, pressing it against her breast
savagely. But I had turned against her devotion. With love,
like praise, it is the source which counts. Floy was a beautiful
slut, with a tongue ringing in her head as irritatingly as that
of a tinny bell. Her father was a chairmaker with six children
and a wife who took in washing, with one room across St
George's Fields. And I was going to abandon her. She would
starve, or delay it a year or two by turning whore. Yet I was
determined. I consoled myself that gentlemen in society
treated girls as badly. I had still one hazardous card, which
might win my way across the Atlantic. I should play it on the
morrow.

From the cupboard I took books, inkstand, paper and
quills, sitting at the chenille cloth, turning up the lazy wick of
the lamp, setting beside it from my fob my father's watch,
which ticked extremely loudly. I shivered, the room already
growing unpleasantly cold. But I had my self-imposed duty of
recording the events of my day, which now arms me to write of
times far past without the fuzz and fading of memory, confident that my facts can be rung against history and not found
counterfeit. These yellow notes shall make a pleasant bonfire
before I die. With all my other papers, for I would spare my
literary remains the fate of being savaged by clever young
dogs.

Before retiring, chilled and fagged, I opened one of the
leather-bound books which my father had left me with his

chemicals and debts. It was entitled *Researches, Chemical and Philosophical, Chiefly Concerning Nitrous Oxide*, written in 1800 by Sir Humphry Davy, who my father always implied to have been a close friend of his youth. Davy was a Cornishman of brilliance and charm, my father told me. He had early made the valuable acquaintanceship of the physician Thomas Beddoes, who was taking a quiet spell in Cornwall to unravel the Plutonic and Neptunian theories in geology. Beddoes was so struck by Davy, he immediately offered the youngster the Superintendent's post at his 'Pneumatic Institute' at Clifton, near Bristol, which treated disease of both body and mind with inhalations of newly discovered 'factitious airs' like oxygen and the gas of carbonic acid. But Davy was a chemist, not a medical man. His researches on nitrous oxide, which I now opened at my bookmarker, he later dismissed as 'the dreams of misemployed genius which the light of experiment and observation never conducted to truth'. As for my father, I doubt if Sir Humphry had ever met him, or been aware of his existence.

I read once again how Humphry Davy had produced nitrous oxide gas from zinc and dilute nitrous acid. And how he had tried its effects by inhaling it – bravely, when it had been thought more deadly than the breath of Charon himself, even if wafted across the human skin. Davy found he could breathe it easily, for minutes on end, experiencing not agonal convulsions but the most delightful sensations from top to toe, enjoying simultaneously the strength of Hercules, the energy of Alexander the Great and the visions of Joan of Arc – until he fell asleep.

I turned the pages. Once more I read how one day Davy suffered a headache, which he ascribed to indigestion, and cured with a whiff or two of the gas. And on another he had an inflamed wisdom tooth, which responded to the same remedy, though the pain returned each time the inhalation was stopped. So nitrous oxide gas relieved pain, while it was inhaled and for as long as its effects lingered. Exactly as discovered in Hartford, Connecticut, by that involuntary scientist, Sam Cooley.

I looked up, noticing the lamp beginning to smoke. Now, Robert Liston must certainly have known of Humphry Davy's book. He had surely read those very passages. Yet their significance had never struck him. How much suffering the world might already have been saved! I thought, had Liston, or any other surgeon, put a simple two and two together. But that is the most difficult sum in all human experience.

Should I return to Clifford Street the next morning, book under arm, and point the passage out to Liston? I could not forbear a smile, thinking it unlikely he would thank me for such instruction. I shut the volume and replaced it in the cupboard. My debt to my father's eccentricity is infinite. The scientific atmosphere which came so pungently to my youthful nostrils silvered the novelist's mirror which I have since turned upon the world. My 'scientific' novels are my best – or my most successful, or my most lucrative, all three terms being utterly different. Admittedly, H. G. Wells swims better in deeper philosophical waters than I, and has thundered spectacularly to golden shores on the mighty rollers of his imagination. I have rubbed shoulders with him, though I fancy I am more aware of the friction than he. 'What scientific training did you have, Romilly?' he asked a year or two ago, in that high-pitched voice. Like any shop assistant with the luck to get a second-rate technical education, he venerates the subjects exposed to his intelligence. 'What qualified you to write such books?'

'My father was a gifted amateur scientist,' I replied. 'That was qualification enough.'

'My father was a gifted professional cricketer,' returned H. G. Wells. 'But I didn't find that sufficient qualification for myself attempting to play for Kent.'

6

THE NEXT MORNING I dressed again in my best. I did not tell Floy where I was going. She never seemed inquisitive, though she must have been curious over a thousand things about me. She was too loving to chance irritating me with midge-bites of questions. And too timid, because she knew that much of my business about Town would be beyond her comprehension. There are advantages in a man's attaching to himself a female companion of limited intelligence.

When I left the lodgings past noon, Mrs Arbuckle was dead and cold, perhaps already dissected. Across the street I saw the hot potato man, to whom I tossed a ha'penny with the air of a grandee scattering largesse, instructing him to supply the lady in the first floor front. That left me in my pocket – and in the world – one penny and one ha'penny. Were my impending business successful, such poverty would look trifling. Were it not, my life would seem no less dismal had the pair of copper coins the comforting company of a ten-pound note.

My route lay much as the night before. The sky was glowering, I was afraid that rain might spoil my smart appearance, but it held off until I reached the gardens of St James's Square as Wren's church in Piccadilly was striking two o'clock. I had chosen my time carefully. A lady of Lady Aubery's quality would never be seen out at such an unfashionable hour. She would certainly be at home, but whether to visitors, and particularly to me, was problematical.

Aubery House half-filled the west side of the Square. I gave a double knock. Instantly the door flew open, in the hands of a page barely three feet high, dressed in a pigeon-breasted green jacket and trousers striped like a guardsman's.

'Is her Ladyship at home?'

In reply, he extended the fingers of his white kid gloves for my visiting card – these were not wafted genteelly on silver salvers about the greatest houses. I had to satisfy him by saying simply, 'My name is Mr Guy Romilly.' With a look of scorn, the child disappeared.

I waited barely a minute atop the five broad steps before the page returned with a young footman, in livery finer than Robert Liston's, with silk stockings, brilliantly pomaded hair and smelling powerfully of eau de Cologne. 'Lady Aubery is at home, sir,' he announced blandly.

I entered with some excitement, while trying to give the impression of performing such social exercises every afternoon of my life. Handing hat, stick and gloves to the page, I crossed the huge chessboard of the marble hall floor, into which poured a cascade of Carrara forming the staircase – *not* used only on special occasions, as in meaner establishments. From the walls looked down Frenchy, Fragonard-like paintings in delicate blues, young women disporting on swings or amid unaccustomedly clean sheep, each set as a medallion in a border of thick gold. Above, the chandeliers could each blaze with a hundred flames. Lord Aubery employed his town house only for dinners, salons and the like, his guests selected with careful calculation as possibly useful politically to himself. He would not be under its roof at that hour of the day. He slept there, doubtless spinning webs of intrigue in his dreams. He was a born politician. He was a Tory, flesh, breath and bone. I believe he bestowed patronage by smiles from the cradle, and that now his every action was motivated politically, even blowing his nose and farting.

For its singular mistress, the house was but a frame as extravagant as those encompassing the medallions on the walls. She received me in the downstairs morning-room, sitting on a lemon-coloured satin sofa, beside the fire in an elaborately-carved grate. She wore a silk dress of dull gold – which was the fashion – a shawl of Norwich silk across her shoulders. Lady

Aubery did not sit like other women. One white, lace-fringed hand lay along the back of the sofa, as though she were eager to be busily up and about.

I bowed. 'Lady Aubery, your servant.'

She nodded cordially in return.

'I must ask your Ladyship's forgiveness for calling so early, and so unexpectedly.'

'Young people in society are privileged to make their own rules,' she replied accommodatingly, smiling. She was tall for a woman, strong-boned, lean, dark-haired, a neat, pointed chin giving an elfin look to a face alive with intelligence. Two features always struck me in Lady Aubery. Her eyes were as green as emeralds, and as sharp. Her smile was pleasant, but controlled with precision. So I believe was every other expression of her countenance, every intention of her mind and every emotion in her breast. She was twenty-six. Lord Aubery lumbered goutily under the burden of fifty. They had no children, and all London laughed that it was his Lordship's fault, not hers.

'I hope your pen is ploughing you a fine fortune, Mr Romilly?'

'It ploughs, ma'am. But I'm afraid the harvest is always uncertain.'

'Perhaps you're right to show such caution. Most young gentlemen these days would agree with Pistol that the world's their oyster, to be prised open as violently as he.'

'I assure you it is a caution I should gladly throw to the winds on the slightest encouragement. And there is none better for a young man of letters than a few guineas.'

'Do you suppose your father would have smiled on the career you have chosen?'

'Undoubtedly. He considered that writing was not work, and therefore not demeaning for a gentleman. Exactly like the study of natural science.'

She laughed. 'I was fonder of your father, I think, than anyone outside my immediate family.'

I accepted the posthumous compliment with a short bow. Lady Aubery was my second cousin, the child of my father's own cousin, and my toehold in the aristocracy. My father the scientist was the younger son of a family distinguished for eccentricity and extravagance, even when such were commonplace among English noblemen. He was the descendant of a young spark in Sir Francis Dashwood's Hell-Fire Club – who dressed as monks to sport with ladies coifed as nuns, until ferreted from the wicked caves of West Wycombe Hill. The examples set by my own uncles were admonitory rather than inspiring. One sailed, after a month of ceremonial banquets, for the heroic exploration of Africa, but reached no further than Venice. A second pledged himself to refashion our family estates on the best agricultural principles of William Coke, if he could tear himself away from White's. The third raised money in the City for gold mining in Greece, on which he lived comfortably in Athens. The fourth recognized in himself the talents of a great painter, but succeeded at nothing more than living in Paris, where he rapidly perished from zeal towards the kitchen, the cellar and the bedchamber.

And my father ... about the time of Napoleon's death in St Helena he married a French actress, who gave him a few years of bliss, of which I was the only remnant. After spending his money she disappeared with an Italian opera singer. She had probably not yet learned of my father's death, of which I felt unemburdened with the duty of her enlightenment.

Lady Aubery made me a motion with her hand to take the chair opposite. 'Well, Mr Romilly. Have you yet been received by Mr Liston?'

I sat, carefully arranging my coat tails. 'I have been received, ma'am. And verbally eviscerated, exsanguinated and deboned.'

She looked playfully startled. 'I certainly know Mr Liston to be a man of bitter words. But did he show no interest in this pain-killing gas?'

'He dismissed it as some dodge, like mesmerism or phrenology, unworthy of attention by a practical surgeon.'

'Yet you say it works?'

'Yes, indeed,' I replied forcefully. 'I read again last night the passage of Sir Humphry Davy, of which I spoke when you last received me.'

'Well, Sir Humphry himself did not take its practical possibilities seriously either, surely?' Lady Aubery had a singular interest in philosophy and science. She had as a girl protested shrilly against male *chauvinisme* towards such academic subjects, her frightened family marrying her safely beyond reach of such ideas as quickly as possible.

'Well, ma'am, Sir Humphry said in his book that the gas could be used in surgical operations, where no great effusion of blood took place.'

'But Sir Humphry did nothing to further this notion?'

'Nothing whatever. He became more interested in chemical matters.'

'So? What's your next move? If you intend to make one.'

'However severe the surgery I received from Mr Liston's tongue, I do not think it right to keep contained in my breast a process which could possibly bestow limitless benefit on mankind.'

'Indeed, you must send it forth, like Noah's dove. It may return with an olive leaf from the grove of Academe.'

'For that I would need money.'

'Money?' She looked at me with a surprise which was only half-mocking.

'I know that is a word never used in this house.'

'Well ... perhaps we think of money as something which can become a matter of concern only to the common people, like the cholera.'

'I have neither money, nor what is worse, the prospect of attaining any,' I confessed.

'You must marry for it,' she recommended teasingly. 'Which shouldn't be difficult. You have inherited your mother's good looks. You're up to your ears in debt, I suppose, like every young gallant in Town?'

'I am only a *little* in debt.' I said this shamefully rather than modestly. In Lady Aubery's world, even a young man's debts had an arrogant, heedless extravagance. 'But I want to go to

America.' It was the first unfolding to her of my plan. 'I must see the effects of this gas with my own eyes.'

'That's bold. You may not be received as a welcome visitor. Now we are at each other's throats like two wild dogs, with the Oregon border as our bone.'

'I shall invade their shores even with *Fifty-four Forty or Fight!* volleying round my ears,' I replied, smiling.

That was where Americans set their northernmost boundary, while we asserted that everything north of 49 degrees was Canada. But I doubted if Peel wanted a scrap, or President Polk, once safely elected on that bellicose slogan.

'Natural science is certainly taken seriously in America,' Lady Aubery observed. 'And scientists afforded the honour which our own society dissipates on useless clerics and disastrous generals.' She paused. 'You are looking to me for your fare, sir?'

I let my silence, and my expression, imply my agreement.

'But how can I?' This came bitterly, almost as an outburst. 'A woman has no money, beyond a few pence. She is a chattel herself.'

'I wondered if your Ladyship might recommend my expedition to Lord Aubery? He might think that a loan, insignificant to him, was worth his patronage of such relief of human suffering. I assuredly should sprinkle his name across all I wrote, like the sand itself.'

'I don't think Lord Aubery finds much attraction in technical matters,' she replied shortly.

'Then I shall remain in London, and the gas doubtless will remain in Boston.'

'Pray don't give way to self-pity, Mr Romilly. It is the most sterile of emotions. As well as the most irritating to all within earshot.'

'If I do miss this chance, I swear I shall never enjoy another day's contentment in my life,' I told her forcefully.

'Nonsense, sir! Contentment is conceived in the heart as the child in the womb. It grows, or it dies, perfectly impervious to external circumstances.' There was silence. I noticed her fingers drumming on the sofa-edge. 'Very well. Come back this day week.'

I jumped up, uttering expressions of gratitude, which she cut short with a gesture. 'I can promise nothing. Pray understand that. You may simply have a *rendezvous* with disappointment.'

Before I left, she gave of her own 'few pence', five sovereigns from her purse. I think Lady Aubery had a genuine tenderness towards me. There was an unmentioned bond between us, which to a sensitive man and woman can be as satisfying as an embrace. Perhaps – now I cannot recall, and she is long dead – there was a sketchy *amour*, but our respective stations in life made impossible its ever being filled with the lurid colours of passion.

I returned a week later, to the very hour by St James's church clock. Lady Aubery was not at home. But the butler handed me an envelope. I tore it open on the pavement. There was no letter, just a second envelope inside addressed to Coutts's the bankers. It was a draft for a hundred pounds, drawn by Lord Aubery in favour of his wife. Lady Aubery had endorsed it over to me.

The same afternoon I called at a shipping agent's counting-house in Lothbury, in the City. Three weeks later I was aboard the *Britannia* steam-packet of twelve hundred tons, in Coburg Dock, Liverpool. She was the mail-boat awaiting the tide, bound for Halifax and Boston. Another hour, and the paddles turned. A few more, and I was watching the retreating mouth of the Mersey through our scudding black smoke, to my right the Welsh mountains in their purple coverlet of evening mist, to my left the open sea, composing my emotions on leaving my country for ever.

I was downcast at quitting England. I was guiltful at abandoning Floy. When a man takes up lightly with a girl below his station, I reflected, he must steel himself for one day being hard-hearted. But I told myself also there was suffering enough already in the world, and no greater shame than adding to it.

7

I SAILED FROM Liverpool on Wednesday, May 13. The weather on the crossing was fine, though Halifax, that shyest of ports, was as usual invisible behind a bank of fog. The whole voyage took nineteen days, a good average for steam. Our approach was telegraphed into Boston early on the morning of June 1, a Monday.

The date and day of the week, the precocious hour, the clear air and the bright sky which dominated the strange shores all emphasized the fresh start I was making in life. Boston itself struck me as brand-new. It seemed put up that morning, with the paint still wet, its wooden buildings so flimsy after London brick-and-mortar they seemed in danger of crushing by next winter's snowfall. The dwellings were smart enough, white with shutters of inevitable green, some elaborately colonnaded. At the centre, timber gave way to stone round the State House on its hill, from which the whole city could be viewed in a glance. A domed building hard by the river impressed me. From a passer-by I learned it to be the Massachusetts General Hospital.

I eagerly explored the main streets, which were paved, with broad 'sidewalks', lit by gas and visited regularly by the water-cart. Signs at every second corner promised OYSTERS IN EVERY STYLE! The Bostonian seemed much addicted to the oyster, which he consumed with indifference to the season, generally in huge, steaming stews. He had also a fondness for flat-boned beefsteak at breakfast, for cranberries, and for Cock-tail, Gin-sling, Timber Doodle, Sherry-cobbler,

Mint Julep and Sangaree, which I found to be not names of racehorses, but drinks full of power and mystery.

Boston was lively, its traffic as heavy as London's. The people had broad brims to their bonnets or hats, many of the young men with the habit of turning down their shirt-collars, and men of all ages and ranks spitting tobacco juice with the profusion of a volley of musketry. There were three or four newspapers to claim my attention, each occupied that morning equally with the war in Mexico and the vexed question of a Negress slave sold in pregnancy and dying in childbirth. Who should be the loser, buyer or seller? Within my first hour ashore, I discovered everyone to be shamingly pious. And within the second, to be great enthusiasts for the almighty dollar.

As with all emigrants, the excitement and expectation of my voyage outshone the reality of my arrival. I soon found that the almighty dollar unhappily showed no magnetism towards myself. I presented myself to the *North American Review*, imagining the editor agog for a young gentleman with a year at Trinity Hall, and therefore full of English culture. But this apparently was precisely what he did not want at all. I rapidly slid down the intellectual scale of publications, while the indifference shown towards me slid matchingly into contempt. I felt that, from my welcome, the Boston tea party could have occurred but the previous afternoon. But I was offered lavish employment in the way of carting, digging and sweeping, which I declined with steadily diminishing disdain.

I took a small, spare room in a hotel, from which I viewed life with alarm. I had not the money to turn for home. Nor the faintheartedness. Nothing is so stimulating as the smell of your burning boats. I changed my plans. I should not first seek the security of employment. I should go straight to Hartford, discover Charlotte, and beseech a demonstration of the miraculous gas.

Transportation was simple. The railways then were still threatening to invade the lands they have since conquered, but they were well advanced in this corner of America. I left Boston by the Great Western Railroad on the evening of

Wednesday, June 10. I travelled neither first, second nor third class. In America, equality dictated no such divisions. There was only a gentlemen's car and a ladies' car, and of course a Negro car. There were some fifty of us to a coach, sitting in pairs aside the aisle, in the middle of which an anthracite stove must, in chillier weather, have attempted to suffocate everyone. I discovered my companions' aim for spittoons sadly undermined by the motion. The track was single, the scenery felled forest, all gone for the white walls of Boston. The locomotive engine was a noisy beast, with shrieking whistle and tolling bell, and when night came bright sparks from its high chimney fell about us like bright snowflakes.

I spent the remainder of that night at Worcester, forty miles inland. The next day, I took the train another forty miles to Springfield, near the State border with Connecticut. At daybreak on the Friday morning I started my final twenty-five miles, by paddle steamer down the Connecticut River. Despite Charlotte's letters, I knew little of my destination. I had heard of one Captain Wadsworth in Hartford blowing out the candles to filch King Charles the Second's charter from under the nose of the British Governor, hiding it in an oak tree. And of the town's 'Blue Laws', which consigned anyone kissing his own wife on a Sunday to the stocks. And that it had recently been graced by Charles John Huffam Dickens, who declared the rich well-wooded soil to be carefully improved, showed his customary unhealthy preoccupation with the insane asylum and the deaf-and-dumb institute, mentioned that the very steamboat I took was more suitable for the transport of dwarfs than ordinary human beings, and that the bedrooms of the local hotel were very conducive to early rising.

Leaving my two bags at the wharf, and providing myself with directions from a stevedore, I set on foot for Elm Street. Hartford was another bright, wooden, white-and-green-shuttered town, with the impression of growing in size and prosperity by the hour. Its people were doubtless, like Bostonians, devout in their commerce and businesslike in their religion. Though the brand-new Wadsworth Atheneum which I passed indicated their minds to be as carefully improved as the rich well-wooded soil. The Wadsworth oak I noticed to be preserved and revered. Later in the century the town became a Valhalla of life-insurance companies.

Now lathered with excitement at the prospect of meeting Charlotte, I hurried hot, hungry, dry and sweaty along the broad main street, its mud dried hard, diestamped with innumerable hooves and wheels. I was at last in sight of the house – prosperously porticoed – where, I could barely believe, in a minute I should be holding my darling in my arms. The door was opened by the slave, a fat Negress in black bombazine. My inquiry as to having the honour of being at Colonel Otis' residence, and my request to see Miss Charlotte the English governess, were met only with extravagant head-shaking and eye-rolling. Then it sank into my head that Charlotte had left. I frowned. Surely, she had not been discharged? I saw her starving in a garret in this foreign land, to be saved by my unexpected arrival, a picture I found most agreeable.

The Negress directed me to another porticoed house at the end of the street. This time a white-haired Negro manservant in red-and-white striped waistcoat answered my knock. I explained that I was Mr Guy Romilly from England, who wished to present his compliments to the lady of the house, with the object of addressing her English governess.

'There ain't no governess here, sir,' he told me solemnly. 'No, sir.'

Irritated, distrustful of further directions from servants, I asked shortly, 'Is the lady of the house herself at home?'

'Sure, sir. Mrs Tooms is at home. Come on in.'

He opened the door wide. There was in America a refreshing lack of fussy formality with cards and the like. He showed me directly into the front room. Charlotte was sitting in the inevitable American rocking chair, doing some embroidery.

'Charlotte!' I stood open-armed in the doorway.

She leapt up, embroidery flying, giving a loud shriek.

I waited to be embraced. She stood stock still, wide-eyed, bright scarlet, hand to gaping mouth. My arms slowly fell to my sides. She remained dumb. I realized my appearance in

Hartford that morning was a shock, a cruel shock. But there had been no time for a note from Boston to precede me. 'Did you have my letters?' I asked eagerly. 'From London. And on arrival at Boston?'

'Oh, yes,' she said faintly.

I approached smilingly, reaching for her hand. This triggered her into action. She sprang away, spinning round and staring through the window, her back to me, her hands clasped inaccessibly under her chin.

I was more mystified than affronted. 'Charlotte, you're not angry with me? For following you to America? But there were so many, many times before you sailed away that we spoke together, and wept a little together, anticipating this exact happy moment.'

She turned to face me, eyes full of tears. I understood. She was overcome with joy.

'Guy . . .' She swallowed. 'Something has happened.'

'The Americans?' I spoke with deep concern. 'They've been unpleasant to you?'

She shook her head vigorously. 'No, not for one moment . . . you see, I *am* an American.'

'You've taken their citizenship?' I said in surprise. 'So soon? Well, I don't suppose it'll signify.'

'Guy . . . Mr Romilly . . .' She stiffened her back. 'I am married!'

She burst into sobs.

We stood looking at each other. I then noticed the ring on her finger.

'Oh, Guy! I meant to tell you, but somehow it was all so difficult. I never *really* thought you'd come all this way, you see. Not till I had your very last letter from London. But by then, you'd already be in Boston before I could send a reply. I'm Mrs Tooms,' she announced, most miserably.

Seeing by my frown the name to be faintly familiar, she added, 'Mr Tooms is a friend of my former employer. He is a lawyer by profession. Oh, Mr Romilly! How can I ever forgive myself? Putting you to the discomfort and danger of such a long journey.'

I dabbed my forehead with my bandanna. 'Would it be impolite of me to request a glass of wine? As a restorative?'

'Not impolite, but I fear impossible. Mr Tooms does not allow of such items. Like any person of consequence in Hartford.' I recalled with resignation that we were in the dry dominions of the Congregationalists, their Central Church built but a few hundred paces away over the bones of its founders. 'But you may have a cup of buttermilk, if you care.'

'I think not.'

'Poor Guy . . .' She looked at me with a tenderness which was now maddening. 'Have you a position in America?' I shook my head. 'Perhaps Mr Tooms can help you find something suitable?'

'I should prefer not to become acquainted with Mr Tooms.'

'I am sure you would soon be as brothers,' she predicted hopefully.

'I must decline, not through jealousy or hostility, but to save ourselves embarrassment. The harshest pain, fortunately, to which gentlemen are subjected these civilized days. Or has Mr Tooms been made privy to the secret of my existence?'

Even as I spoke came the clip of hooves and crunch of wheels outside. Charlotte nodded towards the door. 'Mr Tooms,' she indicated nervously.

A minute later, and there he was. Large and florid, middle-aged in the thirties, with jowls like bladders of pink lard, his head poor pasture for hair, whiskers we now call muttonchop and a moustache which overhung both lips like the eaves of a roof. His stare of surprise congealed to a frown at Charlotte's unobliterated traces of distress. But by the words which tumbled from her lips, he ascribed such signs to feminine emotion at meeting a fellow-countryman and friend of childhood. He shook my hand heartily, told me that any friend of Charlotte's was *ipso facto* one of his, and warmly invited me to share their midday meal. I preferred hunger.

'And what brings you to our fine city, Mr Romilly?' he asked, hands clasped behind full-skirted black frock-coat, feet astride before cold iron stove, master of his house, of Charlotte and of my own despairing spirits.

I had come to marry his wife, but I could hardly say so. 'We have been hearing stories, sir, on the far side of the Atlantic, of a gas with the magical effect of relieving pain for tooth-pulling, surgical operations and the like. As I am a journalist by profession – which I hope shortly to resume in this country – I have an interest in investigating these rumours, and sending a dispatch to London.'

'Oh! You must see my good friend Dr Wells,' he said cordially. 'He and his partner Dr Morton have achieved great fame with painless tooth-pulling hereabouts.'

'I should much appreciate a meeting with the two gentlemen,' I said humbly, wondering how Charlotte could possibly have coupled herself to such a grim grotesquerie.

'No sooner said than done.' Mr Tooms waved his large hand with accommodating airiness. 'Leastways, in respect of Dr Wells. Dr Morton left Hartford some while back, for practice in Boston. I shall give you a letter of introduction to Dr Wells directly, sir,' he announced smilingly. 'Though I have not seen as much of the doctor this last twelvemonth as I should have wished. He is in indifferent health, I hear. I am not even certain if he still performs tooth-pulling. It is high time we paid a call on Dr and Mrs Wells, my dear,' he added to Charlotte. She was staring distractedly through the window. 'Mrs Tooms,' he added loudly. She turned, flustered. 'Have you any news recently of Dr Wells?'

'Yes. He is giving exhibitions with a troop of singing canaries.'

'The doctor is a gentleman of wide interests,' Mr Tooms passed off this unusual news.

The lawyer sat his bulk against a bureau in the corner of the pine-walled room, busily scribbling my note of introduction. This left me a minute to stare at Charlotte's trim back, she having turned to look hard again through the muslin curtains. I felt I was not indulging in self-flattery by suspecting that she would dearly have loved to grab my hand, flee with me from that house, and never set eyes on her portly lord again. But a woman can untie her marriage knot hardly less easily than that of her shroud. I had to reconcile myself to

Charlotte vanishing from my life, though I doubted if she would ever vanish from my thoughts. And never could I reconcile myself to the blow she had struck me, it seemed with such airy casualness.

Her good-bye was faint, with the gratification of another tear or two, hastily brushed away behind her husband's back. Mr Tooms took me to the front door, arm round my shoulders in the familiar manner of the Americans. 'So you knew Mrs Tooms when she was in short skirts?' he asked jovially. 'Mrs Tooms has told me everything about you.'

The comfort of his tone indicated that Charlotte certainly had not. 'We were the children of neighbouring houses, and my family worshipped at Mr Conybeare's church,' I explained. With what pangs I recalled our glances, so shy, sly and subtle, across the pews during her father's interminable and unmemorable sermons!

'Mrs Tooms has grown to be a mighty fine lady. She has handsome looks, sharp intelligence, skill in household management, grace in entertaining visitors and an excellent singing voice.' He slapped my back heartily. 'I thank the Lord daily for my good fortune. What more could a man ask Him to bestow?'

'Nothing . . . nothing at all,' I managed to say.

'There is, Mr Romilly.' He held up a big forefinger, eyes twinkling quite savagely. 'Next time you are in these parts, which I hope will not be too long distant, Mrs Tooms may be on her way to the ultimate attainment of womanhood.' I looked puzzled. 'The supremest of God's gifts towards man's happiness. A large family.'

I turned. The fellow was as subtle as a dead pig. I could say no more. I wanted to be sick.

8

THE DENTIST'S HOUSE was smaller than the lawyer's. I found it a street or two away, but in the same genteel area of the town. It was steep-roofed, wooden, on two floors with five windows up and two down, a picket fence retaining a small garden, and the inevitable portico. I had expected a board announcing Dr Wells's profession, a 'shingle' as the Americans called it, but there was nothing. The place had a neglected air, the step dirty, the shutters closed on the downstairs windows, the paint not up to the gleaming whiteness of its neighbours, like a bad tooth in a smile. I faced the front door for a whole minute, bracing myself for the interview. I had reached the second of the two targets on which I had aimed at such long range. But any excitement had been dispersed by the *mauvais quart d'heure* just endured.

My knock was answered not by a servant, but by the lady of the house herself. She was pleasant looking, well dressed, young, staring at me with an apprehension ill-suppressed.

'Good day, ma'am.' I stood hat in hand. 'May I introduce myself? I am Mr Guy Romilly from London. I should much appreciate a word with Dr Wells.'

'The doctor is no longer in practice.' She started to shut the door.

'I have a letter of introduction from Mr Tooms, of this city.'

She hesitated. I noticed how drawn her expression was. 'Give it to me,' she commanded curtly.

As she took the folded paper a voice came urgently, 'Who's that? Who's there? Is it someone about the shower-baths?'

'Wait.' She disappeared quickly. I stood on the doorstep,

uneasiness rising inside me. The unwelcoming and nervous atmosphere, the references to singing canaries and the doctor's ill health, the abandonment of his profession, combined to create in my mind a suspicion. That the miraculous gas was akin to that which gives the pale, deluding light to Jack's lantern over mire and marsh, or lit the St Elmo's fire which blazed in the rigging of my ship.

Mrs Wells returned, and with an air partly apologetic and partly frightened showed me into the dental surgery.

It was a room at the back of the house, its walls like Mr Tooms's of pine, its fireplace stone, its purpose declared by an instrument cabinet, a stout high-backed leather chair and a capacious spittoon. The heavy curtain of red velvet across the door I surmised hung less to prevent the intrusion of draughts than the escape of screams. The room did not seem to have filled its official role for some time. Everything was untidy. Paintings were propped face inwards against the wall, the stuffed bodies of birds and small animals covered a desk under the window, beside which a cage of a dozen or so canaries twittered and chirped most distractedly.

At first it seemed a cell without its Prospero. Then I noticed in the light of half-drawn curtains the dentist observing me guardedly, half hidden by a folding screen which stood against the leather operating chair.

'What do you want, sir?' He asked this quietly, even submissively.

I bowed. 'I have travelled from London, sir, in England, for the honour of this meeting. Intelligence has reached us there of the gas you employ to perform your famous painless extractions.'

He made a noise half snort and half laugh, moving from the shadows into a shaft of sunlight. He was younger than Mr Tooms, handsome though pudgy, his head large, his face rosy, his eyes large and blue under straight brows, his hair thick and reddish, his upper lip and chin bare but his whiskers luxuriant. Like Mr Tooms, he wore the uniform of a professional gentleman, a wide-skirted black broadcloth coat with a high starched collar and jet silk cravat. Though respectable, his clothes shared the insalubrious and disordered appearance of his room. He moved a little towards me, so hesitantly and timidly he almost crouched.

'Are you a medical gentleman, sir?' I noticed the softness and fullness of his mouth, suggesting at once an emotional and volatile nature.

'I am a journalist, sir.'

This drew a look of interest, even of admiration. How different from the scorn my profession excited in Robert Liston! But in America journalists were respected, like men of science or men who made money.

'You don't say?' he asked in a much friendlier tone. 'What paper do you work for? The *Courant*, right here in Hartford?'

'In London I write for *Lloyd's Penny Weekly*, a paper known to every household of the Kingdom,' I assured him earnestly. 'I have just arrived in your country, and am engaged in selecting a respectable periodical for my services.'

'I've written a manual of dentistry. Do you know it?'

His voice had the eager assumption of every author that his work achieved universal cognizance, if not readership. I courteously confessed ignorance.

'I guess I'm going to Europe pretty soon, Mr Romilly.' His eyes strayed from mine, to roam the room. 'To Paris. To buy some pictures.'

'Paris is the centre of the civilized world, equally for science and art,' I assured him gravely.

He was silent. The heat of the shut room was overpowering, the noise of the canaries aggravating. 'Could you favour me with a demonstration of this nitrous oxide gas, doctor?' I asked, trying to muffle my impatience.

'No,' he replied shortly. 'I've lost interest in it. I guess it's ineffective.'

My spirits, steadily sinking, grounded. My trouble, and Lady Aubery's money, seemed wasted. 'But sir!' I insisted. 'Can you not tell me something about it? Of your first-hand experiences?'

In reply, Wells rummaged among the stuffed animals on

his desk and handed me a rolled-up sheet of stout paper. 'That was the first I ever heard of it.'

It was a poster in exuberantly variegated type, as might be seen stuck to any wall in the city. I read it by the window.

A GRAND EXHIBITION OF THE EFFECTS PRODUCED BY INHALING NITROUS OXID, EXHILERATING OR LAUGHING GAS! it began, with poor spelling. IN THE UNION HALL. TUESDAY EVENING, DECEMBER 10, 1844.

With some excitement I recognized this advertisement for the lecture delivered eighteen months ago by 'Professor' Quincy Colton, as related by Sam Cooley to my dear, lost Charlotte.

Forty Gallons of Gas will be prepared, and administered to all in the audience who desire to inhale, it went on. *Eight Strong Men are engaged to occupy the front seats. They will prevent those under the influence of the Gas from injuring themselves and others. This course is adopted that no apprehension of danger may be entertained by the audience. (Probably no one will attempt to fight.) The Gas will be administered only to Gentlemen of the First Respectability. The Object is to make the entertainment in every respect a Genteel Affair.*

The poster continued in smaller and smudgier type, as though running out of breath. *Those who inhale the gas once are always anxious to inhale it the second time. They seem to retain consciousness enough not to say or do that which they would have occasion to regret. No language can describe the delightful sensation produced. Robert Southey (poet) once said that, 'The Atmosphere of the Highest of All Possible Heavens Must be Composed of this Gas.' Entertainment to be given at 7 o'clock sharp. Tickets 25 cents.*

I rolled up the poster and handed it back to Wells, aware he was studying me intently as I read. 'I have heard, sir, of the drug store clerk, Sam Cooley, and how you had your own tooth drawn —'

'In that very chair.' For the first time his face wore some animation. 'Dr John Manley Riggs pulled the tooth. A dentist of high repute in Hartford, sir.'

I nodded my respect. He was later to be of high repute through the United States, and give his name to 'Riggs' Disease', by which your teeth all go septic, and drop out.

'Dr Riggs came back here, the morning after Mr Cooley inhaled the gas. We had an agreement, the night previous, to push the administration to a point hitherto unknown. We did not know whether success, or my death, confronted us, sir. It was *terra incognita*, but we were bound to explore it.' This was spoken with no *braggadocio*. 'There were four or five other gentlemen in the room, to hold me should I run amok, though in the event they were not needed. But only Dr Riggs and myself knew to what point the inhalation was to be carried. I inhaled with the gas-bag on my lap, until my arms fell to my sides and my head lolled back on the rest, when Dr Riggs quickly pulled the tooth.'

'It must have been a most frightening experience, sir,' I said in a heartfelt voice. 'You were risking your life.'

'I wasn't scared. No, sir. But I guess Dr Riggs sure was. He was risking his career, and maybe his liberty. I didn't feel a twinge, no more than using a toothpick. I saw great possibilities, enormous possibilities! It was the greatest day in my life . . . and now it seems my last happy one,' he ended pathetically.

'Then what went wrong?' I asked quickly, to hold his confessional mood.

'What went wrong? Everything went wrong.' He paused a moment, his mouth working. 'I had a partner, a Dr Morton, a man of goaheaditiveness like myself. We worked in Boston with our new dental solder – it doesn't turn black in the mouth like the others – but I didn't think we'd make a go of it, for one reason and another, so I came home here to Harford. Dr Morton being attached to me by . . . well, if not exactly the bonds of friendship, by the usual esteem of professional gentlemen who have worked together, when I wished to impart wider fame to my discovery, and receive wider respect and reward, I travelled to Boston to see him. Dr Morton knows several important people there – Professor Jackson, the famous chemist, with whom he lodges, and Dr Warren, the surgeon at the Massachusetts General Hospital.'

Wells tossed the poster among his stuffed animals. 'Dr Warren was interested in my experiments, and treated me with much kindness. He invited me to address a medical class on the subject, and to administer nitrous oxide to one of his patients, who was to have a limb amputated.'

'So!' I exclaimed, 'The gas has been employed for a capital operation? Not only for the drawing of teeth?'

Wells shook his head. 'The patient decided against submitting to an operation, which is a usual enough occurrence. I was happy to demonstrate on the removal of a tooth. A large number of students and several well-known Boston physicians had assembled to see the operation, and one of the students having a sore molar opted to substitute himself for the original patient.'

Wells fell silent. 'It was a success?' I jogged him eagerly.

He shrugged. 'I guess the bladder of nitrous oxide was withdrawn too soon. It's ironic, when I was prepared myself to inhale unto death. The patient protested forcefully when the tooth was withdrawn, though afterwards he testified to almost complete painlessness. But by then they were hooting at me.' He added bitterly, 'I should never have demonstrated before medical students, which gentlemen comprise the most critical of audiences, and the worst mannered. They laughed and hissed, imagining I was affronting whatever dignity they presumed to with some sort of hoax. Not that Dr Warren was better. Having afforded me a sarcastic introduction as a gentleman who *purported* to have something which would destroy the pain of surgical operations, he now expressed his opinion that it was a humbug affair. *That* was all the thanks I got for my gratuitous service. I had gone to Boston expecting no pecuniary advantage whatever. I accordingly left the next morning for home.'

I could not help feeling sympathy towards the poor man, after so painful a failure which would have daunted many more resolute souls. 'But however they treated you in Boston, doctor, you know at least the gas to be safe?'

'Oh, sure,' he answered mildly. 'The patients lose their colour, they breathe like furnaces and take a dusky sheen ... their pulse races, they may kick and jerk their limbs, but these are all signs of healthy activity in the nerves and circulation.

Their lives never stand in the slightest danger. And they feel nothing. On occasion, the slightest tug as the tooth comes out, that's all. Would you be interested in buying a shower-bath, Mr Romilly?'

Startled at this change from the philosophical to the commercial, I replied, 'I am in lodgings, sir.'

'Take a look at this patent shower-bath.' He indicated a spindly device in bronze, which I had thought an item of dental equipment. 'It's the coming article, yes sir!' he added with a salesman's enthusiasm. 'It'll be seen in every respectable home in New England before long. You mark my words. And hey, sir . . . when you write for your newspaper, say something about the patent shower-bath. I've the concession, you understand. Mighty useful, getting something in the papers.'

He turned to the canaries, which he started to furnish with birdseed. The dentist struck me as a decided oddity. I made my excuses, and searching for a final question as he accompanied me no further than the door of the room, I reflected on the accolade of Robert Southey (poet), and asked, 'People inhale the gas for pleasure, do they?'

'Since way back. In Vermont, over the last fifteen years, so I've heard. "Frolics" they call them, the folk hereabout. It has the same effect on a man – or a lady – as taking strong drink. And if the gas is the air of the gods, drink sure is the water of the devil.'

I left Hartford by the same paddle-boat, that very night. I have often reflected on Dr Wells's final remark. The two most powerful transformations in human life since the birth of Our Lord have been wrought by gunpowder and anaesthesia, both ot which were invented for amusement. Chinese of great, if indefinite, antiquity mixed saltpetre, charcoal and sulphur to create diverting explosions in their ceremonial fire-crackers. New Englanders of the nineteenth century inhaled nitrous oxide, to enjoy sensations familiar to we who live within the smile of grape and grain. It is all perfectly reasonable. Mankind is always at its most ingenious in the pursuit of fresh pleasures.

9.

WITHIN A DAY of my returning to Boston I found employment. This was of a literary nature, if somewhat specialized. I was hired to write handbills for a haberdasher's, or what the Americans called a dry goods store.

My first *feuilleton* invited the ladies of Boston to honour Cornelius and Son, conveniently situated by the Common, with inspection of their latest corsets, just off the boat, and as encircled the shapely and fashionable waists of Paris. I felt compulsion to match the elegance of the garments with that of the prose. Anyway, all writing must command its author's best effort, as a courtesy to his readers, even if it be only lettering a signpost.

But I found Mr Cornelius a critic of harsher taste. He was an enormous pink-faced jelly-jowled man swaddled voluminously in black broadcloth, breathtakingly skilful as a spitter of tobacco-juice, firing dead centre into the cuspidor even over his shoulder. He thought my work lacked force, was wishy-washy, slip-slop, and without the 'goaheaditiveness' so cherished by New England, the city of Boston and his own establishment.

The man who pays the scribe calls the plot, as I had learned so usefully from Lloyd of Salisbury Square. Recollecting advertisements in the *Penny Weekly*, I tried,

PRESIDENT POLK SHOT

continuing in much smaller type beneath,

an admiring glance at ladies in our summer dresses.

73

Or,

HENRY WADSWORTH LONGFELLOW DYING
to be seen in one of our silk hats.

I was delighted to find Cornelius tickled by these absurdities, though perturbed over their dignity. I won greater enthusiasm by trying another wrinkle favoured in *Lloyd's Weekly*, plundering current events.

> *Across the Rio Grande, General Taylor leads his heroes,*
> *Though Mexico may burn, like the Rome of Nero's,*
> *Cornelius's Store still respectfully brings*
> *Ladies of fashion their own pretty things.*

I began to wonder if my talents lay possibly in versifying rather than prose.

But Cornelius paid pitifully. I grew shabby. The collar which I wore turned down like the other young men became frayed, my boots were on the point of introducing my feet to the sidewalk, I was often hungry, I had forgotten the taste of wine. That August in Boston was stifling. I had quit my hotel for a bed in a rooming house, shut airlessly behind a never diminishing stack of timber down by the harbour. I passed my days in sad contemplation of my comparatively rosy circumstances in the Borough, my thoughts inevitably concentrating on Floy. I stood incredulous at my own callousness towards her. My only cause for thankfulness towards my Maker, as I tossed sweating in my room, was that I could still afford to avoid sharing it with one of the Irish navvies who teemed in the dock area and reeked violently of rum.

My notion of seeking out Wells's former partner Dr Morton sprang from the insubstantial hope that he might provide me with sufficient detail of the poor dentist's drubbing at the hospital that I could write an article about it. It might draw a welcome guinea across the Atlantic from Lloyd. And there was little risk, in America, of a clamant journalist earning a rebuff.

Wells had mentioned Morton's lodging with Dr Charles Jackson, whom I quickly discovered to be a man of consequence in Boston. He was a professor of chemistry, and official geologist to the States of Maine and New Hampshire. It appeared from Boston conversation that Jackson had invented the electric telegraph. It was to him, not to Samuel F. B. Morse, that the world was indebted for the wondrous transmission on May 24, 1844, from the Supreme Court room in Washington to Baltimore, of that most pertinent of inquiries, *What hath God wrought?* And that very summer Jackson was claiming in the Boston newspapers, with heat which matched the weather, that he and not Herr Christian Schönbein of Basel had discovered the new explosive, guncotton. Everyone in Boston knew Jackson's residence up on Beacon Hill, where at four o'clock one baking afternoon I presented myself.

Dr Morton no longer lived there, the Negro informed me. Disappointed, but reluctant to leave empty-handed, I besought an interview with the professor himself. He was at home, and condescended.

'Mr Romilly? A newspaper-writer? Just out from England?'

'From London, sir.'

'A city I should much care to visit. I hold your Royal Society in the highest esteem, sir.'

Dr Jackson (the academic title itself was in those days not an invariable prefix to the learned holder's name, on either side of the Atlantic) was a tall, lean man about forty, cleanshaven, his dark hair brushed forward like a cap, his face round and schoolboyish, gazing at me closely through oval metal-rimmed glasses. I noticed he had the tic of repeatedly pursing his lips. He received me in the downstairs drawing-room, a plain apartment without indication of the scientific calling of its occupant, but distinguished with one of the new American organs – or 'harmoniums', as an Englishman would call them.

'The Royal Society, I can assert without fear of contradiction, sir, is an institution which bestows the honour for any invention where it is due,' Jackson continued. 'In this country, any honest man's brains are likely to be scavenged of ideas, like the navvies scavenge anything they think of value from the garbage in the gutters of Quincey Market.'

My expression graciously accepted the compliment on behalf of the Royal Society.

'Dr Morton left my establishment back in May,' Jackson explained. 'He was one of my pupils here, being eager to expand his knowledge of natural science, rather than pass his life as a mere tooth-drawer. His wife was expecting her first child, and hence in a state which could render her mighty awkward.' He paused. 'Dr Morton is a sabbath-school teacher at our near-by Congregationalist church. This caused me regularly, once a week, to await his appearance before the serving of my noon meal. It was *mighty* annoying.'

He fell silent, though his lips busily continued their involuntary twitching. I could assemble in my mind the scene of this weekly domestic drama.

'He sent me a travelling-case to make up for it,' Jackson added solemnly, 'A mighty handsome travelling-case.'

'Perhaps you could enlighten me, sir, on Dr Morton's present address.'

'Oh, sure . . . they have gone into rooms, but you'll find Dr Morton at his office, No 19 Tremont Row.' I murmured my gratitude and was moving towards the door when Jackson stopped me with, 'Pray, Mr Romilly, what business have you with Dr Morton?'

He was eyeing me narrowly. I explained that I had met Dr Wells, and wished to know more about the experiments with nitrous oxide gas. 'They struck me of interest to the general public,' I said. 'Which it is my duty, as a journalist, to keep informed.'

Jackson responded to this with unexpected fierceness. 'I *told* Dr Wells that pain-killing gas was the notion of a crazy man. Right here, in this house, in this very room, when he came down from Hartford bouncing with excitement, like a schoolboy who's learned to play a new game. I warned him, but he paid no heed. So what happened? He was hooted, hooted from the hospital, as any quack deserved. Had he listened to me, he would have been a happier man today. A dentist should not presume to meddle with matters of scientific philosophy. The gas is now discredited as hopelessly unreliable.'

'I knew as much from Dr Wells, sir, and it is sad news to me. I had word of the gas in London, and it seemed worth braving the Atlantic to see. It is a lesson to me in rashness.'

Jackson gave an unexpected smile, and continued in a more intimate tone, 'Despite your green years, I take it that as a journalist you are adept in gathering information? With discretion?'

'Those are the elements of my craft, sir.'

'I have done you a service in providing Dr Morton's whereabouts. You shall do one for me. Dr Morton is deeply involved in *something*. What it be, I know not. But it is certainly not dentistry. Heed me a minute. At the end of June Dr Morton took into partnership another of our Boston dentists, a Dr Grenville Hayden. I happen to know that Dr Hayden was brought in for the specific duty of performing all the extractions, of superintending the employees who make the false teeth, and generally running the office in Tremont Row. Leaving Dr Morton free for *some other interest*, into which I understand he has thrown himself urgently. I wish to know what this interest is.'

His suggestion of my spying on a man I had not yet met I found distasteful. I was anyway mystified by such inquisitiveness, Dr Morton seeming a man much humbler in the profession of science than the great Jackson. I suspected it was not simply good-hearted interest in the activities of an old pupil. Jackson had struck me as a slippery fish.

I replied evasively, 'Dr Morton may not be forthcoming, sir. Even William Cullen Bryant can't make a man talk, if he's determined not to.'

Jackson found my objection too trivial to notice. I had anyway picked the wrong name in the scholarly, serious, self-restrained Puritan poet who was editor-in-chief on the New York *Evening Post*. I had intended to imply some hectoring, inquisitive editor, but I had been in the United States only long enough to gather a colourful garland of superficial impressions.

'I have suspicions, Mr Romilly, that Dr Morton is experimenting with a liquid which *I* suggested to him, two years back. A liquid for painting on the gum, that the pain might be deadened in filling a sensitive tooth. *Maybe —*' He screwed his eyes up. 'Maybe Dr Morton has a mind for passing it off as his own invention. You keep sharp eyes and ears, Mr Romilly.' I held my silence. 'Meanwhile, I must entreat you to leave him in ignorance of our conversation this afternoon. Say you had his address from my servants.'

I gave no more thought either to this underhand suggestion or to this new, magic pain-deadening liquid. It seemed there was no balm in Gilead – nor in New England. But I was determined to see Dr Morton the next morning, on the assumption that a journalist must push open every door, in the hope that, even if he find inside an empty room, another door may lead from it beyond.

The next day was additionally significant for me, because it marked my graduation from handbills to an advertisement in the *Daily Journal*. (This started, *Cornelius's Store for Unparalleled Apparel*, and achieved Keatsian voluptuousness in the matter of the corselet bodice.) I easily found Morton's dental surgery, or 'office' as the Americans generally had it. I was not prepared for its alarming aspect inside. There were a pair of dental chairs with spittoons, where a young man with a swollen face dolefully awaited attention. But my eye was taken by a vast glass showcase half filling the room, crammed with innumerable sets of false teeth. These massed, disembodied grins, set amid isolated fangs arranged as tastefully as ivory necklaces in Bond Street, had a horribly chilling effect. I was staring fixedly when a voice at my elbow announced perkily, 'There's one hundred thousand false teeth in there. Yes, sir! One hundred thousand gnashers.'

I turned to find a pale, pimply, spindly young man in a dark frock-coat, no older than myself. 'Are you sure you've counted every one?' I enquired solemnly.

'Sure thing. Every one.' I fear the air of New England induces a numbness to the funny bone. 'Say, you're a Britisher, aren't you?' I nodded. 'Well, that showcase is destined for the London Exhibition. Make quite a stir, I guess,' he added proudly.

Deciding from his combination of lean years and formal dress that the enthusiast was a dental apprentice, I explained that I was a journalist, and would appreciate the favour of an interview with Dr Morton, whenever convenient.

'The doctor is always ready to receive acolytes of the Press,' he said amiably. The apprentice led me towards an inner door, from where I was already aware of a noise curious in a dentist's surgery. It was the regular thud of a steam engine, which I discovered puffing away in a small factory with four or five busy workmen. Amused at my surprise, my guide said, 'This is Dr Morton's tooth-mill, sir.'

In the middle of the room, which was unbearably hot, stood two revolving stones, as any miller uses. But instead of wholesome flour, they spewed a hard, glittering white powder. 'Only the finest quartz and spar is selected by the doctor,' he continued ardently. 'All quarried in New Jersey and brought to Boston by the railroad. Makes mighty fine teeth.'

Confrontation with such industry – and its fruits – made me anticipate Morton as a man of intense 'goaheaditiveness' indeed. I found him in a small cubicle beyond the tooth-mill, writing busily amid a confusion of books, papers and bottles, yet on learning of my profession instantly pushing his letters aside and cordially inviting me to take the other chair. We sat so close our knees touched. He was tall and slight, carefully dressed in black frock-coat with velvet collar, his features regular with deep-set eyes, his thick brown hair parted on the left and flopping over his right brow, his mouth decisive, his eyebrows straight, his cheekbones and somewhat pointed chin softened by a fuzz of beard. He was a vigorous twenty-seven.

'Are you connected with the newspapers of this city, sir?' he asked at once.

'I represent those of London, England.'

'Then you wish to write up my showcase of false teeth?'

I shook my head. 'I was given your name, sir, by Dr Horace Wells of Hartford. I understand the gentleman was your partner.'

Morton looked Heavenwards. 'God has not given Dr Wells faith in his own talents. Had he not backed away from my new

79

process of dental soldering, in a fit of faintheartedness, he would assuredly have made a fortune. I guess Dr Wells is not sharp enough by half for these times.'

I recalled that Morton was a sabbath-school teacher, and that shrewd commercial enterprise so often accompanies devout and active Congregationalism.

'I was interested less in dental matters, sir, than the nitrous oxide gas which Dr Wells demonstrated here. And achieved what I believe theatrical people call a *fiasco*.'

Morton nodded. 'Had the exhibition been a success, in such a place as the Massachusetts General Hospital, and in the presence of such a figure as Dr Warren, Dr Wells could have been on the path to untold wealth. I fear he did not pray hard enough beforehand.'

'I sought you first at Dr Jackson's —'

'And what had Dr Jackson to say of me?' he demanded abruptly. Morton's manner was brisk, his voice forceful, his every gesture decisive. Now he gave the impression of energy boiling within, like the steam of his engine thudding just beyond the door.

'He spoke of a liquid you were rubbing on the gum to kill dental pain.'

'Oh? Did he claim it to be his own notion?' I nodded. 'Dr Jackson is a man of genius, and like many geniuses most unsettled. He has a weakness for seizing the fame of every new invention with which he has enjoyed the most slight connexion. Naturally, a gentleman of Dr Jackson's standing in both Harvard University and Boston itself is always favoured in every controversy. While a man like myself ... a practical man ... I am a dentist, he is a doctor. Dr Jackson taught me anatomy at the Massachusetts Medical College, where I am engaged in medical studies, in addition to my many other pursuits. I am, in that respect, merely one of his pupils. So I am bound always to be in the wrong against him. Not that any Boston newspaper would dare contradicting Dr Jackson. In writing of myself and my work, Mr Romilly,' he added earnestly, 'I only ask you to be fair.'

'Fair play is the Englishman's leading quality.'

He nodded thoughtfully at this. I had been aware for some time of a faint but penetrating smell in that little room, spirituous, musty, evasively familiar. My memory was jogged by my nostrils to recall something in my childhood, of a medicinal nature, but precisely what, or even for what ailments, was beyond me.

'Well, Mr Romilly, you would seem to have your wits about you. I will confide that I am indeed experimenting with a new pain-destroying method – nothing to do with Dr Wells's gas, nothing to do with Dr Jackson – as I'm sure many people hereabout know well enough. I have tried it already on an animal, my own spaniel. With complete success!' he exclaimed, slapping his thigh. 'The dog became insensible, completely insensible, with my every effort to rouse him, all my pinching and pulling, quite in vain. Yet after removal of the vapour, within just a few minutes, he was as right as rain, and as lively as ever. Now, attend this, Mr Romilly. By a curious accident, the dog frisked into the jar containing my liquid and broke it. I soaked the substance up with my handkerchief, and deciding there and then to risk inhaling it myself, discovered the effect perfectly remarkable.' His voice became more excited. 'I was overcome by a feeling of lassitude, which became more and more intense, until ... I lost consciousness, Mr Romilly! I fell back in my chair, the handkerchief dropped to the floor, and I woke to the knowledge that Heaven had bestowed upon me the duty of pursuing a great discovery to benefit mankind.'

It flashed upon me I had been made party to some wholly new pain-killing preparation. Perhaps Morton afforded me the journalistic importance in London I had dared to imply. I asked at once, 'And what is this substance?'

'I'm not saying,' he returned as quickly. 'This remedy is *my* invention, *my* property. I won't see it pirated. I am forced even to buy its ingredients at different pharmacies, establishments where I am not known. But I assure you it is effective, and *safe*. Absolutely safe. I have tried it on my two apprentices, without the slightest harm. I was ready to try it on a patient for the extraction of a tooth, and sent the apprentices last month down to the wharves, offering five dollars to any labourer who would permit the experiment to be performed on him.'

'And it was performed with success?' I asked eagerly.

'Unhappily, all declined coming,' he added with disappointment. 'Have *you* any troublesome teeth, Mr Romilly?'

'Oh, no! Mine are all in capital condition,' I told him quickly.

'An opportunity will arise. Soon I shall be able to receive my patients in the front room and extract all their teeth, convey them into the back office and fit them with a new set and send them off without knowing the first thing about the operation.'

I could but admire such confidence.

'I should consider it a rare privilege, were I invited to witness the experiment,' I said tentatively.

'Indeed, it will be among the greatest moments in the history of mankind,' Morton asserted. 'And so you may ... on one condition. That you write of my work quite impartially. That you would not be swayed by any faction in Boston to discredit me.'

'I give you my word on that, as an Englishman.'

He nodded. 'Then where might my apprentices find you?'

I disclosed my address, adding that I should be moving to more salubrious surroundings once settled. But Morton saw my circumstances, and drawing from his waistcoat pocket a gold five-dollar piece, pressed it into my palm with, 'Take this on account, for such literary services as I might require. I think I have summed you up as trustworthy, Mr Romilly. And no word to Dr Jackson, about my preparation or my experiments, if you please.'

I rose, murmuring my thanks, but adding, 'I hope you did not think it necessary to *buy* my discretion?'

'I did not. But Dr Jackson is sly. The Lord be with you.'

I walked in the bright sunlight back to my lodgings, my brain absorbing the unexpected booty of my halfhearted foray to Tremont Row. Were there anything in this new pain-killing drug – and I had grown jaundiced in my views after my quest for nitrous oxide – I had won myself a splendid position from which to shout its tidings to the world. I wondered why Morton had favoured me. He clearly feared Jackson making some claim upon his new drug, as upon the electric telegraph and upon guncotton. He thought perhaps that as a foreigner I had some independence from the Boston Press. Or he may have taken me for Jackson's spy, and simply bought me off. That five dollars in my pocket now bound me as liegeman to the dentist. Dr Morton was sly, too.

I sat on the three-legged stool in my stifling room, trying to conceive another advertisement for Cornelius's imported whalebone stays.

THE AUTUMN – THE FALL, as the Americans call it – is the legendary season of gentle melancholy. The heat and vividness of summer have grown tiresome, with relief the eye absorbs a more restful world in blurred, suppressed Turneresque hues. Crisp, crackling winter is to come, with snow and mighty fires, and Christmas. Then spring, soft and green, with lambs and pink blossom, to reassure us tenderly of mankind's immortality. Many poets have wallowed cosily and prettily in their sadness, as they have bid farewell to one cycle of husbandry in full confidence of the fairly punctual start of the next one. But to a man impoverished and friendless in a foreign land, the outriders of winter induce nothing but sickly foreboding and painful nostalgia.

I longed for home. I received no letters, because there was no one to pen them. I could not communicate with Floy, because I had no notion of her whereabouts and anyway she was totally unable to write. Meanwhile, I continued creating advertisements for frocks, millinery, underwear and, Cornelius's being an enterprising store, tonics and embrocations to relieve all conditions from lack of hair to lack of progeny.

> *Fingal's Pills, above all others,*
> *Turn barren wives to loving mothers,*

was one of my prouder compositions.

I saw Jackson's name occasionally in the newspapers, mostly connected with activities at Harvard. From Morton, I was content with a silence which left me untroubled for some return on his outlay of five dollars. I heard nothing of Wells. They seemed on reflection a strangely quarrelsome trio, and I remembered my father warning me that scientific men and academics in their backbiting could be perfectly feminine.

I was dressing on the morning of Thursday, October 15, when a loud knock came at my rickety door, followed instantly by the appearance of the lanky, spotty youngster I had met in the dental surgery. 'Mr Romilly, you're to come at once. To Dr Morton's office.'

This was clearly a command, not a request. 'Why? What's up?'

'Something important about Dr Morton's new preparation. Not a minute to waste, he says.'

We hurried through the streets, the messenger infected with the enthusiasm of his master. His name was Leavitt, and with his fellow-apprentice Spear he had several times inhaled the new specific. He told eagerly how the world had swum before him, consciousness had fled, and he was informed afterwards of kicking about in excitement. Remembering Sam Cooley, I asked, was this another laughing gas? But he refused to divulge its nature (had he known it) saying only that it was pungent, and inclined to make a man cough and choke.

The dentist's office was full of frock-coated gentlemen, with an air of great activity. A thudding from within indicated the tooth-mill ground as busily as ever, but the display case of teeth had, thanks be, disappeared. Morton greeted me with his usual animation.

'Mr Romilly, I beg you to pay the closest attention to everything you see and hear.' He led me by my lapel into the corner. I noticed the same medicinal smell of my former visit, but was still unable to place it. 'God has sent the greatest moment of my life. Tomorrow I am to perform a demonstration at the Massachusetts General Hospital. Look—'

He thrust a note at me.

Dear Sir: it began. *I write at the request of Dr John Collins Warren, to invite you to be present Friday morning, October 16, at 10 o'clock, at the hospital, to administer to a patient who is then to be operated upon the preparation which you have invented to diminish the sensibility to pain.*

Yours, respectfully,

C. F. Heywood.

House surgeon to the General Hospital, October 14, 1846.
Dr Morton, Tremont Row.

I looked up. 'Dr John Warren?' I asked doubtfully, remembering the surgeon who sent the hapless Wells packing with 'Humbug!' ringing in his ears.

'One of the most respected medical gentlemen in New England, perhaps in the entire Union.' Morton spoke with awe. 'He has given me the privilege of his acquaintance, receiving me at his house in Park Street. His influence is beyond all worth. Overnight, I could become one of the richest men in Boston.'

'If it works,' I said bluntly.

'It *has* worked!' Morton slapped fist into palm, eyes gleaming. 'Listen. One Wednesday night, a fortnight ago, about nine in the evening, God sent me a patient. One Mr Eban Frost. You shall meet him by and by, have the story from his own mouth. He suffered a toothache so violent, that he agreed to inhale my new preparation for the extraction. No others had been driven by their suffering to such boldness. I gave him some on my handkerchief. Within a minute, he was asleep.' Morton clutched my elbow. 'A minute more, and he was awake again, amazed to see the tormentor was plucked from his jaw, without so much as a twinge. He felt nothing! Nor did he suffer any untoward effect afterwards. He walked into the street in a state of happy astonishment.'

'This was Dr Wells's gas?' I insisted, suspecting it might be chemically convertible to a liquid.

'No, no, *entirely* different,' Morton returned fiercely. 'I've tried it on myself countless times, asleep for ten minutes by my watch, there in the operating chair.' He pointed dramatically. 'Its innocuousness I now regard as beyond dispute. The time is ripe for its wider application. Hence I made my preparation known to Dr Warren.'

'But surely you can tell me *something* of its nature?' I insisted.

'Out of the question.'

'It speaks little for your trust in me.' I could not keep the resentment from my voice. 'Holding me in ignorance, like a child among adults. Does it come in a gas-bag, or a bottle? Or does it burn like a candle?'

He searched my features closely. 'Yes, it is better for you to be in the secret,' he decided. 'But you must swear solemnly before God not to divulge it.'

'Before God. And my Queen,' I added for good measure.

He clutched my elbow again, so powerfully that at night I found bruises on it. 'Its chemical name is ether. Sulphuric ether. It is mentioned as causing stupefaction in Jonathan Pereira's book, *Elements of Materia Medica*.' He was speaking with great rapidity. 'Which was published in your own city of London, some five years ago. No reader apart from myself seems to have taken action on, or even notice of, this interesting fact. You've heard of "ether frolics"? Among students and young people, who inhale ether for the sensation of the moment? People who are always searching for new excitements.'

Then I remembered the smell. Physic prescribed for coughs and bad chests nearly always contained ether. I must have swallowed a fair quantity of the medicament from the hands of my mother, before the intrusion of the Italian opera singer. The secrecy in which Morton insisted on muffling his 'preparation' was made more intelligible in the next minute by a further visitor to the surgery.

'This gentleman is Mr Richard Eddy,' Morton introduced him. 'The son of Mr Caleb Eddy. Who is a close friend of Dr Jackson's,' he added, with a sidelong glance in my direction. 'Mr Eddy is our Commissioner of Patents here in Boston.'

'Yes, sir,' confirmed Mr Eddy. He was a young man with the serious mien which, I believe, affects even Boston babies in the cradle.

'You may have heard, perhaps through your father,' Morton continued to the Commissioner, 'that we here in

Boston are very go-ahead in finding some means of relieving pain in surgery?'

'Yes, sir.'

'Tomorrow, with God's help, I shall be performing such a service at the General Hospital. The preparation which I shall use, which I alone invented, I intend to patent. Why should my brains and toil be plundered by any knave out to turn a quick dollar?'

'Yes, *sir*.'

'Well, Mr Eddy. Pray give your opinion. Would a patent be granted in Washington, or not?'

After a long period of thought, interrupted by solemn but equivocal pronouncements, the young man suggested that patenting such a process was something of a novelty, and he would have to consult the law. Morton plainly found such prevarication galling. Once Eddy had withdrawn, he divulged to me, 'I had to visit Dr Jackson, the very day before I pulled Eban Frost's tooth. It was a weary chore, not of my own choosing. I wanted the loan of a gas-bag, having in mind the delivery of the ether vapour by such means. Dr Jackson didn't oblige, the bags being stored in his attic. I explained my request with some tale of making a nervous female patient insensible through breathing ordinary air from the bag. As condemned criminals were once said to be killed through their imagination, by blindfolding them and having them believe they were bleeding to death, with nothing worse than warm water trickling down them.'

I was amazed at this elaborate hoodwinking, perpetrated by one member of the liberal professions upon another. Equally, I was lost for its reason. Morton continued in a low voice, 'Dr Jackson knows of sulphuric ether, naturally, he is a chemist. It was that substance he suggested I rubbed on painful gums.'

'But Dr Jackson would know nothing of ether being *inhaled*?'

Morton hesitated. 'To tell the truth, Mr Romilly, I mentioned administering ether vapour, in a casual way. Dr Jackson has greater knowledge and authority in such matters than myself. I needed his assurance the procedure would be completely free of danger,' the dentist admitted. 'As he opined it was, provided I used the purest preparation.'

I suspected the web which Morton wove did little but blind its spinner. He seemed eager to drop the topic of Jackson. While speaking, he was leading me to a workbench set against the far wall of the surgery, the teeth which normally occupied it swept to a horrid pile of grins at one end, in their place pieces of chemical glassware, such as my father had occupied himself with so painstakingly for a lifetime.

'These are our failures.' Morton picked out a tube which recalled the yard of ale I essayed to empty at Cambridge. 'The folded handkerchief I used for Eban Frost is too uncontrolled to serve a capital operation.' He reached for a glass globe with a neck, like a transparent Orb of State. 'Unhappily, such appliances have made some patients no more than drowsy, while others have leapt about and screamed. But Mr Chamberlain, the philosophical instrument maker, is preparing something very special for tomorrow.' He ended with his usual confidence, 'Now you know what's afoot, Mr Romilly. You must meet me here in the morning, no later than nine o'clock. I wish you to accompany me, to record events at the hospital.'

I went pale. 'You mean, sir . . . to accompany you into the operating theatre?'

'Yes, I can arrange the matter quite easily with Dr Warren,' he said casually. 'It may be necessary to pass you off as one of my apprentices. I shall vouch for you. It is but a small deceit.'

'But I should become insensible myself, looking at such sights!'

This did not seem to have crossed his mind. 'You must control yourself as best you can. Pray hard beforehand. Good morning to you, Mr Romilly. I rely on you not to be late.'

I felt more nervous than if I were myself to be operated upon next day. I rued ever involving myself in this process of killing the pain which accompanied the shedding of blood. But I was quick to see my advantages. Could I but retain my senses – and should Morton's method work – I could become famous overnight. I should be much sought by editors on both sides of the

Atlantic, my future secure. And Charlotte would be shown to have backed the wrong matrimonial horse. The prospect was thrilling.

And why *should* I give way at the sight of a capital operation? I asked myself. I had witnessed executions enough, without even a heave of the stomach. I hoped ardently that in the morning Morton would prove as neat-fingered as Calcraft at Newgate.

11

I PRESENTED MYSELF at the dentist's surgery that Friday morning as the clocks were striking nine. Those of Boston contrive no better to proclaim the hour in chorus, rather than as a straggle of solos, than those in London. I was surprised to find the place empty, apart from the lean and spotty apprentice. He told me that Morton had already left.

'The doctor's at Mr Chamberlain's, the instrument-maker's,' he explained, bright-eyed, sounding a little breathless. 'A lot of things have been happening during the night. Yes, sir, a mighty lot! The doctor's hardly been to bed, sitting up drawing diagrams with Mr Chamberlain. He's got an absolutely brand-new inhaler, to be made ready for him by nine o'clock. But the doctor rushed away, to see how the work was going. Couldn't control himself. I've never seen him like it. I guess Mrs Morton hasn't, either.'

'Where's the shop?' I asked urgently. 'I'd better join him there.'

'Far end Cambridge Street. You can't miss it.'

I stepped back into Tremont Row, my day begun with some foreboding. To change horses in midstream may be inadvisable. To change them before starting out indicates an alarming lack of confidence.

The shop was barely wider than its own bay window, which displayed one or two bright brass instruments striking me as astronomical in nature. The inside was empty. But the workroom door being open, I saw at a bench beyond a stout, grey-maned man in a green smock whom I took to be the instrument-maker, with Morton bending intently over his shoulder.

I stood in the doorway, but neither turned his head nor appeared to notice me.

'I should much prefer it, doctor, if you found yourself in less haste,' Chamberlain observed dryly. 'Couldn't you give me another day? I should do much better.'

'The demonstration *cannot* be put off.' I was startled by the anger in Morton's voice. 'If I don't show up on time, they'll think I've shirked. They'll just go right ahead with the operation. I shan't have a second chance offered me, you may be sure of that. They'll simply suspect that I've no confidence in my preparation. It's now or never. Please understand that, Mr Chamberlain.'

'I'm doing all I can.' Chamberlain sounded more resigned than resentful. 'But this work simply cannot be rushed.'

'I must take what you've got,' Morton returned shortly. 'I'm sure it will do perfectly well.'

'I hope so, I do hope so,' sighed Chamberlain.

'Why must those valves still stick?' Morton demanded impatiently. 'Haven't you been using prime leather?'

Peering forward with curiosity, I saw the new instrument to be another globe, small enough to be cupped in the palm of the hand. But this globe had two necks. One was open, the other ended in a cuff of brass, from which protruded a mouthpiece set on a glass flange, like a cup in its saucer. Looking more closely as Chamberlain turned the inhaler in his hands, I noticed the brass cuff had a stubby, square side arm, through which, I gathered from his conversation, our unknown patient was to breathe *out*, by virtue of the leather valves. He was to breathe *in* through the body of the flask, into which Chamberlain was squeezing a small, pale marine sponge. It struck me as a considerable elaboration of those glass appliances I had seen in Tremont Row the previous day. The intervening dark and lonely hours had caused Morton's scientific caution to get the better of his natural bubbling enthusiasm.

'Hurry, hurry ...' Morton pulled out his watch. 'Great Heaven, it's almost half past nine. At ten they're expecting me.'

Morton glanced at me restlessly, hardly noting my presence.

Some time passed before the extreme tension of this active scene was broken by a hearty voice from the outer shop.

'Good day to you, doctor! I followed you here, to be on hand, as directed. Your satisfied patient Eban H. Frost.' Morton vouchsafed him only a distracted nod. 'And you, sir?' A short, stout, red-faced middle-aged man held his hand towards me. 'You are with the doctor, sir?'

'Mr Guy Romilly, at your service. A journalist.'

'From your accent, sir, you would be British?'

'I am from London, sir.'

'Then you are perhaps acquainted with Charles Dickens?'

'I regret that I have not that honour, sir. London is a sizeable jungle in which to meet literary lions.'

'*A Christmas Carol!* A mighty fine book, sir! As good as anything penned by Nathaniel Hawthorne, I'll assert any day. You will have read it?'

'Mr Dickens's works are many, sir, and we journalists' leisure is little.'

'Dickens visited us here a year or two back. Though we didn't take much to him,' Frost admitted. 'I am a teacher of music, sir, and I too have precious little time to enjoy the great masters, Mozart, Beethoven, Lowell Mason. His songs are very touching. Mrs Frost sings them repeatedly.'

I comprehended that Morton was dragging the man along to the hospital, as a prepared position to fall back on if his demonstration ended in defeat. I doubted gravely if the sight of such a walking testimonial would pacify the same audience which had booed and hissed so savagely at Wells.

'Do you know Nantwich well, sir?' Frost asked.

I frowned. 'Who, sir?'

He looked offended. 'The city in England. I have an aunt living there.'

Our conversation was mercifully terminated by Morton giving a great shout, 'It's near on ten!'

'They shall have to wait,' said Chamberlain.

'They mustn't wait. They *won't* wait.' With no more ado, Morton wrenched the globe from Chamberlain's hands, and grabbing his silk hat ran for the street door. The instrument-maker stared in astonishment. But I wasted no time in trotting behind, as we left him shouting protests from his shop door. I supposed that Eban Frost, too, was dutifully lumbering in the rear.

I caught Morton up, and said by way of encouragement, 'Never fear. The Duke himself confessed to feeling uncertain on the morning of Waterloo.'

'My mind's a turmoil.' Morton was staring fixedly ahead, not slackening his pace, his words coming distractedly. 'Don't you see? This instrument's untried. It may not work. Or it may work only too well. My preparation's dangerous, you know, deadly dangerous.'

'But you declared to me repeatedly it was perfectly safe!' I exclaimed.

'May God forgive my falsehood! I had to pretend so to others. I had to pretend so to myself. There have been cases of prolonged stupefaction ... of death ... I have read about them, in books on *materia medica*. Your countryman Michael Faraday wrote of it thirty years ago.'

'But shouldn't you break your silence about such things, before administering the preparation at the hospital?'

'My work will find detractors enough, here in Boston, without that. But I have no illusions. If my patient dies, this time tomorrow I shall be in court on a charge of manslaughter.'

I could but admire Morton's courage. I doubted it would be matched by the patient's, had he been furnished with equal knowledge of the dangers approaching with such rapidity.

'Mr Romilly – take heed, not a murmur about the true nature of my preparation.'

'Won't the medical men recognize the smell?' I objected.

He patted his coat pocket. 'The bottle is dark glass, and I have scented it with *Eau de Mille Fleurs*.'

We arrived at the hospital.

I was familiar enough with the outside of the building, hard against the Charles River. It was long and narrow, of three storeys, with a massive portico of six columns, its wings stretching in each direction for the distance of twenty windows, having been doubled in length during the past ten years. The roof was surmounted by a flattish dome with a lantern atop, about fifteen feet across, a chimney stack at each of four corners. The hospital abutted a wharf, stacked with more timber, though its grounds were as well-kept and pleasing as any English gentleman's park. I remember noticing at that distracted moment that the hills surrounding Boston looked singularly beautiful.

The main entrance under the portico was gained by two matching flights of stone steps with iron handrails, up the nearest of which we dashed. I had never before been inside any hospital, God mercifully having spared me the necessity. Now the headlong rush from Chamberlain's shop, the agitation of my cicerone, the stakes which turned on the fall of the next hour, and the expectation of high drama, hurried me through the forbidding doors without a second thought. I noticed only that the place had the smell of a butcher's in midsummer.

Morton made directly for the stairs, neither speaking to a soul, nor slackening his pace. I managed to tug out my watch as we hastened upwards. We were almost fifteen minutes late. We had shed Eban Frost, the Lord knew where.

The staircase seemed unending. It came upon me that the dome, which might fittingly have housed an astronomical telescope, contained the hospital's operating room. Morton flung open the door, and I found myself in a well-lit apartment with some half-dozen rising rows of benches lining most of its circumference, filled with grave-faced men of all ages. The atmosphere was solemn, like a funeral without sobs.

In the centre of the constricted floor-space stood a tall, lean, grey-haired man with a face like crinkled parchment. He wore a jet-black frock-coat, a black silk cravat carefully tied round his high collar. He was tight-lipped and severe, his fierce dark eyes striking as great a contrast to his pale skin as glowing coals flung into snow. 'Ah, here is Dr Morton,' he observed, with no warmth of welcome.

'A thousand apologies, Dr Warren,' Morton stumbled out. So this was the man the Boston doctors held in awe. The professor of surgery, whose opinion, so I heard, could build or demolish their careers, and their bank balances. Warren was then sixty-eight, himself the son of a professor of surgery in Boston – who by coincidence had advocated in the early years of the century just passed the inhalation of ether vapour in the treatment of tuberculosis. Later, I discovered Warren to combine hard principle with the tenderest humanity, a synthesis beyond the rigid mentality of everyday New England Puritanism.

'I was in the act of informing those present that, as you had not arrived at the agreed time, I presumed you were otherwise engaged.' The professor's voice was sarcastic.

Morton made no reply. I fancied that he would have preferred to quit the room with the haste which had brought him to it.

'Well, Dr Morton, we need waste no more of *your* valuable time,' Warren added, as forbiddingly.

Morton looked round wildly. He had nowhere to put his hat. I saved the ridiculous situation by taking it from him. I tried to examine more coolly this strange room and its occupants, all leaning forward intently, packed tight for the special occasion. Against one wall a row of sloping glass-topped cases, like those displaying draper's wares in Cornelius's store, presented a shining array of knives and saws which made my stomach turn over. Various appliances were scattered about, the use of which I had no conception, but which looked hardly friendlier. On the wall was a notice requesting the students to eject their tobacco juice into the boxes provided, and not to discolour the stairs.

To the left of the door, on a long, stout table as might embellish any gentleman's kitchen, were arranged pewter bowls, towels neatly folded, a water jug with a glass. In the centre of the floor, separated from the audience by a low screen, in the majestic, homage-demanding isolation of a throne, stood a chair. Not an ordinary chair. It was in three sections, capable of arrangement into a flat couch. It was covered by a sheet, on which lay with head slightly raised and feet slightly down, a man of my own age. He wore dark trousers and a shirt open at the neck, with no mark of disease I could see upon him, but was staring round restlessly and chalky white.

Close round this throne pressed the lords-in-waiting, middle-aged and elderly gentlemen in sombre dress, though one had allowed himself the dazzle of a check waistcoat. Among the remoter courtiers on the rising benches were many grey heads, but most were the students who I expected to give us short shift should anything go wrong. No one seemed to notice so insignificant a 'super' as me in the drama. The conception of myself, a foreigner, a writer of advertisements for Cornelius's store, amid the most eminent medical personages in Boston almost made me laugh out loud.

Morton advanced into the room, every neck craned to see the inhaler in his hand.

'Well, sir, your patient is ready,' Warren continued in his dry way. He added to the audience, 'You are well aware, gentlemen, of the astonishing claim – the quite astonishing claim – made by Dr Morton here. That his preparation would render the person operated upon free from pain. You must also be well aware how desirable an objective I personally have always felt this to be. So strongly so, that I have allowed Dr Morton to perform this experiment before us today.'

These words struck me as a warning signal hoisted on a halyard of disbelief. But Morton could go only forward, into the innermost circle of the court. He took the young man's hand, speaking quietly and earnestly. I could catch little, but the gist seemed an assurance that he would partly relieve pain during the operation, if not entirely prevent it. 'I have already a dental patient who can testify to its success,' I heard him add. I was heartened by Morton's striking recovery of composure. Then I remembered that I had previously observed the like in men immediately about to be hanged.

'Are you afraid?' asked Morton.

'No, doctor, I am not,' the young patient replied firmly. 'I'll try to do just as you direct me.'

I was suddenly aware that the silence in the room had an *active* quality, like the silence of the jungle night before the leap

97

of the snarling tiger, or that of the battlefield before the springing of a mine. Warren moved to the long table, picked up a knife, and turned. Morton poured a quantity of ether from his dark bottle into the globular flask, the smell penetrating its orangy disguise and assuredly introducing its true name at once to the assembled doctors. Morton was facing me, leaning over the patient, behind his head, inserting the flange in his mouth. For some minutes nothing happened. The young man's chest rose and fell. The pallor of his cheeks suffused with red. I became aware of a regular noise, half hiss and half click. It was the leather valves in the apparatus. In the stillness they sounded like the opening and closure of iron gates.

Perhaps ten minutes passed, perhaps more. It demanded much steeliness from Morton, withholding his patient from the surgeon until satisfied of his moment. Later, Morton told me how valuable had been the tininess of Chamberlain's improvised inhaler. The liquid ether had been effectively vaporized by the warmth of his palm.

Morton reached for the patient's pulse. He stared hard into the face. He removed the globe and straightened up.

'Dr Warren, your patient is ready,' he announced, almost casually.

Morton stepped back against the wall. The patient's head was moved by the assistant with the check waistcoat. I noticed for the first time a red tumour the size of a plum below the left angle of the lower jaw. A plain chair was produced, on which Warren sat, and with no hesitation made a cut beside the tumour. There was no response, no murmur. Warren looked up. He exchanged a quick glance with Morton, but that was all.

The knife cut again, now deep into the flesh. Blood ran down the young man's skin, soaked his shirt, seeped on to the operating couch, fell in regular drops like an overspilling gutter on to the floor. It was a sight which could have woken me in terror from a nightmare. But I barely noticed its horror. As there came no sound, and the patient remained insensible, it grew upon me that I was in the presence of a miracle. I might have been at Christ's side by the Pool of Bethesda, when he commanded the man of thirty-eight years' sickness to take up his bed, and walk.

The patient's arms stirred, not violently, but groping slowly towards the knife picking away like a razor-beaked vulture at his neck.

'Gentlemen, I am now dissecting deeply, to insulate the veins before ligature.' Warren's voice was no longer sarcastic, only explaining and excusing the patient's movement.

The man moaned loudly, gave a suppressed cry, shouted something about water, ships, horses – all nonsense. Morton stood impassive, arms folded, inhaler cupped in hand. Warren continued busily with his work. 'Twine, Heywood,' he said to the man in the check waistcoat.

I was amazed to see the wound stitched with needle and thread, as Floy had mended my torn shirts. The man's head moved sluggishly, eyes still shut, so much blood outside his body I felt there could not possibly be any left inside it. But I felt no nausea, no fear, only excitement at the whiff of victory, like a soldier realizing that he had survived his baptism of fire without a scratch.

Bandages were applied. The onlookers were now stirring eagerly in their seats, but silent, perhaps in disbelief at their eyes. The patient's lids opened, he stared round uncomprehendingly.

'Gilbert Abbot,' said Warren. It was the first time I learned the name of the sovereign for whom the court was assembled. 'Did you feel any pain?'

There was a pause, the man struggling to recover his full senses. 'Pain . . .' Again a silence, trying for us all, Our Lord knows how agonizing for Morton. 'No, sir. No pain.'

'You felt nothing?' Warren asked sternly. 'Nothing at all.'

The man answered in a low voice, 'No, sir.'

Warren was insistent. 'Were you aware, Gilbert Abbot, that you were undergoing an operation?'

'Well, I guess I . . . I felt that my skin was being scratched with a hoe. That's all.'

Warren turned to the benches. 'Gentlemen . . . *this* is no humbug.'

At once the taut line on which the morning's events had trod like a tightrope snapped and threw all into agreeable confusion. There was hubbub, a clap or two, suppressed by Warren's, 'Gentlemen, I pray remember where you are. Applause is not proper in an operating room.'

A slight movement of the mouth in his parchment face betrayed Warren's emotion. Morton himself stood with bowed head, closed eyes and moving lips. He may have been devoutly praying. Or he may have been calculating, at fifty dollars an administration, how much his preparation would fetch him a year in Boston alone.

12

LORD, WHAT FOOLS we mortals be!

God created us in His image, but the mould He used was cracked. Perhaps He cracked it deliberately? He deserves some amusement from the antics of His creatures. Heaven must otherwise be a place of much joy but few diversions.

That Friday morning at the General Hospital was a sublime moment for mankind. It should have proved transcendently uplifting for its actors and its witnesses, for Boston, New England and the whole Union. Instead – alas! It struck the starting-bell for a free-for-all so sordidly malicious, so squalidly mercenary, and, I suspect, so sorrily mendacious, as to disgrace in my own eyes for ever the learned participants I had formerly revered.

'Some men are fine fellows,' George Meredith once wrote to me. 'Some, right scurvy. Most, a dash between the two.' Morton, Jackson and Wells were neither saints nor knaves. But the effect of a discovery so superbly beneficial to mankind, yet so unexpected, stumbled upon in black ignorance illuminated by the briefest if most brilliant flash of intuition, was to unbalance all three of them. Though I suppose, had they been humdrum, stolid fellows like the rest of us, pain-killing for operations might have stayed undiscovered for another hundred years. We cannot object to genius and madness being bedmates, if we are so eager to adopt their offspring.

I must confess that the following morning I myself was less uplifted at participating in mankind's sublime moment than at seeing my name printed in the *Boston Examiner*. I had gone directly from the hospital to my room, to work on the article all afternoon with great ferocity. If I were incredulous at its not enjoying greater prominence, this was not through awareness that a furrow of agony had been smoothed for ever from the human brow, but the natural response of any journalist to any editor's impassive appraisal of his work.

I did not see Morton until the morning of the following Wednesday, October 21, when I was summoned to 19 Tremont Row by a single-sentence letter. It was the beginning of six weeks in my life more argumentative, tumultuous and wearying than any I can remember since, even during my later days on the rough-and-tumble platforms of radical politics. (Platforms which I am forced, as an old man, to mount again, by our wicked war in South Africa. My sense of duty stays sharper than those of sight or hearing. Yet my contribution is a mite beside such as my friend Miss Mary Kingsley, the intrepid author of *Travels in West Africa*, who is driven to play Miss Nightingale among the Boer prisoners of Simon's Town.)

In Morton's dental surgery I found the same fervid atmosphere of my last visit, the day before the operation, now much intensified. There was no longer any pretence of dentistry being performed there, all its impedimenta swept aside and neglected. Torn journals, letters, disordered newspapers, open books lay everywhere, earnestly being marked and scissored by the pimply apprentice, his fellow and Dr Hayden, who seemed overwhelmingly confused by such an unexpected turn to his newly joined practice. Men continually hurried in, conferred briefly and hurried out again. Morton, too, I found touched in brighter hues. The immediate aftermath of the operation had left him stunned with success, his energies drained by the torturing anxieties which had borne him to it. Now his manner had even greater vigour, his voice a fresh incisiveness, his words a new grandeur. As I waited, he sat, stood, wrote, spoke, exited and entered with a rapidity which even the onlookers discovered very tiring. In the back room, the tooth-mill ground on imperturbably.

'Well, Mr Romilly, God has sent reward for my skill and daring,' he greeted me, striding across the surgery with a sheaf of papers in his hand. 'Look at this —' He excitedly thrust forward two letters. 'A testimonial from Dr Warren. Another from Dr Heywood, who removed an adipose tumour from a woman's arm on Saturday, while my preparation had rendered her completely insensible. Dr Warren and Dr Heywood! With such names behind me, I am made! They will provide a capital start for the exploitation of my preparation right across the Union.'

The pride in Morton's voice could not have been topped by Napoleon after Austerlitz. Only once more in my life did I see a man so blazing with self-confidence. On Christmas Day 1866 I interviewed Arthur Orton, the pretender in the Tichborne Case, as he landed in England from Australia to claim a baronetcy and a fortune. Arthur Orton ended with fourteen years' penal servitude. Had I in Boston more experience of men, I might have saved Morton from the shadows which were to fall on him as inescapably as those of night.

My mildly self-appreciatory remark about my article he brushed aside with, 'Oh, it's got in all the newspapers. Not only right here in Boston, but even in New York. And see this—' A folded magazine was poked at me. 'Read what the *Boston Medical Journal* says this morning.'

The item was short and vague, speaking merely of strange stories circulating in the Boston newspapers of some wonderful preparation, by which a patient was affected just long enough, and just powerfully enough, to suffer surgery without suffering pain. But Morton was cock-a-hoop over it. 'That is my first recognition in a *medical* paper, Mr Romilly. With God's help, soon my preparation shall be known to every medical man in the entire world. I shall publish pamphlets, put out advertisements, trumpet my success round the earth! I shall have great numbers of the inhaling apparatus made, which I shall present to various surgeons and charitable institutions at home and abroad. I shall send them – very costly ones – to the chief sovereigns of Europe.'

The notion of King Louis-Philippe, Tsar Nicholas, the Emperor Ferdinand and our own Queen perplexedly turning over in their hands these possibly gold-embellished and diamond-studded additions to their regalia, I found very diverting. But I contented myself with some remark about Morton's means of bringing sleep having paradoxically woken the world from its worst nightmares.

'I have never known such times,' Morton continued fervidly. 'I have hardly enjoyed one full night's rest, or one regular meal, this last week. But I have completed a system for licensing my preparation. Heed me carefully, Mr Romilly. I shall license dentists to use it at fifty dollars for five years in cities of ten thousand or less inhabitants, rising to two thousand dollars for three years in cities of over a hundred thousand. That is a very reasonable charge, I believe. For surgeons, I have a different method. I shall take twenty-five per centum of their fees. I shall also charge a royalty on the inhalers.'

Some perplexity on his reason for pressing this information upon me was resolved by his next remark. 'Mr Romilly, I have a proposition for you. I am so overwhelmed with communications that I am obliged to employ a secretary to answer them. I also need a gentleman – a literary gentleman – to assist me with a circular, to communicate the success of my preparation to the general public. Would you honour me by accepting the post?'

His offer came so unexpectedly that I begged to consider for a moment. I was by then installed comfortably in the esteem of Cornelius, who had been particularly taken with my

ENORMOUS EXPLOSION
of delight over our winter furs.

And my

> *To satisfy a spinster's hope*
> *Wash yourself in Babbitt's soap.*

(Had I persisted in writing advertisements rather than novels, who knows? I might have enjoyed the fortune of our Mr Barratt, the trumpeting archangel of Pears' Soap.)

I was swayed by suspecting that Morton's present mood would incline to generosity in the line of salaries. His own grasp for dollars I found not the slightest objectionable, immoral or inordinate. I had been in New England long enough to learn that the pursuit of wealth lay in the marrow of all men's bones, and was accepted in America without hypocrisy like any other bodily attribute. I agreed to the proposition. I happily found my suspicions to be correct.

We had barely sealed our compact with a handshake when through the street door came Richard Eddy, the Patent Commissioner. Morton said hastily, 'Remember, Mr Romilly, that no one – *no one* – must ever get to know that the true nature of my preparation is sulphuric ether. Ether is a chemical to be bought anywhere, any druggist can make it at a few cents a bottle. Once that secret is out, I am lost. Well, what news from Washington?' he demanded from the visitor at once.

'I have taken the opinion, sir,' Eddy answered in his irritatingly suspenseful drawl, 'of none less than Mr Daniel Webster. Who is the most distinguished man of law—'

'I know that,' Morton said snappishly. Webster's name was not yet familiar to me, as the New Hampshire farmer's son who became the greatest orator in a country never poor in such talents. 'But what did the gentleman tell you, pray?'

'Mr Webster is of the mind, sir . . . I can give you the exact words by and by, I have them noted down in my office . . . Mr Webster is of the opinion, sir . . . of the sound opinion . . . there can be no obstacle whatsoever to your discovery being patented in a regular way by the United States Patent Office.'

Morton was capable only of half-suppressing an excited cry. 'God be praised! There can be nothing now between me and the road to fortune.'

'Dr Jackson called on me yesterday,' Eddy continued in an even voice.

Morton responded sharply, 'What's the affair to do with Dr Jackson?'

Eddy expressed, or perhaps assumed, some surprise. 'Well, I guess Dr Jackson's the joint discoverer. His name will have to go along with yours, Dr Morton, on any application for a patent.'

I saw Morton flush. 'How can you say that? How can he claim as much? Dr Jackson has done nothing, nothing. He simply gave me some trifling advice, something which any chemist in his position would feel obliged to dispense free to a younger colleague.'

Eddy's own face kept its habitual lack of expression. 'Happens Dr Jackson was talking to my father Mr Caleb last night.'

Morton grunted.

'Dr Jackson says, sir, you paid a call on him at Beacon Hill last month. He suggested you used the inhaled vapour of ether to pull a tooth. That's what Dr Jackson says.'

'He suggested nothing of the kind. Nothing whatever. Dr Jackson mentioned only applying ether to the tooth itself, locally, to create numbness. He had no notion in his head that a person who inhaled . . .' Morton paused. He had been too distracted to notice Eddy's casual mention of the chemical itself. As I had suspected, the secret of the 'preparation' was inevitably seeping out. 'A person who inhaled *ether*,' Morton continued in a low voice, 'could have his flesh cut with the knife, yet experience no pain. Dr Jackson had no notion of that at all.'

'Dr Jackson says that you were a reckless man, for using ether when you did,' Eddy returned calmly. 'He says you'll kill somebody yet.'

'Dr Jackson's reputation as a gentleman must suffer for such . . . such travesties.'

'Dr Jackson asks five hundred dollars for his advice,' came the impassive response.

There was a silence, in which I saw Morton struggle to take control of himself. 'I should be honoured if I might call upon Dr Jackson.'

'I guess there's no obstacle to that.'

'Meanwhile, pray go ahead with drawing up the application for a patent.'

'In both names, sir?'

'Yes, yes, whatever you like,' Morton told him half impatiently and half resignedly.

As the young lawyer left, Morton observed to me bitterly, 'Dr Jackson is a scientist, a person much thought of. And what am I? A man of not much science and even less cultivation.

How do I look in the eyes of the professional circle of Boston? A man out to make money and a reputation.'

'You richly deserve both.'

'Oh, they see me only as an upstart. Or worse. As a thief trying to steal those two particular items from themselves.'

I remembered Morton's admission, the day before the operation, of having asked Jackson's assurance that inhaling ether was safe. 'Was it only *trivial* advice which Dr Jackson gave you, sir?' I asked pointedly.

'Yes, trivial, trivial. I forget now exactly what it was.'

The human mind, by and large, recalls only that which it desires. Which is another mercy afforded mankind by God.

My duties began there and then. Morton set me composing a notice to be printed and posted to everyone in the New England medical community. I decided the correct note of dignity would be struck by the style I used for Cornelius's more intimate ladies' netherwear.

TO SURGEONS AND PHYSICIANS, I began.

The subscriber is prepared to furnish a person fully competent to administer his compound to patients who are to have surgical operations performed, and when it is desired by the Operator that the patient should be rendered insensible to pain. Personal or written application may be made to

W. T. G. MORTON,

Dentist
No 19, Tremont Row, Boston.

This circular was printed in elegant copperplate script on a single sheet of paper, which was folded to go through the post. I learn there still exists in Massachusetts a copy postmarked November 20 addressed to a Dr J. Mason Warren of Boston, and another posted on November 23 to Dr Henry Wheatland of Salem. They are prized as museum specimens. The remaining copies of my early printed work have, alas, vanished like Cornelius's handbills.

My second concern was to sort, and prepare draft replies to, the day's cascade of mail, a task which the pimply apprentice was relieved to relinquish. Almost the first letter I unfolded was from Dr Wells in Hartford.

Dr Morton. Dear Sir, I read. *Your letter dated yesterday is just received; and I hasten to answer it, for I fear you will adopt a method in disposing of your rights which will defeat your object. Before you make any arrangements whatever, I wish to see you. I think I will be in Boston the first of next week – probably Monday night. If the operation of administering the gas is not attended with too much trouble, and will produce the effect you state, it will undoubtedly be a fortune to you, provided it is rightly managed.*

Yours in haste, H. Wells.

It seemed that Morton had not embraced his former partner in confidence over the nature of his 'preparation'. And that Wells's natural caution, which Morton had dismissed as timidity, stood estimably against Morton's own grandiose schemes. But Morton observed as he read the letter, 'Dr Wells is still feeling the rough handling he got at the General Hospital, I think. He sings in a minor key.'

'As I see it,' I ventured, 'it was his misfortune to use nitrous oxide gas at the hospital, and your good fortune to use the vapour of ether.'

'It is not a matter of fortune and misfortune,' Morton said severely. 'Write to Dr Wells saying I expect the pleasure of his visit. I have in mind offering him the position of my agent in New York, an excellent advancement, disposing of licences to use my preparation, and of shares in the many companies I am about to form.'

As I sat down with my quill, for the first occasion in some weeks I thought of Charlotte. A man who cannot afford to butter his bread must forget, too, the taste of woman.

My new position required my accompanying Morton three days later, on the morning of Saturday, October 24, when in company with Richard Eddy he called upon Jackson. I found the chemist in the same posture before the log fire, legs apart, lips working incessantly. If he felt any surprise at re-encountering me so abruptly, he quickly suppressed it.

'Dr Morton, my request for five hundred dollars in return for my advice I think eminently reasonable,' Jackson started almost at once.

'If I make even as much by the patent,' Morton countered.

'Oh, come. Well, perhaps you are not being unduly modest,' Jackson admitted, I think to Morton's surprise. 'In light of the antics of the dentists of Boston in the last day or two. Following the lead of Dr Flagg, your professional brethren have lost no time in publishing a manifesto against your right to patent such a preparation. On the grounds of its holding such wide benefit for all mankind. They say it is the equivalent of trying to patent sunlight or moonshine.'

'A month ago, they were rubbing against me like cats,' Morton said acidly.

'Yes, but *then* they were not aware that you would shortly represent absolutely unassailable competition to their own practices and livelihoods. Are you aware that they have organized a committee of vigilance?' Morton shook his head. 'To ascertain and publish every instance in which your preparation fails, or has ill-effect.'

'They are moved by greed and jealousy. May God forgive them.'

'They have already taken a title, *The Boston Immortal Seven*.' Jackson seemed amused, perhaps largely at Morton's discomfiture. 'They start with the confidence their names shall shine through history, at least. I assure you, Dr Morton, you must take them seriously. It is my experience among men of science, that a committee set up for any purpose, even to prove the moon is made of green cheese, will think up a string of logical arguments to make its point, and *ergo* indicate its usefulness. It is much as a man pinches himself to stay awake. Any such instances as they seek may not be hard to find.'

'Or hard to fabricate.'

'Dr Morton . . .' Jackson stared at the ceiling, lips working. 'You must be aware by now that every medical magazine in the Union has come out not *for* etherization – and let us have no quibbles among friends that ether is your agent – but against it. In Philadelphia it is dismissed by Dr Robert Hunter as a will-o'-the-wisp. Why, *The Medical Examiner* in that city throws up its hands at recent events in our General Hospital, and gives the warning that physicians and quacks will soon constitute one single fraternity. In Baltimore, Professor Westcott has made some sport about *Morton's sucking-bottles* to stupefy crying babies.'

'I am only aware that the medical magazines right here in Boston are enthusiastic,' Morton returned firmly.

'In Boston the influence of Dr Warren is paramount.'

'Well, my enemies can holler as much as they like. It's the Boston surgeons who matter in New England. With Dr Warren close behind me, none dare stab me in the back. I'm not concerned over a pack of uncultivated tooth-pullers.'

I found this contempt pleasantly distracting.

'Be that as it may. I have a proposition for you, Dr Morton. I shall not press you over the five hundred dollars for my original advice. Instead, the patent shall be taken out jointly, in both our names. I learn from Mr Eddy here you have already acquiesced to this reasonable request.' Both other men nodded. 'I shall then assign my rights to you, under a separate agreement. For ten per centum of the profits. If any profits there be.'

I saw at once Jackson's slyness in denigrating etherization to the point of worthlessness. Morton seemed to suspect the same ruse, remarking warily, 'That is indeed generosity, Dr Jackson, if the prospect of a profit is as unlikely as finding gold in California.'

This was more than a year before the fervid metal was struck at Sutter's Mill, and three before the great 'gold rush' of '49. Men in Boston spoke of digging their fortunes from the ground, but to the sober, remote New Englanders such talk was mostly as fanciful as nursery-tales.

'You overlook the prestige of my name,' Jackson said. '*My* support makes etherization a much more virtuous and meritorious prospect. And look upon the other side, I pray you, Dr Morton. The lethal potential of sulphuric ether is yet untapped. But it is likely to be, any day of the week. We cannot close our eyes to such discouragements. Suppose suit were filed against you? Who would be called as the principal hostile witness? Why, myself! *Ergo*, it is better to have me on your side from the start.'

Morton said nothing. He seemed suddenly overwhelmed by these arguments, which I suspected had been well rehearsed. Then abruptly he said, 'I agree.'

Jackson acknowledged this sweeping victory with a restrained nod. The scientific birdnester had claimed his share in the discovery of etherization, as he had claimed in the electric telegraph and guncotton. He was at least disinclined to concern himself with inventions less than world-shaking.

I felt that Morton's day of glorious brilliance had turned somewhat thundery, and the storm was evoking its first flashes of lightning. It was I who made the cuttings from the journals and newspapers, and I had come to take the opposition more seriously than my master. Americans are a sceptical people, a natural response to the advertisements which continually harry them. Medical men are conservative, an attitude equally natural with new treatments blowing along like thistledown. Though to read every day of the bitter and often vindictive rejection of a process, which my own eyes told me to be of immeasurable benefit to humanity, was beyond my comprehension or my indulgence. I did not envisage then, standing in a Boston parlour, that my own countrymen would prove even worse than Morton's.

'There is one further point.' Jackson folded his hands under his coat-tails. 'The by-laws of the Massachusetts Medical Society, of which I have the honour to be a senior member, forbid the keeping of any remedy whatever a secret. I would add that Dr Warren is particularly of this opinion himself.'

'In that case, we can save Mr Eddy here the trouble of making the patent application,' Morton returned sourly.

Jackson smiled. 'Men's promises are made to be broken. And by-laws are made to be bent.'

I was aware that Eddy, standing close beside me, was bubbling with some contribution to the discussion. 'Say, if you two gentlemen would care to cut me in for twenty-five per centum, I'd run the whole business for you. Yes, sir! Turn you into the two wealthiest citizens in New England, you mark my words.'

But neither new partner seemed inclined to accept the offer, nor even to hear it.

13

WELLS ARRIVED IN Boston, as promised, the following night.
I was alone in the dental surgery, lit only by the lamp aglow
on my table, busily copying out letters from Morton's scribbled drafts. Most of these protested his right to patent, in
company with Jackson, his 'secret' process. My employment
demanded loyalty to his view, yet I sympathized with the
arguments of his outraged fellow-dentists, however selfishly
applied, that such benefit should not be withheld from a single
sufferer by the rein of a patent. I did not wish to risk the accusation of running with the hare and hunting with the
hounds. Though from a distance, hare and hounds often
appear indistinguishable.

My work seemed more of a drudge than for Cornelius's Store.
The two apprentices had gone home. The tooth-mill had
ground to its nightly halt. Only Morton himself was left,
among the bottles and india-rubber bags in the cubicle where
he had first received me, and where he had the increasing
habit of locking himself for hours on end.

Wells did not knock, but came in directly, looking round in
his timid way. I had already identified myself in my letter
confirming the appointment, and as I rose from my stool he
gave a nod of his large head with a smile of recognition.

'I'll fetch Dr Morton "right away",' I said, using the expression fashionable in Boston. But I paused to ask, 'Pray tell
me, sir, how is Mr Tooms?'

'Mr Tooms is very well,' he replied in his gentle voice.
'And mighty busy, busier than any man in Hartford, I'd say.'

'And . . . er, Mrs Tooms?'

'Mrs Tooms, too, enjoys good health.'

'Are they perhaps to ... to be blessed with a little visitor?'

'Having conversed with Mrs Tooms yesterday, sir, I can assure you that such an event is not in the immediate offing.'

I wondered why I had asked. Charlotte was a deserter from my affections. Were I a sensible fellow, I should drum her out of my memories.

'The office here has changed somewhat,' Wells observed, looking round. 'Dr Morton doesn't appear to practise much dentistry.'

'Dr Morton is greatly occupied with his new preparation.'

'Oh, sure,' said Wells vaguely.

The two former partners greeted each other cordially. 'It's exciting news, isn't it?' Morton asked.

'Your preparation is *not* nitrous oxide gas?' Morton shook his head. 'Then it must be sulphuric ether.'

'Why should you think that?' Morton demanded, looking startled.

'Because I myself had in mind the use of ether or of nitrous oxide at the General Hospital last year,' he explained quietly. 'I guess I picked the wrong horse.'

Morton made a gesture of impatience at yet another claimant for the honour of his invention. (And who, to his lifelong distraction, was not to be the last.) 'I will not disclose the nature of my preparation, as long as God gives me breath. Not even to you.'

'If it isn't ether, it's the same principle,' Wells told him mildly.

Morton diverted the conversation to the offer of his agency in New York, which he made appear more bountifully profitable even than the current financial game of 'milking the railroads'.

'I shall command one of the biggest businesses in the Union,' Morton ended grandly.

'And one of the most dangerous.'

Morton looked irritated again. 'Why should you say so?'

'You'll kill someone with it some day.'

'That's the voice of a man defeated before he starts. But I have faith in God, and faith in myself.'

'I advise you to make every cent, friend Morton, while the excitement runs high. For myself, I'm travelling, going to Paris. There's a fortune to be made buying and selling pictures.'

'And a fortune to be lost.'

'Maybe. But a charge of embezzlement is preferable to one of manslaughter.'

Morton did not show offence. As Wells would be of no help, he was eager to be rid of him. They exchanged some small coin of conversation, and the dentist from Hartford shortly left.

I did not set eyes on Wells again. (Neither, indeed, did Morton.) Wells took his expedition to Paris, but whether he made money dealing in art I know not. I *do* know that he used the visit to importune the scientific gods of its *Académie* with his claims to have used ether before Morton had even thought of it. He would seem to have impressed the hard-headed Frenchies. I learned recently from my worthy friend Monsieur Emile Zola that a bust by the sculptor Bouthee is being raised to the *chirurgien americain sympathique Horace Wells* in the new *place des Etats Unis*, formed by redevelopment of the 16th *arrondissement* of Paris. So he got at least a lump of bronze for his pains.

There was more trouble for Morton before the end of that bustling and seminal October. 'Now Dr Warren's turned his coat,' he announced to me bitterly, a few mornings later. 'I've just learned at Mr Chamberlain's shop that Dr Warren sent the house surgeon from the hospital for another glass globe. When the house surgeon returned with the intelligence that a patent was under application in Washington, Dr Warren at once forbade the use of Letheon—'

'What's that?' I interrupted, puzzled.

'The name given to my preparation,' Morton answered off-handedly. 'It was suggested by some doctor at the General Hospital with literary leanings. If word passes round that surgeons there are refusing to use Letheon, no one will chance his reputation with it. Everyone will suspect some hidden danger, and shy away from it like poison. It'll end up a nine-day wonder, and by Christmas the Union will have forgotten it. How can Dr Warren have encouraged me this far towards making my fortune, and then snatched it away from my grasp?' he ended dejectedly.

It seemed that Jackson's assuming the rules of the Massachusetts Medical Society to be as malleable as glowing iron on the blacksmith's anvil was overhasty. Morton's ebullience in the aftermath of the famous operation had now gone. It left him distraught, dejected and suspicious of every professional man in Boston. The dispute over the secrecy of 'Letheon', fulminating like a carbuncle, came to a head in the first week of November. A young woman named Alice Mohan had lain in the General Hospital most of that year with a putrefying disease of the knee, and Warren had already invited Morton to administer his preparation for the capital operation of amputation. To keep this appointment, on the morning of Saturday the 7th the pair of us left Tremont Row in a carriage, Morton determinedly clutching his inhaler.

The hospital was an astounding picture of unseemliness. Every doctor in the State seemed to be there, in the lobby, on the stairs, beneath the portico outside, all arguing, and even quarrelling, making more noise than an unruly crowd of schoolboys. Morton looked nervous, but plunged among them. We were elbowed, and subjected to looks and shouts both hostile and encouraging, but all undignified. We made doggedly upstairs, to find Warren himself outside the closed doors of the operating room under the dome, the centre of a fiercely contentious knot, his dark eyes and parchment face as calm as ever.

'Here is Dr Morton himself,' Warren remarked quietly. 'Whose opinion is hardly impertinent to this matter. Though I shall not ask for it in public, in view of the heated faces I observe round me.'

Warren produced a key to unlock the doors of the operating room, all three of us finding seclusion inside.

'You did not write to put me off, sir, so I came,' Morton began defiantly.

'I wished you to come, doctor,' Warren said imperturbably. He half-turned to me. 'I do not recall that you introduced your colleague.'

We shook hands, Warren giving a wintry smile. 'An Englishman? We are cousins, Mr Romilly. My family comes from Tiverton in Devon, a city you doubtless know.' My expression indicated intimate knowledge of Tiverton. 'I was in London as a young man, at the beginning of the century. I was charged by your Dragoons.'

I found myself saying, 'I am most extraordinarily sorry, sir,' as though personally responsible. He did not enlighten me on this alarming adventure, and I assumed the young visitor had stumbled into one of the *émeutes* with which London enlivened the humiliating later days of William Pitt.

'My position in this lamentable business is difficult and uncertain,' Warren continued to Morton. 'But clearly, it would not be etiquette for you to keep your remedy secret.'

'The processes of dentistry are by convention secret,' Morton countered.

'The medical profession expects more liberality.'

'It's nothing but a conspiracy! A conspiracy to deprive me of my money.'

'Come, sir! Are you not over-sanguine in believing you have a secret to keep? Yours is *un secret de polichinelle.*' Like all New Englanders, he had a poor French accent. 'A secret you might have as readily imparted by "stage whisper" to your audience. I recognized your preparation as sulphuric ether instantly, so did Dr Heywood and every other in the operating room. Dr Jacob Bigelow, our professor of *materia medica* at Harvard, is this very day busying himself with experiments to prove it. Though all required is a shrewd pair of nostrils.'

Morton said nothing to this. In his heart, I knew, he recognized that Warren was right. The surgeon continued in a kinder tone, 'I pray you, doctor, heed this. Next February I am resigning from the hospital staff. That is confidential as yet. Now, I would not wish my last days to be tormented with controversy, which could overshadow such memories as people will keep of me.'

He paused, making a sudden, weary motion of fingers across brow. 'It has all come upon me so unexpectedly. That morning of your demonstration, I was more interested in my experiments in the medical college, which it interrupted. My mind was occupied with the renovation of decayed bones with white or black glue – the white gives the better appearance, the black gives the better strength. Frankly, Dr Morton, I had little vision of your success. But I saw at once that you had found a mode of mitigating human suffering. Which may become a valuable agent in the hands of careful and well instructed practitioners, even if it may not prove of such general application as our imagination tempts us to anticipate. Great Heaven, I have discussed the relief of surgical pain in lectures endlessly, and have experimented upon it repeatedly. I should embrace the use of your preparation at this hospital, but if you insist on keeping it secret, and taking out a patent, I must set my face against it.'

This appeal was addressed with a dignity and feeling which clearly affected Morton greatly. His objections continued falteringly, and when I ventured a suggestion that the patent be suspended for the hospital alone, and the secret of 'Letheon' imparted to such doctors as Warren instructed, the pair accepted the British compromise with rapidity and relief.

'My preparation has done nothing but make me wretched,' declared Morton miserably, as Warren made to open the door. 'And Mrs Morton wretched. She is, as you know, in a delicate condition. I wish sometimes that God had not guided me towards my discovery.'

Alice Mohan had her operation. I was present. I heard for the first time the awesome rasp of saw on human bone. The patient woke, amazed to see her severed limb lying on the floor. Morton gave ether for a second operation that day, the treatment of spinal paralysis by the application of white-hot irons to the back, but the hiss and stink of the blackening, crisping flesh precipitated my withdrawal. Five days later the patent was issued from Washington, No 4848. Morton remarked only that it wasn't worth a continental copper.

Morton's failure to make an immediate and immense profit

had an effect on my own fortunes more drastic than I foresaw when detachedly observing the miserable haggling. Towards the end of November his natural enthusiasm began again to boil. He spoke of fortunes still to be made away from Boston and asked out of the blue, 'Mr Romilly, have you found fulfilment in this great country of ours?'

'I should have been unduly optimistic expecting to conquer America in six months. It took Caesar himself over six years to conquer Gaul.'

'Would you consider returning to your native land?'

The words ignited such excitement that my answer was formed almost without benefit of deliberation. Now Morton's discovery was general knowledge, the Boston press had no use of me. My future as his secretary, I could not help fearing, was extraordinarily insecure. I had no Charlotte. In London, Lloyd would surely pay eagerly for the scenes I had witnessed. And how I longed for the soot-picked walls, the Stygian alleys, the glowing gin shops, the noise, the dirt, the deplorably delightful Godlessness and fecklessness! I inquired why he suggested my going.

'My discovery is endangered in Europe, where I have best hopes of seeing some return on it. That is clear from the stratagems of Dr Jackson. He enjoys considerable influence in Paris and Berlin, and I must have a reliable man at hand to protect my interests. I intend to go further, to take out a separate patent in London – without Dr Jackson's knowledge – and I am already in correspondence with an attorney there, a Mr Moses Poole of Middlesex. You know Middlesex?'

'As the back of my hand,' I assured him.

'As I understand only a subject of your Queen can obtain a British patent, it shall be in your name.' He was misinformed on this point, I later found. 'You see how I trust you, Mr Romilly?' he added smilingly. 'I hereby invite you to be my agent in London, on a commission. I shall, as a matter of course, attend to your fare.'

I had budgeted for all my days to be spent in the Land of Opportunity. Instead, I was there precisely six months. I left Boston by the Cunard steam-packet *Acadia* on the evening of

December the first, a bleak storm-scowling Tuesday, and Morton came to the quay to see me off. He was in good spirits, saying my mission was to stake another claim for him, in a land more promising than California. But the mine 'Letheon' contained no gold, and finally took the lives of all three prospectors.

His last act as I stepped aboard was showing me a letter just arrived, which I read in the glim of the gangway lantern.

My dear Sir – Everybody wants to have a hand in a great discovery. All I will do is to give you a hint or two, as to names, or the name, to be applied to the state produced and the agent. The state should, I think, be called 'Anaesthesia'. . . .

I looked up, mouthing the word.

'It sounds well enough,' Morton decided. 'Anaesthesia . . . I am gratified the writer adds his opinion that the term will be repeated by the tongues of every civilized race of mankind.'

'Who is the writer?'

'The literary doctor I mentioned, at the General Hospital. He who suggested the earlier name "Letheon". He would seem a competent wordsmith.'

I peered down at the signature.

Yours, respectfully,
Oliver Wendell Homes.

14

THE WEATHER WAS FOUL. For fifteen days the *Acadia* rolled regularly from side to side, then forwards and backwards, and next quite excruciatingly with both movements together. The great paddles churned and roared in their boxes, our stout sides quivered as if to spring their timbers, the rigging sang like a harp and the smudgy record of our passage on the sky was instantly erased by an angry and resentful wind.

I had a bunk with a slip of horsehair mattress in a general cabin, which smelt of tar, boiling onions and human spew. Luckily, I seemed immune from *mal de mer*, though I had noticed some fellow-passengers turning green in Boston harbour. I had five cabinmates, two civil engineers returning from constructing the fine new Halifax harbour, a pair of Yorkshire merchants come to swaddle New Englanders in their cloth, and a man of my own age claiming kinship with a Duke, a nobility I noticed to have achieved him an official farewell from the Boston Police Department.

Each day passed as the others. I rose in the late dawn's dimness, struggled to shave in the light of the bull's-eye above the washing-slab, and breakfasted at eight, with a few other sturdy stomachs, in a saloon with glasses and china racked along the roof. I spent the morning over the stove reading anything at hand, mostly out-of-date newspapers. A copy of *The Times* six weeks old read to me like a journal from remotest China. So Lord John Russell was Prime Minister. Whig had ousted Tory, Peel was gone. And no one had told me. But the news-papers of Boston were, like the population, inclined to the parochialism which lent much of the fury to the controversies beating round Morton's head.

At noon, we 'lunched', to use the verb then newly risen from the servants' hall. At three we dined, on either boiled mutton and capers or boiled beef and onions. Meals were our main amusement, with the vagaries of the table-service each good for killing an hour or two. There was cribbage and backgammon, and a Scotsman who persistently played the accordion, from which we took compensation that it might have been the bagpipes. On deck there was often a sail to be spied, or an iceberg to be respected, and our smokers were allowed to puff away aft of the funnel. Every afternoon I scrambled astern to inspect 'the milk', a cow with an air of forbidding melancholy reasonable in one accustomed to broad and immobile pastures. We took tea at half past seven, and brandy-and-water was drunk incessantly by every gentleman aboard.

I fell to chatting with Dr Fraser, the ship's surgeon, who had read in the Boston papers about 'Letheon'. He became greatly interested on learning I had been present during the operation at the Massachusetts General Hospital. He explained that his father practised as a surgeon in Dumfries, and that he must purchase a specimen of the magic liquid his next voyage, so that it might be employed in Scotland before the rest of the United Kingdom, as was befitting.

'Though it is nothing but ordinary sulphuric ether, I understand,' Dr Fraser added. 'Such as we have been using freely for years to alleviate complaints of the lungs.'

'Yes, it is ether,' I agreed, thinking it stupid to persist in exuding an atmosphere of mystery round 'Letheon'. 'Though I fear, doctor, no one may use it in Scotland or anywhere else without paying the prescribed fee. It is patented in Washington and I am travelling with the specific purpose of establishing Dr Morton's rights equally firmly in London.'

'You may take out as many patents as you like, sir,' Fraser told me bluntly. 'But no medical man would let such a detail stand between himself and the relief of human suffering. That trick has been tried time and again with various medical processes in Britain.'

'The United States Patent Office —'

'Oh, nobody gives a tinker's damn for that, sir.'

Though Dr Fraser practised only on seasickness and sailors' broken limbs, this rediscovery of stale arguments I found discouraging.

At last the wind dropped, and the paddles beat steadily through still, icy, grey water, until one night we heard the look-out's cry 'Land-ho!' from the barrel of the crow's nest. Excitedly crowding the deck, we saw within minutes the sweeping flash of the Holyhead light. Our gun was fired, our speed slackened. A small boat bobbed from the darkness towards our wooden sides, and we watched open-mouthed as the well-muffled pilot grasped our rope-ladder nimbly to haul himself aboard. That seasoned and kindly fellow brought us his daily newspaper, which he cheerfully tossed into our midst, where it was seized as a tender-looking Christian among the lions. By six the next morning, on Wednesday, December 16, 1846, I was back again in Coburg Dock, Liverpool, and through a familiar prankishness of the human mind with the feeling that I had never left it.

I travelled to London by the railroad, first class. I could not bear the joy of my homecoming to be chilled with a draughty, sooty journey in the second or third. I had a half-bench to myself, opposite a whiskery old gentleman in a well-brushed silk hat intent on *The Times*, my box in the guard's van, my umbrella lodged in its rack, my legs covered with my tartan travelling-rug. How delightful it was to sink into the upholstery and appreciate the *oldness* of everything outside the windows! In America, whole cities seem to have been nailed together the week before, white-painted the day before, and awaiting knocking down the following week for re-erection elsewhere. But in England even the factory chimneys, the pitheads, the ever-groping railroad tracks – in those days of 1846 still but green shoots of our country's present flowering prosperity – seemed features of the landscape as well established as the castles and manor-houses. Then I saw a hunt! Across the dormant wintry acres of the shires, in full cry, the sleek horses, the pink coats, the striving pack, so quintessentially English! I tried to fancy I heard above the roar and rattle of the train the quickening blast of the horn, as they cheerfully sought their wily prey.

The mail train was fast even in those days. I quit Liverpool at nine and was in London by three. At Euston Square, the familiar glum sandwich men, plodding to advertise Holloway's Universal Ointment, Madame Tussaud's Exhibition, and Manockjee Poonjiajee and Sons' Bombay curry-powder and chutneys, shone with a new light in my eyes. No smell came sweeter than the steaming urns of a London coffee-stall, all at a penny a cup. And the inevitable begging, barefoot street arabs were for once as entrancing as a whirling flock of starlings rather than an intolerable nuisance.

I stowed myself and my box aboard a chariot, this being before the years of glorious profusion in cabs, directing the man to the Star Inn, near the Angel. Then weariness and worry fell on me together. In London, I stood amid my debts and my remorse over Floy. I had but five sovereigns in the world. My last dollars had been dissipated aboard on brandy-and-water, the steward's fee allowing only one gill of spirits a day, though a reasonable quantity of port, sherry, madeira and claret was issued, as advertised, with all meals save breakfast.

I had hastily to find some reasonably priced lodging. The boots at the Star directed me to a French pastrycook's at Covent Garden, where he had heard of a room to let. It was up a rickety stair, small, shabby, dirty, reeking ominously of turpentine applied lavishly against the little gentlemen in brown, mixed with the delicious smells of baking *pâtisseries* which were already beyond my pocket. The French language imbibed with my mother's milk set me immediately on good terms with the pastrycook, a squat, explosive, jet-bearded Parisian, and I spared barely ten minutes to take possession before making up the Strand towards the office of Lloyd's newspapers in Salisbury Square.

In my coat pocket was an article on 'anaesthesia', as I must now call it, giving a somewhat theatrical account of my experiences in Boston, yet packed with scientific fact. It was written amid swinging oil lamps and slopping brandy-and-water aboard the steam-packet. The tornado of excitement which Morton's invention aroused in Boston had not yet ruffled London, there being no earlier mail-boat than the *Acadia* since the first operation at the General Hospital. My unpretentious figure was the herald of magnificent tidings for mankind, which would appear, equally prosaically – the *Penny Weekly* having stopped publication – in *Lloyd's Penny Sunday Times and People's Police Gazette*, or perhaps in *Lloyd's Monthly Volume of Amusing and Instructive Literature*.

I strode through the frosty morning, the sun beginning to disperse the inevitable London mist. The familiar jangle of the hackney-coaches and the ponderous rumbling of the wagons, the cries of sweep, street sellers and importuning beggars, were musical with the charm of homecoming. Even the noisome, abounding smells turned almost fragrant.

But Edward Lloyd was not interested.

'Another form of mesmerism, is it, Mr Romilly?' He was a red-faced man about thirty, top hat pushed back on pale hair, sitting busily thumbing through my manuscript. 'I'm afraid we've had a deal too much of that. The very sight of the word is enough to send our readers to sleep.'

Utterly disconcerted, I tried to explain that anaesthesia was a chemical, not a mental, process, and one creating jubilation among the staid doctors of the sober city of Boston. But to no avail. The editor failed to be moved, either through a journalist's cynicism towards human enthusiasm for anything whatever, or through pure ignorance.

'Now, steam heating, Mr Romilly, that's different,' he told me. 'There's a hotel shortly to be opened in Boston, the Eastern Exchange, heated entirely by steam. The very first public building in the world to have the system. You know all about it, of course?'

I shook my head. Lloyd's glance clearly implied that I had wasted my time in America.

'Our Yankee friends harness much of their ingenuity to the pursuit of comfort,' he observed. 'For two years now there's been a hotel in New York where you could book a bedroom with a *bathroom*. Attached, completely private, for your own use. Imagine, such luxury! If you could do me an article on those lines ... mechanical inventions and the easement of human life ... then I should be *very* interested.'

This stunning rejection left me bereft of any plan. I supposed I could try my luck with *Reynolds' Miscellany*, a journal newly established. I had known George Reynolds slightly as editor of the *Illustrated London News*, and he was a man of Radical outlook like myself. But if Lloyd turned me down, I was likely to find that other editors thought alike. I wandered disconsolately past St Bride's church and along Fleet Street. The qualmish effluvia of its eating houses, steaming up through the iron gratings, reminded me that I had breakfasted early and must dine soon, but cheaply. I groped my way into some cavern-like tavern basement, choosing the ordinary at sixpence, hot pork, bread and cheese and beer, though relieved with a good helping of pease pudding and crackling.

I reflected over the meal that my traveller's tales would never be taken seriously unless anaesthesia with sulphuric ether were demonstrated as successfully in London as in Boston. But how could this be engineered? Why should medical men take me more seriously than Lloyd had? I contemplated seeking from Lady Aubery a second introduction to Robert Liston, but was disinclined to show my face in Aubery House when she had so recently taken such trouble to dispatch it across the Atlantic. Then a breathtaking notion began to shimmer in my mind. It quickly took an outline of hard resolve. I should that very evening present myself at Clifford Street, demand to see Liston, and refuse to be turned away. It would need brazenness. But I had acquired much of that valuable commodity in America.

It was a hateful midwinter day when the gas is doused after breakfast only to be relit at tea, and the cold was sharpened by everyone taking pains to inform me I had missed the hottest summer in memory. I grew increasingly tremulous. As the afternoon passed and the clocks struck six, it was desperation which brought me to the surgeon's broad, chequered front step, guarded with its twenty spearlike cast-iron railings.

The same young footman answered my knock, his manners not matured in the interval. He failed to recognize me, seeming to suffer the *idée fixe* I was a patient, unable to believe a visitor of such insignificance could be drawn to the house other than by need of surgical attention. I declared that I had an urgent message for Mr Liston, but feeling that the names of Morton or Warren would convey little outside their own remote and inconsiderable country, I said impulsively it was from the President of the United States.

I was admitted to the oak-panelled gaslit hall where I had passed down to dinner. Now it was crammed with people, men and women of all ages, a child or two whining among them. Everyone was perched or leaning wherever they could, surveyed haughtily by the tall-pedestalled marble bust of some classical figure, doubtless very learned. In those days, there were no appointments with doctors. With messengers few and costly, and the penny post still suspect, patients simply appeared on his doorstep and hoped to be attended. The richer ones had the surgeon to stay until they recovered – or died. Little wonder servants grew off-hand with the daily horde of intrusive strangers, but the visitors had more on their minds than to heed such shortcomings. And if they were obliged to tarry long enough, the butler appeared to provide them with wine and biscuits.

I took my place in this melancholy company, all of whom searched my face and figure for some hint about the cause of my joining them. I tried out of sympathy to look a little ill. Within a quarter of an hour the butler appeared in his blue coat and brass buttons, calling my name in a loud bleak voice, as though a jailer summoning me into court.

I was shown into a square front room which faced into Clifford Street, alongside the stone-flagged entrance hall. It was empty. This room, too, was oak panelled, with two doors, the shutters drawn across its pair of tall windows, candles brightly lit, coals glowing in the grate. Against the wall stood an open bureau, quill stuck in pewter inkstand, untidy with papers, as though the writer had been summoned hastily away. I turned to the glass-doored bookcase, locked like a tea-caddy.

Eustachius, Fabricius, Bichet, Versalius, Scarpa ... authors who could have been familiar, had I been better educated. I noticed *Practical Surgery*, Liston's own name on the spine. In one corner was a table of rosewood inlaid with mother-of-pearl, on which were set, as casually as the carvers for dinner, two knives a foot long, pointed like a guardsman's bayonet, both edges ground finer than a razor. Beside was a little open leather wallet of instruments, some strange to my eyes, others like the familiar needles and bodkins of any household. These unexpected reminders of Liston's grisly profession aroused my interest, when two months before they would have set me aghast.

The door was thrown open.

'You would seem to have returned somewhat precipitately from the Americas, Mr Romilly.'

I turned, bowing my head. 'I assume you heard from Lady Aubery of my voyage, sir.'

'I heard she had given you the money for it. Or was it some deceit, and you preferred to put the cash to less exerting use? There are plenty of young men in London, I should think particularly so in your line, who must clip the coinage of rectitude to make their way.'

I protested, suppressing my indignation at the slur, 'I assure you, sir, I landed only yesterday by the *Acadia*. If you had inquiries made from the shipping intelligence at Lloyd's Rooms, they will verify her arrival.'

'There's no need. You have developed a pronounced Yankee accent.' I was surprised. But such changes, like bad habits, are insidious. Liston sat heavily in a round wooden chair before the bureau, sticking out his long legs in their Wellington boots. I remained standing, having no invitation otherwise. 'My servants say you bear me a message from President Polk?'

'I apologize for some ... er, exaggeration, sir. I can only assure you it is one of comparable importance.'

'Well?' Liston tucked his left thumb into the armhole of his shawl vest, poking the orangewood toothpick into his mouth. 'What do you want of me?'

He had at least not had me kicked into the street. I had the feeling that, despite its roughness, his manner suggested a more amiable opinion of me than at our last meeting.

'I have witnessed anaesthesia, sir, in Boston,' I explained humbly.

'What's this?' He looked mockingly. 'Some strange new disease? Some play? Some charming lady?'

'My apologies, sir,' I continued hastily. 'The name is newly coined, to describe a state of insensitivity, induced by a chemical, during surgical operations.'

'Indeed, Mr Romilly, you make me feel quite uneducated.'

'If you would have the grace to read this, sir . . .' Hand trembling, I thrust towards him the slip cut from the *Boston Examiner* bearing my name.

Liston did not take it. He stared in silence while I stood with racing heart. 'What you saw was not nitrous oxide gas?' he asked soberly. 'Not a gas at all? Rather, the heavy vapour of a liquid?'

'If you would read my account, sir —'

'I have already done so, Mr Romilly.' I looked astounded. 'It was enclosed in a letter sent me this afternoon by a professional acquaintance. A Dr Boott of Gower Street, an American, a Harvard man. Dr Boott is in turn acquainted with Dr Jacob Bigelow in Boston.' He took up a paper from the open bureau at his elbow. 'You may read what Dr Boott had to say to me. The letter he received from Dr Bigelow must have crossed on the same boat as yourself. You have been eating and sleeping on top of it for a fortnight.'

I read quite breathlessly,

> *By hand of messenger.*
> *Gower Street, Bedford Square,*
> *Thursday, December 17, 1846.*

My dear Liston,

I send you an account of a new anodyne process lately introduced in Boston, Massachusetts, of which I heard only this morning from Dr Bigelow. It promises to be one of the important discoveries of the present age. It has rendered many patients insensible to pain during surgical operations, and other causes of suffering. Limbs and breasts have been amputated, arteries tied, tumours extirpated, and many hundreds of teeth extracted without any consciousness or the least pain on the part of the patient. The inventor is Dr Morton, a dentist of Boston, and the process consists of the inhalation of ether to the point of intoxication.

Dr Bigelow's daughter Mary has in his presence undergone the removal of a molar tooth by Dr Morton, without the slightest knowledge of the extraction. She inhaled the ether about one minute, and fell asleep instantly in the chair. In another minute she awoke, smiled, said the tooth was not out, had felt no pain. It was like some magical illusion.

I am inviting Dr Robinson to perform a similar operation on a similar subject as soon as practicable. Meanwhile, should you consider using this process in a capital operation, I venture to suggest you may find it of at least passing interest.

Your servant,
Francis Boott.

'Of passing interest!' I exclaimed. 'I warrant, sir, you shall find its importance more demanding than that.'

'Well, I have certainly no wish to share public ridicule with the unfortunate Captain Warner.' Liston took the letter back. 'Have you read in the newspaper? He has some secret apparatus for destroying ships, and so forth, while they are out of sight. He persuaded our illustrious Secretary of State for War and the Colonies to permit his demonstrating it. Upon a distant tree, in Anglesey. But even this inoffensive target survived safely intact.'

I began to protest that I brought news of no hoax, but Liston cut me short with, 'I am not ablaze with enthusiasm, Mr Romilly. But you may ascribe that to my Scots caution. I shall try your Yankee dodge. I would try anything – anything reasonable – to blunt the edge of my knife in my patients' —'

With that word, he was torn with a sudden, violent bout of coughing. For more than a minute I stood alarmed, wondering if he were choking, my mind occupied with the propriety of a layman like myself offering aid to a distinguished surgeon. I was contemplating the bell-rope when Liston began to recover, explaining between gasps, 'I had a blow from the boom of my boat ... I fear it may have touched the lungs ...' He rasped a coda of coughing into his handkershief. 'It will recover by and by,' he dismissed the visitation, dabbing his streaming eyes. 'Well, Mr Romilly, I intend to give this dodge of yours a try on Sunday. I have a suitable case lying in the North London, a butler with chronic arthritis of the knee, due for amputation at mid-thigh. One Frederick Churchill. His name may pass into history if your dodge is successful.' Liston seemed to be recovering his good spirits. 'And if it is not,' he continued more sombrely, 'the poor man will in three days from now be freed from all his earthly troubles and sorrows.'

'There has been no fatal outcome from ether yet, sir,' I told him eagerly.

'I wish I had your ability to tell a fine day from a glimpse of the sunrise. You have witnessed this inhaler?' he continued in a more commanding tone, reaching for the slip of newspaper again. 'You have observed its use by this dentist ... what's-his-name ... Morton?'

'On repeated occasions.'

'I shall need to make use of your recollections. Pray be at Squire's the apothecary's in Oxford Street – you know the shop? – at noon on Saturday. Squire is an ingenious fellow, and will construct something handy for me.'

In my elation that Morton's invention was about to be demonstrated in London, and by the best-known of its surgeons, I had overlooked the essential reason for again finding myself in my native capital. 'That the agent is sulphuric ether, sir, is an open secret,' I began boldly. 'But I have the duty to indicate that the process is safeguarded by patent, granted by the United States Government.'

'Patent? Fiddlestick's end.' Liston tugged the bell pull. 'And pray, sir, wear your collars turned up decently, like a gentleman. Door, Reilly,' he directed, as the young footman appeared.

'But sir!' My protest came with some anguish. 'It is solely through Dr Morton's vigour and inventiveness —'

'Door, Reilly,' Liston repeated. He nodded at me, with a cold look. 'Your way lies there, sir.'

I left, the footman seeing me into the street with well-practised briskness.

15

MOSES POOLE of Middlesex had an office in Gray's Inn Lane, hardly bigger than the cabin which had confined me and my five companions aboard the *Acadia*. He had a short, skimpy frame, and was bald, with an equally threadbare short-tailed black coat and a matching napless tall hat on the hook over-head. He sniffed repeatedly, like a locomotive going uphill. Feet apart, he stood between glowing fire and high desk, excluding an air of infinite slyness which his clients must have found most heartening.

'So we may have our arms and legs – and even our heads – cut off without even so much as noticing? Very interesting. *Very* interesting.' He sniffed several times rapidly. It was the morning after my bearding Liston. Poole had just read through Morton's official letter appointing me as his European agent, then through my slip from the *Boston Examiner*. A few sharp jerks of his wily head were enough to shake into it the principle of Morton's invention. 'I trust your "Letheon" is fully effective, sir?' He stared at me, wiry grey eyebrows raised quizzically. 'I should feel greatly inconvenienced, permitting some sawbones to be at me, then discovering your specific to be of no more use than . . . well, than our canny Mr James Morison's Universal Pill turns out to be against the cholera. *Most* inconvenienced, sir.'

'I assure you, sir, I have repeatedly seen it work like a charm. A charm as effectively sleep-making as dispensed by Prospero's sprite, Ariel. Furthermore, Mr Robert Liston is to perform a capital operation under the process at the North

London Hospital on Sunday. And no gentleman of his reputation would risk so public a failure.'

'Morison's Universal Pill is patented, to be sure. So are Parr's Life Pills, which are held to stimulate the beauty of our ladies as the June sun our rosebuds. I am of the opinion that "Letheon" must be on all fours with these, and other popular empirics. Yes, sir. I should say that your application to the Patent Office to secure Dr Morton's rights throughout England and the Colonies must succeed.'

I accepted this advice with gratification, but added cautiously, 'In the light of certain arguments which arose in Boston, would you suspect that difficulties might arise in obtaining all monies due to me as Dr Morton's agent?'

'That is inevitable with any patent, sir.'

'But how might such difficulties be overcome?'

'That, sir, must remain an exercise for your ingenuity, not mine. The fee for my consultation will be six and eightpence.'

I called directly at the Patents Office, where my business went briskly, an official entering particulars in a ledger with the resigned appearance of a man paid to humour lunatics. I dined again on sixpence, and returned to the pastrycook's, writing at once to Morton that his affairs were in capable hands.

The next morning – Saturday, December 19, 1846 – I made north from Covent Garden towards Oxford Street. It was a dull day, bitterly cold but dry, everyone's breath a cloud, the snowfall of yesterday glass under the iron of hoof and rim, white lumps falling from the roofs of coaches newly harnessed. The traffic was the worst I could remember, shafts, spokes and springs jammed together, sometimes apparently beyond hope of separation without the use of machinery. Gentlefolk were starting to turn Christmas into the most elaborate of festivals, in reverence less for Christ than for Charles John Huffam Dickens, who had raised benevolence from the level of a virtue to that of a fashion.

Yet the noisy, bustling overcrowded streets, which I saw through eyes sharpened by travel, warmed me with the magnificence and sumptuousness of London. The shops were profligately lit with flaring gas, their windows displaying with haughty casualness brilliant floods of silks and velvets, jewellery to enhance the slightest of hands or snowiest of bosoms, every glittering or sparkling article of adornment from every shore in the world. There were burnished metals exquisitely wrought, rich materials turned delicately into dresses, shawls from China, golden lamé from India – even coffins and shrouds of the finest make – and everywhere a profusion of tempting delicacies to stimulate the most jaded of appetites or enliven the most humdrum of feasts, peered upon hungrily by ragged ballad-singers, crossing-sweepers and flyposters, through a sheet of plate glass more impenetrable to them than the walls of the Tower of London itself.

That murky noon found me standing in the glaring green and scarlet lights shining through the double bay front of Squire's chemist's shop, well known to everyone in Town. Each window was lit through a huge bulbous flask of coloured liquid, the signal of his trade. I stared through the panes at the delft-ware jars, painted with names mysterious to my eyes – *Petrol. Lig.*, *Tr. Rhei Co.*, *Colocynth Husks*, *Golden Balls*, *Tr. Zingib. Co.*, all powerful drugs for the sick. In one corner stood a big blue jar of leeches. I was giving my boots the attention of the scraper, while reading beside the establishment's day and night bells an advertisement for its medicated lozenges, infants' food, feeding bottles, sponges and marking ink, when Liston's horse came walking along the cobbles. He dismounted, tossing the reins unheedingly to the inevitable barefoot boy who seems to spring from the very flagstones. I reflected that Christmas would be a hollow celebration for this ragged guttersnipe, and so it would be for me, friendless in my garret. Though I was warmed with the hope that my Aladdin's Cave would shortly open, to the rub not of a lamp but of a globular inhaler.

I greeted the surgeon by asking respectfully about his health. 'I'm hunting next week, and that's the best treatment in the world for anything,' Liston replied gruffly. 'It does the liver a power of good. Though this season's been an atrocious one. You hunt, Mr Romilly?'

'Unhappily, my family's fortunes never permitted it.' Unwisely trying to impress him, I added, 'Though in childhood I regularly followed the hounds in Sussex with my uncle, who was Lord Horsham.'

'*Never trust a man who hunts south of the Thames,*' Liston quoted shortly, pushing through the double front door into the shop.

I should have been mindful that Liston shot with squires and rode with peers. I found later that his mind curiously linked his skill at surgery with that at sport, amputation of the leg in twenty-five seconds a feat to compare with downing a high, fast bird with a cool, perpendicular shot. This was a particularly British attitude. It could never have entered the thinking of Dr Warren in Boston. Meanwhile, I had to curb my tongue, if I wished to be accepted in medical matters as his loader.

'Good day to you, Squire.' Liston ambled into the shop, orange-stick in mouth and thumb in armhole. With a nod, he introduced me briefly as, 'Mr Romilly, the Homer to our Odyssey.'

Peter Squire was pleasant-looking, dark-haired, middle-aged, I could see at once a friend of the surgeon. Beside stood his nephew William Squire, who I gathered from the greetings to be walking the hospitals so to join Liston's profession. The shop was small, with no counter, dominated with a pair of porcelain urns two feet high on a shelf, each emblazoned with an eagle and crest and the word underneath *RHUBARB*. One wall was occupied with small drawers – there must have been 150 of them – each lettered neatly in gold-leaf with *Amyli P.*, *P. Seidlitz*, and suchlike. Another had shelves with more jars, some with the Royal Arms, labelled *Camphora, Sennae, Aloes, Honey*, and the inevitable pill-rolling machine with mortar and pestle. The air was warm from a leaping fire, and with that characteristic smell compounded by essences from all corners of the earth and medicaments from all ends of man's imagination, sweet and sharp but predominantly camphorous, which may soothe or frighten the customer, depending on the gravity of the illness which drives him there.

I was invited to tell the story of Warren's operation. Liston declared approvingly afterwards, 'They're sharp, these Yankees. *I*'d certainly support nothing with quackery or humbug about it, as I wrote in Syme's subscription book at Minto House, where he set up shop in Edinburgh. Thus causing our learned professor to pursue an action against me for libel. Which I lost, great Heaven!' Liston gave a loud laugh. 'Though I dare say my comparing an ape's skull to his own in the lecture hall had something to do with his ruffled feelings.'

This engrossing aside remained unhappily unelaborated, Squire leaving a boy in the shop and ushering us into an inner room. This was chilly, pungent, and crammed with carboys muffled in straw amid items of chemical glassware in varied and weird shapes. On a small, rough wooden bench stood a glass bell about a foot high, into the top of which fitted a bulbous glass stopper. The stopper itself was hollow, and received the stem of yet a third and smaller glass vessel. From the rim of the bell itself extruded a yard or two of stiff, flexible tube leading to a semicircular metal mouthpiece, familiar to me from medicinal inhalers in daily use.

'Have you any knowledge of natural and physical science, Mr Romilly?' asked the chemist.

'My father was versed in the discipline.'

'This is a Nooth's apparatus, which I have just adapted for our new purpose,' Squire explained. 'It was originally designed by Joseph Priestley, its proper use for the production of carbon dioxide gas. The gas is made from marble chips in the base of the bell here, on which sulphuric acid is dropped from this middle section.' His finger indicated the bulbous glass stopper. Liston stood over us, chewing his orange-stick in silence. 'This uppermost vessel of all would ordinarily contain water to absorb the newly formed gas. Now, to my mind, the apparatus could be used with the Read's inhaling tube and mouthpiece you see, for administering ether vapour. Did the clever Bostonians contrive it much the same, Mr Romilly?'

'Dr Morton used a globe, and a mouthpiece fitted with valves.'

'There would be little difficulty in valves,' Squire said thoughtfully. 'Otherwise, I suspect our principle is the same as your Dr Morton's. Well, we can easily see,' he added cheerfully, directing his nephew to fetch a beaker of sulphuric ether and a sponge.

The apparatus was charged. I told young William to hold his nose and take a breath through the tube. He gasped, coughed violently, and flung the mouthpiece from him. 'It's worse than chlorine,' he said angrily.

I returned, somewhat tartly, 'Pray don't surrender to the first blast, sir. Had the Americans done as much, the world would still know nothing of this blessing.'

Liston supported me, to my relief. 'Ether vapour is wholesome enough. Even our most delicate invalids inhale it for the lungs. The air of the seaside could make a man gasp, if he weren't accustomed to it. I have my rounds to finish, so I must bid you good day, gentlemen. Mr Romilly, come with Mr Squire tomorrow morning. You must be about the hospital, in case your experience is needed.'

I felt pride, even conceit, at being the only soul that side of the Atlantic who had seen the 'Yankee Dodge' work. But remembering my duty I began, 'Dr Morton's patent —'

'Pray speak no more of patents,' Liston said severely. 'Inventions or improvements which tend to alleviate suffering cannot be the subjects of patents. That's all there is to it. Such would be the height of illiberality.'

I returned calmly, and bravely, 'I am aware of such doubts existing in certain minds, sir. But I cannot see why the individual who by skill and industry invents or discovers the means of diminishing – or in this instance annihilating – the depths of human suffering, is not as much entitled to compensation as he, who makes an improvement in the manufacture of woollen of other fabrics. Indeed, he is entitled to greater compensation, because he has conferred upon mankind a greater benefit.'

Liston replied to the speech with another loud laugh. 'Save that for the *Penny Weekly*,' he advised, leaving the shop.

I began seriously to fear that I should not turn a penny piece for Morton, or for myself. Or that Liston might cheerfully contrive to have me walking the treadmill for fraud.

But the operation was postponed. As Mayfair was going to church that Sunday morning, I presented myself again at the chemist's shop. Squire told me that Liston had ridden up Bond Street to say that the light was too poor, and the patient's condition had grown suddenly low, though expected to rally. I was disappointed and disconcerted. Were the patient to sink and die, another might not be suitable before Liston's interest in etherization waned. It could then be months before another surgeon of comparable boldness took upon himself to test this artifice, barely tried, newly arrived from a land largely primitive. How might I support myself in London meanwhile? Even a patent which nobody seemed inclined to recognize was more valuable than one which nobody seemed inclined to use.

I regarded the weather through my skylight window the next day with some attention. It seemed bright enough. I called on Squire during the morning, and received the encouraging news of a message left by Liston, to present myself at the North London Hospital by one o'clock. The operation had been fixed for two-thirty. I was to meet a Mr Douglas Bush, one of Liston's dressers, a student, who would attend me.

The day grew unseasonably warm. The thermometer outside an instrument-maker and cutler's which I passed in Gower Street was registering fifty degrees. I knew little about that part of London, save that it contained Euston Square Station, and that its early hours were rent with the lowing and baaing of cattle and sheep, driven down its long straight roads to Smithfield Market from the farms of Middlesex and Hertfordshire. My destination was easily found. The long, low building of four storeys, with its massive pediment, struck me as a stark shadow of the new Buckingham Palace, then being raised by Mr Edward Blore on foundations of financial trickery by the ousted Mr John Nash. Carved in tall letters between ground and first floor was NORTH LONDON HOSPITAL, though everyone was already calling it University College Hospital, as to this day.

Despite my adventures with Morton in Boston, I approached the hospital with a sickening feeling. As that which touches a man, even a young and healthy one, on encountering the plumes and pall of a funeral clattering its sombre way on the cobbles. The butcher's shop smell was stronger than at the Massachusetts General. The front steps led between railings into a lobby shaped like a cross, giving off half a dozen rooms the purposes of which I did not care to think of. Hurrying about were men of various ages and social classes, whom I took to be doctors and hospital servants. No patients were to be seen, save a blackbearded weatherbeaten man making his way out of doors cheerfully enough on a wooden leg. I confronted unexpectedly a stout, pink-cheeked female of well-scrubbed appearance, in dark dress and an ample cook's apron, on her head a quaint half-cap of muslin with a generous frill and a bow tied under her chin. My shock that a decent gentlewoman should work in so dreadful a place gave way to my admiration of these estimable deaconesses, who dispense their lives in attendance on the sick poor.

In the middle of the lobby three young men of my own age were standing chatting, hands in pockets, indifferent to the bustle round about them. One was fair-haired, a dandy, with light, tight trousers, bright blue coat with shining buttons, and an extravagant frill to his shirt. He looked up, after I had been regarding the scene for some time forlornly, inquiring languidly, 'Mr Romilly, sir, I take it?'

'Your service, sir,' I said.

'May I introduce myself as Mr Bush?' he continued in the same tone. 'This gentleman is Mr Joseph Clover.' He indicated a solemn-looking, bright-eyed, lean, dark young man with a fringe of black beard. 'And this, Mr Joseph Lister. Who is not, under any circumstances, to be confused with our professor, of slightly different ilk.'

I inclined my head again. I found young Lister a handsome fellow, with thick dark hair, broad of brow and mouth, and restrained in the way of whiskers. The pomp with which Bush performed these introductions evaporated with his heartfelt, 'Capital fellows the pair, I'd give my word any time. And this is Mr Romilly, the well-known man of letters.' I fear he mocked. 'Mr Romilly has been all the way to Boston – in *America*, can you imagine that, my cronies? To witness the marvels which this afternoon shall be displayed to us be-nighted natives of London.'

'I assure you, sir, the anodyne process will prove of infinite benefit to humanity,' I said earnestly.

'Great Heaven, let's keep humanity out of it.' Bush looked greatly shocked, or affected to. 'We aren't concerned here with *humanity*. We're concerned in turning ourselves into doctors with a sound digestion for guineas.'

Clover smiled, either at this remark or the baffled expression with which I received it. 'We'd best make haste, if we want a good place,' he urged. 'The word's got round that Liston is out to try something new. Half the doctors in London will be trying to push into the theatre.'

'Is our scribe venturing in?' Lister asked, also grinning.

'Into the *opisthodomos* of the Temple of Hippocrates,' proclaimed Bush. 'Indeed, the very *adyton*.'

'I was present at the earlier demonstration at the Massachusetts General Hospital,' I replied assertively.

'Perhaps you should suggest to the professor that he invites you to perform today's operation?' suggested Bush. The other two laughed loudly, but I thought the gibe ill-placed.

'I *shall* venture in,' I said firmly. 'If I am afforded the privilege. Which I shall respect.'

'Please yourself,' agreed Bush lightly. 'Should you be obliged to vomit, kindly do it into your hat.'

I discovered the operating theatre roughly like that at Boston. It smelt more, because of the post-mortem room next door. The benches, with their iron bars for leaning, were already bursting with students. Grey heads and bald heads were squeezed uncomfortably on the seats of honour inside the railing. The four of us pushed into the second row from the floor. Bush's condescension had doubled my determination not to flinch from the coming gruesomeness, from the spectacle of pain which men must inflict upon one another, in either the anger of war or the mercifulness of healing, that good might come in the end. The journalist must greet human misery and human happiness with equal coldness.

An hour passed quickly. Just before half past two, the

buzzing room suddenly petered into silence. The doors slid apart with a crash. Liston strode in. He wore the same bottle-green coat with its velvet collar, with light worsted trousers secured under the arches of his Wellington boots. Behind came a balding, youngish man of apelike looks, William Cadge, his assistant. Then Ransome the house surgeon, waxed hemp ligatures ready in his buttonhole, immediately busying himself gathering saws and knives from the tall instrument cabinet, and setting them on a towel laid across the squat chair in company with a bowl of sponges.

'Palmer, read the notes,' ordered Liston at once.

A younger man whom I took as a student, the last to enter, obediently opened a long leather-covered journal. (Which I have seen again but this past month, Robert Liston's case-books being preserved in the Medical School of University College Hospital. I read those same pages written in Edward Palmer's close, neat copperplate, though the notes are finished by Edward Franklyn, another student whose turn came to succeed him as Liston's dresser.)

Palmer explained that the patient was one Frederick Churchill, _aetat_ thirty-six, admitted on Monday, November 23 last, for the past sixteen years butler at No 37 Upper Harley Street, previously a footman.

'He is unwed,' Palmer continued the man's intimate story in a colourless voice. 'He is of regular habits, though sometimes up late these last two-and-a-half years. His food is of good quality, he has a strong appetite, especially for breakfast. He sleeps soundly, but in a rather confined room these last fifteen years. He has lived the past twenty-five years in London, though his occasional months away total some five to six years.'

Everyone was stirring on the benches, impatient for the student to finish and the promised excitement to begin. But it seemed that formality must be preserved, as the rigmarole in a court of law. Liston stood impassive, thumb in armhole.

'The patient is five feet eight inches tall, fair complexioned, his state of mind cheerful. His father died ten years ago from an abdominal complaint, his mother is alive and well, _aetat_

141

sixty-eight. Brother and sister alive and well, none died in infancy. He suffered gonorrhoea eighteen years ago, and again ten years ago, treated by Dr Mayo.' I was shocked to hear this sin of the poor man so casually aired. 'For the past five months he has suffered from a skin disease on the arms, probably eczema. He has a small stream of urine.'

As Liston had derisively suggested, I knew that these personal items, appertaining to one of the lower orders, might live long after the man himself were dust. The student turned the page. 'History of present condition. *Aetat* five, pain in right hip. *Aetat* fifteen, hackney coach ran over right leg above the ankle. For past six years, right knee swollen and painful, more severe after a fall with violent bending of the knee two years ago. Iodine applications were prescribed. A swelling developed over the right tibioperineal articulation, which was opened three weeks ago, and a number of irregularly shaped bodies pressed out. They were preserved in alcohol, and varied in size from a pea to a horsebean. They were enough to fill a two-ounce bottle, and consisted mainly of fibrous tissue.'

He continued, 'A sinus developed, which the professor probed on November 25, bare bone being distinctly felt on the head of the tibia. Water dressing and complete rest were ordered. The patient suffered fever and night sweats with inflammation of the lungs. It was subsequently decided to remove the limb.'

He shut the book.

'We are going to try a Yankee dodge today, gentlemen, for making men insensible,' Liston announced at once.

At this remark, Peter Squire appeared through the sliding doors, followed by his nephew William. Everyone craned to see the apparatus in the elder man's hands. I heard the words passing round, 'Why, it's a Nooth's,' in tones of disappointment. Clearly, all were expecting some device of engineering as elaborate and ingenious as those from the brain of Mr Isambard Brunel. As Peter Squire set the inhaler on a low table, placed for the occasion by the operating table, the audience began to sniff, and mutter sapiently to one another, 'It's ordinary ether,' seeming even more crestfallen.

'Is there any gentleman present who would care to try it?' Peter Squire inquired pleasantly. There was silence. It appeared that medical men preferred to afford their patients, rather than themselves, the privilege of undergoing momentous experiments.

'What, no one?' the chemist exclaimed mockingly. His eye fell on the huge porter. 'Come on, man! Let's see if we can put you under.'

The audience began to titter and shout, 'Come on, Sheldrake!', who with an unsure grin felt himself impelled to show courage. He lay on the thin mattress of the operating table, stout legs dangling over the edge, and sucked the tube while Squire pinched his bulbous nose.

Unlike young William Squire, Sheldrake took to the vapour as a babe to milk. His eyes closed, his face flushed, his breathing fell into the gentle regularity of a sleeper's. The onlookers fell silent, impressed. Then with the roar of a bull, the man flung himself from the table, hurled the mouthpiece aside, scattered the distinguished doctors, vaulted the railings, and plunged his way through the students, who prudently dodged his massive flailing fists. At last he calmed sufficiently to spit lavishly several times and make for the upper door, shouting through the hubbub, 'No more of that damned stuff for me.'

I felt this an unpromising start for the afternoon.

In my mind adapting Voltaire, I knew that Squire was administering a drug of which he knew little, by an inhaler of which he knew less. And should the *fiasco* be repeated, I was confident the London students would afford the same reception as those in Boston gave Horace Wells with his nitrous oxide gas. But once recovering themselves, the audience seemed much amused. And I had anyway no time for forebodings, because already Liston had his shirt sleeves rolled up and was testing the blade of his long pointed knife against his thumbnail.

'Ready, Mr Ransome?'

'Ready, sir.'

'Have the patient brought.'

A nod from Ransome to Palmer. Almost at once the man

appeared, borne by two porters on a stretcher. Pale, emaciated, lined, even to my eyes he was very sick. He was laid on the operating table, staring round, an animal already stricken, finally trapped, ringed by its pursuers.

'Churchill, you shall have an inhalation to render you insensible during the operation.' Liston's tone was so quiet, so solicitous, so unexpectedly self-effacing, that I was more startled than had he shouted. 'You're not afraid?'

'I know I've to lose my leg, sir,' the man replied weakly. 'It's that or meet my Maker.'

'Do as this gentleman directs,' ordered Liston, nodding towards Squire.

I realized I was gripping hard the rail in front of me. How closely the operation had so far followed events in Boston! It was as two performances of the same play. But I knew the drama could turn into tragedy, or farce, as readily as provide us with a happy ending.

Two students took their accustomed positions, to hold the patient down. Squire applied the mouthpiece to Churchill's lips. Two or three minutes passed. He gave a hurried command to the nephew, who produced a dark bottle from his coat-tails and dropped more ether into the top of the inhaler. Liston stood testing blade against thumbnail, increasingly impatient. No one in the room stirred, nor I believe was any longer aware of his neighbour.

Squire looked up. 'I think he'll do, sir.'

Liston nodded. Squire withdrew the mouthpiece, placing instead a plain folded handkerchief. 'Take the artery, Mr Cadge,' the surgeon commanded.

Cadge plunged his thumb into the inner angle of the man's leg to stop the huge pulse of the femoral artery. 'Now, gentlemen . . . .' Liston's voice had the rasp of urgency. 'Time me, time me!'

Watches exploded from every pocket. I saw Clover shaking his crossly, peering across at Lister's. I wondered abruptly what Dr Warren of Boston would have thought. He scorned operating 'against the clock'.

'Right, gentlemen . . . now.'

There followed the most amazing display witnessed in my life. Liston's massive left hand grasped the thigh at the same moment as his right plunged the dagger-point of his amputation knife into its middle, just in front of the bone, piercing the flesh clean through. It was less agony to cut from within outwards. Two or three movements, part sawing, part cutting, but so swift they became one, and the knife appeared, bloody, above the knee. Liston's left fingers slipped underneath this bleeding flap, flipping it back on itself, exposing white bone. The knife thrust again, at the angle of the wound's gory mouth. A second flap was made at the back of the leg, Liston's thumb holding back the oozing muscle and skin as the rind of a lemon is decoratively peeled by a French cook. Next the saw, held ready, handle outwards, by Palmer. To waste not a second, Liston took the blood-smeared ebony handle of his great knife between his teeth, a trick learned from Edinburgh butchers on busy market days. Six swift sawstrokes and the limb was severed. Liston's movements were so dexterous, so exact, that jerk of saw and slit of knife seemed to flow into the same.

Instantly there was uproar.

'Twenty-eight seconds, sir!' cried young William Squire, timepiece in hand. Ransome dropped the leg with a thud into a box of sawdust already scarlet.

'Twenty-six,' objected Bush, at my elbow.

'Twenty-five, sir,' declared Clover and Lister, over the one working watch between them.

'It was twenty-five, sir,' stated Palmer calmly, being accepted as timekeeper with a brief smile from Liston.

It was only then, as the excitement of Liston's performance died away, that the onlookers began to grasp a notion almost impossibly elusive to the human mind. That already such merciful dash in surgery was obsolete.

But there was no time for congratulation or jubilation. There is still much to do after lopping a diseased human branch. The severed end of the femoral artery, bloodless from Cadge's grip, was impaled with a sharp hook and tied with waxed hemp, like a cord shutting a purse. Lesser arteries demanded to be staunched, spouting their strings of red beads.

Lint dripping with water was placed between the two oozing flaps by Ransome and Palmer. The patient lay as quiet as a corpse. Only when Squire uncovered his face from the handkerchief did he raise himself on his elbows, and half-spoke, half-moaned, 'When are you going to begin? I can't have it, I can't have it! Take me back, I can't have it done.'

'Look,' said Liston quietly.

The man saw his stump. Relief and wonder burst from his heart. He began to weep aloud. So was he borne back to the bed from which he had been plucked five minutes before with terrible expectations. Now Liston could bare his excitement to our eyes. He stammered, words hardly able to tumble out, as he exclaimed to us, 'This Yankee dodge, gentlemen, beats mesmerism hollow.'

How smugly I recalled Warren's, *This is no humbug!* Though I would admit both welcomes for the miracle of etherization fell short of the poetic.

The room was abuzz. I felt relief and pride, pride in Morton's triumph, by proxy, across three thousand miles of salt water. But Robert Liston was not a man who allowed miracles to interrupt the brisk flow of his business.

'We shall now try the same process, I trust with equal success, to remove the nail in a case of onychia of the great toe. This is one of the most painful operations in surgery.' For the first time, his eye caught mine. 'Homer . . .' He smiled. 'You may withdraw, if you wish. We no longer need you. We have the Golden Fleece.'

16

THAT NIGHT THERE was a dinner party. After my last dusty reception at Clifford Street, I was gratified to be thrown an invitation by Liston as he left the North London Hospital that memorable afternoon. I came to learn that he erased much rudeness and appeased much resentment with his lavish and lively table. And I came later to reflect that my inclusion was a pleasant foretaste of a sudden upsweep in my fortune and social position.

I steeled myself for another evening of Liston *en famille*, searching my mind fruitlessly for diverting shipwrecks. I hoped that piracy in China would play the satisfactory substitute. But at seven o'clock I was surprised and delighted to be introduced in his drawing-room to a pair of beautiful and charming ladies.

Miss Hattersley and Mrs Wilcox, Liston explained with unblushing vanity, were actresses.

'Mrs Wilcox was acquainted with Mrs Fanny Kemble,' Liston told me. 'Before we lost that lady to the plantations of southern America.'

'I was acquainted with Mrs Kemble when *I was a child*,' Mrs Wilcox pointed out, smoothing the skirt of a printed green and red silk dress, bright to the verge of gaudiness. The other lady had yellow curls, a waist as neat as a sapling, a fair skin with a high colour for which Nature had invoked some assistance, and a bosom sufficiently exposed to tax little of a young man's imagination. I wondered where Robert Liston had found such dazzlers. He certainly proved himself, most agreeably, as no snob. I wondered also the whereabouts of Mr Wilcox. The correlative question about those of Mrs Liston was answered by the surgeon's explaining for my benefit that his family was at Duddingstone House, in Edinburgh, for Christmas, a puny festival beneath a Scotsman's notice. He would follow for Hogmanay. Standing with his long legs astride before the fire, he spoke complainingly at length about the journey by coach, or by coach and railroad, more complicated and in many ways worse. He declared that he preferred the sea route from Thames to Forth, even in midwinter.

'I love the sea, ma'am,' he told Miss Hattersley. 'I should have taken His Majesty's commission in the Navy as a young man, had my father not talked me out of it.'

'Had you gone to sea, sir, you would never have released the magic spell you were telling us of, at the hospital today.'

'It *is* magic, which has changed in a single afternoon both surgery, which is a science, and operating, which is an art.' He was interrupted by a bout of coughing, so fierce that I noticed the two ladies exchange a glance of subdued alarm. But he as quickly recovered, waving his hand as though the attack were of no consequence.

'I trust the due education of surgeons' fingers will not become lacking, by reason of the new process,' he continued, still dabbing spittle from his chin. 'It is criminal to prod and poke about, to give pain with want of adroitness, to leave the patient on the table – great Heaven, even to consult with colleagues! – while the poor man lies bleeding and full of awful expectations. I should not care to think our new invention relieved the operator of *those* responsibilities. A patient, even insensible, remains a human being.'

Wishing to make some mark with Miss Hattersley, I put in, 'If you would allow a literary opinion, sir, it would have seemed true magic in the past. There are lines in Thomas Middleton's *Women Beware Women,*

> *I'll imitate the pities of old surgeons*
> *To this lost limb, who, ere they show their art,*
> *Cast one asleep, then cut the diseased part.*

The ladies are perhaps familiar with the play?'

148

But both looked mystified, protesting they played only comedy.

A carriage was heard below. A minute more and William Cadge was in the room, red-faced from the cold, rubbing his hands and preoccupied.

'How's Churchill?' Liston asked at once.

'Tolerably fair, sir. At about three-thirty, he had a pulse of ninety, with much pain in the stump —'

Cadge broke off, glancing at the two fair guests to whom Liston, in his impatience for news, had not yet vouchsafed the ceremony of introduction. He reddened more at his impropriety of mentioning such matters in their hearing. But Liston said hastily, 'Pray go on, Cadge. These ladies are worldly. They know all about the operation.'

'We are agog,' Miss Hattersley assured him, open mouthed.

'Excruciatingly,' concurred Mrs Wilcox breathlessly.

Cadge still looked uncertain, but continued. I find medical men seldom hesitant to seize the privilege of shocking young ladies with the details of their trade. Nor are the young ladies themselves reluctant to savour the gory tale, and its teller. 'When I left the hospital just now, we had brought the two flaps together and secured two more arteries. One was the small artery running in the centre of the great sciatic nerve.'

'That's how many ligatures in all?' demanded Liston.

'Ten, sir, including the double one on the femoral artery. We applied strips of isinglass plaster, and the pain has now almost ceased.'

'The pulse?'

'Still ninety, sir. His expression of countenance is cheerful, notwithstanding.'

'Has he any memories of the operation at all?'

Cadge gave a sagacious little shake of the head. 'It's curious, sir, all he remembers is "something like a wheel going round my leg". He had a great sensation of cold, but no pain until some minutes after being returned to bed.'

Liston gave a nod. 'I've sent a note round to Boott, with permission to pass the news along to the *Lancet*, if he feels inclined.'

Mrs Wilcox was alarmed and confused by the dialogue. 'Is the poor man sinking?' she asked tremblingly.

'Surely he is lost?' declared Miss Hattersley, soft hand fluttering at snowy bosom.

'I assure you, ma'am, he will rally,' said Liston with all his authority. 'Another two months, if his fortune holds, and he will be discharged as cured.' He finally introduced Cadge, as the butler appeared at the drawing-room door. 'Let us dine,' Liston continued, rubbing his hands eagerly. 'I have a claret tonight of which Lord Palmerston was envious.'

I have lost my note of the *menu*, but the wine doubtless merited Lord Palmerston's coveting. As we sat to table I noticed on the sideboard, next a glass bowl piled with fruit, the Nooth's apparatus used at the hospital that afternoon. I was surprised that Liston made no reference to it, my own eyes repeatedly straying in its direction, as some intrusive stage property distracts the audience with the enigma of when it will enter the action. Liston talked much during the meal about body-snatching, perhaps deliberately, to produce gratifying horror in the ladies.

'But why must surgeons stoop to such horrid practices?' demanded Miss Hattersley, blue eyes wider than ever.

'Only when we have acquired dexterity in the dead subject, ma'am, are we justified in interfering with the living.'

'But the men who . . .' Mrs Wilcox swallowed. 'Who *do the deed* must be out and out rascals, surely?'

Liston gave a laugh. 'Why, ma'am, in Edinburgh I was considered a thoroughly accomplished resurrectionist. A sack-'em-up man.' Both shuddered, very prettily. 'When I was a student, we'd go down to the churchyards about six or eight o'clock in the evening – those were the days before they posted a watch on them. It was the easiest of operations, I assure you. We'd dig a hole down to the head of the coffin, pitching the earth on to a canvas, using a short spade like a dagger, made of wood so's it shouldn't ring on the stones. It would take us an hour, working in relays. Then we'd get our iron hooks, break the coffin lid, and have the body out by the ears —'

Miss Hattersley gave a little shriek.

'It was as simple as drawing a pheasant,' Liston assured her with relish. 'Ears, ma'am, make remarkably convenient handles. We had to take care over reburying the grave-clothes, for to take those would be theft.'

'Then the poor ... poor *person* would be in the ... in the ...?' Delicacy crushed Mrs Wilcox to silence.

'A corpse and a baby are indifferent to such things, ma'am. There was nothing – no law whatever – against carrying off the body. There was only the fury of the bereaved, or much worse, the fury of another anatomist if we happened to be invading his territory. Why, Dr Barclay, who once taught your servant, used to send along a student as look-out man, to stand astride any fresh grave, to reserve it for him. I fired a pistol at Dr Barclay once,' Liston added casually.

'You *fired*!' I felt that Miss Hattersley could not have been more stricken were she in the presence of Captain Macheath himself, nor more admiring.

'But the bereaved took to such devices as the mortsafe – a cage for a coffin – to baulk our designs on anatomical material. We were obliged to turn to the professionals in the game. I used a low fellow called Crouch. He'd go along in his dog-cart at twilight, and seldom return empty handed. He did well out of his business, £7.10 to £10 a sack.' The ladies shivered again.

'Sometimes there was a subject I wanted specially, who I knew was about to die ... I remember a hydrocephalic boy, with a huge head ...' The ladies now gave the appearance of imminent succumbing to the vapours. 'The boy's grave was guarded well, for weeks on end. But Crouch got him. He had him aboard a fishing brig in the Firth, and he turned up in my dissecting room in a parcel delivered by a liveryman. Crouch charged me seven pounds for that one.' Liston tossed back his claret. 'The Anatomy Act has set such adventures to rest these ten years back.' He seemed quite regretful. 'Though I get a brick through my front windows, now and again, from folk who dwell on the past.'

The grimness of his subject, and the playfulness with which he disposed of it, showed Liston to be in capital spirits. I was never to see him so sparkling again. We had reached the champagne, shortly the table was cleared, and the ladies were preparing to leave. Liston turned to me and asked, 'Mr Romilly, pray fetch that decorative piece of glassware.'

The two actresses looked with interest as I set the Nooth's apparatus on the bare dining-table. Liston asked if they knew its function. Both shook their heads sweetly. They looked astounded as he explained it was the very 'Yankee dodge' used for the operation.

'But how does it work?' cried Miss Hattersley.

'I shall show you,' Liston replied promptly. 'Cadge! On the table, if you please.'

Cadge looked at me, looked at Liston, gripped the sides of his chair, and seemed strongly desirous of being elsewhere.

(William Cadge is still alive. He resigned from University College Hospital during the '50s to practise in Norwich, where he became so agreeably rich he rebuilt the local hospital from his own pocket. He tells me that he remembers his alarming experiences at the dinner-table that night more sharply than the afternoon's operation.)

'Come on, Cadge,' repeated Liston, commanding rather than urging.

Obedience to his surgeon sorely tried, the young man rose slowly and lay the length of the dining-table. The ladies laughed and clapped their hands, bright-eyed with this exciting novelty. Liston poured ether from a dark bottle on the sideboard, and applied the mouthpiece. Cadge sucked away dutifully, turning more scarlet than before he arrived. The ladies were quite overcome, Mrs Wilcox managing to utter between spasms of laughter, 'Mr Liston, sir, I won't stand for it! You'll kill that poor young man.'

I think Cadge was inclined to the same idea. He tried to raise his shoulders from the table, moving his arms in half-sensible gestures. Liston gave a loud laugh, and instructing me to keep the mouthpiece applied, set upon the poor fellow's prominent ears with his powerful thumbs, pinning his head to the woodwork.

'Enough, enough!' cried Miss Hattersley, eyes running with joyful tears. 'I can't stand any more, I can't!'

Cadge might have been plunged playfully into a stupor which verged on death, or even went beyond. Or we might all have been blown to bits, no one appreciating the explosiveness of ether vapour in the naked flames of our gas and candles. A Davy lamp is required when the substance is given at night. But Liston suffered another bout of coughing, which stopped his sport. Cadge began to stir, incapable of litttle but moans. I then reluctantly had to leave. I did not care to part company with our charmers, but I had the night to fill with writing. I knew that should I miss but one day in exploiting the afternoon's operation, there would be plenty of others overjoyed to step in and perform the service for me.

That night I wrote an article which appeared shortly in the *People's London Journal*, on which I still look with pride at my youthful exuberance, if at nothing else.

Hurrah! Rejoice! I began. *Mesmerism and its professors have met with a heavy blow and great discouragement! An American dentist has used the inhalation of ether to destroy sensation in surgical operations, and the plan has succeeded in the hands of Drs Warren, Heywood, and others, in Boston. Now it has succeeded in those of Mr Robert Liston at the North London (University College) Hospital in our metropolis. In six months' time, no operation will be performed without this precious preparation. Rejoice! Hail the happy hour! WE HAVE CON-QUERED PAIN!*

What good news comes from our brothers in another land, with whom we were lately going to war! It comes with no firing of cannon from the Tower, no banners, no drums and fifes. How well might our poet John Milton say, 'Peace hath her victories No less renowned than war'. Benevolence has its triumph! The knife performs its friendly office, robbed of all its terrors. Rejoice!

I had already, that very afternoon, written my first account of Liston's operation, for which, through fear of my taking it to any competitor, Lloyd paid more than for the accumulated previous earnings from my pen. I had still the duty to scribble brief intelligence of our success to Morton himself. Then I went to sleep, nearer dawn than midnight, and woke to a world which suddenly found me rich and famous.

17

IT WAS *The Times* newspaper which unexpectedly lit the touchpaper of my rocketing fortunes.

By the end of the year 1846 all London was buzzing with news of the wondrous new drug. Doctors dissertated on it to their patients, often in ignorance, sometimes implying they had just such a thing in mind themselves. Smart men upon 'Change, who would never in their lives discuss such un-commercial matters, spoke of the discovery on City corners. Clergymen exulted from pulpits, judges remarked on it from the bench, to show they were as up in modern affairs as any man, and sent their prisoners to transportation or the gallows with grim little jests in their ears about suspended animation.

Punch made a proper and predictable joke, of John sitting sucking a balloon in his parlour, shrewish Jane with nagging face and wagging finger at his elbow, underneath inscribed, *WONDERFUL EFFECTS OF ETHER IN A CASE OF SCOLDING WIFE* – *Patient: 'This is really quite delightful – a most beautiful dream.'* Mamas threatened their naughty children with sleeping all next Christmas. Even footmen mentioned it to grooms, and crossing-sweepers had something chirpy to say on it as they accepted your farthing. I believe 'etherization' even intruded into the breathed conversation of lovers.

A dread which ever lay in the back of the human mind, only a shade away from death itself, had abruptly been erased. Today our courage is taxed little by a surgical operation. We accept oblivion as a matter of course. The state of wakefulness, which fifty-four years ago decreed for the surgeon 'more haste less pain', has become as impossible for our minds to grasp as splitting the atom.

The last day of 1846, a Thursday, found me during the morning at Lloyd's office in Salisbury Square. Someone said casually that a man from *The Times* had called, asking after me. A true journalist never affords to let slip a commission, even when his pockets are full. And *The Times* was already established in British folklore as 'The Thunderer' through the editorship of Thomas Barnes, dead some five years, the man who could blow warm or cool equally with Whig or Conservative. I walked without delay towards the river at Blackfriars, where the newspaper had its office in the old King's Printing House.

I gave my name to the porter. I had a long wait, before a threadbare-looking man with a ragged moustache and a tall hat with a distinct greenish tinge introduced himself as one of the staff. It seemed that *The Times* did not want me to write for them, but they to write of me. I was agreeable enough. The man expressed his gratification and suggested we repaired to the nearest tavern, all in one breath, which smelt of spirits. I had expected a more scholarly representative and more austere venue, but once we sat over brandy-and-water in the Mermaid, he produced a huge notebook from his side pocket and questioned me closely about the new anodyne process in both Boston and London.

I had imagined I might rate a paragraph in the next morning's paper. I was sufficiently content to have my name puffed at all in such an organ. I was amazed and delighted to find that two stylish columns about me had emanated from its seedy scribe. The print applauded me as the luminary who had brought the immeasurable blessing to England from America, describing me as the young colleague of Dr Morton, and associate of such learned Bostonians as the Drs Jackson, Wells and Warren. I was presented to the public rather as Sir Henry Stanley, after his perhaps less consequential discovery at Ujiji on November 10, 1871. I blushed for the exaggerations in private, and as unblushingly sustained them in public.

I had been happy enough to enjoy a modest rise in fortune which had enabled me to buy a greatcoat from a slopseller's and a pair of highlows from the bootmakers. Now a cloud of inquirers after me settled upon Liston's house in Clifford Street, with a subsequent shower of invitations upon my lodgings. Many of these were businesslike. I was asked to write, and to lecture to societies of varying erudition, to all of which I dashed off my acceptance, and named my fee. Others were social, which I sorted carefully, not wishing to miss the chance of establishing myself in the best society. The pastry-cook's was now clearly below me. I moved to rooms in Cadogan Place, at £5 a week. It was a convenient address which suggested neither the haughtiness of Belgrave Square nor the raffishness of Chelsea, or as much, or as little, of either as I cared from time to time to express.

But I had still to remember my employer, without whose provision of my steamship fare I should not be enjoying such delights. I decided to drive my point home where the timber was stoutest. I delivered a letter to the office of Dr Wakley's *Lancet*, which he printed in his first issue of the new year, alongside Liston's letter about our success, passed on by Boott.

Sir, I declared, *I take this earliest opportunity of giving notice, through the medium of your columns, to the medical profession, and to the public in general, that the process for procuring insensibility to pain by the administration of the vapour of ether to the lungs, employed by Mr Liston, is to be patented for England and the Colonies, and that no person can use that process, or any similar one, without infringing upon rights about to be secured legally for others.*

What dusty answers it brought me! In the very next issue Dr Boott quoted in detail the opinion of Queen's Counsel that such a patent could not possibly be valid, adding that 'It would be most deplorable to have any interruption to such mitigation of human suffering'. The irascible editor himself attacked the letter with a vinegary leading article. My hopes of establishing a profitable agency for Morton were dwindling, as steadily as the sand in an hour-glass. Luckily, hopes for myself were accumulating with matching steadiness else-where.

Liston did not go north for New Year's Eve. The excitement kept him in Clifford Street. The transcendental inequality between us diminished, even my faint insistence on Morton's rights leaving unaffected the friendship he began to show to-wards me. He brushed all mention of the patent aside as my passing fad. He seemed possessed with the notion that a reporter should record his acts and words, before they flew into the infinite space of human forgetfulness. (I imagined this to be part of his vanity, but the urge came, I think, from sad and secret self-knowledge.) I was repeatedly in his operating theatre and at his side in the hospital that January of 1847. I came to appreciate his fine qualities, his zest and gusto. I came to learn of his favourite surgeon-philosophers like Paré, Desault, John Hunter, Chiselden and Ashley Cooper. I learned his concern that the world should know an operation, *a deed of blood* as he called it, was not always some cruel if needful mutilation, but could repair as well as destroy.

'Surgeons are too often asked to admit that operations are the opprobria of their art,' he told me. 'And in some sense there is not much room for dispute, when cruelty must be practised to save life. But when the object of the operation is to restore rather than to deform, when it is to regain lost appearance and symmetry rather than to cripple, to re-establish suspended functions and capabilities, then the deed is surely placed beyond the cavil of all whose opinion merits attention.'

That was the afternoon he repaired a young woman's cleft lip at the North London, the student Palmer stupefying her first with ether. He had a second case that day, before the light faded. Another girl, who had fallen into the fire as a child, now so scarred as to draw her head down upon her breast, and her lower lip from her mouth, allowing her spittle to dribble continually. This repulsive spectacle was to be relieved by Liston's cutting the bands of white scar which pulled her features about like ropes. Her distortions made anaesthesia in-advisable, if not impossible. She was tied to the operating table, and before many minutes was entreating to be loosened and let remain as she was, her cries more and more terrible until one of the students fainted and others had left the benches, saying they had work to do elsewhere, but in truth unable to stomach the scene. A scene, thank God, that need then but seldom be repeated.

The next day, in Clifford Street, Liston repaired the nose of a young man shot that early morning in a Hyde Park duel. The case seemed to awake in him both amusement and memories. Duelling was becoming rare in England. It was almost twenty years since the Duke had called out Lord Winchilsea, and established himself then as a very old-fashioned sort of fire-eater. The Duke's opponent had chosen pistols, though Liston declared that only the rapier was the weapon of a gentleman, and confided that he had once himself stood as surgeon to such a contest at daybreak. 'Surgery has much akin to fencing,' he instructed me. 'I made the point in my book *Operative Surgery*, and was much attacked by many righteous ninnies in the profession over the comparison. But I should have thought it obvious enough.' I felt he was unjust, because it was only himself who operated with the same dexterity and controlled pugnacity as a fencing master.

The young blood was half-carried, half-bundled into Liston's house from a carriage with its blinds drawn, by two young companions as ashen-faced as himself. He sprawled in a chair in the small downstairs room, stinking of brandy and sending up a *feu d'artifice* of oaths. And I could scarce blame him, the deviation of an inch in his opponent's shot sufficing to blow his brains out. He was of my age, of higher social position, being titled. (I cannot give his name, because he is alive, and distinguished, and over half a century has doubtless concocted some ready explanation for the scars of his rash youth.) Yet I could not see myself exposing the thread of my precious life to th' abhorred shears to spite some slight. The insult which brought him to Liston's finger-tips was most likely trivial, or misinterpreted, or imagined. Young men with passions boiling for a fight needed not to look far, in those days, to find a playmate in their grisly games.

Liston cut a slice of the man's forehead, which he swung

down and stretched in place of the missing flesh. Ransome from the hospital administered ether from the apparatus still in the dining-room. 'It is not beneath me to make noses as well as stumps,' Liston observed afterwards with satisfaction. 'Besides, Romilly, noses are profitable. A dexterous surgeon may make them from the buttock, you know,' he added engrossingly. 'You beat the flesh like a beefsteak.'

I came also during that busy period to appreciate Liston's intolerance, his pig-headedness, and his impulsiveness. I was at his side in the North London Hospital when he came to the bed of a poor man who, in desperation at his life, had some days before cut his throat. The death which he then sought was now close upon him, though his wound had been sewn up by another surgeon in the hospital. Liston did not, it seemed, agree to the stitching of cut throats. He preferred to flex the neck and let them heal. And because Liston preferred a method, it was the only one, with all others unthinkable. 'Cooper could not have considered very well what he was about,' announced Liston in a loud voice, referring to his own senior surgeon. 'In consequence of his ill-timed interference, and misdirected attention, every ray of hope has been shut out from this poor sufferer.'

Yet within an hour of such crude censure Liston was brought to a boy with a swelling like a plum in his neck, which Ransome diffidently suggested to be an aneurism – a sac in the great carotid artery – because he could feel pulsation. 'Pooh,' Liston told him with shrivelling contempt. 'Whoever heard of an aneurism in one so young?' Before this opinion could be digested, Liston had with characteristic promptitude taken a lancet from his waistcoat pocket and plunged it into what, he supposed, was a ripe boil. Blood spurted as from a fireman's hose. The boy cried, fell to the ground, was borne on a stretcher to the operating theatre. The artery was sought with a hook, Liston tied a waxed hemp ligature round it, but to no avail. The unfortunate little fellow died under our eyes, the first soul I have observed depart, except when I sat at the bedside of my father. And the very same severed artery may still be seen by the curious observer, preserved for eternity in a jar of spirit

159

in the University College Hospital Museum – Specimen No 1256.

In a month of many excitements, the one most to set aquiver my heart was an invitation from Lady Aubery to a *soirée* shortly to be held at Aubery House. I could not restrain myself from accepting with <u>indecorous</u> immediacy.

The *soirée* was on Wednesday January 20, a cold dry day, with the lake in St James's Park frozen over, and a man dead through falling through. I had bought myself an entire new outfit, short square-tailed coat, white vest, brand new Irish linen and a cream silk stock. I hired a fine coach for the occasion – wastefully, it becoming jammed before arrival among the more glorious aristocratic vehicles which I found filling St James's Square. I paid the man off, making my way among the link-boys with their smoking torches and the running footmen with their glaring flambeaux, towards the steps of the massive front door, triumphantly brilliant in gaslight, up which moved society it had hitherto been beyond my dreams to penetrate.

A footman deprived me of hat, topcoat, stick and gloves, so deftly I was hardly aware of it. I crossed the chessboard marble of the hall, which itself now sparkled with candle-flames as brilliantly as the ladies with gems. I squared my shoulders, reminding myself that I was related to noblemen, and was thus simply taking my rightful place in life, among those stations into which God has seen fit to divide the world. I thought of my poor father, performing his sterile, mad experiments in poverty, bereft even of a comforting wife . . . were he watching from Heaven he would have been proud of me, if our spirits are capable of such ignoble emotions. I made my way upstairs with such self-satisfaction that tears pressed behind my eyes.

I gave my name.

'Guy Romilly, Esquire!' thundered some gorgeously-liveried functionary.

I advanced into the huge reception-room, already half full, an unseen string band playing a subdued polka. Lady Aubery was dazzling. She wore a white silk gown, full-skirted in the fashion, cut low, edged with the most delicate lace, spattered with pearls as casually as raindrops, her neck aglitter with diamonds. Her dark hair covered her ears, drawn back in a bun. All society aped our young Queen, though to tell the truth she was regularly out of society's sight, through so dutifully increasing the Royal establishment.

I bowed. Lady Aubery smiled. 'Mr Romilly, you have been enjoying some extraordinary adventures among the surgeons, so I read?'

'I hope your Ladyship is pleased that my voyage to America was profitable?'

'Oh, you are quite the scientific Columbus,' she returned flatteringly.

I bowed to Lord Aubery, at her side. He was a stout florid man with tiny pale blue eyes and shiny white hair, who made no response, nor seemed aware of my presence within a foot of his squat pug-nose.

I made into the room with languid pace, suggesting I attended such functions with stifling regularity. The human mind is a sardonic jester. I found myself thinking of Floy. Supposing she were destitute? Dead in the Thames? Worse still, alive and about to confront me that evening as one of Lady Aubery's servants! Sweat sprang from my skin. How would the splendid company in which I moved respond to the revelation of my past? I told myself severely that, if it is never safe for any man to discount his chances of falling from respectability into meanness and sordidity, the exact reverse can hold just as awkwardly.

In a further room I glimpsed supper laid – lobsters and huge raised pies, champagne, vast silver bowls of punch, urns steaming with coffee. Most satisfactory! But I grew ill at ease. No one found himself burdened with the slightest obligation of speaking to me. For all the social intercourse I enjoyed, I might have stayed by my fire in Cadogan Place. After some minutes, in which I gave the appearance of searching for anticipated friends, but without too great desperation, I became conscious of two gentlemen my own age, with decorative waistcoats and elaborate whiskers, standing a pace away.

I was uncomfortably aware of being inspected – indeed, dissected – through their quizzing-glasses.

'Oh, law! Look at that cwavat!' exclaimed one, languidly and loudly.

'Why, it's quite yallah,' agreed the other in the same tones.

I turned, careful not to appear the slightest affronted. They continued their examination of me, unruffled. Their own cravats were enormous, as exaggerated as the lapels on their coats, which had tails reaching to the middle of their calves, and the collars which sought to engulf their ears. They were *fops*, birds of passage and distinctive plumage through the *salons* of London. I should not have expected their delicate patent-leather boots to have trod Lady Aubery's august carpets.

'This cream cravat, sir, I recently purchased in America,' I lied. 'From where I have just returned. I assure you they are all the rage in Boston. The collar there, by the by, is generally worn turned down.'

They were instantly filled with curiosity about such peculiarities of dress, a subject which doubtless filled their natural mental vacuum. But as enthusiasm might be expressed for nothing whatever, the first drawled, 'How demned horrid for the Yankees.'

'One is kept in *such* a constant state of *soiréety* in London,' sighed the other. 'That one has barely vigour enough left to study the news from abwoard.'

'Abwoard is a baw,' decided the first.

'You say you have been lately in Boston, sir?' A grizzle-haired man with a kind face stood at my elbow.

'Yes, sir. I travelled to study the new anodyne process for surgical operations.'

The first fop shut his eyes tight, saying it made him feel quite poorlyish.

'Then you must be the famous Mr Romilly?' inquired the kind-faced man.

'Your servant, sir.'

I found myself immediately in an eager knot, agog to hear of Warren, Morton and Liston. The fops melted away, either through lack of interest in so serious matters, or through queasiness. I of course clothed my experiences in thick draperies of delicacy for the sake of the ladies. How my spirits climbed, and then soared! I was making a pronounced hit at Lady Aubery's *salon*, albeit in one small corner. The crowd parted, and I saw Lord Aubery advancing upon me.

'Mr Romilly —'

I bowed. 'Your servant, my Lord.'

'Mr Romilly, you have done a vast disservice to your country.'

My cheeks suffused, almost to match his own colour. As I was incapable of speech, he continued in a voice which I felt could be distinctly heard throughout the huge room, 'You have imported into Great Britain, and are now engaged in puffing – in even the most reputable of newspapers, I know not how – a process designed to sap us of our character.'

I managed to stammer, 'M–my Lord, etherization is purely a benefit, I assure you —'

'*You* assure *me*?' His scorn was thunderous. 'Attend me, sir! I will assure *you* that no good can come of this devil's invention. Pain exists in the world to be endured. And its endurance is the mark of a *man*.' He was now declaiming as though addressing the House of Lords. All eyes were upon me, those who had heard nothing of my own words craning to glimpse the curious, ill-mannered creature who had drawn their host's wrath, and so digracefully marred the smooth pleasure of their evening.

'What an insult you pay to our gallant soldiers and sailors, sir,' Lord Aubery continued even more furiously. 'They are men who enter Her Majesty's service, prepared to bear pain on Her Majesty's behalf. That is because they are men who set their country before themselves. You denigrate them, sir. You devalue the currency of their courage.'

'Nothing . . . nothing of that nature was in my mind, my Lord,' I managed to utter. I was paralysed mentally, even physically, by this violent assault. To one who had witnessed the precious benefits of anaesthesia, it was perplexing, almost inconceivable.

'Then so much the worse for you, sir. What is your wretched

invention?' he demanded with contempt. 'Nothing but a device for turning men into cowards. Have you ever smelt powder, sir?'

I responded to this fierce question with but a dumb shake of the head.

'I was with His Grace at Waterloo,' my adversary announced crushingly. 'Do you believe that day would have gone as it did, were the British troops not steeled with *pain*? As a knife is ground on stone? Do you, sir? Do you suppose our men could have fought so splendidly, had they nothing to fear from a wound, nothing that would be in the slightest uncomfortable? Why, sir, you would have a soldier go into battle without the heart to defend himself from a musket-ball, if it were to afford him no more inconvenience than a splinter in his finger. How do you answer *that*, sir?'

I could not answer it. I was still stunned. But I should have required to be much more thoroughly stunned, to fail perceiving his Lordship's arguments as not entirely rational.

'How would you discipline our ranks, sir?' he continued. 'If you would absolve them from the effects of a flogging? Your invention is a mutineer's godsend. I have suffered pain enough in my life – I cannot answer for you, sir – and by bearing such pain, I have formed my character. It is such that Her Majesty was graciously pleased to entrust me with the responsibilities of Government.'

Lord Aubery had come to office on Peel's coat-tails, to be ousted by Lord John Russell and the Whigs the previous summer. My mind began to resume some function. I sought the reason for this savage attack on myself, and on my innovation from Boston. Its fury seemed as unnecessary as its content was illogical and pointless. I wondered if perhaps Lord Aubery's anger was assumed, as politicians have the trick when the effect suits them. But why should he attack me, a person of no political significance, so crudely and so openly? I had certainly been invited that evening specifically for the office I now so miserably filled. My feelings towards my benefactress Lady Aubery turned like Othello's towards Desdemona.

'Not all persons enjoy the fortitude of your Lordship,' I rejoined in a meek voice.

He charged my other flank. 'How does it work, this invention? Tell me that, sir.'

'It induces sleep, my Lord.'

'You are not very flattering over my ability to read the newspaper, Mr Romilly. But how does it produce sleep?'

I became aware that the whole room had fallen silent, the string band unconcernedly playing away Frédéric Chopin's *Trois Valses Brillantes*, music which I cannot hear even today, in my old age, without a pronouncedly sinking feeling in the stomach.

'I don't know,' I confessed.

'Nor does anyone in the world, my dear sir.' This came haughtily from a tall, bald, lantern-jawed, bloodless-looking old gentleman at Lord Aubery's left elbow. I perceived that his Lordship had brought two henchmen across the room with him, for my social assassination. The other was a fat pink bishop in full canonical fig, as de Quincey would have put it.

'I should not venture so far as that, sir,' I returned, relieved to be shot at by artillery of smaller bore.

'On the contrary, you could venture further,' the man continued in the same tone. 'The manner in which ether produces its effect – an effect which is both profound and dangerous – is unknown in Heaven as well, to all conscience. Allow me to introduce myself, Mr Romilly. I am Sir Anthony Noon, surgeon to Gresham's Hospital, and to many others.'

I politely inclined my head. I had heard Liston speak of him – scathingly.

'I have certainly tried your invention, Mr Romilly. On one occasion, for a capital operation. I should not care to repeat the experiment, neither for my patient's sake, nor for my own. The ether certainly fulfilled its intended offices, but the shock to the patient! The healing was delayed, the loss of blood – forgive me,' he broke off to the audience. But all were too engrossed in the unexpected entertainment I was providing to give play to their sensitivities.

Sir Anthony wagged a long finger. 'Pray, sir, counsel your

patrons in Boston that their artificial means of inducing oblivion may produce a *very depressing* effect on the nervous system. It deprives a patient of that reactive power so necessary for the reparative process. I have no hesitation in deciding where *my* opinion lies. And it is an opinion not unaccustomed to be followed by the greater part of the surgical profession.'

'Pain is surely our great safeguard,' Lord Aubery concurred briskly. 'That's a matter of common sense. Without pain, every hour of the day we should be running ourselves into danger. How otherwise would you have a burnt child dread the fire?'

'Pain is a healthy indication, and an essential concomitant to surgical operations, amply compensated by the effects it produces on the system as the natural incentive to reparative action,' the surgeon concluded with majestic smugness.

'And it is God's will,' added the bishop, more complacently still, perhaps because he was quoting the highest authority available.

I had with foresight prepared an answer to this argument, because nothing new could escape proscription as against God's will, whether railroads, the electric telegraph, omnibuses or bathing-machines. 'With great respect, my Lord,' I returned quickly, '*And the Lord God caused a deep sleep to fall upon Adam, and he slept; and He took one of his ribs, and closed up the flesh instead thereof.*'

The bishop looked outraged. 'You don't understand, sir. The sleep of Adam occurred before the introduction of pain, in the state of Innocence.'

'Then it would appear to me, my Lord,' I told him, 'an example of our Creator being more merciful than we ourselves.'

My triumphal feeling of striking back was momentary. 'My dear Lord Bishop of Greenwich.' Lord Aubery used a bored voice. 'Mr Romilly would not understand the store we British set by fortitude, being himself half a Frenchman.'

My breath was taken by this sneer. I never believed Lord Aubery would attack in public my parentage, which he had known long enough from my second cousin, his own wife. I faced him squarely. 'I am proud of my mother being a French lady.'

'Still? In view of her interest in the Italian opera?' He gave a laugh.

I managed to reply with some coldness, 'I must feel flattered, that your Lordship has taken such pains over a detailed study of my family.'

'Oh, you are far too modest. All London knows of your family. The Hell-Fire Club is still capable of stirring our imaginations. It would seem to me that your father reached his end in their best traditions of lunacy.'

'Your remark, my Lord, makes it necessary for me to leave your house.'

'Pray do, if you wish.' He spoke with offensive amiability. He had anyway finished his work with me. With a nod, he indicated the anteroom. 'You shall miss your supper tonight.'

I bowed. I strode from the room. The crowd opened for me, as for royalty. All wanted to make clear they held the same view of myself, and of etherization, as their noble host. I wondered what the two fops were thinking. I saw Lady Aubery, still at her position by the door. I stared hard at her, but her expression remained a blank on which I could draw any meaning I cared.

18

MY REPUTATION, made in a month, seemed gone in an evening.

I had retired to bed with faint hopes that the hammering I received from Lord Aubery would resound no farther than his own reception-room. Early next morning these were dashed. The *Chronicle* carried a long account. It enjoyed greater glory through sharing a prominent page dampened by the tearful joys of Charles John Huffam Dickens, who had previously returned for Christmas in England from four months' incarceration at the Villa Rosemount in Lausanne, where the dour Swiss peasantry were sadly deprived of such jollities.

EXTRAORDINARY SCENE AT LADY AUBERY'S RE-CEPTION! the merry piece began. *Mr Guy Romilly, lately returned from Boston to introduce the new pain-killing process for surgical operations, invented by Dr Morton, a dentist of that city, and demonstrated last month to the satisfaction of Mr Liston, F.R.S., has found himself so attractive to members of the Press, not to mention of the general public, particularly those eager to exhibit the fashionable concern with matters scientific, as to be emboldened to correct Lord Aubery on other matters concerning the conduct of State. Mr Romilly decidedly over-reached himself in his Lordship's own reception-rooms, where the well-known protagonist of the anodyne process was so monopolizing the conversation as to render upon his hearers exactly the same effect as etherization. . . .*

I groaned.

The *Daily News* was short. *The Times* held its tongue. Lord Aubery had clearly seen to my appearance in the *Chronicle*, whose columns made him into a champion of good sense, rebutting with statesmanlike argument the presumptions of a small-minded quack. I was wounded, angry and puzzled. Why should a man of Lord Aubery's position engage himself so painstakingly in this exercise, so trifling compared with his customary intrigues of State?

I decided to take counsel of Lloyd, to whose office in Salisbury Square I had resort later that morning by hackney-coach.

'You would seem to have enjoyed a lively evening, Romilly,' the editor greeted me jovially from his desk, tall hat pushed back on head. When I protested there was no word of truth in the *Chronicle*, he declared airily, 'Oh, all puffery is sound puffery. It'll do you good.'

I handed across in silence my bundle of manuscript. I had composed over the past week a 'penny dreadful' serial, with a new approach. The hero was not, as customary, a dashing nobleman in disguise, but a handsome young medical man. The heroine herself remained, as ever, an innocent girl of lowly social position much given to fainting.

'It stands out a mile, doesn't it?' Lloyd continued cheerfully, when I inquired pathetically why Lord Aubery should turn on myself. 'Aubery wants to be Prime Minister. It's all over London. Peel certainly won't get his old office back, not now he's supporting Russell and the Whigs. But the Tories will turn up again some time. That's in the nature of things with our country. Aubery wants to lead the new Government. He also wants to become a duke. I don't know if he much cares which of the two events befall him first.'

'But what's the man's political ambition got to do with the process of etherization?' I asked, bewildered.

'Why, he wants a good popular cause. That's all there is to it. Something to whip up the people. It could have been vaccination, the cholera, the penny post. He's a fine orator. You can feel flattered he picked on you,' Lloyd added with cold comfort. 'There's a dozen political fellows in Westminster who'd jump at the chance to be known as his adversary.'

'But he must be a madman. Who would seek popularity by restoring pain to surgical operations?'

'You must be a realist, Romilly. Let us blow exuberance from the truth. How many shall benefit from your discovery? How many a year suffer an operation? Why, but a handful, compared with the whole population. Most folk care to pretend they'll be spared the knife. Just as they care to pretend they'll be spared death itself. You'll serve yourself best by forgetting his insults,' he continued sagaciously. 'That rigmarole about insulting Her Majesty's soldiers as cowards . . . Aubery's trying to set himself up in the Queen's opinion as the embodiment of all which is virtuous and staunch in her subjects. Particularly her aristocratic ones. So I hear, leastways. I also hear the Prince detests him, and that Baron Stockmar is inclined to leave any apartment which Aubery enters.'

'I'm sure our Swedish baron, at least, would turn a tin ear to such ravings,' I said disgruntledly. 'Stockmar being a physician.'

'Well, you must expect plenty of the same medicine from Aubery, but you must hold your nose and swallow it.' Lloyd flicked his thumb through the pages of my new story. 'The public will still read you. They'll read anyone who interests them, even if he's swinging from a scaffold. But I'll give you some advice, young fellow. Etherization is indeed a wonder which'll run its full nine days. But no more. Nothing ever does. Find a new line. Agreed? Tomorrow to fresh woods, and pastures new.'

I did not wait until the morrow. That night I started on a novel, of the regular three-volume kind. For years, its thoughts had been scurrying behind the skirting-boards of my mind, and like mice occasionally running into the daylight of consciousness. Its theme had first come to me while living in the Borough with Floy. I should depict life round the docks, contrasting the teeming, squalid alleys and lanes with the latest in the engineer's art for handling ships, and the cargoes they brought with the ease of steam from the Empire and the world. I had always a fondness for romanticizing the technical, of rendering its methods and phrases intelligible and exciting for ordinary men and even women. The novels I have written since are occasionally honoured by some critics through comparison with those of Monsieur Emile Zola.

(*I* think it an honour, if Zola's multitude of literary detractors would not. Before Zola returned to France in 1899, he spent part of his enforced year's holiday in our country, after the shocking *Affaire Dreyfus*, in my company. He was amused when I showed him copies of such reviews. Less so, perhaps, when I suggested chaffingly that if *La Bête Humaine* wearies you as a novel, it is a reliable source of information about the working of railways.)

I like to hit on a title before starting to compose, by way of raising my colours to the masthead. I decided on *The Water Gate*, a book which I venture to claim has diverted a good many readers since it was first published in 1850, and has the distinction of entering the new century still kept in print by my admirable publishers, Messrs Chapman and Hall.

Next morning's post brought a letter from Morton, forwarded by Moses Poole. The sight of a Boston postmark filled me with guilt. In my preoccupation with myself, I had almost forgotten my American benefactor.

> *19, Tremont Row,*
> *Boston,*
> *Mass.*
> *Thursday, December 31, 1846.*

Mr Romilly, Dear Sir – it began.

I have had no word of you from London, but I learn at the harbour that the mail-steamers, which should leave Boston regularly the first of each month, are much delayed by bad weather at this time of year. I trust, therefore, that God granted you a safe arrival.

I now learn of open treachery by Dr Jackson, who is, after all, my partner and co-signatory to the agreement proportioning royalties from my patent. Contrary to all assurances, Dr Jackson wrote last November to Dr Elie de Beaumont, a professor at the Paris Academy of Science, an intimate friend of his, claiming for himself sole honour for my own discovery. His letter was published, a copy of it reaching me by the Brest mail, and I hasten to acquaint you with its calumnies.

Dr Jackson writes of a discovery which he has made, to the relief of suffering humanity and of great value in the art of surgery. He states that five years ago he noticed insensibility could be produced in the system by the inhalation of sulphuric ether, which he took himself to cure a cold from inhaling chlorine. He then has the boldness to say that he 'persuaded a dentist of this city' to administer ether vapour for the extraction of teeth. And later 'requested this dentist' to attend the Massachusetts General Hospital, to administer ether to a patient, for an operation on the jaw!

Such brazenness, without even the mention of my name, takes my breath away. His misrepresentations are compounded by describing as his own the inhaling apparatus which I had Mr Chamberlain make from my designs, and by recounting the success of his administration for Dr Warren! He ends by inviting the Academy to appoint a Commission to see for themselves the wondrous effects of HIS discovery.

I now see Dr Jackson to be a man with neither truth nor honour in him, as I must confess to long suspecting, and long struggling to disbelieve. I have not confronted him with his conduct. Knowing Dr Jackson's wiles, I prefer to seek him armed with affidavits from Dr Warren, Dr Heywood, and others, for which reason I request you to swear your own statement of events last October before Mr Moses Poole, in due form as prescribed by English law.

How that quarrel among scientific men of Boston already seemed to me as remote and irrelevant as the Trojan Wars!

Neither has Dr Wells shown any persistence of friendship toward me, Morton continued. *He writes in the Hartford 'Courant' claiming he intended to use ether for his 'humbug affair', but was dissuaded by Dr Marcy of Hartford. I greatly doubt his word. Dr Wells is bound for Paris, or already there, where I fear he will serve as reinforcement for Dr Jackson. It may be well for you to journey there, with your knowledge of the language, to uphold my rightful claims, at my expense.*

I found this a more attractive suggestion than swearing affidavits.

Everyone in the Union is using ether, yet no one pays a penny. I am desperate trying to enforce the patent. I have written to the Secretary of the Navy, and to the Surgeon-General of the Army, suggesting the use of my discovery for the relief of suffering among our soldiers and sailors in the Mexican War. I offered to send agents to Mexico, this very month, whose expenses to the Government would be but a few hundred dollars, while the apparatus would be furnished at wholesale price, the ether costing but a cent or two for each patient treated.

I noticed Morton's characteristic amalgamation of high thinking and business detail.

But they rejected me, he continued. *Though I know well from the newspapers that anaesthesia is performed as a matter of course in the campaign. God knows, it is hard for a man to avoid bitterness, particularly when he finds himself with debt the only reward of his considerable pains. Mrs Morton is likely to be brought to bed with child at any day. Pray exert yourself over the patent in England and in Europe, and remit me the royalties you have in hand to date. God will sustain me.*

W. T. G. Morton.

This sad and desperate letter, with nothing of the self-confidence of our parting in Boston, resolved me only to resign forthwith as Morton's agent. There were no English or European royalties. There never would be. I should return him my fare, as soon as I could afford to. It is a cruel paradox, but a man can get nothing from an invention which has a value beyond price.

I wrote to Morton that very day, renouncing his agency. I wrote to Liston, begging to be excused further attendance on him. My rooms in Cadogan Place were comfortable, I had a little put away with Baring Brothers. I had neither wife nor friends to distract me. I was just turned twenty-two. I could settle down to pen *The Water Gate.*

I wrote as if inspired. The inspiration, I must confess, of a young man on the make.

19

IT WAS NEARING a month later, on Tuesday, February 16, 1847, a crisp, frosty day with the pale, rheumy eye of a winter's sun peering down at London as best it could through the perpetual muslin of smoke from sea-coal. I sat at my table in a long-skirted, heavy silk dressing-gown of tartan design, in which I had indulged extravagantly in the Burlington Arcade, off Piccadilly. I was writing busily with one of Mr Perry's patent new Birmingham steel pens. My cloth-covered table, astrew with sheets of paper, stood in the middle of my front room, bright enough with its red Kidderminster carpet and its yellowish 'paper-hangings' (as wallpaper was then known) embellished by eternally climbing lurid red roses.

I had received by first post a pleasant letter from Robert Liston, accepting my withdrawal as his chronicler and telling me that Frederick Churchill had been discharged cured on February 11. He added, 'The wound healed by secondary intention with the exhibition of laudable pus. The ligature on the femoral artery sloughed away on the twelfth day after operation. The diagnosis of the case was chronic arthritis of the knee.'

'Laudable pus!' How ancient the term seems today, when our surgeons operate in laundered white jackets, when the box of bloody sawdust in the operating theatre is replaced by a porcelain receiver, when the knives are boiled over gas-rings, and the dressings handled with forceps by nurses in clean aprons and oversleeves. Frederick Churchill was doubly fortunate. For every patient who died from pain and shock during the operation, or whose life flowed away with his blood on to the encrusted floorboards, ten more died in the pus-stinking wards afterwards from infection.

On the December afternoon of Churchill's operation, Louis Pasteur was twenty-four years old, the son of one of Napoleon's old soldiers who followed the trade of a tanner in the little town of Dôle in the foothills of the Jura. And Robert Koch was a child at Klausthal in the Harz. Koch became a country doctor in Wollstein, where he studied the dread disease of anthrax, which may attack both animal and man. He scotched the idea of infection being caused by 'miasmas', which everybody blamed but nobody understood or even could identify. He declared it caused by microbes, which swarmed invisibly round man more dangerously than snake or tiger in the Bengal jungle. He founded 'bacteriology', as the Germans have begun to distinguish the new science.

Pasteur was a chemist, at Lille in northern France, where it struck him that the fermentation of wine, the souring of milk, and the putrefaction of flesh, were not separate processes, but one and the same, all caused by something imperceptible in the air rather than the air itself. These principles were twenty years later applied to surgery by the handsome young fellow at my elbow during Liston's operation, the student who shared his timepiece with Joseph Clover, whose name needs no illumination in my pages.

Four years after the operation, Joseph Lister went to Edinburgh for a month, and stayed seven years. There, Robert Liston's former pupil not only attached himself to Liston's _bête noir_, Professor James Syme, as his house-surgeon. He married Syme's eldest daughter. 'Poor Joseph and his one patient!' Alice Lister would sympathize to me, for her husband was too busy sowing the seeds of discovery to reap the guineas of practice. In March 1865, then Professor of Surgery in Glasgow, Lister first used carbolic acid to kill germs, in an open fracture of the leg. Afterwards he used it from a spray, worked by hand and later by a steam-engine. So within my lifetime, in the two decades between Christmas 1846 and Easter 1865, came the inventions of anaesthesia and antisepsis, which immeasurably lessened suffering and impeded death, and opened to the surgeon's hand the vital organs of the abdomen itself. Joseph Lister is now, like myself, in his mid-seventies. He is a Baron, and President of the Royal Society. And he still asks me to tea.

But *that* morning, in 1847, I had allotted to preparing an article for the *Christian Lady's Magazine* in answer to my own question, *Is Ether Safe?* I decided that it was. I added that Americans had been inhaling it for years at 'ether frolics', suiting my audience by adding it had a far less horrible moral effect than strong drink. In the afternoon, I had to finish another 'penny dreadful' for Lloyd, about another handsome medical man and another innocent girl so repeatedly in need of *sal volatile*. Then in the evening, *The Water Gate*. Charles John Huffam Dickens himself could not have been more industrious with a pen-nib.

Shortly before noon I heard the clatter of a carriage, and glancing through the window saw a fly at the front door. It was being paid off by a man of middle height and slender build, in dark frock-coat and well-brushed hat, in his hand a black dressing-case. I returned to my work. Another minute and my landlady knocked to say a Dr John Snow desired to see me.

I frowned. The name was unknown. But I permitted her to usher in the stranger who was shortly to shape my life as forcefully as Morton or Liston.

'You'll pardon the intrusion,' were his first words to me. His voice had an odd huskiness, and the flatness of his vowels marked him as a Yorkshireman. He stood looking at me shyly, but seriously. 'I'd been intending to pay a call on you, Mr Romilly, for some time. We have a mutual interest in etherization.'

'Pray sit down, sir.' I indicated my best red plush chair by the hearth, with a leaping, pale yellow, neat morning fire. Snow took the seat with an abrupt, jerky movement, setting the dressing-case carefully at his feet. He was in his early thirties, balding, with well-clipped whiskers. I saw him to be dressed most plainly, his frock-coat of austere cut, with grey worsted trousers and a matching waistcoat. His mouth was broad, his eyebrows heavy, the eyes themselves bright and ever darting about the room. His expression was sedate, but indicated the *active* repression of a natural inner liveliness. He struck me like a Church of England cleric battling against the indecorum of exhibiting enthusiasm.

Snow nodded towards the table, covered with my papers. 'I fear I have interrupted your literary endeavours.'

'It is only the interruptions which make so solitary a life as the novelist's in the slightest bearable,' I returned, smiling.

'I never read novels. The hours devoted to them are hours thrown away,' he said in his forthright way, without any contemplation of rudeness. 'Though in anticipation of my visit, Mr Romilly, I perused this morning a copy of the latest penny serial paper. It is impossible for any woman to faint so often as your heroine, unless she were suffering some affliction of the circulation so serious that no gentleman would care making advances to her.'

'The poor lady's condition shall be improved in my next,' I promised amiably. 'Will you take a glass of wine, sir?'

I could have made no more *gauche* an invitation. 'From the age of seventeen I have been a total abstainer, sir. Since that time I have also held the view that the vegetarian system of feeding is the only true one, as well as being the oldest. It enabled me to swim against the tide longer than my omnivorous friends.'

This information was given in a dry, dull way which left me disconcerted and bereft of chat. My visitor added simply, 'I was a noted swimmer,' and abruptly crossing his legs and folding his stubby hands against his vest fell silent.

The conversation thus being brought to a halt, I sought urgently some topic politely to divert so strange a caller. 'You have performed the etherization, doctor?'

In reply, he said a shade shyly, 'Mr Liston suggested I made myself known to you.'

'Mr Liston is well, I trust?' I inquired, seizing on this subject.

'No. He is not. He is suffering some trouble with his swallowing. It is due to a blow from the boom of his boat, so I understand.' This was delivered bluntly, with no commiseration. 'But Mr Liston's only notion of proper treatment would seem to be long walks, and days in the saddle. He thought you would be interested in my inhaler,' Snow added without pause, indicating the dressing-case with the toe of his boot.

'Most assuredly,' I said politely. 'We seem these days to be surrounded by inhalers of all shapes and sizes, like ladies' hats in the season.'

'Oh, indeed. Mr Sibson of Nottingham has produced one to make men look like horses, and Mr Hooper of Pall Mall has an etherizing nose-bag which seeks to make horses look like men.'

I shifted my manuscript into a pile, making room for Snow to open his dressing-case on the table. He took from it a japanned box the size of a stout octavo volume. One half remained closed, the other half formed the lid of a compartment from which he drew a green and yellow woven tube an inch wide and a yard long, one end with a triangular valved mask to cover mouth and nostrils. 'Do you know, Mr Romilly, early this year I was leaving St George's Hospital when I met a druggist of my acquaintance, bustling along with a large ether apparatus under his arm.' Snow screwed one end of the tube into an aperture in the sealed half of his box. 'I said good morning, to which he replied, "Good morning to you, doctor. Don't detain me – I am giving ether here and there and everywhere, and am getting into an ether practice. Good morning, doctor," he says, and off he shoots. *Rather peculiar*, I thought. Rather peculiar, certainly. Would *I* entrust *my*self to a mere druggist as my guide to Lethe's walk? The man had not the remotest physiological idea. Yet if he could get an ether practice ... perchance, I thought, some scraps of the same thing might fall to a scientific unfortunate. The whole box has a capacity of a hundred cubic inches,' Snow continued without interruption.

'I place water in it, at sixty degrees Fahrenheit.' His stubby
178

index finger moved to indicate the closed half. 'This lid covers a circular section six inches in diameter and one-and-a-quarter in depth, with a spiral baffle-plate attached to the top. In that I place two ounces of ether. Its vapour being heavy, it holds to the bottom, and each inspiration is drawn by the baffle across its surface four or five times. One ounce of ether will produce insensibility for any operation. I am the only man in London to know that,' he ended, making a point of fact rather than a boast.

The complexity and ingenuity of the apparatus was so in advance of Squire's simple glass bell, I saw how his unassuming manner had deluded me from recognizing him as a first-class administrator. Certainly one more able than the usual, who might well be the hospital porter. 'You have made much scientific studies, sir?' I asked diffidently.

'I have performed certain work on asphyxia and resuscitation of newborn children,' he replied in a modest voice. 'And on matters appertaining to the removal of the retained placenta in childbirth. I had the honour of addressing the Westminster Medical Society on these subjects, some two years back. I have also invented an apparatus for performing the operation of paracentesis of the thorax.'

'And you wish me to write up your inhaler, like so many others, in the popular papers?'

'Oh, no. I didn't call with any intention of interesting you in my inhaler. Not at all. I am here on a matter entirely different.'

He started packing his box away again, in another awkward silence.

'*What* matter, sir?' I asked, somewhat impatiently. Despite my earlier pleasantry about interruptions, I was itching to get back to my pen. 'I assure you that I am at the service of any gentleman recommended by Mr Liston.'

'The cholera.'

I gave a slight shrug. 'Well, sir . . . we always have it with us, like the poor.'

'And among the poor. Now, heed me, Mr Romilly . . .'

He had turned, and was standing near me, and with surprise

I saw the fire in his eyes. 'I nailed up my colours as a practitioner in Frith Street, near Soho Square, in the autumn of 1838. There hasn't been a summer since, without a hundred people perishing from cholera in the area. And I'm no stranger to the disease. I was in Newcastle – articled pupil to Mr William Hardcastle, surgeon – during the great epidemic of 1832. I was sent to Killingworth Colliery, to do what I could, but they died like flies. Or worse than flies, wallowing in their own vomit and excreta.' He looked at me sternly. 'The miners and their families died. Not the coal-owners.'

'But surely . . .' I objected. 'The poor live in conditions which generate bad air. That's known to everyone.'

'Cholera is caused by *a poison*,' he said emphatically. 'A poison which acts on the alimentary canal, by being brought into direct contact with the alimentary mucous surface. It *cannot* be due to the *inhalation* of any effluvium. In all known diseases, in which the blood is poisoned in the first instance, there are developed certain general symptoms – rigors, headache, quickened pulse. They precede any local demonstration of the disease. But in cholera the rule is broken. The symptoms are primarily seated in the alimentary canal, and all the after-symptoms of a general kind are the results of the flux from the canal. I have made a close study of the disease, sir. It was my main occupation before ether came along, perhaps wickedly to divert my fancy.'

I remained puzzled at so enthusiastic a lecture. 'But why should you wish to interest me in cholera, sir? I am no medical man. I was thrust into etherization as a mere observer.'

'Where do you suppose the poison of cholera comes from?'

'I would have no more idea than a bootblack.'

'Water,' said Snow firmly. 'That and the excreta of the patients, which often adds up to the same thing. That is *my* view. It is one to lose me friends. Well, I have a way of direct speech, and of direct thinking, which must offend sometimes. And where does the water come from?'

'I would suppose from the water company.'

'Exactly, Mr Romilly! Now, attend me carefully. Of 286

fatal attacks of cholera occurring last year in the south districts of London, the area supplied by the Southwark and Vauxhall Company had *over fifteen* times the death rate of that supplied by the Lambeth Company. Which supplied pure water, free of faecal impurities.'

'That is, I am sure, of much significance, sir. Though, with respect, hardly to myself.'

'Soho is supplied by the Clerkenwell Water Company. Of which the chairman is Sir Magnus Pymm. Who is the creature of Lord Aubery, the landlord of the whole area.'

Snow clasped his hands behind his coat-tails, and turned sharply to stare through the window.

The reason for his dissertation was now stark. I said slowly, 'You wish me to thrash his Lordship with my pen?'

Snow spun round. 'If you do, I'll keep you handsomely supplied with scourges. You should see the hovels, the pits, the holes those poor people live in. By Heaven, Mr Romilly, were such properties mine, I should not sleep o' nights. I'd drive the inhabitants into Finsbury Fields, and I'd operate on the buildings with gunpowder. My tenants would be better off without roofs over their heads. They'd be less likely to die of cholera.'

I should have been inhuman had I not found the chance of striking my aggressor where he was vulnerable a pressingly attractive one. Yet I had no wish to bear the banner of a crusade. I hated injustice and cruelty quite as much as I hated Lord Aubery, but I would be content to follow men of more challenging mind. Besides, my time was filled with the necessary business of making a living for the present, and assuring one for the future.

'Come and see for yourself,' Snow invited pressingly, as I remained silent. 'Can you be at my house a week today? In the afternoon, at three o'clock? No 54 Frith Street.'

It seemed unenterprising to refuse. 'Very well.'

Snow picked up his dressing-case. 'Now I must walk up to St George's,' he ended in his usual flat voice. 'Mr Cutler is shortly operating.'

I noticed how the time had gone. 'Could you not stay for

some luncheon? I'm sure my landlady could accommodate you with something suitable, in the line of boiled potatoes or a cabbage.'

But he declined, to my relief. I could not have eaten my chop and drunk my madeira in so austere company without suffering the pangs of guilt and indigestion.

20

THE FOLLOWING MORNING the fog, which all winter hangs as a threat over London, descended on its rooftops. I woke thinking it still night. I had to light my candle to dress, as usual, in what faint heat remained in the grey ashes bottoming my bedroom grate.

Outside, the world ended after three yards. Beyond that lay something different from yesterday's composition of bricks and mortar and flesh and blood. It was one of strange, yellow blurs of gaslight. Of groping bull's-eyes. Of muffled heels and hooves. Of stumbling ghosts, communicating by coughs. Of damp-coated dogs who never barked, and cats with bedewed fur who leapt briefly from infinity to infinity.

I took my coffee and toast and raspberry jam contemplating without relish the journey I must make with my new 'penny dreadful' to Lloyd's office by Fleet Street. I decided wisely to walk, in my greatcoat with yards of white muffler protecting my throat. I progressed faster than carriages drawn by stumbling, neighing horses, their breath a thicker fog still, each preceded by the bearer of a flaming torch, who could be either in gold-braided greatcoat and cockaded hat, or in patched trousers and ragged jacket with collar up against the raw morning – it mattered not to the passengers, such servants being invisible.

The days before John Snow's visit had been wet, which offered the extra inconvenience of streets deep in mire, with prodigious splashing from the wheels grinding past. The still air contained but one motion, the steady rain of specks of soot from the reeking chimneys. So I finished my tedious journey, bumping into every fifth lamp-post of Piccadilly and the Strand, with my lower half like a plowboy's and my upper with a rash like some black smallpox.

Lloyd greeted me breezily with, 'I notice your noble friend has been paying you fresh attentions. You read the paper?'

The newspaper had not arrived in Cadogan Place because of the fog. He threw the *Chronicle* across his desk, from which I learned that Lord Aubery had spoken strongly against ether in the House of Lords, expressing the certainty of widespread stupefaction by its agency, depriving householders of their valuables, passers-by of their watches, girls of their virtue, and probably everyone of their lives. Already there had been a robbery reported in Thrale Street, and another on London Bridge, by ruffians armed with ether. I saw my own name printed, and that I was awarded prime responsibility for all such crimes performed, and yet to be committed, in Her Majesty's dominions.

'He'll have you yet where the coaches can't run you over,' said Lloyd, meaning in prison.

'I can't see much pleasure in taking a girl's virtue when she's sound asleep,' I observed. Though I was sick at heart with the report. Lord Aubery was using the privilege of the House of Lords to attack so defenceless, and I thought inoffensive, a target as myself. I consoled myself that at least my medical friends, whom I valued the most, could tell where the truth lay. I handed across my second 'penny dreadful' to the cheering news that the first had already proved popular.

'Why don't you do a tale about aeronauts?' Lloyd suggested.

'I know nothing whatever about ballooning.'

'You can easily find all that out in Paternoster Row. A gentleman has no need for the pains of education, if he knows where to look everything up.'

I promised to consider it. (I did – but thirty years later. By then, Monsieur Nadar's enormous balloon had raised its two-storey cottage of wickerwork, containing such luxuries as a photographer's dark room, a printing press and a privy. In 1873, the *Daily Graphic* in New York constructed an even bigger one, for crossing to Europe a mile in the sky. It came to nothing, but the idea inspired my *Men With Wings*, which had the stoniest of luck to appear the same year as Monsieur Jules Verne's utterly overshadowing *Le Tour du Monde en Quatre-vingt Jours*.)

I left Salisbury Square to grope my way home. It was noon, but of no significance, the sun having for the day deprived the world of its services. I began to envy the encapsuled security of a hackney-coach, but none was to be seen. Finding myself at the end of Chancery Lane, I decided to call on Moses Poole. He might have news of Morton. It would be worth escaping from the fog and warming myself by his fire, even if he charged me six and eightpence for it.

The attorney was sitting at the stool of his high desk, on which I noticed breadcrumbs and a rind of cheese with an empty tankard. I explained I had written to Morton on January 21 relinquishing the agency, and expected a reply by next month's mail-steamer. The little man shook his head, sniffed like a blacksmith's bellows, and insisted I was making the mistake of a lifetime.

'But I have collected precisely nothing in royalties,' I objected.

'Then you must sue.'

'Who? Every surgeon in the Kingdom is using ether.'

'One would suffice. A test case.'

'Mr Liston, I presume?' I asked acidly.

He took me completely seriously. 'A surgeon so well known, whose words carry such weight, would be an unwise choice of defendant. You must find some lesser doctor. Then we would seek an injunction from the Court of Chancery.'

'But the whole world has decided that etherization is not the proper subject for a patent,' I insisted.

'The Lord Chancellor and his Vice-Chancellors do not form opinions in the manner of ordinary people.'

'It would be a complicated affair.'

'Not a bit. The law can be very simple, or very complicated, according to use. That is its great beauty.'

'It would cost money.'

'If money is not spent, plainly money shall never be received.'

'Well, where shall this money come from? Dr Morton's letters speak of debt, and I am a man of the slenderest resources.'

'Sell a share of the British patent.'

My eyebrows rose. 'Dr Morton would not care for that.'

'Possibly, but otherwise he shall not get so much as a kitchen candle's end.'

I warmed my hands before the coals in silence. I was averse to complicating Morton's affairs, or my own, by resort to the Court of Chancery, which might well not decide anything until the sky rained turnips. But the scheme seemed sound, if only as a last resort. And I had a moral obligation towards Morton to take any advantageous decision open.

'If I sell, who should be the buyer?' I asked doubtfully. 'When everyone knows it will be as uncertain as trying to enforce a patent on eating beefsteaks.'

Moses Poole sniffed decisively. 'The City's full of men with money to risk, now Mr George Hudson's railways are running out of steam.'

'Well, if you know where such gentlemen are available . . .' I acquiesced doubtfully. 'But I should prefer the search not to be advertised.'

'Discretion, sir, is the second name of Moses Poole.' He drummed the side of his nose with his finger-tip. 'I can recommend an excellent silk-gown to lead your case. Mr Vawdan. Sharp in all departments. Like a porcupine.'

I escaped with the attorney suggesting no charge for the consultation, which I took to indicate confidence in greater pickings to come.

I mentioned nothing of the meeting to John Snow when we met the following Thursday. I cared neither for my medical friends, nor Lord Aubery, to discover that I was moving to enforce the patent by law. Though I was pulled badly with doubts, and would have liked Snow's sensible counsel. It was a fine, sharp afternoon, and I found his neat, three-storey house, about a hundred years old, one down from the corner with Bateman Street. He greeted me with some disquieting news. Ether was killing people.

'A woman has died at Grantham, in Lincolnshire,' he told me. 'One Ann Parkinson, wife of a hairdresser. After three days in coma, following removal of a tumour from the leg. The coroner's verdict was *that she died from the effects of the vapour of ether, inhaled for the purpose of relieving pain, and not from the effect of the operation nor any other cause*. Most specific, you'll agree?' he added dryly. 'I hear too of a similar fatality at the Essex and Colchester Hospital.'

'But I thought ether was perfectly safe!' I exclaimed. 'As safe as wine ... or laudanum, rather,' I corrected myself hastily.

'We shall see. We may be in for a difficult time. The favour of the public is like a spring tide, and may suddenly recede and leave us high and dry. We shall need all our faith in our method.'

So we took our stroll along Cholera Alley.

Soho Square and Golden Square themselves were both fashionable addresses, where any gentleman in London might set up his household. The little courts and twisting lanes behind the main thoroughfare provided accommodation for the low class and the poor, as was natural in London and all large cities. I had never ventured into these indescribably dirty, profligate and felonious 'slums', as people were beginning to call them. A gentleman went through life without the need to, and in his right mind would never seek the obligation to. But a doctor must venture everywhere that sickness imperiously beckons. Snow was perfectly at home, wherever we strayed. More so, he was greeted all round with friendly cries and smiles, when his fine clothes and tall hat would otherwise have attracted a flying brick or dead cat.

That afternoon was a sickening and shaming revelation to me. Within yards of tolerably well-swept main footpaths lived human beings in conditions which no sensible farmer would bestow on his cattle. I had seen poverty in the Borough, but there it was a comparatively genteel affair; its sufferers threadbare but not ragged, hungry but not starving. The bleak little houses within the Rules of the Bench were mansions compared with the tumbledown, rat-riddled, broken-windowed, doorless, stinking hovels owned by Lord Aubery. Yet these unspeakably squalid and ugly dwellings might have been the most pleasant, popular and salubrious in Town, from the numbers of people crammed into them. Every door, every window was filled with pinched and pale faces. They were human rookeries, with walls that seemed to totter and chimneys that seemed hesitating to fall. The muddy footways, under poles of washing with a perpetual look about them, with heaps of garbage and ashes in all directions amid stinking pools of foul liquids, were crowded with men, women and little mites, talking, arguing, fighting, scavenging, smoking, drinking and drunk. As we passed, there was borne into a doorway – marked LOGINS AND BEDS FOR THRAVELERS, may God help them – casually on the shoulder of a workman, an empty coffin some two feet long. The waiting cold little body somewhere inside seemed no discouragement or inconvenience to the residents of all ages leaning and shouting from the upper windows.

'There's no cholera about just now,' Snow informed me in his matter-of-fact way. 'It comes in epidemics, and is a summer phenomenon.'

I could smell spew – or worse. Then I saw against a wall, almost brushed by the feet of passersby, a pile of excreta, not animal but unmistakably human. The sight turned my stomach more powerfully than any I had met in the hands of Liston or Warren. There and then I decided to march as John Snow's standard-bearer. I openly called myself a Radical, the name no longer being of low reproach, but the title of a class who gloried in it. My family circumstances really left my political views little option. I pitied these poor people, though I knew they would prefer crusts to condolence. Pity is useless without action.

It is strange, at that same time a German agitator, Frederick Engels, was moved the same way by the same sights in Manchester, where he had gone to work in a cotton-mill. And but two years later, the alleys I trod were scrutinized by another factioneer, a German of the Jewish persuasion, one Karl Marx, who came to live near by after his expulsion from Paris. Engels and Marx, both today dead, later produced revolutionary articles in the British and American Press, and wrote books published on the Continent of Europe, which received serious attention from students of such fiery matters. My own response could from my nature not be so violent. But I felt the time had arrived to dip my pen in vitriol. It had enjoyed a sufficiency of being dipped in syrup.

21

MY ARTICLE ABOUT the Soho slums was a rousing success. It made me the envy of many other green sprigs in the area of Fleet Street. Lloyd ran it prominently in his *Penny Sunday Times*. On the Monday, I had messages asking for more from the *Illustrated London News*, *Reynolds' Miscellany*, and *The Churchman's Monthly Penny Magazine*. It seemed that cholera was always a diverting topic.

But I could never be a reformer in the line of Wilberforce or Shaftesbury. I lack the dash and resolution. I worried that I might have already been too rash in baiting Lord Aubery, though his only response was to inform the House of Lords that cholera was not contagious, and so that was that. As the days passed, and no counter-attack was launched, I began to feel braver, and pleased with myself. How casually, and foolishly, in exercising my youthful indignation did I miscalculate the power and malevolence of my adversary!

Not before March had I a reply from Morton, imploring me in a sentence to remain as his agent. The rest of the long letter was a further account of his wrangling with Jackson, which by its complexity, and the distance of the protagonists in space and memory, I found impossible to follow. Though, to tell the truth, I made but little effort to try. I had distraction enough with Morton's affairs in London. It was on Saturday, April 17 – a day on which I noted, for what reason escapes me, that eighteen-year-old Catharine Foster, who gave arsenic to her husband, was hanged in Norfolk, a proceeding to which the newspapers reported she showed complete indifference – that I presented myself by appointment at Moses Poole's office. London had enjoyed another downpour, the horses with mud to their bellies, the traffic a squelching mass, myself slithering on every crossing. I was introduced to a fat man with a flowered waistcoat and a bunch of seals at his fob like gold grapes. We both signed a document gay with scarlet wax, and the 'syndicate' now owned 51 per centum of the British patent for ether.

Morton's remaining share apparently necessitated my appearance the following week at Lincoln's Inn Hall, where the Court of Chancery sat. (The Queen's Bench sat in Westminster Hall, and our splendid new Courts of Justice in the Strand had not even been started.) Moses Poole introduced me outside to Mr Vawdan, a man as stout as a tub, with whiskers like wings and a voice like a bassoon. He was apparently ready loaded and primed with the case, and needed but the spark from a judge's eye to explode and demolish all in sight.

Moses Poole conducted me into the Hall, sniffing like a seasoned sailor approaching the sea, or a schoolboy opening the door of the jam-cupboard. It seemed we were *making a motion*, though how, and in which direction, I was at a loss. The Hall was pleasant enough, with two bay windows at each end and a fine beamed roof. It was jammed with barristers sitting on benches, their wigs resembling a flock driven to the sheep-dip. In front, in a well with matting walls, attorneys sat scribbling amid mountains of paper. Then came the red table of the bewigged clerk, and the padded red dais of the judge, who sat gloriously amid crimson curtains with no table or desk, and his thoughts apparently far elsewhere. There were bored officials with maces, even more bored and scruffier reporters from the newspapers, messenger-boys climbing about with armfuls of documents representing immeasurable hopes and untold money, and a handful of men and women I understood from their utter perplexity to be litigants like myself.

The afternoon passed. Silk gowns stood to orate at great length. The judge stayed seated and said nothing. The broad shoulders of our own champion remained wedged in place.

'Motions are taken strictly on the seniority of the advocate,' Moses Poole explained in a low voice. I thanked him for the information. 'We shall be on our feet by and by,' he encouraged me. 'Mr Vawdan is no chicken.'

The candles were glowing bright when our silk gown rose. He spoke for an hour. The judge spoke for a minute. 'An adjournment,' sniffed Moses Poole. I shortly hurried away from the fount of justice, needing my dinner. I do not know what transpired, but I heard no more of the case from that rainy day to this. The next morning I obtained a draft from Baring Brothers, to the value of Morton's outlay on my steamship fare, which I sent at once to Boston. Thus I broke the association begun the previous June with his five-dollar piece.

On the last day of April, a Friday, I was at home in Cadogan Place during the morning, working hard on *The Water Gate*, when my landlady knocked to say that a gentleman had called to see me.

I frowned. 'Has he no card?'

'No, sir. I think he may be a servant.'

I had him shown up.

He was certainly dressed like a gentleman. He was my own age, his hair well larded with pomade and smelling of *eau de Cologne*. I judged him either a clerk in some fashionable business or a successful dressmaker's husband.

'Your servant, sir,' he greeted me. 'I am Mr Jeavons, from the Royal Academy of Arts.'

I inclined my head in return, puzzled by the visitation. I have suffered all my life from blindness towards anything on canvas. Paintings which I have heard others extol or execrate strike me simply as decorations to relieve a blank wall. Then I felt a flutter of excitement: Was it possible that my fame demanded my features be preserved in oils?

Jeavons produced an envelope. 'I represent the Secretary, sir. He presents his compliments, and asks you to accept this invitation to the private viewing of the Summer Exhibition, to be held at the National Gallery on Monday next.'

'Very kind,' I murmured. Why should *I* be asked? I

wondered. And were all guests summoned to the occasion personally by such exquisitely turned-out gentlemen? But the private viewing was always a fashionable affair, one that started the London season, and it was flattering enough to be included at all.

'The Secretary respectfully suggests that you be at the National Gallery by four o'clock in the afternoon.'

'That would be perfectly convenient,' I replied, reading the copperplate of the invitation-card. 'I have no other engagements that day.'

'The Secretary also urged – with respect, sir – that you pay particular attention to Mr Edwin Landseer's work *Deer Shooting.*'

I said immediately, in great alarm, 'I am hardly in the position to purchase it.'

The man drew himself up. 'The picture is already bespoke, sir,' he said, with that most irritating condescension of the knowledgeable underling.

'Well, I shall do my best to eye it with the appreciation it doubtless deserves.'

'Good day to you, sir.'

'Good day, sir.'

After Jeavons had left, and the smell of Cologne had faded, I grew more mystified. Why should I be there at a definite hour, as though for the rise of a theatre curtain? Why in the name of great Heaven should I be recommended to *Deer Shooting*? I decided the artist expected me to write something for the popular papers about the picture. Even Royal Academicians are not above engineering puffery, so long as it appears to come spontaneously.

On the Monday afternoon I donned my new tail-coat, carefully brushed my new Lock's hat, took up my silvertopped cane, and slipping the inevitable notebook into my pocket set out for Charing Cross. The weather being fine and my time ample, I walked, hoping my boots would not become too sullied for such glistening company. Well before four o'clock I arrived in Trafalgar Square, where John Nash's monument to Lord Nelson – so familiar today, it would seem to have been towering there even before the birth of the Admiral himself – wore its Devon granite still grey, not encrusted with half a century of London soot.

Outside the National Gallery stood a throng of admiring onlookers, mostly female, of the sempstress and servant class. From an unbroken procession of carriages brilliantly dressed ladies, escorted by smart gentlemen of all ages, were handed down by footmen in a rainbow of liveries, to make their way in a tide of gorgeous colour breaking on the steps and washing through the eight columns of the massive portico. It was the hour of the day when the most fashionable of society was astir. I merged discreetly among the marvelling poor on the pavement, with the particularly warm contentment of knowing that in a few minutes I should be joining the *élite*.

As four struck from St Martin-in-the-Fields I entered. I found the portion occupied by the Royal Academy towards my right. I moved among the crowd, who were chattering noisily and animatedly, like a gorgeous barnyard thrown a few shovel-fuls of corn. I clasped my hands behind my back and assumed the air of being perfectly at home, an art I had taught myself in such diverse surroundings as Lady Aubery's reception-room and Robert Liston's operating theatre.

I joined the edge of a throng eyeing through their quizzing-glasses, all with expressions of acute perception, the two pictures drawing most attention, Etty's *Joan of Arc* and Paul Delaroche's *Napoleon at Fontainebleau*. I moved sedately to another knot of connoisseurs – from the stridency of their comments, all present must have been connoisseurs – who were appraising Landseer's quest for venison. I tried forcing my mind into some critical judgement of it, but could decide no more than it was the best painting I had ever seen on the subject of deer shooting. I was about to turn away, when the assembly opened like corn in the wind. I was face to face with Lady Aubery.

I stepped back, startled, at the same time looking with some disquiet for an accompanying Lord Aubery. But he was elsewhere. He had doubtless decided that a visit to the Royal Academy could have not the faintest advantage to his political career. Lady Aubery was accompanied only by a female companion, a respectful pace behind. How strange, I thought, the coincidence of our meeting! I bowed silently, preparing to disappear backwards into the crowd, having no wish to exchange words with my deceitful ensnarer.

'Why, Mr Romilly —' She stopped, smiling. 'How pleasant to find you here.'

I bowed again. 'Lady Aubery, your servant.'

'And how advantageous! You are a fine judge of art. Come now. Tell me what you think of Mr Landseer's picture.'

For a moment I thought her badly muddled over my abilities, then it came to me how adroitly the scene had been stage-managed. If Lady Aubery had something to tell me, it would seem worth the hearing. I stood close at her side, both of us facing Landseer. My heart began to race. My second cousin was handsome. She was dressed in golden silk with an embroidery of white flowers, and a three-quarter bonnet with ruffles under her chin. She had the smell of Atkinson's *millefleurs*, with that faint but powerfully moving odour of the female. I had lacked a lady for a long time. And that Lady Aubery had gone to such pains, and taken such risk to meet me by stealth, unbeknown to her husband, indicated her retaining some regard for me.

'You must feel in my respect as the shorn Samson towards Delilah,' she said in a quiet unimpassioned voice.

'I was indeed bitterly angry that you should so lure me to my humiliation in your house.'

'I knew nothing of what was to happen that night.' Her fingers were extended, as though referring to a detail of the picture.

I hesitated. 'I should like to believe as much, ma'am. But human faith is not infinitely elastic.'

She turned, her imploring expression impossible to have been incited by view of the Landseer. 'You must believe me, *please*.'

'Why was I asked, then? If not to act the spittoon for Lord Aubery's spleen?'

The crowd had drawn back, in deference to her rank in

London society. In the middle of a throng we were enjoying a *tête-à-tête*.

'I knew nothing of what lay in his Lordship's mind when you were invited, or when I received you in his house.'

'He merely wished to buy cheaply some political *kudos*, by attacking the new process of etherization. Every journalist in London has been telling me that. My own feelings were beneath consideration, in a matter of such selfish importance —'

'You must not attack my husband to my face like that.'

'I apologize.'

'I'll admit that all you say seems to be true. Lord Aubery does not make me privy to his political stratagems. Nor to his thoughts, beyond those directed occasionally to domestic affairs. No woman is believed to have a mind of her own, whatever her station. Or if she has a mind, it must be numbered like her other possessions among the property of her husband.'

These unveiled remarks affected me. I knew how irksome so spirited and intelligent a woman would find so clumsy a yoke. 'From all I know of you,' I said, 'and I have known you since childhood, my heart, if not my head, has already told me all that you have this afternoon.'

I could see this stirred her, however she sought to hide it. 'I should have written earlier, or sent a message. But my husband might have found out. The servants are not trustworthy. That would not have been the best for either of us. Besides, I preferred to explain my innocence myself. It is what you deserved. You know I have always had a fondness for you.'

'I assure you, such regard is matched,' I told her warmly. 'And also, that I don't give a fig's end for your husband.'

'Listen, Mr Romilly . . . my foremost reason for arranging this meeting was to warn you. You must stop writing in the newspapers about the cholera.'

'I shall write exactly what I like.'

'Don't be stupid.'

'If Lord Aubery is murdering his tenants wholesale, it seems over-nice to hush it up.'

'Now you're sounding self-righteous. There is no possibility of the water causing cholera.'

'There is. I have it from Dr Snow.'

'Who's Dr Snow? The greatest medical authorities hold that cholera is not a contagious complaint.'

'I prefer to believe Dr Snow. He has cholera on his doorstep. The greatest medical authorities have not.'

'You're using cholera as a stick to beat Lord Aubery, and I'm warning you that a stick is no use against steel. Cholera and this trivial business of the flogging.'

'It was not a trivial business for the man concerned,' I told her.

An unfortunate sailor at Spithead had recently been 'Flogged Round the Fleet', awarded a hundred lashes on one afterdeck, covered with a blanket, taken down the ladder to the ship's boat, rowed to the next in line for another hundred, and so on. He was accompanied on his journeying by a surgeon, presumably to keep him alive that the pantomime might not be disappointingly curtailed. I had written scathingly on the episode for *The London Pioneer*, to elicit some protest in the House from Lord Aubery that 'The Navy must be protected'. But I had not felt his Lordship unduly outraged on this score.

Lady Aubery made a small gesture of impatience. 'You don't seem to comprehend the adversary you have presented yourself with. Lord Aubery is a dangerous man.'

'What can he do to me? We live in the land of free speech. He can't send me to the Tower, as befell John Wilkes.'

'There is *nothing* my husband would shirk, once he decided on it. You must know well enough he has a reputation short of angelic. You have surely heard of men ruined, ostracized, exiled? There are worse things – I know of them, few others do. There must be even more which I've no awareness of.' She stopped for a moment, her mouth a tight line. 'Remember that Lord Aubery grew to manhood during the great wars against the French. He fought Napoleon's armies. In the days of the Regency the world was less peaceful, and men were more ruthless, rougher in their manners, less bound by feelings of delicacy in their business with one another. There was a duel every dawn, a challenge every night ... he is *dangerous*,' she repeated. In that stifling hot room, she shivered.

'I'm afraid of no man.'

'So you say, and so would any gentleman of self-respect in London. Take my advice. Be *brave mais pas téméraire*, as the French put it. The line between courage and foolhardiness is faint but fatal. You are an eminently sensible man. I pray you, apply your brains rather than your passions to your perils – which you have sought out yourself.'

'I did *not* seek them. Lord Aubery attacked me with his tongue. I replied with my pen. It happens to be a duel where both parties may enjoy the choice of weapons.'

'The weapons may well become more material. Please, Guy.' She glanced at me softly. 'Promise me you'll halt this campaign against Lord Aubery.'

'He sent you here to ask that, did he?'

'I *should* feel angry and insulted at that remark,' she replied calmly. 'But you are perhaps entitled to such suspicions. I merely give you my word that they are false. Do you accept it?'

I smiled. 'I accept it.'

'Then accept my advice as well.'

'I'll sleep on that.'

'Then you may well wake to a safer morning. We have passed time enough talking to have criticized the entire exhibition. Which is distressingly banal, as every year. I hope that one fine day you shall tell me all your adventures in Boston.'

'And I hope so, too. One fine day.'

'Good day to you, Mr Romilly.'

'Good day to you, Lady Aubery.'

She turned, and was in an instant lost among the crowd.

22

I STOOD WHERE I WAS. My mind was too overloaded to budge. I remained isolated from the throng, who were inspecting me through their glasses with far more interest than the exhibits.

'Who *is* that man?' demanded a male voice loudly, with that peculiar indifference of our upper classes towards the bodily presence of inferiors they wish to discuss.

'But don't you know?' returned a female voice shrilly.

'Never set eyes on him.'

'Never seen him in Aubery House,' said a second man, on an equal assumption that I was stone deaf.

'He's the Comte de Neuilly, of course,' the female instructed all in earshot.

'Who's that?'

'The famous Parisian art expert. *Everybody* knows him.'

'Oh!' said the man, succeeding in investing the monosyllable with a contemptuous disappointment I found quite crushing.

The crowd began to stir. I could drop my brief prominence. I strolled past the rows of pictures, but seeing none. I believed Lady Aubery. She knew nothing of her husband's plans for my social and moral assassination. I believed she had sincere regard for me, the same as inspired her to furnish my expenses to America. I could believe also that Lord Aubery's springs of malevolence flowed deep and fast. I had the sickening premonition of a knife in my back in the dark.

My sombre reflections were interrupted by coming face to face with Floy.

It was not Floy. It was the painting of a neat-waisted, bare-breasted young woman, clothed in nil but a cloud of blue muslin and gold sandals, sitting outdoors in a dreamy state on a tree stump. It was a largish work, almost lifesize. The resemblance to Floy of the pale, calm face, the lustrous eyes, the parted and plaited jet hair, was breathtaking. How often had I seen her with the same distant expression, the same bend of back, the same folded hands, the same delight in indolent repose, beside our humble grate in King's Bench Walk! I peered for the artist's signature, but it was indecipherable. Startled at the coincidence, and curious, I approached a white-haired haughty-looking man in the corner with a ledger in his hands.

'That work there, sir —' I pointed with my cane. 'Pray, who is the artist?'

'That is a Maddox, sir.' His tone was of stating something obvious to a child in reins.

'The pictures exhibited here may be purchased, I believe?'

'Most certainly,' he replied, more warmly.

Was hard cash mentionable in the temple of Aglaia, Thalia and Euphrosyne? I wondered. I asked diffidently, 'Could you state the price?'

'Ninety-five guineas, sir.'

'Ninety-fi —!' I swallowed.

'Maddox is a rising young painter, sir,' he said in his original voice. 'Some would say, quite rocketing.'

The woman on the canvas would have made a pleasant keepsake. But not for a fortune.

If a knife was forged for my shoulder-blades, it did not strike. I began to forget Lord Aubery. *Cowards die many times before their deaths*, I told myself. *The valiant never taste of death but once.* Instead, I set earnestly to enjoy myself with such delights of the London season as lay within my pocket. I went to hear Jenny Lind, singing Alice in *Robert le Diable* at the Italian Opera House in the Haymarket. (An expedition with some disadvantage, in recalling the disappearance of my mother.) I went to see that most ingenious of comedies *London Assurance*, its amiable heroes five-o'clock-in-the-morning men, a class of young fellows quite edifying to witness.

I wrote much. My novel, and for the periodicals. I was soon provided with another flogging to denounce. Private White of the 7th Hussars had 150 lashes on the triangles at Hounslow for insubordination on June 15, and died in hospital on July 11. Three doctors certified that 'death was in no wise connected with corporal punishment'. That the trio were Army doctors possibly clouded their judgement. Smelling a rat – or a bucket of whitewash – the vicar had refused to bury the body. A *post mortem* examination was held. There was fluid in the chest, the back muscles were turned to pulp. Death was found undeniably to be the laggard servant of the lash. The coroner's jury gave a verdict with horror.

I came across the sorry story because I turned the pages of the *Lancet* now and then, that I might find some item to interest the wider public. When I wrote it up for the *People's Journal*, I flattered myself that barely a man in the country could forbear to mutter 'Shame!', not a woman suppress a sob. Barely a man save Lord Aubery, who wrote to *The Times* again reviling my name and stating that flogging was necessary for the soldiers' well-being and peace of mind, quite as much as the branding of deserters with a large 'D' by the regimental farrier.

Another case I pulled from the *Lancet* – like a balloon to be inflated for the entertainment of the commonalty – even Lord Aubery could not take offence over. I recounted in the *People's Journal* how Mary Ann Hunt, being found guilty at the Old Bailey for the murder of a crone, interrupted Mr Justice Platt in the very motion of donning his black cap with, 'I believe I am in the family way'. Why, she did not so much as address him as 'My Lord'! These eight simple words stopped the law in its tracks, diverted it to a different course. The judge immediately empanelled a jury of twelve matrons to decide if Mary Ann was big with quick child, or not. They decided not. Black cap was replaced, suspended sentence passed.

Mary Ann went to gaol, to pass her last three Sundays on earth, an interval which fortunately lent more substance to her plea from the dock. Even the prison Governor noticed it. A medical man, hastily summoned, reported that the convict was quick. Mercy was shown to mother and unborn child, who were transported for life. Which proves that twelve women are as likely to be mistaken in such matters as one.

There was a General Election on July 27, which permitted Lord John Russell to continue ruling sedately, and Old Pam to continue keeping matters in hand abroad. Though John Bright, newly returned for Manchester, was to growl and snap round the Cabinet's ankles, though the Non-conformists were as noisy as screech owls in the woods, the Corn Laws had been repealed and well-fed men forget old grievances. I who was born long ago a Whig and shall shortly die a Radical, concede happily enough the coach of State began then to run on smoother road, the harsh tensions of its springs relaxed, for Britain to arrive at the pre-eminence among all nations which is our destiny today. Prince Albert became Chancellor of Cambridge University, and Her Majesty again in a delicate condition.

In early October I had a cordial letter from Liston, inviting me to dine on the second Saturday in the month. I had not set eyes on him since the end of January, after my savaging at the *soirée*. I was eager to enjoy again the stimulation of his company, and his excellent cooking. I still had an interest in etherization, to which the French had taken with customary *panache*, which had won in Germany a thorough testing by Professor Johann Friedrich Dieffenbach – a military surgeon who had wielded sabre as well as scalpel – and which was even sniffed by the great Russian bear (though 'sniffed' is not the exact word, because Professor Nikolai Pirogoff insisted on administering the fluid by a route quite unmentionable).

I repaired to Clifford Street at seven. The young footman was still insolent. I was shown at once into the small room with the bureau and bookcases, where Liston was waiting.

There is a story by Count Tolstoy, which appeared a year or two back, called *The Death of Ivan Ilyich*. It contains a passage of hauntingly universal application. Ivan Ilyich's brother-in-law, a healthy florid man, just arrived to stay, looks up from unpacking his portmanteau to greet his host. For a second the visitor stares without a word. That look tells Ivan Ilyich, the sick man, everything. The brother-in-law opens his mouth to utter an exclamation of dismay, just checking himself. That movement confirms everything. 'I've changed?' asks Ivan Ilyich. The guest has to admit that he has.

So it was with Robert Liston.

His huge frame was so spare it seemed but a peg for his clothes. His face was drawn and bloodless, his eyes as dull as the ashes of last night's fire. As he turned from the bookcase to greet me, I feared he would totter. For a moment we exchanged a glance. He saw into my startled mind. I saw that he saw.

'Well, Romilly, our Homer ...' His voice had a huskiness which, in my ears, echoed John Snow. 'I ... I have been poorly of late.'

I recovered myself. 'I am sorry to learn that, sir. I hope it is only a passing illness.'

'Aye, it'll leave me by and by. So my colleagues tell me.' His words were leaden. He asked as he shook my hand, 'Do you care for porridge, Romilly?'

I was surprised. 'At your table, sir?'

He managed a look of good humour. 'And haggis?'

'I would not know, sir. Having taken the precaution never to taste it.'

'It's the heart, lights and liver of a sheep, boiled in its maw. A dish fit to place before an anatomist.'

I wondered where this strange conversation would lead, or if he were, in addition to his bodily pains, out of his mind.

'We Scots are taken by you English for a nation of haggis-fed rustics,' he continued, though with sad lack of his usual liveliness. 'But your country revelled in the dish, until you decided to lose the taste for it the day Queen Anne assented to the Act of Union. And the bagpipes. You enjoy the bagpipes?'

'I prefer them to the sermons of Dissenters, which have much the same tone.'

'All these delights you shall shortly enjoy, Romilly. At the end of this month you leave for Edinburgh.'

23

TWENTY-TWO IS an adventurous time of life. I decided to make the whole journey by train. It *was* an adventure then. One inconceivable these days, when the railway companies, to the glory of their directors, literally race one another up the east and west coasts of our island.

Our modern grouse-shooter may dine late in Mayfair, and breakfast early in Aberdeen. Though I suspect that his wife and her companion, his children and their governess, his servants and his dogs, all have less enthusiasm to be propelled towards the butts at sixty miles an hour, and endure less hardily than their master the unremitting shake-up from King's Cross to Kinnaber Junction. At the time of my first journey to Scotland, the 'direct route' – an exaggeration and a euphemism – had been open only since the previous first of July. And in those times, half the speed enjoyed by today's sportsmen was recorded as inducing nervous weakness, quite to the edge of prostration, in the system of Mrs Jane Welsh Carlyle.

One irksomeness of my long journey north has hardly eased over the past fifty years. Nowadays, the traveller has still to stop and wait for his engine to be changed as he passes from the custody of the Great Northern to the North Eastern, or the London and North Western to the Caledonian. In 1847 I travelled the 'East Coast Route', operated by Mr Hudson, through Rugby and Derby. I was obliged to dismount, with all my luggage, for the waterbreaks at Tyne and Tweed, which we bridged in a jolting, overcrowded, four-horse onmibus. I sustained myself only by recalling that the coach took four days to York alone.

I had hoped to travel second-class all the way. I lived well, and not prodigally by the standards of other young men of my social position, but with no immediate return on my novel I was beginning to see the need for prudence if not stringency. And the second-class coaches were then becoming fairly comfortable, closed at the sides, well-sprung, and offering some privacy with low partitions. But the expresses north from York were first-class only, three carriages and a luggage van, so I had no option but the extravagance of travelling *en prince*. Late in the evening of Wednesday, November 3, I was finally deposited at Edinburgh General Station, as dismal and as unwelcoming a cavern as might be found outside the infernal regions, and a good deal chillier.

I mounted in a hackney chariot to the level of Princes Street. It seemed for a moment that I had taken a carriage across the Highland grouse moors. The drawing-rooms of the great houses on its northern side were black, being either heavily shuttered, or their occupants having with Scots godliness removed themselves from the temptations of evening enjoyments by retiring to sleep. The opposite side was equally stygian, being uninhabited gardens, which the Edinburgh and Glasgow Railway Company had been recently licensed by Parliament to violate. There was gas, to be sure. But it was sparser, or weaker, than in London, and burnt with a grudging, bluish flame. I directed the man on the box, whose speech I could understand no better than he mine, to drive me to the George Hotel. I recalled as a faint but pleasing coincidence that Dr Warren of Boston stayed there once as a young man.

I had notified the hotel of my arrival, and found a letter waiting. I opened it as I thawed before the fire in my bedroom.

> *52 Queen Street*
> *Edinburgh*
> *Saturday, October 30, 1847*

Guy Romilly, Esquire. Dear Sir,
I am apprised by my good friend and colleague Mr Robert Liston

that you will shortly be visiting this City. I am acquainted with the works of your pen, and I think I can assure you of an occurrence or two of some interest. If your journey is successfully accomplished by November 4, pray take supper with me that evening, at seven o'clock.

Faithfully yours,

J. Y. Simpson.

The invitation being for the morrow, I immediately wrote my acceptance and descended to find a porter who might bear the message. The entire staff seemed to have joined the guests in slumber, at an hour when the drawing-rooms of Mayfair were alive with chatter over the coffee-cups. At last I found a man to do my service, and another to fetch me food and drink – a quartern loaf to slice myself, a mutton chop, a potato baked the Scots way. I sought the reinforcement of brandy-and-water, despite his persistence in bringing me tea. The Scots are as addicted to tea as avidly as to oatmeal, which they eat as porridge, or as a coffin for their baked herrings, or drink quite disgustingly as bowls of groats, and present to their University students by the bagful one Lenten Monday of the year – 'Meal Monday' – as a present to their ravenous parents in their distant crofts.

The next morning I saw Edinburgh. A study of greyness – grey stone, grey plaster, grey skies, only the people shiny and red-faced, like cherries on a shovel. The Castle glowered down thunderously on Princes Street, where the houses seemed dropped in respectful curtsy, like a line of *débutantes*. I made reconnaissance for my evening's expedition, spying out Queen Street. I found it another grey, grave line on a steep north-facing slope, overlooking more public gardens, with a view in the pale, brief sun aslant the Forth of low hills and little houses across water lively with fishing-smacks from Newhaven Harbour.

I had little leisure that day to explore either New Town or Old. I had to find myself lodging less costly than the George. A house in Beecham Place took me in, and offered me tea and bread four times a day. The proportions of the landlady, a gingery well-scrubbed body whose speech was hardly more comprehensible to me than Hindustani, gave comfortable indication that I was unlikely to starve. These first impressions of Edinburgh stay fresh in my mind, despite the many visits I have made since. That is perhaps because the City has not contrived to change over the past fifty tumultuous years. It was seemingly carved out of one single block of granite, and left completed.

Promptly at seven o'clock I presented myself at No 52 Queen Street, which lies between its corners with Castle Street and Frederick Street. The house was narrow, of four storeys and a basement, nicely proportioned, three windows across, those of the first-floor drawing-room tall enough to dominate the façade. There were two steps up to the front door, heavily porticoed, the area railings lit by a gaslamp. The construction was of course stone, as would have phlegmatically weathered besiegement with the trebuchet. Having risen to such elegances, I produced a silver case and sent my card by ancient footman to the professor.

As I waited in a small, neatly swept hall, warmed by a fire in a Gothic grate, to my surprise singing broke out somewhere above. My immediate expectation of a carousal was extinguished by its sacred timbre. The footman creaked downstairs. I ascended. I was shown into the drawing-room, where elegance made only a perfunctory struggle against comfort. The fat fire radiated a self-satisfied brightness, the massive brass clock on the mantelpiece chimed seven and ticked on with easygoing loudness, the oil-lamps gave a snug and rosy glow. The room was empty, save for a plumpish young lady of eighteen or so with dark ringlets, wearing a neat frock of fine brown holland embroidered in scarlet, sitting in a tapestry chair by the fireside, and emitting the same air of contentment as the other furnishings.

I bowed. 'Mr Romilly, Miss. Your servant. From London,' I added, thinking it afforded me some cachet.

'Miss Agnes Petrie, sir,' she returned. 'I am Dr Simpson's niece. The professor is at prayer.'

I bowed deeper, in appropriately solemn acknowledgement of this fact.

'I should be at prayer too, sir. But I was given the duty of receiving you.'

'I am sorry to be the unwitting cause of your impiety.'

'Och, this is *far* more comfortable.' She spoke in the business-like way of the practical-minded Scots gentry, her voice soft but with a tang to it, like their peaty water. 'The chapel is *dreadfully* cold.'

I reflected silently on the godliness which constructed a private chapel in a private house, even one so generously proportioned as befittingly to ensconce Dr James Young Simpson, professor of midwifery at Edinburgh the past seven years. I later found the place of worship to be as correct as any official one, even to stained-glass windows. The singing next door stopped. 'Psalm thirty-four,' Miss Petrie informed me. 'Please be seated.'

I took a small round red velvet chair, which of course looked invitingly comfortable.

'In London, do you know Lady Blantyre?' she asked.

'I have not that pleasure,' I confessed.

'Or the Marchioness of Douglas? Or the Duchess of Cambridge?'

'I am humbled – indeed, shamed – to admit not.'

'Och, it's a pity. We should have some mutual friends to discuss, to pass the time till the company appear.'

'You are well acquainted with these ladies?' I asked, a little surprised.

'No, I am not. But my uncle the professor has recently delivered all three of child. From his descriptions, I feel I know each quite intimately. Perhaps one day my uncle shall take me to London, and I shall meet them.'

I took these singular bonds of friendship as indicating Dr Simpson's acceptance on the highest levels by London society, for which Scotsmen have a flair. They so often prove themselves useful, yet may be taken up without embarrassment, through possessing no more definite social standing than itinerant Turks. This pair of attributes led even the despicable Boswell to some success in the *beau-monde*.

'Do you admire the novels of Sir Walter Scott?' asked my comely welcomer.

'Very much.'

'And which is your favourite?'

'I have never read any of them.'

'Then how dare you answer me thus, sir?'

'One can admire things by their effect on others. I need not trek to Rome to admire the Colosseum, nor to Egypt to appreciate the Pyramids. I am prepared to take any responsible critic's word for them.'

She gave me a long, steady look. 'That's how people talk in London, is it?'

'Quite often,' I enlightened her amiably.

The door was opened by the elderly footman, to admit the party released from their devotions.

Simpson came in first. He was thirty-six, short, strongly built, with a large head and thick auburn hair. My first impression was a startling resemblance to Horace Wells of Hartford. He wore a melancholy look, but his face was mobile, his expression eager to leap from its usual gravity, his eyes always illuminated with a keen interest in his fellow-beings. His benevolence was *active*, rather than the passive tolerance we all affect towards our fellow beings, as less exerting. He had a strong humorous mouth, a lumpy nose, whiskers, but shaven chin. He wore a high collar, a linen shirt with a white silk cravat, and a suit which had felt the hand of a London tailor. On second glance, I thought him the head of Jove on the body of Bacchus.

'Mr Romilly—' We shook hands warmly. 'You come with Mr Robert Liston's recommendation, of which there could be none better. Neither to myself, nor I warrant to any medical man in his old home of Edinburgh. With one or two self-evident exceptions.' I recalled that James Syme, *the ninny*, was professor of surgery at the Royal Infirmary in Edinburgh. 'And how is Mr Liston? I have not met him for some months.'

'I fear he has been somewhat poorly, sir.'

'Oh?' Simpson looked concerned.

'It was from some slight accident on his boat.'

'I expect he'll drive himself back to health. You know, he'd put a dying man on a horse, to shake his liver into salubrity. Mrs Simpson, this is Mr Romilly, the well-known author.'

The profundity of my bow matched the misinformed flattery. His wife was handsome, large-eyed and small-chinned, her mouth full-lipped, her teeth white and good, her dark hair parted in the middle and drawn back across her ears in the London fashion – if some six months behind it. She had a pretty dress of russet silk, her bosom well curtained in muslin, pinned by a cameo no bigger than a fourpenny-piece. 'I am sure you esteem the novels of Sir Walter Scott, sir?' she greeted me.

'Indeed, ma'am, an esteem which can but grow on more intimate acquaintance. My leisure is short.'

'The children of the busy cobbler go barefoot,' said Simpson pleasantly. 'And a doctor's children are always ill. May I present Captain Petrie of the Royal Navy.' I bowed to Agnes's father, who was tall, red-faced and white-haired, some twenty years Simpson's senior. 'And Mrs Petrie, who is Mrs Simpson's sister.' The resemblance was apparent, but she was tubbier, like the daughter. 'And my two assistants from the Lying-in Hospital, Dr George Keith and Dr Mathews Duncan.' Our party was completed by two tall, dark-haired, amiable-looking men, the first with a gaudy tartan waistcoat, the other with a spotted cravat. 'Well, tell us the news from London,' Simpson invited.

I thought so wide an invitation needed a fitting reply. 'You may perhaps know, sir, we shall be blessed with a new little prince or princess next March.'

'Her Majesty sets a splendid example. No, it is news to which I am not privy, although I have the honour to be one of Her Majesty's Physicians in Scotland. An honour which came to me the very week I first used sulphuric ether to deliver a woman without pain. I confess I was more interested in the second of these events at the time. Though flattery from the Queen is not common flattery, to be sure. Did you know that Her Majesty was herself delivered into this world by the hand of a lady?' I shook my head. 'Dr Marianne Siebald, a graduate of the University of Geissen, who accompanied the Duke and Duchess of Kent from Bavaria for that event of May 24, 1819. Their Graces thought the outlay of a guinea worth crossing the Channel to have the child born in Britain.' He gave me a humorous look. 'But they didn't care for Sir Richard Croft laying hands on the Duchess, after he slaughtered Princess Charlotte through sheer incompetence when delivering her of a stillborn son. He shot himself later. Well, shall we go down to supper directly?' Simpson's dazzling fizgig of regal information abruptly expired, to my disappointment. 'I have already kept you waiting, Mr Romilly,' he apologized to me, 'because I came very late home myself today. Those of us who choose to play Nature's handmaiden must be prepared to dance attendance at all hours.'

We made downstairs, host and hostess last. I took down Agnes, searching my mind for shipwrecks. But that winter seemed to have brought only commercial ones – the City of London had become a shoal strewn with bankruptcies – which unfortunately lacked the physical perils so tickling to young ladies.

The dining-room's pair of windows shared the ground floor with the front door. The door leading from the small hall was curved. Another in the matching corner led down stone steps to the kitchens, between them an arbour containing a heavy wooden cabinet filled with leatherbound journals, which I assumed to be Simpson's casebooks. The ceiling was moulded, the floor covered by a red Turkey carpet, relinquishing its extremities to the product of the Linoleum Manufacturing Company. The table was oval, under a fine linen cloth, with ample space for the eight of us, in the middle a porcelain warming-dish of Chinese pattern awaiting our repast. The silver was Aberdeen, of great solidity. On the mantel above a square grate with a good fire stood a pair of Dresden shepherdesses, two decorated jars and a porcelain clock – banal decorations, but enlivened by an overlooked stethoscope like an upturned wooden flower-vase. We were lit by five oil lamps in candelabra. On side tables, my eye discovered not one massive family Bible, but two. I saw that I must rein my regrettable tendency to ungodly flippancy.

I was honoured to be on Simpson's right, Agnes beside me, Dr Keith of the tartan waistcoat opposite. 'Have you lived here long, sir?' I asked politely, unfolding my napkin.

'Near on three years. It's very convenient. There's a staircase front and back, you see. So I may see my poor patients without keeping them waiting, yet not incommode my rich ones with the knowledge. What do you make of *this*, Mr Romilly?'

He showed me a small gold cross on his watch-chain. Before I could find a reply, he had touched a spring, and from it protruded the sharp blade of a lancet. 'You see, sir, if we incorporate our practical skills within our Christian ideas in the manner this instrument suggests . . . then we shall make our best contribution to the world we live in.'

With Liston in mind, I asked, 'Are you the son of the manse, sir?'

'Oh, no! I'm the son of a baker.' He laughed. 'The seventh son and eighth child.'

'Then you were the scholar of the family?' I suggested, a little put out.

'I was not. My parents decided to *invest* a University education in me.' He chuckled again. 'We see these things differently in Scotland. But you have Celtic blood?'

'My mother was a French lady.'

'*My* mother was of Huguenot descent.'

'Indeed, sir?' We seemed to be extruding points of intimacy, like snails' horns after rain.

The door from the kitchens opened to display the butler with the dish of viands. Simpson touched me on the arm and said quickly, 'Pray, attend closely to all that happens later tonight, Mr Romilly. You may startle those jaded Cockneys of yours once again. Now thanks to God.'

We all bowed our heads for grace, an observance which Robert Liston did not find necessary to impede him from his dinner.

24

I HAD HOPED for pheasant, the season being open and six shillings a brace being well within the professor's pocket. We had beef. Though it could have been mutton. Or even buffalo. The Scots manner of pot-roasting rendered it greasy, grey and tasteless. But the potatoes were plentiful and the 'neeps' – the humble turnip – had an unexpected juiciness. We drank sherry and claret. My host spent most of the meal reminiscing over Robert Liston's days in Edinburgh, his voice filled with the respect and relief in which we recall great tempests blown-out in our youth.

'He and Mr Syme argued over everything,' Simpson observed. 'Perfectly automatically, like dogs over bones. They never took the rights or wrongs into their minds, I think. If but they knew the amusement it caused the medical body, they would have instantly become bosom friends through mutual shame. When Mr Liston was expelled from the Medical House – before I was even a student back in the twenties – the whole of Edinburgh was divided. Town was against Gown, there were disputations on every street corner, religion for once took second place as our main topic of argument. A court was convened, you know, to look into the matter, with no less than the Lord President of the Court of Session in the Chair. I quite forget now what was decided. I know that Mr Liston wrote letters to absolutely everybody in Edinburgh, from the Lord Provost down.'

'I have been privileged to see such correspondence, sir.'

'But Mr Liston is the most skilful operator. The greatest I have seen.'

'It has been my privilege to observe that, too.'

'As I gathered from your writings. Of course, he makes mistakes. All of us do. I think his enthusiasm is too fresh a horse for his judgement, and occasionally unseats it. Nor does he rush, exactly, to publish accounts of his errors, that others might avoid them. But we must be charitable. The gleam of his knife will not be tarnished by his occasional lapses into pettiness.'

I mentioned with raised brows that Mr Liston perhaps enjoyed a reputation in Edinburgh for speedy work outside the operating theatre – in the open air.

'No one thought twice of *that* when I was a student,' returned Simpson, perceiving my reference to body-snatching. 'You've heard of our infamous Dr Knox, Mr Romilly?' I nodded vigorously. 'I sat at his feet myself, in the lecture room. I remember the day Burke was hanged – it was a Wednesday, January 28, 1829 at eight in the morning in the Lawnmarket. Hare turned King's evidence, of course, and saved his neck. There were twenty thousand to watch him drop, and twice as many went to see him spread on the slab the next day, dissected by Professor Munro. The scandal drove Dr Knox from Edinburgh, and from his scientific work.' Simpson shook his head in regret. 'There was a lot of emotion, of uninformed opinion, of outright jealousy directed against the man. I can't abide prejudice. But a closed mind and an open mouth too often exist in the same head.'

'There was scandal, too, sir, was there not, about the appointment of Professor Syme to the Chair of surgery? Or so I understood from Mr Liston.' I was mischievously hoping to invite more revelations of surgical chicanery.

Simpson paused thoughtfully before replying. 'It is a long story, Mr Romilly, which I think even your pen would be tested in tracing. James Syme is much respected here. He is the son of a Writer to the Signet, he was born in Princes Street, he was a boy at Edinburgh High School – he is essentially "an Edinburgh type of man", as we say. When he was young, he was a good-looking chap, rather sharp-featured, a bit dandified. He has grown into a practitioner who never wastes a word, or a drop of ink, or a drop of blood. I would distil his character into *verax, capax, persipicax, sagax, efficax, tenax.*'

Simpson took another mouthful of that dreadful meat. 'Mr Syme was only thirty when he applied for the staff of the Royal Infirmary. Robert Liston was there already, and the Managers feared the pair might start squabbling under the eyes of the students – an awful prospect I think deliberately planted in their minds by Mr Liston's friends.' With a knowing shake of the head he added, 'We all know our Liston, don't we? Well, Mr John Lizars was appointed instead, and Mr Syme went off to buy Minto House, a private residence, and turn it into his own surgical hospital.'

I recalled this as the establishment where Liston had written in the subscription book so forthrightly as to invite a libel action. Though there was also the item of his comparing an ape's skull to Syme's.

'Some fifteen years back now, Mr Syme was appointed to the Royal, as professor of surgery,' Simpson went on. 'There was certainly a bargain struck, in which he pensioned off the retiring professor at £300 a year. I assure you, Mr Romilly, it looked more honourable in Lauriston Place than in Gower Street. And it was money well spent. Whatever Mr Liston says – and it is never difficult for his friends to imagine *that* – James Syme has opened the eyes of surgeons all over Europe to our new reputation here in Edinburgh. His operation for amputation of the foot, which saws away both ankles and disarticulates the joint between them, will become one of the classical procedures of surgery, I am sure of it. Pray do not let your mind be poisoned against him by our mutual friend, who can be more careless with his tongue than with his fingers.'

'Men have their pet hates like their pet dogs, I think, sir, and would be quite uncomfortable without regular opportunity of exercising them.'

'Well, Mr Syme has one cleverness beyond Mr Liston. As a student, he discovered a chemical method of rendering cloth waterproof. This has been patented and developed by a manufacturer in Glasgow named Macintosh. When you wear your 'Mackintosh' cape bless the name of our Professor

Syme. Whose talents, I hope, will never need to be directed more intimately on your body.'

As the meat was followed by a pudding of equal anonymity, the conversation became general. Captain Petrie gave a stirring account of his adventures in the East Indies. Or perhaps it was the West Indies. Or the Antipodes. I noticed the company received it as some over-familiar drawing-room song. But I thanked my stars for my silence on shipwrecks, about which it occurred to me the Captain had a professional knowledge, and possibly a certain touchiness.

We were on our fruit before the topic of anaesthesia was mentioned, by way of Simpson demanding jovially, 'Well, Mr Romilly, do you suppose I'd have made a good lawyer?'

'Had you been *that*, James, we should have eaten our meals on time,' his wife replied on my behalf.

'I nearly became a law student, and that was through the agency of Mr Liston. It was my first encounter with surgery. He was amputating a girl's breast, and he performed it in a flash, beautifully. But the blood, the screams, were too much for me. I suspect they were too much for every young fellow in the operating room, but they were better at dissembling, or perhaps braver than me. Or perhaps more cowardly, because they were afraid of dropping a brassy face, and showing themselves as the weak beings God has made us all. So I presented myself at the Faculty of Law. But my conversion lasted barely the day. Medicine had already claimed my life. Besides, the *smell* of the law, the musty offices, the dust, the creaking parchments – they soon dissuade a young man with an active mind and a sound pair of hands. But from that time I have searched to make operations less degrading spectacles, so you can imagine how I was affected by your account in the newspaper, Mr Romilly. I saw that a miracle had happened, one that not even Our Lord had achieved.'

Simpson continued by informing me that Baron Dubois in Paris and Dr Walter Channing at Harvard had been using ether to mitigate the pains of childbirth. He had himself been giving it since January, as an improvement on mesmerism. 'But it stinks,' he declared. 'It irritates the lungs, like chlorine.

The patients become as sick as dogs. Why, you must use gallons of the stuff! And the apparatus is an awkward bundle in some of the chimneys which pass for Edinburgh staircases. Besides, metroperitonitis has occurred after ether, though in hands other than mine. So I have been searching all summer among other volatile fluids, which your presence tonight inspires me to try upon myself. You shall record our success – or failure – as Mr Liston suggested in London. Dr Keith, fetch me those bottles from the corner table. We may do without port tonight, you see.'

'May we all stay, uncle?' asked Agnes excitedly.

'Och, the ladies need not withdraw from *this* pastime. We shall hold a family sniffing session.'

The footman and butler cleared the table, but leaving the cloth. In front of Simpson was placed an oblong of coconut-matting, on which bottles had left their thumbprints as many-hued rings. As all leant forward eagerly and tugged in their chairs, the atmosphere recalled that among ladies and gentlemen more inquisitive of the next world than this, at the start of a *séance*. Amusement was mingled with self-consciousness, and the comforting expectation that nothing particularly alarming was to happen struggled against the exquisitely exciting one that something *might*.

Keith set on the matting a dozen small dark bottles of different shapes, all securely stoppered. 'Remember the rabbits!' cried Mrs Simpson loudly.

I was mystified, until Simpson explained casually, 'I was going to try inhaling ethylene bromide, but Dr Lyon Playfair – a chemist at the University – insisted I tried it on a brace of coneys first. He had some justification.' Simpson unstoppered one of the bottles. 'In the morning, both animals were dead.'

I felt some apprehension that I might be offered first sniff of another untried chemical and follow the rabbits. I inquired if Simpson had himself risked any other preparation. 'I have enjoyed the most fragrant of summers,' he assured me. 'I recall trying carbonic acid, carbonic oxide, cyanogen, hydrocyanic acid, Dutch liquid – that is the chloride of hydrocarbon,' he explained, as I glanced inquiringly. 'Also ammonia, nitrogen, amylovinic ether, allyle, cyanide of ethyl, chloride of amyl, a carbo-hydrogen from Rangoon tar, and puff-ball smoke. But without success. Sniff this.'

While talking, Simpson had poured about a teaspoonful of a clear liquid into a saucer, which I politely, if gingerly, inhaled. 'It would appear a distillation of rotting fruit, sir,' I announced, wrinkling my nose.

'It's acetone. Do you feel any narcotizing effect?'

I sniffed more heartily. 'No, sir.'

The saucer was handed round, but none claimed more stupefaction from its fumes than I had. Simpson decanted the remains back into its bottle, and sent for a kettle of hot water, which was brought on a spirit-lamp. The next preparation he poured into a tumbler, which he stood in a saucer of hot water for better vaporization. The experimenting was continued, with much lively talk in between, until well towards midnight. Of the liquids tried I knew nothing, not even the names, except they all smelt repugnant. But there was no indication that any could entice us on Lethe's walk more effectively or agreeably than Morton's sulphuric ether. 'It's like sampling a bin of bad clarets,' Captain Petrie gave the disgruntled opinion.

Our supply of bottles exhausted, we at last prepared to leave the table, Simpson clearly downcast. 'Perhaps we are following nothing more real than a corpse-candle,' he declared glumly. 'Those "dead-men's lights", you know, which country folk see flicking in the churchyard, and shake in their shoes at the omen of another death.'

'The "corpse-candle" is at least an effective demonstration of some natural gas,' Keith pointed out, even more despondently.

'I must apologize, Mr Romilly, that your arduous journey has been in vain,' Simpson said. I tried to seem indifferent to this, but in truth I was angry that the guineas I had scattered on my expedition should be the seeds of a fruitless crop. We dropped our heads for grace, and Simpson gave thanks to Our Lord, I presumed inclusive of the inhalations.

'What about that other stuff, Dr Simpson?' asked Mathews Duncan, on the heels of our amens.

'What other stuff, Duncan?'

'We threw it away,' said Keith.

'Och, it was altogether too heavy,' Simpson explained. 'It would have no likelihood of suiting.'

'Go on, uncle, try it,' urged Agnes, hopeful of prolonging the entertainment. Keith was already rummaging in a basket in the corner, producing a small bottle from the discarded papers and handing it to Simpson. I inquired the name.

'This is *chloric* ether – not your *sulphuric* ether,' Simpson explained. 'That is, a solution in spirits of wine of a drug called chloroform. It was invented by Monsieur Dumas, and has been used for some time in chest complaints, as has ether. Also, to cure the gripes.' He poured a little into four wine-glasses, saying humorously that the three medical men and myself would exchange toasts. 'This specimen was specially prepared by Duncan and Flockhart, our esteemed Edinburgh chemists,' he told me. 'It is also *dreadfully* expensive.'

The three raised their glasses, and we inhaled together. I certainly found the odour agreeable. It was sweet, and free from pungency. I felt encouraged to sniff again, more deeply. I was filled with a feeling so pleasantly warm, so comfortable, that I drew an enormous breath, both hands round the glass. Dr Keith suddenly threw back his head and gave a loud shout of laughter.

I looked up. Simpson was eyeing his hilarious young colleague with a smile of utter benignity.

'Here, that stuff looks as useful as Nelson's blood,' exclaimed Captain Petrie. 'Give me a glass of it.'

In my original notes, from which I now compose this narrative, I tried to record events with the detachment and calm which are essential for good journalism. I regret that I have no more record of this famous evening than one scribbled in Beecham Place the following morning.

Hang me, if we weren't all blind drunk at the end of it! I've had not such a revel since Trinity Hall. One young doctor on the floor, snoring like a steam engine. The other attempting to send chairs and dining-room table through the window. 'Far stronger than ether,' said Simpson, quite unnecessarily, for with the words he slid to the floor. The noise was like an iron-foundry. I recall Mr Miller, the surgeon who lived next door, coming round in alarm at the din and discovering Simpson under the table-cloth. The time was then past 3 in the morning.

That night brought my first mention of chloroform. And chloroform is the only reason for these memoirs to be penned at all. It happened thus. Two summers ago, in 1898, I was sharing a hansom with my friend Mr George Bernard Shaw to his mother's house in Fitzroy Square, from a political meeting he had addressed in Islington. Shaw is a *belletrist* and a debater, and at the time was serving as dramatic critic on the *Saturday Review*. Like most dramatic critics, he is a playwright *manqué*. He knew of my experiences in the 1840s, and prompted by our rattling past the old University College Hospital suggested I put them on paper, explaining he had for some time the notion of writing a play about chloroforming. We could divide the royalties, he suggested airily. 'I had the same arrangement with my fellow-critic William Archer. Archer can construct passable plots, while I am capable of reams of fluent dialogue. The result was *Widowers' Houses*, which you remember we put on at the Royalty in December '92.'

I told Shaw that I did not regard this as a promising precedent for our collaboration, the play having got the bird, of aquiline proportions.

'I shall do it either about chloroforming or about Professor Almoth Wright's phagocytes,' he told me, undeterred. 'There's a dozen plays to be written of those mischievous charlatans of Wimpole Street, whose reputation is made by the number of dukes who die in their hands.'

'You cannot surely see chloroform as anything but an immense blessing to mankind,' I protested.

'On the contrary, chloroform has done mankind a great disservice. It's enabled any fool to become a surgeon.'

Conversation with Shaw needs the adroitness of Blondin crossing Niagara on his tightrope.

I acceded to Shaw's request. If he writes about phagocytes instead, let these words stay unread until they are as old as I myself today – another seventy-five years on. Then perhaps they may have some antiquarian interest. Though my executors will have to stand fast, to save these pages from the printer in face of my publisher's blandishments. Nothing increases an author's popularity so much as his death.

25

MONDAY, NOVEMBER 8, 1847. Just after four in the afternoon. A ragged boy gave a double knock of the front door of my lodgings, with a note addressed to me. It said simply,

> Come at once.
> *J.Y.S.*

I plucked up my hat and hurried downstairs, leaving my tea and baps half-finished, to the consternation of my landlady at good vittles going to waste. Nothing in the world could have stayed me another second. I was to have an experience entirely new, one I would share with no male in the Kingdom outside the medical ranks. I was to witness the birth of a baby.

I knew the address, No 19 Albany Street, about half a mile down the slope from Simpson's house in the direction of Newhaven. Simpson had told me in his drawing-room the night before – between returning home from one patient and immediately leaving it again for another – that the mother was a Mrs Jane Carstairs, who had come across the water from Fife. She was a doctor's wife, returned home to have her baby, her husband still serving in India. I soon found the house, the knocker muffled. I was admitted by the servant-girl, pale, freckled and gingery, with that smug, knowledgeable expression so common among females in attendance on another giving birth.

Simpson was in the hall, unruffled and benevolent as usual, his sealskin coat and black leather bag on a chair.

'You made good time, Mr Romilly,' he greeted me genially. 'A regular Phidippides.'

'Am I late?' I asked breathlessly. 'Is it all over?'

'My dear man, it has not properly started yet. You are behaving quite like a husband.' His manner became graver. 'Now, pay heed to me. I must acquaint you better with the nature of the case. As this is the very first use of chloroform, I would wish you to report it to Mr Liston in an informed manner. We must pray God our new drug will prove a success.'

'When Dr Morton first gave ether successfully in Boston, sir, I assure you that anxieties and doubts beat round his head like vampire bats.'

'Yes. But now there are two lives at stake, not one.'

'Yet only one reputation, sir.'

He made a dismissive gesture. 'What is my reputation in comparison to a dead mother or a stillborn child?' he demanded severely. 'What is any man's? Mr Romilly, I must enjoin you never to reveal your presence here today. The laity must not be privy to our secrets, for they are performed upon other human beings at their most wretched. Though to be sure, Dr Thomas Chalmers has been present at operations performed by Mr Miller under etherization. Dr Chalmers is our professor of divinity, and a chemist, which perhaps gives him some standing, and the leader of the "Wee Frees", the Free Church movement. He is also, I thank God, unlike many of his cloth an advocate of the anaesthetic process. But it is *most irregular* for *you*, Mr Romilly, to gaze upon the private parts of a woman.'

'An artist may see a woman naked without opprobrium, sir. And the profession of artist is surely akin to that of a man of letters?'

Simpson did not seem impressed by this argument. 'Keep your thoughts Godly, sir, I pray you. This is the lady's second child,' he proceeded in a more businesslike tone. 'The reason I have chosen her for chloroform lies in her terrible experience with the first – when I was *not* the obstetrician. It recalled the death of Princess Charlotte, which had occurred in similar circumstances almost thirty years ago to that day.'

I nodded, though I confess to thinking of another Charlotte, and wondering if she had caught the same complaint as the patient upstairs.

'Mrs Carstairs's first labour was long, three days. The mother, poor creature, was exhausted near to death. She could not expel her dead child ... you must understand, Mr Romilly, the process of birth is not so simple as the many smiling faces of children around us would suggest. There may be discrepancies of size between the mother's bony pelvis and the child's head. In Mrs Carstairs's previous labour, such imbalance had perforce to be corrected to save her life. Resort was made to craniotomy.'

'What's that, sir?'

In reply, Simpson opened his black bag and handed me an instrument like a stout pair of scissors, but in place of the blades a pair of sharp spikes. 'That is to perform craniotomy, the perforation of a dead baby's head. I am working to improve the design somewhat.'

I had a feeling of sickness. 'But why should you perforate the baby's head?' I asked blankly.

'To let escape the brains, that you might crush the bones to a smaller mass. Some obstetricians would leave the opened head for a day, so mummification might affect the child's body, and render it more easily expelled. I myself expedite matters by using these —'

He produced a second instrument like a pair of tongs or pliers. 'These are craniotomy forceps, by which you may break off portions of the baby's skull *in utero*. Or you can use a cranioclast, to pull the open head through. Or the *forceps cephalotribe* of Monsieur Baudelocque, which protects the mother by keeping the scalp intact, but crushes the head to force the baby's brain matter conveniently through the eyes and nostrils.'

Simpson added, 'Of course, it is sometimes better simply to decapitate the baby, and remove the body with crotchets in two portions.'

The hall seemed to shimmer before me. I wondered if I had allowed my vanity to overestimate my stoicism towards such sights. In 1847, such heroic measures were sometimes necessary to save a mother's life. If obstetrics has advanced since then in step with the fecundity of our age, much of the credit was Simpson's. He adopted the subject when it was the lowest and most ignoble of the medical arts, and he left it a science numbering among its present professors many of the most distinguished of our modern physicians. I learned later that Simpson's reputation as an obstetrician and a chloroformist became worth £80,000 a year to the Edinburgh *hotels*.

To my relief, my instruction on the use of Simpson's instruments was interrupted by a woman's voice from the stairs. I looked up to see a figure in black bombazine, a fawning example of faded gentility, clearly the lying-in nurse. This was an occupation much favoured by widows with not even an outside chance of remarrying. We all three entered the large bedroom on the second floor, my heart racing. On the bed, covered only by a sheet, lay a comely woman with fair hair in two plats, eyes shut, groaning, hands clasping an enormous belly. I would never have believed a female could have advanced to such a size. There was no need for Simpson's explaining me away, the patient being so distracted with pain she would hardly have noticed the presence in the room of her own butler. Simpson nodded, and felt her pulse. After a few words of murmured encouragement, he removed the sheet. I was no *ingénu*. I had lived with Floy as a husband. But the abrupt baring of a woman's most intimate part shocked me. The more so as Simpson, with no further ceremony, inserted his hand up the *pudendum muliebre*.

His examination completed, he turned to me. 'The pains have been going three hours. I think we shall start the chloroform, for which I need your assistance.' He took from his pocket a clean handkerchief, which he made into a funnel. 'I have a simple mind, Mr Romilly, and I fancy this will do as well as Mr Squire's elaborate contraption.' From the same pocket followed a dark bottle and a teaspoon, which he passed me with instructions to pour half a spoonful on the handkerchief to start with. I performed my office with confidence, knowing how in London it was often entrusted to the handiest hospital porter.

To my gratification as much as Simpson's, the mother stopped her groaning. She lay quiet, breathing shallowly, her features composed, for all the world in a natural sleep. 'So much smoother than your nauseous ether, Mr Romilly,' said Simpson smugly. 'You can send that back to those rough fellows in Boston.' Her arms moved slowly, groping towards her face, exactly as I had observed in Warren's patient. 'Another few drops,' Simpson directed. 'The baby is coming.'

I hardly knew to which end of the poor woman to direct my attention. Simpson produced from his tail pocket another instrument, and I had horrifying visions of babies' heads pierced and squeezed of their brains like oranges. But he explained this was his 'forceps', which he laid on the bed ready in case the child needed expediting. Then suddenly came a high-pitched cry. As though electrified, I had the realization of not four human beings in the room, but five.

'A little girl,' Simpson announced. 'You had best continue the chloroform, Mr Romilly, until the delivery of the placenta.'

I had no knowing what the placenta might be, but it was a peculiar red object. There seemed a great deal of blood about. Simpson applied some rags between the mother's legs. The nurse swaddled the infant and bore her into the next room. By then I had withdrawn the handkerchief, and the mother began to stir and moan. Not in agony, but as one in nightly sleep.

Simpson was looking jubilant. 'She'll soon be right, as long as she makes an effort. There's not much puerperal fever about this time of year – the raw uterus performs like an amputation stump,' he explained to me. 'This chloroform is quite capital, and much less is needed, so the expense is no greater than ether in the long run. From this evening, Mr Romilly, ether is as out-of-date as mandrake root.'

The mother opened her eyes. 'I've enjoyed a sleep,' she murmured. 'A most comfortable sleep. I required it, indeed, as I was so tired. I will now be more able for the work before me.' Seeing Simpson smiling over her, she asked weakly, 'Am I to take some labour tea?'

'Such infusions will not be necessary. You have passed beyond the need of ergot.'

'My pains assuredly seem to have gone off . . .' A cry came from outside the door. Simpson called the nurse. But instead of being overjoyed at her painless delivery, the mother gave a gasp and asked angrily, 'What is that child?'

'Your daughter, ma'am.'

'Oh, no. It's some impostor, some changeling. I've not had my child . . .' She turned to Simpson in terror. 'Oh, my Lord, do not say it is dead like the last?'

But her bewilderment was short. Soon mother had child at her breast, amazement replacing anguish. I did not tarry long. I had to write an account of the new anaesthetic for the newspapers – the pen is a nimble instrument in the hand which feels an emptying pocket. Simpson said good-bye warmly, asking me to be at his house at ten the following morning.

I wrote an article about chloroform for *The Scotsman*, and next day presented myself promptly at the familiar door. It is a door grown even more familiar during my lifetime, for I make the pilgrimage to No 52 Queen Street on my every visit to Edinburgh. The house stands much as it did that winter of 1847. It is indeed so solidly built, it will be standing there a century or two yet. The dining-room with the curved door is preserved, dignified with a label *The Discovery Room*. I hear the place will be used by the Church of Scotland as a hostel for missionaries on furlough, who I hope will enjoy sleep as sound as ours that November night.

But that morning I received only apologies that the exigencies of work prevented Simpson seeing me until two days hence, on the Thursday, November 11, when he would be pleased to afford me luncheon.

Even then, I was robbed of my meal. I arrived to find the hall full of black hats. He was suffering an unexpected invasion of clergymen.

'The professor says you're to go up, sir,' the elderly footman directed, in a state of some agitation.

The drawing-room contained a dozen strange, stern faces. In the middle stood Simpson, regarding me with the expression which must have illuminated the Duke's face on Marshal Blücher's appearance at Waterloo.

'And here is Mr Romilly himself,' he announced. 'The very author of the article in yesterday's paper.'

The Scotsman then appeared only on Wednesdays and Saturdays. The stern heads nodded briefly at me. I was dismissed as but an imp attendant upon a wickeder devil.

'Chloroform is a direct contravention of *Divine Will*, Dr Simpson,' continued the cleric who seemed to have assumed spokesmanship of the group, and presumably of God himself. His face was as grey and granity as Edinburgh's, his voice as hot and Scots as the inside of a boiled haggis. 'And so is any other form of narcotization at the sublime moment of childbirth. The Lord set his primeval curse upon woman, that she must *suffer* in giving birth. That was His word, given in the very Garden of Eden.' He wagged a long finger at the obstetrician, like an irate schoolmaster's cane. 'It is writ in the Scriptures, perfectly plainly, Book of Genesis, chapter 3, verse 16, *Unto the woman he said, I will greatly multiply thy sorrow and thy conception; in sorrow thou shalt bring forth children.*'

A murmur of approval came from the others like an amen.

Simpson seemed unconcerned. 'My dear Mr McCorquodale, may I refresh your mind of two items in the following verses of Genesis? *Cursed is the ground for thy sake*, the Lord told Adam. *Thorns also and thistles shall it bring forth to thee.* Yet the agriculturist promptly pulls up these thorns and thistles, which are the primeval curse of our earth to bear. Would you ride out among the crofters, telling them how wicked they are?'

'Dr Simpson, that is not at all the same thing.' He was plainly affronted at the laity daring to quote the Bible against him.

The ancient footman appeared at the drawing-room door to announce that the ladies had already passed into luncheon, but was dismissed impatiently. '*Not* the same, Minister?' Simpson demanded. 'Well, you will recall in that same passage how man is destined to eat bread in sorrow all the days of his life. Yet he contrives to dine as comfortably as his means and health permit. I hope you all breakfasted before paying me the honour of this visit?' he inquired benignly, looking round.

'And I hope your porridge and baps caused you no pain. If they did *not*, then you are not attending to the Lord's curse. If they *did*, I fear you must consult me professionally before leaving.'

A small pink and sandy cleric spoke up from the back. 'The word *sorrow* is not a precise translation from the original Hebrew, sir.'

Simpson rounded on him. 'Indeed, you are right, sir. In anticipation of the attentions you gentlemen pay me, I consulted Professor Gesenius's *Lexicon*, to discover that *sorrow* signifies those severe muscular efforts of which parturition essentially exists. Particularly *human* parturition, the uterus being more powerful, and the mechanical obstacles to birth being more numerous, than enjoyed, for example, by the domestic cow. There is therefore more toil in human birth. That is all God's curse implies. We can reduce it to a faint echo.'

But religious arguments are, by their very nature, unanswerable. And intolerance is a respecter of neither bad nor good intentions. A thin pale clergyman like a woebegone skeleton declared, 'Women who are members of my own church have come to me, saying they would feel sinful to take chloroform, or the like. They see it as a decoy of Satan, apparently offering itself to bless womankind, but in the end hardening society, and robbing God of the deep, earnest cries which arise in time of trouble for His help. How can a mother love her child, sir, if she does not suffer for it?'

Simpson turned on him thunderously. 'Pain is never ennobling, only degrading. And do not be afraid, sir, that there will ever be too little of it in the world to spare mankind its "purification". There will always be human groans enough to fill the sails of *that* argument. But I am a practical Christian. Unlike *you*, sir, I relieve suffering, wherever I see it. Your ladies would not object to warm baths, to mitigate labour pains? To opium? It is the same principle.'

'*I* would not voluntarily surrender up my mental consciousness,' asserted the skeleton.

'Indeed, sir? Do you not sleep o'night?'

The footman reappeared. 'The Mistress says, will ye no come down for ye fud?'

'Leave us,' commanded Simpson, though my own stomach was rumbling pitifully for relief. '*Therefore to him that knoweth to do good, and doeth it not, to him it is sin,*' James, chapter 4, verse 17. You see, sir, I could not refuse the benefit of chloroform, without breaking God's command. May I also remind you of Timothy, chapter 4, verse 4, *And every creature of God is good, and nothing to be refused, if it be received with thanksgiving*. I assure you that the creatures of God who inhale chloroform submit the most profound thanks to both me and their Maker.'

Holed by his own ammunition, the clergyman sank. Simpson stared round, dominating the silent room. 'You would abolish smallpox vaccination? You would accept that awful disease as a Holy visitation, not to be interfered with? Och, I know the Reverend Delafaye preaches regularly against Jenner's discovery, but he has seen none of his loved ones stricken with pox. You gentlemen would not interfere with any natural function, simply because it *is* a natural function? But you ride? Why not walk? It is the more natural. A carriage saves you from fatigue. Chloroform saves my mothers from pain. Which is the more important to be done away with? Your weary legs, or the screams of womankind? How did you come this morning from Kirkcaldy, Mr McCorquodale? By steam-boat? You should be ashamed of yourself. You should have swum. I would set my face against chloroform only on *medical* considerations, with figures, Bills of Mortality before my eyes, not vain notions. Meanwhile, medical men shall soon be administering it everywhere,' he ended on a practical note. 'Because our patients themselves will force it. Now I must upon my afternoon rounds.'

As none dare stay him, the meeting broke up. The clergymen were disgruntled, a little cowed, but I suspected they left the house wearing exactly the same opinions and hats as they entered it. I had the chance for a snatched word with Simpson in the hall, as he was getting into his sealskin coat, black bag already in his hand. I made my *adieux*, explaining I was shortly leaving for the south. Simpson nodded towards the backs of

his retreating visitors with the remark, 'Even with such gentlemen at large, my mothers do better than one Eufame Mac-
Alyane, of this city. In the year 1591, the poor lass sought help
to relieve the torments of childbed, at which she gave birth to
twin boys, and for such impiety she was buried alive on Castle
Hill.'

'It is an unfortunate dispensation of Nature, sir, that the
parties you have just addressed cannot give birth themselves.'

'I sometimes despair at anything less bringing them to their
senses. Well, you are off, Mr Romilly? I'm sorry you shall be
unable to see more of our work with chloroform. I persuaded
Mr Miller, who rescued me from the carpet the other evening,
to administer it for a capital operation at the Royal Infirmary
this morning. It was for the removal of a septic bone in the arm
of a Highland boy, six years old, who spoke only Gaelic. It
went well, very well. The child slept soundly while the seques-
trum was extracted, and woke half an hour later as though
from a natural sleep, like our Mrs Carstairs. He felt no pain
whatever – as we found from an interpreter among the
students, neither myself nor Mr Miller nor anyone else
from Edinburgh seeming to speak our native tongue. My
best respects to Mr Liston. I hope he soon recovers full
health.'

I could not alone join the ladies for their meal. I went to a
tavern for a tankard of beer and a strange pastie called a
'Forfar Bridie'. The deputation, though ending in Simpson's
spirited victory, had left me saddened. The best mind makes
a poor horse between the shafts of bigotry. Yet praise be, the
empty ranting against new ideas is as soon forgotten as the
squabbles of children in the street. (The same occurred fifteen
years later, when Charles Darwin indicated that man was
descended from monkey, rather than all of us being struck in
the Heavenly mint from God's image, like so many millions of
sovereigns, or farthings. How Darwin's detractors scurried like
beetles from the woodwork of high table, pulpit and bench!
At that British Association meeting in Oxford in 1860, Bishop
Soapy Sam Wilberforce was as incapable of understanding
scientific reasoning as forecasting a horse-race. Though in

truth, his scientific adversary Thomas Huxley was always so pig-headed he could scarce see another's argument as a drunkard a lamp-post.)

On the next morning, Friday November 12, I left Edinburgh for London. I was content with my voyage. With chloroform, I had a new magic token to jangle in my pocket.

26

ON ARRIVAL AT Cadogan Place I found a letter waiting, addressed in Morton's hand. The postmark was Boston, but I unfolded the sheets to find it written from Etherton Cottage, West Needham, Massachusetts. Its date was Thursday, September 30, 1847. It was my first word from him since resigning my agency and returning my steamship fare the previous April.

Mr Romilly, Dear Sir – it began.

My eyes moved back to the address. *Ether*ton Cottage. The unhappy inventor enjoyed, unchallenged, at least the privilege of naming his house after his discovery.

I am surely sorry at not having acknowledged receipt of your letter and your draft for 42 pounds sterling on the house of Baring Brothers, London, paid as you directed through their agent in Boston, by coin on sight. I have suffered distractions greater still through the summer, and my health is not good. I have been advised by Dr Homans to spend some time away from the city, on account of the strain I underwent through my original experiments with ether, the worry of my first demonstrations, and the excitements aroused by the controversies connected with them. I would say myself that the ardour of inventing and proving my method of etherization, though heavy in all conscience, was but a featherweight compared to the wrangling in which I have been torn through my attempts to justify my claim for some reward, and some little honour, in return for my pains.

He went on to accept my resignation with neither demur nor disappointment. My refunding the fare left him saddened that a foreigner should be treating him more honestly than many of his own countrymen.

I have suffered not only in mind and body, but as severely in estate, Morton wrote. *I see nothing but debts where once lay the cheerful prospect of fortune. It is like bleak winter following on spring. I am glad for reasons of economy as well as health to retire to this farm – which, I thank God, I had the prudence to purchase a year or two back when I was going ahead in my practice. Yet there is little respite. I used to think I knew what it was to be busy, but I must confess I really knew nothing about it. I am strained up every moment, and I long for the day when I can sit down quietly and have a little rational enjoyment.*

I saw he had reasonable grounds for such mental exhaustion. It appeared that the United States Army, having earlier refused Morton's offer of etherization at cut rates in the battlefield, now openly spurned the patent and was using ether freely on casualties in Mexico. He continued to be vexed by Jackson, and Wells had returned from Paris with his claims refreshed. Morton had earlier in the year petitioned Congress, travelling to Washington, his baggage crammed with support from the governors and doctors of the Massachusetts General. Congress set up a Select Committee of Investigation – precisely, I reflected, as Westminster would have established a Royal Commission, so that little need be done and less decided. Its only activity, by the time Morton wrote, was issuing a general invitation for all his opponents to stake their claims. Were Congressional Committeemen and Royal Commissioners to gather convivially, how loud and gleeful would ring their mocking laughter!

I fear the public are becoming thoroughly weary of the controversy, Morton continued. *I have now lost heart, because I know that if justice will not prevail in the Congress of the United States, it will prevail nowhere. With this I bracket your Queen's Court of Chancery. Pray tell me without delay how the action proceeds, for I have had no word of it from Mr Poole, nor from visitors arrived from your shores. If the Court recognizes my invention and upholds my patent, no foreign words will ever have struck so well in an American's ears.*

This elicited from me only a sad and sympathetic sigh. He ended,

Dr Warren is agitating that Congress makes me compensation for the benefit conferred on the public by my voluntary relinquishing my patent right – if this is any longer worth a red cent. I read recently that your Dr Edward Jenner of Gloucestershire county, the great benefactor of humanity in the way of vaccination, was awarded by the British Parliament £10,000 in 1802 and a further £20,000 in 1807. Would that the example be followed by the nation which wrested its independence from that same body!

I tossed the closely written letter across my writing table. It was a year all but ten days since I had sailed home from Boston. Its characters, then so colourful, had begun to fade as the tones of a daguerreotype portrait. Morton's troubles were no longer my own. But despite his sharpness, his grasp-ingness, Morton was a true benefactor of mankind. Perhaps a testimonial might be opened in London, to persuade the British to raise a lighter wind than blew upon Jenner? I speculated. As this would need the names of men well-known and well-regarded, I wrote briefly to Robert Liston of the plan. He replied the following week, saying he had some sympathy with my notion, and requesting me to call on Tues-day, December 7, at five o'clock.

Meanwhile, I suffered another cannonade from Lord Aubery.

All that is needed to render any lady or gentleman insensible, I had written in *The People's London Journal,* with modest artistic licence, *is a pocket handkerchief and half an ounce of chloroform. Its sweet odour is so pleasant to the nostrils, and so benign towards the sensitive throat and lungs, that the balmy breeze wafts its victim to the Land of Lethe before he or she becomes aware of anything untoward being done to them.*

Lord Aubery at some City banquet thunderously accused me – I had the honour to share with Dr Snow the spattering of his venom – of prowling the streets and laying girls insen-sible in droves, without so much as introducing myself. Or at

235

least, suggesting the means to others more ill-minded, which was exactly the same thing. 'Hear, hear!' reported the newspapers, proving that his audience were possessed of colourful imaginations, or were drunk, or wanted to keep in with Lord Aubery. Then the Bishop of Greenwich filled his cathedral with the same arguments with which the Scots divines had filled Simpson's drawing-room. Agreement followed from parish pulpits, as predictably and as clamorously as the church bells the following Sunday, while there were always headmasters and retired admirals everywhere to object to anything.

I heard of a petition to be laid before Parliament outlawing chloroform, and doubtless rendering desperadoes like Simpson liable to transportation. I wrote a strong article, which I posted to him, asking him to urge it on *Blackwood's Magazine*. I chose my platform carefully. William Blackwood's journal – *Maga* to its devotees – had then been going in Edinburgh about thirty years, but was famous throughout the whole country for its provision of scandal, satire and personal ridicule. That was in the golden age of such reviews, which formed the opinions of the influential few, before the newspapers and steam-presses arrived to form the opinions of everybody. I knew *Blackwood's* had shown a particular aversion for Leigh Hunt and the 'Cockney School' of poets, as it slightingly called them, but I hoped this had worked from its splenetic system. A defence of chloroform in *Blackwood's* would counter among rational men the vapid blatherings of those who spoke their thoughts as predictably and automatically as clocks chimed.

In reply, Simpson sent his tract newly published by Sutherland and Knox of Edinburgh, *Answer to the Religious Objections Advanced Against the Employment of Anaesthetic Agents in Midwifery and Surgery*, the composition of which he claimed to have agreeably passed a day recovering from influenza. I never heard again of my own article. Doubtless he found it superfluous, or it was forgotten in the everlasting press of Edinburgh maternity. I never, ever, appeared in *Blackwood's*.

On the afternoon of December 7, I set out for Clifford

Street. It was a chilly, gloomy day, gas already yellowing the windows of houses which knew not the word 'extravagance'. The roads were thronged, as always towards the hour of five, when City men rode home, and drays, wagons, carts – almost everything on wheels – were making impatiently for their stabling. I scampered across Piccadilly and made up Old Bond Street. As I turned into Clifford Street, a finger of ice caressed my spine. There was straw spread across the road.

I quickened my pace to No 5. I saw the great black front door open, a man in a great-coat and very tall hat bustling out, briskly entering a waiting carriage to be instantly driven off. I approached as the door was shutting. I saw the knocker muffled in somebody's Berlin glove.

'Here, there —'

The door hesitated, opened again. In the gas-lit entrance-passage stood the young, insolent Irish footman.

'What's the matter?' I asked immediately, adding without much necessity, 'Who's ill?'

''Tis the master himself, sir.' He spoke now in awe, his customary manner shattered, like any jack-in-office exposed to a good fright.

'What's Mr Liston sick with?' I demanded, the footman's face a sign plain enough of its seriousness.

'That was Dr Watson, sir, just been to see the master,' he said in reply, nodding after the disappearing carriage. 'They've been all day – Dr Watson and Dr Williams, Mr Cadge from the hospital. The day before yesterday, Sir Benjamin Brodie himself was here.'

I had heard of Brodie, surgeon to King George IV, King William IV and our present Queen, the man who had recently declared in *The Times*, *Let it never be forgotten that money forms but a part, and a small part, of professional success*, and was well known to make £10,000 a year and never take a holiday. The footman's voice expressed satisfaction at the eminence of the practitioners required by the disease, but I did not care to hear of so many consultations. When many doctors confer, death can slip past them unnoticed. 'Is it something with Mr Liston's chest?' I asked, remembering the coughing fits.

237

'Mr Liston brought up the blood, sir. Last week, when he was seeing patients. He came out to the hall, white as a ghost. "Reilly," he said. "Help me upstairs." Which I did. I took the poor gentleman to his dressing-room, where he fainted. Sudden like, as if you was dowsing a candle. With more blood coming out of him, all over the floor, all over my livery.'

'But is his life in danger?' I said urgently.

'That I can't say, sir. He's having terrible trouble with the breathing. He's been cupped more times than I can count.'

I could hardly believe that a man so vigorous, one to whom God had given the duty of inflicting such pain that he might cure, one who had stood as the sick man's second in innumerable duels against death, could himself be of perishable fibre. I said briefly, 'Please convey to Mrs Liston – to Mr Liston himself, if possible – my sincere wishes for recovery.'

'You'd be Mr Romilly, sir?' At last he had my name.

I nodded. 'I'll call tomorrow, to inquire how he goes.'

'It's bad, sir ... very bad.' He shook his head gloomily, shutting the door.

Fifty years ago, the grave yawned wider. I knew that Robert Liston would soon be dead.

27

ROBERT LISTON'S FUNERAL was on Saturday, December 11, 1847. It was a year, lacking ten days, from his removal of Churchill's leg. Exhausted, nigh bloodless, the surgeon slept the euthanasia at half past ten, the same night as my call. Cadge performed a *post mortem* examination, in the basement on the kitchen table.

A black-edged envelope with a black wax seal had invited my attendance at No 5 Clifford Street by half past ten o'clock that Saturday morning. I dressed in my best, with new black gloves, and black crêpe weepers tied round my hat. The weather was crisp and cloudless, with even the perpetual threat of winter fog fenced off. I walked briskly, thinking the day far too cheerful for its purpose. I could hardly enter Bond Street. The funeral carriages trailed back from Clifford Street, round the corner, confusing the busy Saturday morning traffic, provoking observations from the fashionable shoppers in which asperity was subjugated to delicacy only through the universal awesomeness of death.

Clifford Street itself, a more constricted thoroughfare, was choked with carriages, horses, jostling black-coated gentlemen, and drivers with weepers on their hats, who were agitatedly flicking their whips while trying hard, in deference to the occasion, to repress their customary oaths. Amid them a pair of police constables, stationed specially for the occasion, tried ineffectively to create order by waving their arms with a sensitive solemnity. There were academics in gorgeous robes and mortar-boards or velvet hats, men of my own age whom I took as medical students, and doctors with their countenances extra grave. I surreptitiously pulled my notebook from my tail pocket to jot down an observation or two. It may have been unseemly. Indeed, it struck me as shocking as a 'Knight of the Pencil' performing his essential functions with his betting book in Tattersall's Ring while similarly dressed in mourning. But I was commissioned to describe the obsequies for *The People's London Journal*, and the mind's eye is an unreliable optic. Robert Liston, a practical man, would have unhesitatingly approved.

Prominent in the crowd were many ladies and gentlemen who, from their variegated but often sickly look, or that they hobbled with sticks and crutches, I saw to be patients paying homage to the man who may well have given them a life to survive his own. I recognized Peter Squire and his nephew William, and a face or two which had become familiar over the past year. There must have been 400 persons present. Liston had no need for mutes to pack the ranks of mourners, nor keeners to wail laments. These rang in every heart.

I had the previous morning a message from Dr Snow, who had a place in one of the carriages, and invited me to join him. We had met often during the summer and autumn, when he had honoured me with entry to meetings of his beloved Westminster Medical Society, of which he entertained warm if modestly suppressed hopes of becoming President. I was the only layman present at these assemblies, though the doctors tolerated and even welcomed me, partly through my writings on anaesthesia, and partly through my function as scarlet cloak in the hands of *tauréador* John Snow against the charging bull Aubery.

I found Snow pressed against the spearheaded railings of the house itself. The woollen glove had gone from the knocker, the straw had been piled in the gutter, and through the front door the undertakers moved to and fro, with the purposefulness and professional gravity of the doctors they had superseded. Snow, too, had weepers and black gloves, though his habitually serious view of life spared any deliberate rearrangement of his countenance.

Our carriage was a little to the rear. As we approached it,

there fell an abrupt hush. All hats were doffed. From the front door, the coffin was borne under purple pall on eight shoulders to the hearse, its four horses pawing the cobbles, whinnying and shaking their jet plumes. Behind the coffin came Liston's family, widow submerged in impenetrable crêpe veil, followed by his four daughters in deep black, then his two sons. The youngest boy was only five. I saw him stare bemusedly upon the silent crowd, as though completely unaware of the occasion for which it had gathered, and utterly lost at his own necessity for joining it.

The servants came next in their new mourning. The mantua-makers must have been busy upstairs at No 5 those last three days. They were led by the fat butler, then Reilly the footman, next housekeeper, cook and housemaids, whom I did not recognize. How satisfying, that our social system creates a small world within every household, a microcosm of the large one outside! Within which, those of differing station can mourn their dead with equal pain, and equal unrestraint – and possibly forget them equally quickly. At that most solemn moment, one of the travelling brass bands which insist on delighting the inhabitants of Mayfair on Saturdays struck up loudly, unseen somewhere behind us.

> *Oh, I come from Alabama*
> *With my banjo on my knee;*
> *I depart for Louisiana*
> *My Susannah for to see.*

There were looks of horror exchanged at this popular air, which had just arrived from America, and was homaged by every pair of lips which thought they could whistle, and every instrumentalist who thought he could play. Cries of muted outrage rose towards the hidden and blissfully preoccupied players. I confess the incident warmed and heartened me. Such contrast of gravity and gaiety indicated that mankind is of many parts, and that life goes on eternally – more forcefully and more agreeably than any sermon could.

I climbed into the carriage with Snow. It already contained two middle-aged gentlemen, who were introduced to me as

Dr John Watson and Dr Williams, the practitioners – it occurred to me – to whom we were indebted for the day. I did not feel they were friends of Snow's. As we moved away towards Regent Street, I suspected they were not friends of each other.

'It was a singular case, Liston's,' observed Watson. He was the doctor I had seen hurrying away on the afternoon of Liston's death, a tall spare man with a face as grey as a sliced pork pie.

'Oh, I wouldn't say so,' at once objected Williams, who was short, fat and as pink as a cut penny saveloy. 'When Liston first consulted me . . . that was, before he had the advantage of any consultation whatsoever with yourself . . . I reached the conclusion, there and then, that he was suffering from an aneurism. An aneurism probably of the arch of the aorta. Precisely as Mr Cadge discovered *post mortem*. There was an aneurism the size of an orange,' he recounted with satisfaction. 'Leading from the great aorta by way of a hole the size of a half-crown. Every beat of the heart would have tensed it with blood as hard as a bladder of lard.' He sat back, folding his arms smugly.

'Which is exactly as I diagnosed myself,' returned Watson in a disagreeable voice. 'When I was first called in, the day last July when Liston suffered a haemoptysis of thirty ounces of blood in his dressing-room.'

'*Did* you, my dear sir?' Williams spoke absently, gazing through the carriage window, as we made our way north towards Oxford Street. Our progress was slow, with so many hundreds joining the procession on foot, all walking at a pace appropriate for both the rites and the long distance they had before them.

'*Of course I did!*' declared Watson sharply. 'The pathology was perfectly clear from the patient's history alone. Liston had difficulty in swallowing all year. The last drop drained from a glass always gave him paroxysms, which is absolutely characteristic of the condition – with the head tipped back, the aneurism would abut into the oesophagus. Liston himself hinted it might be an aneurism. He suspected the bleeding

242

had come from its perforating into the trachea. There was no question of my failing to recognize the condition,' he ended bad-temperedly.

Williams turned sharply from the window. 'And what did you discover on examination?'

'Aneurisms of the aorta can be surprisingly lacking in physical signs.'

'Possibly. But *I* found dullness above the left scapula and clavicle, combined with tubular breathing. I *told* Liston he had disease of the chest. At first I suspected phthisis, which his mother and sister died of.'

'I am aware of the history,' snapped Watson.

I exchanged a glance with Snow, who looked through the window and said loudly, 'Do you suppose it's going to rain?'

'Well, sir,' continued the pink Dr Williams warmly, seemingly unaware of our company. 'Mr Liston then passed out of my care into yours. I never saw him again until he was dying.'

'If you are suggesting the outcome could have been any different, sir,' said Watson furiously, as we jolted along Oxford Street. 'That is quite unjustified, perfectly so.'

'The outcome of any fatal case might be different with the proper treatment, sir.'

'I *gave* him the right treatment, sir!'

Williams appeared amazed. 'What, sir? These last four months of his life? He did nothing but take long walks of a morning and ride and hunt.'

'He got relief through strong exercise,' shouted Watson, so loudly I expected the mourners trudging by our carriage-wheels to look up. 'He said that riding a restive horse promoted expectoration. You know his character. He was always trying some feat of activity or strength. All his imprudent acts were done *in spite of my most earnest and reiterated remonstrances.* Which only made him angry,' he ended rather pathetically.

'My friend here,' observed Snow, nodding towards me, 'is a journalist, who reports such matters of public interest to the newspapers.'

This caused the pair to hold their tongues, and to stare at me with matching ferocity.

'I shall write about this to the *Lancet*, sir,' muttered Williams.

'And so shall I, sir,' returned Watson.

Indeed, they did. The correspondence enlivened the issues for December 1847, and may still be read as a reminder that medical manners, like those of society, have grown more squeamish.

The unmannerly disputation ended, the carriage creaked northwards in silence up the Tottenham Court Road. The cortège was swollen by doctors and students from University College Hospital – the North London – as we passed near Gower Street. We crossed the new road from Paddington to Islington and began to leave the metropolis behind us, making for the open country of Parliament Hill and the villages clustered round Hampstead Heath. We were barely half-way, and I could have enjoyed a glass of wine and a biscuit, it being past one o'clock when we ascended Highgate Hill. Whereupon the saveloy-faced Dr Williams drew from one tail pocket a packet of bread, sliced beef and cheese, and from the other a flask of brandy, which he proceeded to enjoy with no indication that he was travelling other than alone.

The funeral was in Highgate Parish Church. Snow and I squeezed in, but many who had toiled from London were left outside. I noticed some of the students move off in search of the nearest ale-house. The clergyman spoke of Liston predictably and at predictable length. Funeral orations are tasteless dumplings, all suet without the salt and pepper. (My own funeral, in which I may claim a fairly immediate interest, shall have instead one minute's silence, in which my few mourners will be at liberty to think whatever they like of me.) Had I been given the freedom of the Highgate pulpit, I should have said in a few breaths that Liston was a man of bad temper, no sense of punctilio, a coarse tongue, and a talent for quarrelling with everybody. A man infinitely gentle with his patients. A man who always left his amazing surgical skill untried, if a cure could be effected by means other than an operation. And that his cases were generally those whom other surgeons shrank from. His epitaph was simply that he cured the incurable.

Outside again, I was amazed to see the crowd had increased tenfold. They were Liston's patients among the poor, come from London after half a day's work. All ended in a rather perfunctory way. The coffin was borne into the adjoining cemetery, and laid to eternal rest in one of the arches of the terrace catacomb, on the top shelf. The sun's eye was blazing redly in the west, and the crowd stood silently until it was extinguished – as inevitably as shall be extinguished all those it shone upon.

It grew dark, it grew colder, and at last and inescapably, foggy. The procession returned to London disorganized, un-led, weary and disjunctive, like a beaten army. The mourners became a pack of individuals concerned more with the stiff-ness of their legs and the void in their bellies than the Life Hereafter. Our quarrelsome doctors Williams and Watson sat mostly in silence until the area of Gower Street, where we were glad to shed both. Snow suggested that, neither of us having been invited to the funeral breakfast, I should pay him the honour of dining at his home in Frith Street. It was an honour I firmly declined. I said instead he should dine at my expense in a chop house, where he might consume his vege-tables while watching me quieten the howling dogs of hunger with red meat and a pint of claret.

I directed our carriage to the Cheshire Cheese in Fleet Street. Snow and I shared a box next a roaring fire of sea-coal, while I ordered fowl with veal stuffing and egg sauce, and some Bordeaux. Snow took a boiled onion and stewed carrots with pease-pudding, to be rinsed down with seidlitz water, to the waiter's dismay rather than disgust.

Over this lopsided feast, Snow told me something of him-self. Though I had enjoyed his company during the year, his natural reticence had left him much of a stranger to me. 'My father was no enemy of the bottle,' he confessed unexpectedly, sipping the seidlitz water, into which I would not myself deign to dip my toothbrush. 'He was a farmer at York, where I was born and spent fourteen years of my life before my apprenticeship to Mr Hardcastle. That brought me some hard days, rough rides and enough acquaintanceship with moonlight. But it was a good gleaning of experience.'

'But surely, you enjoyed some youthful diversions?' I asked, thinking of my own *penchant* for the mouth of girl or bottle.

'Oh, yes. I was busy founding temperance societies in Yorkshire,' he answered seriously.

Snow had come to London ten years before, to place himself on the famous benches of the medical school founded by William Hunter in Windmill Street, off Piccadilly. He had walked the Westminster, and come near top in the London University MD. This information he could bare squeeze out, in his modesty. 'I'm busy enough, with my ether practice, the cholera and my studies of the morbid growth of cancer – which I think is local, from some perversion of nutrition,' he reflected. 'Perhaps I even overload my capacity, like a bad farmer his horses.'

'But your ether practice alone must afford you a comfortable living?'

'I don't sow a crop of gold,' he replied quietly. 'I prefer the harvest of work well done. I am a practitioner, not a philosopher. I try hard to develop my tact in diagnosis, and my recollection of past cases, which assists judgement of the one in hand and foreshadows its results. I have written a book,' he added abruptly.

For one moment I imagined he had penned some fictional work, like *Dealings with the Firm of Dombey and Son*, with which Charles John Huffam Dickens was then delighting his public, by instalments. But it was *On the Inhalation of the Vapour of Ether in Surgical Operations*, just published. He asked if he might present a copy to me, with a tortured expression from being crushed under the weight of his own diffidence. (The autographed work, in the bookcase at my elbow, shall be preserved from the second-hand dealers a few years yet by my doctor-daughter Eleanor.)

I said, perhaps ungraciously, 'But surely chloroform, not ether, is now all the thing?'

He was silent for a moment, dissecting his onion. 'Fatalities have occurred under chloroform.'

This news was a surprise. 'But they occurred under ether. You told me so yourself, the day I walked those dreadful alleys behind Soho Square. It hasn't diminished one whit the public's thirst for ether. The risk seems reasonable, when you consider the terrible alternative.'

'Oh, I agree. I use phosphorous matches instead of a tinder-box. An occasional risk never stands in the way of the ease-ment of life. But there is something peculiar about these chloroform deaths. A girl of fifteen, quite healthy, died after it last week. She was one Hannah Greener, of Winlaton up in County Durham. She had an ingrowing nail to be removed from her great toe by Mr Lloyd, an excellent and careful man, I know from my days in the district. The chloroform was given on a handkerchief, as you described it done in Edinburgh. The girl was frightened and fretting, sitting in a chair ... then suddenly she became blanched, and spluttered, as though in epilepsy. They dashed cold water in her face and gave brandy, but not the slightest attempt at a rally was made. They opened the jugular, and no blood flowed. It was all in two minutes.'

'But surely there was some ... some sensitivity in the patient, for so sudden a disaster?' I suggested.

'That is what the coroner was told by Sir John Fife, who performed the *post-mortem* examination.'

'He would be a reliable witness, I take it?'

'Oh, yes. He is well respected in the north. He founded the School of Medicine at Newcastle, and he was Mayor of the town.' Snow moistened his lips with his seidlitz water. 'Though he won his knighthood not through professional skill. It was for suppressing a Chartist outbreak in 1839.'

I grunted.

'He found brain and lungs congested, the blood dark, the air-passages filled with sanguineous froth, the left portion of the heart empty, the stomach distended. But there was no indication of any cause for such great disturbance.'

'And the verdict?'

247

'Death from the inhalation of chloroform.'

'Chloroform would need more than one gravestone round its neck to drown it.'

'It has already more than one,' Snow returned evenly. 'Another death has occurred within the past few days in Paris, of which I have the scantiest news as yet. But it followed the same pattern. A healthy young person, suddenly seized under the lightest influence of chloroform. It would seem that chloroformization is the exhibition of a very subtle poison indeed.'

'But you will continue to administer it?' I asked, having possessive feelings over the agent.

'Yes, but dancing on needle-points. It has greater strength and more convenience than ether, but more care is demanded in its use.' He munched a boiled carrot in silence. 'Your Edinburgh friends do not take care enough with their handkerchiefs and teaspoons. Why, they even give chloroform on a worsted glove, on a *nightcap* – slovenly and not very cleanly,' he added, with such disgust that an onion he was attacking flew off his plate.

'You don't *enjoy* those victuals, surely?' I exclaimed. As Snow looked pained, I quoted, 'According to the good Dr Johnson, who dined often enough in this very tavern, *He who does not mind his belly will hardly mind anything else.*'

'With the result that not only the doctor's opinions were weighty,' Snow returned somewhat sourly.

'Come!' I urged more humorously than hopefully, raising my glass. 'Will you take wine with me?'

He shook his head. 'If I advocate the principles of the total abstinence reformers, Romilly, it is because I believe the practice of abstinence will become universal, with the improvement of education and sanitation.'

I laughed. 'My dear fellow, I can tell you from my sojourn in the Rules of the Bench – as a visitor to the land, I hasten to assure you – that men are more interested in drink than in drains. And as for education, it releases their fingers from use in counting, but only the better to hold a tankard.'

Snow laughed too, and I ordered more claret for myself. It was a merry enough end for a melancholy day.

Just before Christmas I saw reported as a brief item in the *Lancet* the news that Liston's five-year-old son had, on December 17, at Duddingstone House in Edinburgh, followed his father to God. When I had seen the poor mite at the funeral, he had but ten days more on this earth to enjoy. I assumed that the boy was debilitated by the long journey north, and carried off by the scarlet fever, or the enteric fever, or the Boulogne sore throat (which nowadays enjoys the medical name of 'diphtheria'), which strike with such tragic rapidity at our little ones.

That was the day I had occasion to walk past Liston's house, the wind of a gusty afternoon blowing round my ankles a mouldy wisp or two of the straw laid during his last illness. These few dirty, broken, mildew stalks affected me. They were spread in hope, while life still ran in his veins. They seemed to express the futility of God's puny creatures, battling against the perils of the world which He had created for them.

Liston left only £5,000, a cause of much teeth-sucking and head-shaking throughout London. It appeared that every year he made and spent a fortune, which struck me as an admirable balance of the economy. His family went north, his effects sold. His house was bought by another doctor, and stands much the same today. Lord Palmerston verified his esteem for Liston's wine, by paying 3 guineas a bottle for it. His library was sold, 2,000 volumes, mostly on surgery. I heard later from Snow that *Scarpa on Aneurisms*, Lot No 262, was well-thumbed. So Liston knew of his fatal complaint all along. Even at the moment he amputated Frederick Churchill's leg.

There was the suggestion that Syme be invited from Edinburgh to fill Liston's post. *The offer is an insult to the surgeons of London*, declared the *Lancet*, speaking for Liston from the grave.

28

LISTON'S DEATH MARKED a bleak turn in my own fortunes. Chloroform followed ether into public tedium, but at ten times the speed. The readers of magazines seemed interested only in the new British Museum. I had finished *The Water Gate*, and to my astonishment found that no publisher in Paternoster Row cared to print it. My money was running low. I was obliged to give my landlady in Cadogan Place a month's warning. Suddenly, I saw it would be back to the Borough, and with no Floy to warm my body or my spirits.

The first day of 1848 was a Saturday, bitterly cold, with skaters in the Park and everyone saying the Thames was going to freeze over again. If my credit were negligible, my standing as a literary person was still high enough for a genteel invitation or two, and that evening I was committed to a *conversazione* in Cheyne Row, Chelsea. My hostess was Mrs Elphinstone, a pursuer of literary persons, with all the wildness of the unlettered rich. I heard that the Carlyles were likely to be present. Though in my circumstances, I was more concerned that the edible, rather than the intellectual, fare should be substantial.

I arrived at seven, and leaving hat and great-coat with a footman in lace-bedaubed coat, gold-gartered plush breeches and white silk stockings, I mounted to a large, pleasant drawing-room with greenish-yellow decorations, this colour being considered the latest thing – or *about to become* the latest thing, which was more important to Mrs Elphinstone.

Shakespeare himself could not have been received more cordially.

'Mr Romilly! I really must scold you. You have never yet stepped into my house, not once!'

That I had not been afforded the encouragement of an invitation did not seem to signify. 'Your acquaintance is so wide, ma'am, among those celebrated in literature and the arts, that I would fain offer my own small talent as the price of entry to so magnificent an exhibition.'

She received this well. So well, I fancied she was about to hug me to her warm, heaving, bright pink, large, downy, gem-encrusted bosom.

'But, Mr Romilly, you have rendered yourself *quite* conspicuous, with your accounts in all the papers of these wondrous new methods of suffocation.'

'Stupefaction, I think, ma'am,' I murmured gently.

'It is all the same, surely?' she returned lightly. 'Tell me, may we really have removed our arms and legs, and any bits of us we no longer see the use for, without so much as feeling a scratch?'

'That is true, ma'am. But I am sure there is nothing, in so discerning a patron of the arts as yourself, which even the most scrutinizing of surgeons could find in the slightest superfluous.' Save your brains, I added to myself.

'Mr Romilly, I *do* believe you are trying to flatter me.' She was quite squeaking, like a mouse at the cheese. 'You *are* a naughty man!'

There were other literary gentlemen dammed up behind me. I was passed on to Mr Elphinstone, who was bald, five foot tall and miserable. I said, 'Mrs Elphinstone outshines London with her prides of literary lions, sir. It must be pleasant to live in groves of intellectual culture quite matching those of the giraffes and chimpanzees in Sir Stamford Raffles's Zoological Society gardens.'

To which he replied, 'Good evening,' managing to express in two words more disagreeableness than the outpourings of any Billingsgate fishwoman. I moved away, suspecting that his lady's enthusiasm for my work was occasioned by my being far younger and somewhat better looking than her husband, and indeed than the other pens I saw moving round me. As I recognized no one, I assumed they were all of broader intellectual nib than myself.

The room was already uncomfortably full. My heart sank as I saw a piano, open and primed, fully loaded with sheets of music. I remembered that Mrs Elphinstone was known invariably to sing ballads later in the evening, perhaps to demonstrate the world of art is indivisible. Through open double doors at the far side of the room I spotted tables covered with white cloths, laden with raised pies, hams, joints of blushing beef, a boar's head, silver dishes of lobsters, bowls of punch and bulbous-topped bottles promising a *flûte* or so of champagne. I warmed to see that Mrs Elphinstone's opinions on nourishment were a refreshing improvement on most *conversazione*-givers', with their muddy ices and cup of unsophisticated, washy bohea. It was only unfortunate that she had to sing for my supper.

I found myself standing beside a short young man with bushy black whiskers, gazing in the same direction and with the same interest and connoisseurship. He was wearing a green velvet jacket, a loose cravat with a turned-down collar like the youth of Boston, and conspicuous in the company by unashamedly puffing a large Havannah. 'The grub and bub's good, that's something,' he observed, without introduction.

I was surprised at this low expression from the mouth of a gentleman. He produced a leather cigar case, but I declined politely, explaining I had always abjured the clay, and preferred not being seduced by the pernicious weed in more elegant attire. In truth, I did not admire his brazenness in smoking in a lady's drawing-room before supper. Though perhaps Mrs Elphinstone encouraged such laxity, in the cause of her artistic reputation.

'What do you do?' asked my companion, pleasantly enough.

'I am an author.' I added, fearing I might well be in the company of some smart young man from *Punch*, 'In a small way.'

'Mrs Elphinstone has a powerful fondness for authors. Were an author famous enough, she would be happy to receive him in his coffin, on his way to the cemetery.'

As I gazed among the dowagers and dandies, the misseys and muggins, searching my mind for the identity of this forthright stranger, he asked amiably, 'What d'you make of the company? For myself, I suspect all the men wear gibus hats, and therefore deserve no respect.'

I replied guardedly, 'There would seem a variety. One may converse *selon les goûts*.'

'The women don't go out much in society. You can see that from the draw-creases on their best frocks.'

'They are hardly blue-stockings, either.'

'You like your ladies learned?'

'Unlike Euripides, I do, sir,' I flattered myself in reply.

'I've no objection to stupid women, if they're sufficiently beautiful. To be beautiful is surely in itself severe enough demand of any female? You wouldn't expect a rose to crack witticisms, or a lily to dance the polka.'

I felt it best at this point to suggest diffidently, 'You are an author of distinction, sir, doubtless?'

'Oh, no. I couldn't compose a washing-bill. I'm a painter. As our Junoesque hostess has recently paid handsomely for my performing her portrait, I thought it only courteous to accept her invitation. Besides, I have high hopes of her husband to follow.'

He seemed an easygoing enough fellow. I always expected Knights of the Brush to be arrogant, humourless and explosive.

'I have perhaps had the pleasure of viewing your work?'

'My name is John Maddox.'

This matched one in my memory. I was fumbling for the link when we were interrupted by a noise – half-scream and half-croak – from the direction of the chimney-mirror. The room instantly fell silent, staring. Standing with her back to the fire, with a profusion of jetty ringlets, shoulders bare, in a crimson shot-silk gown with a cameo the size of a muffin, was Floy. Or, it wasn't Floy. It was the lady in the picture in the Royal Academy Exhibition. It was both. It was neither. I was confused.

'Guy—!' Hand and lace handkerchief were at her mouth, her face with every appearance of recent strangulation.

I turned towards my hostess, who was frozen to her very fan. Her husband had his eyebrows working like steam-hammers, looking more disagreeable than ever.

'Forgive me, ma'am . . . ' I stammered, aware of resembling a beetroot newly boiled. 'An acquaintance of childhood . . .'

But Floy was past paying regard for social irregularities. She pushed through the crowd, hands outstretched. 'Guy! Well! Just fancy! I never did!'

Maddox laughed. 'Not Mr Guy Romilly? I've heard a deal about you from Miss Leonora.' As I looked even more confused, he nodded towards Floy, who had seized both my hands. 'Miss Leonora Lopez is my model.'

So the frail barque which I abandoned had been taken safely in tow! I, too, smiled – if largely in relief. The room, remembering its manners, tried resuming its conversation while keeping its eye on the three of us. 'You should never have asked that chloroform fellow,' I heard from Mr Elphinstone, and 'Be quiet, Henry!' returned in reply.

'But I'm still *Floy*,' she said warmly, not letting go.

'The adoption of a *nom de guerre* is not unusual in the profession,' explained Maddox, who seemed increasingly amused by the melodrama, or pantomine. 'After all, the label "Geneva" appears on much honest spirit distilled in Shoreditch.'

'But why Lopez?' I demanded, still fuddled.

'It is customary in a model's occupation to suggest greater familiarity with the Mediterranean Sea than Marshalsea.'

With that disquieting, but familiar, swing of feminine passions across a whole sixteen points of the compass, Floy put her lace handkerchief to her eyes and burst into tears.

I managed to speak, but the words came through my lips like thick linen from the mangle. In truth, I wished I were chloroformed, to wake up in China. Though I was delighted enough that Maddox had played the Good Samaritan. Or was it the Don Juan? I could not imagine Floy as but his manikin, to be folded up and stowed away after the day's use. I reflected that she would seem to have abandoned her reticence to divest herself of clothes in male view.

'Oh, Guy!' She began to recover a little composure. 'What

happened to you, my love? I saw you'd come back from America. I read something what you'd written in the papers. Leastaways, Mr Maddox did.' Her speech had become smoothed, like a fiery peasant wine beginning to mature in bottle.

'I've had various adventures.' Though eager to ask the same of her, I felt it best to leave obscure her transformation from the woman I had seen so often at icy dawn, red nosed in shift and curl-papers. 'I am making my way as a journalist,' I told her. 'And I have written a novel.'

'How clever you are, Guy! You always was, when you was describing all them hangings.'

'What's the novel called?' asked Maddox, lighting another cigar.

'*The Water Gate*,' I told him. 'I have written it, but unhappily no publisher has published it.'

'Oh, publishers! Mere frame-makers,' Maddox said with amiable contempt.

'Well, they do nothing but quote Cervantes at me, *He that publishes a book runs a very great hazard*. They complain I come with no recommendation.'

He puffed away, nodding his sympathy. 'I've a friend – senior in years to myself – with some influence among the gentlemen of Paternoster Row. If you'd care to send your man round with your work, I could pass it on. My friend's word might be of help.'

'I should be eternally grateful for any help whatever in this matter, sir,' I said, my words heartfelt.

He handed me his card. 'After all,' he smiled. 'You have yourself already done *me* one inestimable service.'

A gentleman with a very high collar and whiskers like trailing ivy sat himself at the piano, and Mrs Elphinstone remorselessly started to sing.

29

THOUGH THE NEXT morning was a Sunday, I brought round my manuscript to the painter's house in Glebe Place, near Mrs Elphinstone's. I pushed it at his manservant, hurrying away lest Maddox discover that I did not run to one of my own. Though it was the hour when the world readies itself, or pretties itself, to go to church, I sensed from the drawn blinds and stillness the painter to be still abed. Whether he were enjoying his sabbatical rest in company with Floy, I did not feel it my business to speculate.

A week later, Maddox sent a scribbled card to say that his literary friend was abroad for a while, in Switzerland or Italy, or somewhere. But my precious bundle should be safely delivered into his hands, once he stepped again on our shores. Two more weeks went. I could but rein my soul with patience. My money was growing alarmingly low. I trusted that Maddox's influential acquaintance – I supposed a critic on *The Spectator*, *The Athenaeum* or the like – was one quickly exhausted by foreign travel.

On the morning of Monday, January 24, Dr John Snow called. I had not seen him since the turn of the year, and welcomed him cordially. He entered with his brisk step, his face a mask of deadly earnestness as usual, sitting unbidden at once in the fireside chair with his hands folded. I asked how things went with him.

'Unconscionably busy,' was all he replied.

'I wish I could claim likewise. Next week, I fear you shall have to seek me at some much humbler address.'

He looked startled. 'Are the Muses such hard taskmasters?'

'Devilishly. They pay good wages, then turn you out of doors without a character.'

'I wish you had told me of this before, Romilly.'

'Money is a subject of no interest between friends. Unless one is desirous to borrow and the other has been persuaded to lend.'

But already Snow's hand was in his pocket, from which he produced a fistful of sovereigns, to drop casually on my writing-table. 'That's all I have about me,' he said, with a note of apology. 'Some fees paid today. If you tell me what your needs are, I can let you have more by and by.'

It was a gesture so spontaneous, so characteristic, so open-hearted, yet performed without emotion, nor – as more common in our world – the affectation of it. I protested, but Snow insisted. 'It is a loan, and in the City men are lending and borrowing as a matter of course, circulating money as the systole and diastole of the heart circulates the blood.'

'You can find many better debtors than a struggling author,' I assured him, though the sight of sovereigns glittering on my tablecloth did not inspire me to battle hard against my conscience.

'Frugality is a valuable habit,' he said. 'It affords a man who has modest means great independence in their disposal. An independence often beyond a man of wealth, with numerous appetites to satisfy.' He folded his square-nailed fingers upon his grey waistcoat, as with much gratitude and some shame I piled the money into a wash-leather bag. There must have been 20 *l.*, and a shilling. 'Now to my business, Romilly. You know there is much cholera about, particularly in the area of Soho?'

'So I read in the newspapers.' I locked the bag away in my corner cupboard. 'They say it's unusual for the time of year. Is it because last summer we were spared the infliction?'

'It is *bad*. Very bad. Worse than summer.'

I looked surprised. 'I've heard things in alehouses, across at Fleet Street. But you know how the common folk exaggerate misfortune. To hear them talk, you'd think there wasn't an Irishman left alive, or a single potato in Irish soil.'

'Listen to me – you know Broad Street, by Golden Square, not far from my own house? Within a radius of two hundred and fifty yards from the point where it joins Cambridge Street, the past ten days have seen no less than *five hundred* fatal attacks of cholera. I have inspected the Bill of Mortality, this very morning, in the vestry of St James's Church.'

As I gave a startled exclamation, he continued with unusual animation, 'There's more dead than that, I'm sure. It's impossible to keep a proper tally of those contorted shapes – once human beings, the image of God – which are dragged from their hovels into carts, and tipped from the carts into limepits, as though they were dead cattle, or sacks of rotten mangolds. Anyway, the parish clerk is too frightened for his own skin to pry too closely among the afflicted poor.'

'But why is all this not in the newspapers?' I demanded, bemused.

'Because it would spread throughout London the panic now affecting the vestrymen of St James's, who sit wringing their hands and utterly unable to raise a defence against death's armies. After last summer, people were beginning to say that cholera was a spectre in the past, that it had burnt itself out ... you know how easily the human mind forgets, particularly all that is painful or dangerous. Now citizens are fleeing their homes in Soho, leaving behind all they value most, not caring in their haste whether villains break the doors to steal and destroy. Should this be blazoned in the newspapers, such panic will race through the streets of London as unseen since the Great Plague.'

'But the Press is the watchdog of the nation,' I protested indignantly. (I was still in my state of greenhornism, I fear.)

'Watchdogs may be chloroformed. And the plight of those who lie waiting for their bark is worse than keeping no dog at all. I hear from ... a patient, that your noble friend has a hand in repressing the news. Though I do not care to impute malevolence if I cannot see it proved.'

I told him I was sure Lord Aubery was capable of more vile acts than anyone could think up in a month of Sundays, as Captain Marryat would have put it.

'Any man in Soho may say his prayers in the morning, and be receiving those of his friends at night,' Snow said sombrely. He leant forward, hands on knees. 'Yet I know the very source of the pestilence.'

'Then it had better soon be staunched,' I said warmly.

'That is why I sought you today. Attend me again – in Soho many of the pumps are frozen. Others have been working ill for months. I know, because I make it my private business to inspect them regularly. There is one pump which everyone in the district turns to. That is in Broad Street, between a bakery and a pie shop. The warmth from the ovens keeps the flow going through the severest winter. The water is foul, because it comes within the seepage of cracked sewers. That pump is our murderer.'

'You wish me to write —'

'By the time it is printed, another five hundred will be dead. The vestrymen are this morning meeting at St James's. They generally finish at noon —' He pulled out his watch. 'Fifteen minutes from now. If we make at once for the nearest coach-stand, we can thrust ourselves into their meeting. We shall try forcing these timorous gentlemen to give the Broad Street pump "quarantine for thirty days", exactly as a vessel arriving in the Thames from Naples or some other plague-ridden place. Will you accompany me?'

I was already out of my dressing-gown and into my tail-coat. It needed neither his generosity, nor the malignity of Lord Aubery, to recommend as capital sport the bearding of benighted vestrymen. But my landlady knocked again, to say another gentleman was downstairs and eager to see me.

I glanced impatiently at the card. *Dr William Scott*. It meant nothing, and I knew the names of all important medical men in London. 'I can't see him now. I'm out on pressing business with Dr Snow.'

'He has come from Dumfries, sir,' she said, as an objection.

'He must wait. I'll be back by and by.'

'He is on the point of going back to Dumfries, sir.'

I gave Snow a glance, imploring tolerance for Dumfries. 'He may have precisely one minute.'

The person from Dumfries was small, stout, red-faced and fiery. 'Mr Romilly, sir?' He strode in, still in great-coat, hat in hand. I bowed, not troubling to introduce Snow. 'You have done me a grave wrong, sir.' He had a Scots accent, as rough as a raw turnip. 'You have done a great wrong to the Dumfries and Galloway Royal Infirmary.'

I was making for the door. 'Then I apologize.'

'Look at this!' My visitor waved a dog-eared copy of *The People's London Journal*. 'You state, sir, categorically, that the first operation to be performed under the influence of ether in Great Britain – in Europe, even – was performed by the late Mr Robert Liston, at the North London Hospital, on the afternoon of December 21, 1846. Which is an insult, sir! *I* was the first to operate under ether. In Dumfries.'

'Your memory may be at fault, sir.'

'You mean I lie, sir?'

'No, sir. I imply simply that the truth is too evasive a bird to be netted at a distance.'

'I exhibited ether on December 19, 1846. At the Dumfries and Galloway Royal Infirmary. With the assistance of Dr McLauchlan, the most upright of gentlemen, who will corroborate my word.'

Desperate to pack this bundle of indignation on its way back to Dumfries, I said calmly, 'If I may match your memory with mine, sir, I arrived from Boston with the news of etherization on December 16. I passed this on to Mr Liston the following evening, and even had it become general knowledge among the medical profession before he operated – which it did not – it could not possibly have reached in a single day that remote part of the country you inhabit.'

'You have forgotten Dr Fraser.'

I paused. Indeed, I had. The surgeon aboard the steam-packet *Acadia*.

'The same, sir,' continued my tormentor, 'brought the great news post-haste from Liverpool, as news of the men of Moidart was brought when Prince Charles landed in '45.'

'Come —' Snow was at my side, watch in hand. 'Delay means lives.'

'I demand a retraction and an apology, sir!' The Scot even shook his fist.

I was already down the stairs, Snow on my heels.

'Dumfries was first!' roared my visitor, tumbling after us.

We were through the front door, running towards Sloane Street and Hans Town.

'Damned Sassenachs!' came after us through the frosty air.

'Was there a shilling among those sovereigns?' inquired Snow, puffing.

'Yes. I put it in my pocket.'

'Might I have it back? I have nothing else about me at all, and I insist that I see to the coachman.'

30

'DO YOU SUPPOSE that bad-tempered gentleman's claim was justified?' I asked Snow, somewhat breathlessly, as the coach jogged uncomfortably under his urgent command towards Hyde Park and Piccadilly. 'I remember now, I spoke often enough to Dr Fraser about etherization. Topics of conversation do not flower at sea more luxuriantly than anything else does. Yet how could Fraser have reached Dumfries, on the West Coast of Scotland, in the time? There was no railway from Liverpool, and the boat would take too long. I suppose he could have managed by coach, if he had post-horses waiting and was unenthusiastic over food and sleep.'

'What matters who was first? Your quarrelsome Dr Scott may write to the *Lancet*, if he feels so sorely robbed.'

(As he did, many years after our encounter, on October 19, 1872.)

'I would not care to rob Liston's grave of his honour,' I said.

'I fancy those whose screams have been stilled by the process care little whether one Scotsman used ether two days before the other. Anyway, it was invented by neither your Dr Morton, nor your Dr Wells, to tell the truth.'

I stared in response to this wild statement, so soberly uttered. 'I have heard of no predecessors, outside the Kingdom of Oberon.'

'You have no knowledge of Dr Henry Hill Hickman? A practitioner of Shifnal village in Shropshire? Which was the birthplace of Thomas Beddoes, founder of the Pneumatic Institution at Clifton.' I shook my head. 'Dr Hickman read his Humphry Davy, and his Priestley, and his Faraday. He knew how men shuddered at the idea of an operation, and when performing his own duties as a surgeon lamented that nothing had been thought of whereby those fears might be tranquillized. He made experiments, seven in all, with carbonic acid gas, using dogs, puppies, rabbits and kittens, of which he cut off the ears, tails and legs, quite painlessly. He wrote a pamphlet on this "suspended animation", with a view to ascertaining its probable utility in surgical operations on the human subject. I came across it while I was searching out facts about asphyxia, at the Westminster Medical. It was published at Ironbridge, in Shropshire, in 1824. When your Dr Morton was but a child of five.'

'But why should the world not have heard of him?' I asked sharply.

'No one in England was interested. Nor was Charles X of France, to whom Dr Hickman addressed an appeal, His Majesty being famous for his encouragement of natural science. I have read a copy of this letter, and I do not see how it could fail to stir the heart of any man. But it did not. Napoleon's surgeon, Baron Larrey, had some faint interest, but that was all. Well, Hickman's been dead now these past twenty years,' Snow ended. 'Dead of indifference. Though to tell the truth, the carbonic acid gas he used was too poisonous by far. It was not anaesthesia but asphyxia, which kills both pain and patient.'

'This news would hardly come gladly to Dr Morton, in his fight at Washington,' I said. 'He is already beset with more pretenders to his throne than any of our own imported monarchs.'

'Dr Morton does not deserve to be disturbed by it. In matters of invention, the credit belongs not to the man to whom the idea first comes. It belongs to the man who convinces the world that it works. The second is immoderately more difficult than the first.'

Snow impatiently pulled out his watch. Simultaneously, our coach pulled up with a jerk which all but threw us to the floor. A dray had overturned in Piccadilly, spilling barrels across the cobbles, and a carriage had run into them, snapping a shaft. Its horse was on the ground, neighing and snorting, perhaps with a broken leg. A knot of people had as usual quickly gathered, staring hard but making no contribution to the situation beyond shouting that someone should send for a policeman, who as customary when his services are urgently required was not to be seen. The drayman and the coachman, as their ilk, did nothing but curse heartily and flourish their whips, as though these were magic wands which could restore the *status quo ante* in a twinkling.

'Come on,' urged Snow. 'We have no time left for the troubles of others.'

We jumped down. Insisting, I hastily paid off the coachman. We hurried eastwards along Piccadilly to the fine brick building of St James's Church, which lay almost in the shadow of Aubery House. But as we made across the churchyard vestrymen came hurrying down the steps, their meeting over. Snow stopped one tall, spare man in black, with papers under his arm, whom I took to be the parish clerk.

'You must reconvene the meeting, Mr Lenton,' Snow ordered brusquely.

'But my dear doctor, that is quite impossible. The vestrymen have already dispersed, like bees from their hive. Our deliberations have been long, and they must get home for their dinners.'

'I have the way to check the cholera behind Golden Square.'

'That is indeed fine news. But however welcome your plan, Dr Snow, it must wait until the next meeting, today week.'

'You must call an extraordinary meeting of the vestry. Tomorrow – this afternoon, if possible.'

'*Quite* impossible, Dr Snow,' Lenton told him firmly. 'Our vestrymen have business among the temples of commerce also, you know.'

'But it *cannot* wait!' The phlegmatic Snow seemed in danger of emulating Jack-in-a-box. 'The Broad Street pump – you must proscribe it. It is nothing but a source of poison.'

'But what may *I* do, Dr Snow,' the clerk protested helplessly. 'Nothing at all. I am but the servant of the vestrymen.'

'If I told you that pump were running hemlock, you'd act, would you not? This water is worse than hemlock, which kills but the man who drinks it. One glassful of its water can kill a dozen men – a score of men, and women and children, too. By way of the flux which pours from the poor sufferers' bodies. *Rice-water stools*, Mr Lenton. Thin cloudy excrement, like the water you boil your rice for puddings in.' Lenton blanched at this comparison. 'Well?' demanded Snow, blocking the clerk's way, foot firmly on lowest step, his breath coming in quick, thick clouds.

'I don't doubt your views, Dr Snow, on matters pertaining to the public health. The vestry is well aware ... the vestry did discuss this very morning ... this unfortunate outbreak. But there are other ways of looking at the epidemic, doubtless? I must say, with great respect, that other medical gentlemen have informed the vestry that the water is blameless —'

'Fiddlestick's end! What medical gentlemen?'

The clerk looked as shifty as a gipsy.

'Pray spare yourself the pain of refusing me their names,' Snow told him. 'I know there are doctors enough in London who refute my views. And I know that Lord Aubery would have little trouble pressing them into his employment.'

'Lord Aubery is an esteemed benefactor of this church,' returned the clerk, becoming angry. 'It is anyway universal knowledge that cholera is caused by emanations arising from foul-smelling gases. Like the smallpox, or the scarlet fever. You have bees in the brains about the water, Dr Snow,' he ended rudely.

'Great Heaven! You might as well expect the evolution of such gases should plant a plain with oaks, or a garden with crocuses.' Snow's anger was near matching the clerk's. 'The smallpox may occur over a cesspool, as an oak may spring up through a manure heap. But pray attend to a matter of simple logic. The smallpox would never appear over the cesspool in the absence of its *specific poison*. Nor the oak arise from the manure heap in the absence of the acorn which seeded it. *Surely* you see that, sir?'

265

'I am uninstructed in science,' returned the clerk shortly.

'It isn't science. It's common sense.'

'Sir!' complained the clerk.

'Will you ban use of the Broad Street Pump, or no?'

'Such an action would be *ultra vires*. Your views must sway not just myself, sir. They must sway the whole vestry. Pray return today week and place them before us.' He tipped his hat. 'Good day to you, Dr Snow.'

For a moment, the pair of us stood in silence. Snow's eyes were blazing below the brim of his tall hat. He slapped his black-gloved hands together. 'Come along, Romilly. Look sharp. We've a job to do.'

'What sort of job?'

'Larceny.'

We were off across the churchyard, through the traffic of Piccadilly without seeking a proper crossing, hurrying northwards in the direction of Soho. Snow said nothing. He simply wore an expression more determined than ever – though in truth, I had little chance to savour it, he strode so fast ahead of me. At the corner of Golden Square he darted into an ironmongers and saddlers, and throwing his remaining shilling on the counter demanded a hammer.

I know not what passers-by made of a gentleman, respectably dressed, racing through the streets with this instrument in his hand. Had I not known of Snow's ingrown sobriety, I should have suspected him at the spirits. Two old women and a ragged girl were at the Broad Street pump with their buckets, in the usual company of a stray dog and a cat. Snow thrust aside one of these Rachels, and with a blow or two of the hammer snapped the bolt – which was rusted – attaching the pump-handle. Hammer in one hand, this article in the other, he made off apace towards Frith Street.

The onlookers were at first speechless at such behaviour by a well-dressed party. But soon affront and outrage gave tongue. We found ourselves pursued by the girl, hollering that we had stolen their pump-handle, and inciting the many out-of-door fellows hanging about the back streets to retrieve it. As customary in moments of public excitement, most of those had no notion of its cause, or had the wrong one. The cries of 'Stop thief!' which assaulted our ears set a pack on our heels. Snow began to puff and turn scarlet. A lifetime of vegetarianism and total abstinence was, in the crisis, insufficient to sustain him.

'This way!' I tugged his sleeve at the corner.

'But my house —' He pointed in the opposite direction with the pump-handle.

'Do you want your windows broken?'

I hurried him towards St Anne's Court, opposite which I had spied a hackney-carriage delivering a gentleman to his front door. I shouted my address to the coachman, who set off at a good trot. Snow sat in silence, recovering his breath, looking hugely pleased with himself, clutching his trophy in both hands. 'I am a "practitioner", you see, Romilly,' he managed to say at last. 'I like to bring a practical approach to the problems of my profession.'

'The parish clerk will soon know the culprit,' I warned him. 'The number of gentlemen loose in London stealing pump-handles is remarkably limited.'

'I don't give a fiddlestick's end for the clerk. The handle won't be replaced before the next meeting of the vestry, I warrant that. By then, the plague will be stayed.'

'But if it isn't?'

'Oh, well,' said Snow easily. 'We shan't be the first men of science since Galileo to be incarcerated because we were right.'

Arrived at Cadogan Place, I at once poured myself a gill or so of Madeira, offering the same to Snow with mention of its restorative qualities. His look of censure I thought ill-fitted a red-handed criminal.

31

THE CHOLERA WAS STAYED.

After two days, the Lord was taking a pinch of souls, where before He was taking a handful. After six, there was barely a death at all, and Snow declared these to have taken the contagion from others. When he returned their item of parish property to the assembled vestrymen the following week, he was received with acclaim. With panic not far from the streets, they would have been grateful if Snow had achieved the same effect by chopping off the clerk's head.

I wrote up our foray for *The People's Journal* as *The Adventure of the Broad Street Pump*. It struck at once the interest of the public, and the fee, with Snow's bounty, allowed me to postpone my removal from Cadogan Place. I followed it with an article on *London Smells*. Snow was an immense authority on smells. However obnoxious those which abounded in London, he held, they were as salubrious as the sweet-breathed zephyrs of spring. The word 'pestiferous' should never be applied to smells, however noisome, for they did not in themselves give rise to specific diseases. But this aroused the imagination of my public disappointingly.

In my story of the Broad Street pump I had put Lord Aubery's name clearly, as the landlord and therefore responsible for the area's sanitation. I was emboldened because nothing ill had befallen me, despite Lady Aubery's warning at the Royal Academy's Exhibition almost a year before. Perhaps his Lordship thought me too small a fish to net. Or perhaps, I decided in my more inflated moods, he was like many magnificos secretly afraid of a well-sharpened pen-nib.

These articles appeared towards the end of February. On the morning of Tuesday the 29th – it being a leap year – I was sitting at my fire when a light carriage clattered to the front door. I paid little attention, until I heard two pairs of feet ascending the stairs. My landlady opened my door on a huge fellow in scarlet livery, with a cocked hat under his arm, who pushed roughly past her.

'Mr Romilly?'

I looked up, startled, confessing my identity while the intruder eyed me as though come to take me for a soldier. 'Lord Aubery's compliments, sir. He requests your presence at eleven o'clock tomorrow morning.'

The man at once withdrew. There was no question of my saying aye or nay. I had been commanded.

As I heard the carriage rattle off, I determined to disregard the summons with contempt. No freeborn Englishman could be so ordered about. But as the day wore on, I grew qualmish. Should I not go, Lord Aubery might have me attacked and brought before him, for all I knew. And what had I to fear? A browbeating, which would break no bones. I remembered Voltaire facing up to the Chevalier de Rohan-Chabot, and felt quite pleased with myself.

But I had another appointment already fixed before his Lordship's. That evening I made for a handsome hotel, not long built, in one of the fashionable Mayfair streets between Park Lane and Bond Street. A letter had come the week before, addressed from Liverpool, stating that the sender would be passing through London on his way to take ship out East. Knowing that I had written for the Press about Dr Simpson and the use of chloroform, he had information of interest to impart. The letter was signed *David Waldie*, a name with no meaning to me, however hard I searched my mind.

From the look of the hotel, Mr Waldie would seem to suffer a weighty pocket, an affliction commonly caught in the East. In a hallway bright with gas, I asked the liveried porter in his cubbyhole for my host, whom I was to see at eight o'clock. I was directed to the coffee room, a magnificent apartment, which but a year or two back, before I had acquired the brazenness of a journalist, I would scarce have managed to enter. Its walls were covered with the finest French ornamental paper, its floor richly carpeted, the ceiling white with its cornice fresh-painted in gilt, a huge mirror on the chimney-piece. There was a party of six young gentlemen, in their hats and rather noisy. Also a few solitary diners, one of whom rose from a box by the fireplace on my entry.

'Mr Romilly?' He had a Scots voice.

'Your servant, sir.'

'Pray sit down ... good of you to come ... have you dined, sir?'

Waldie was a thick-set man in his mid-thirties, with a domed bald forehead and a strong black beard. Before him was set the remains of what appeared pigeon pie, and a rind of cheese. I nodded.

'We'll take a glass, then.' Summoning a waiter, he ordered a pint of claret and some biscuits. 'I've read with interest your articles about the new practice of anaesthesia. A very lively way you have with the pen, Mr Romilly.'

I thanked him for the compliment. 'Are you a medical man yourself, sir?'

'No ... that is, I am qualified as a surgeon, at Edinburgh. I am from Linlithgow. I was at the University with Dr Simpson, you know.' He paused, while the waiter poured our wine. 'But I find chemistry the more interesting pursuit.'

'It was the same with Dr Jackson, whom I knew in Boston.' But the name of the inventor of the electric telegraph, gun-cotton and etherization meant nothing to my companion.

'For a while now, I've held a post at the Apothecaries' Company of Liverpool. In the morning I sail for Calcutta, where I have new responsibilities. From your account in the newspapers, you were present the evening that Dr Simpson first experimented with chloroform?'

'I had that honour.'

'I should *not* have thought his own dinner table, in the bosom of his family, the perfect place for conducting experiments in natural science,' Waldie said sourly.

'The professor seemed to take a more human than scientific view of the occasion.'

'And how do you suppose Dr Simpson chose this particular drug – chloroform – to play his parlour games with?'

'It was but one of a variety we sniffed that night.'

'That is not entirely correct, Mr Romilly.' Waldie leant towards me, eyes glittering. 'It was *I* who suggested it to the professor. Did he not tell you as much? Well, I'm surprised,' he said ironically at my denial. 'Particularly as Dr Simpson knew you were going to write it all down for the newspapers. I learned of chloroform nine years ago, from America. I was the first to prepare it here in the pure state, using the United States Dispensatory as my guide. It became widely used by medical men in Liverpool, for afflictions of the chest. Now here's something else for you to write down for the newspapers, Mr Romilly.'

I assured him of my profound attention.

'In October last year – before your frolic at No 52 Queen Street – I was in Edinburgh, and met Dr Simpson at a meeting of the Medico–Chirurgical Society. He introduced the subject of etherization to me – in his easy way, you know – asking if I knew anything likely to answer as a substitute, as he didn't care much for sulphuric ether. I mentioned chloroform. I was well acquainted with its composition, and knew its volatility, its agreeable flavour, its medical qualities. Why, I strongly recommended it to him!' Waldie slapped the table, slopping his untouched glass of wine. 'More than that, I promised to send a purified sample from Liverpool. But I came home to find there had been a fire in my laboratory, which set such promises temporarily from my mind. So doubtless the sample you inhaled came from Duncan and Flockhart.'

'As I remember, yes.'

'Willingly do I acknowledge that the discovery was Dr Simpson's, and the honour his due,' he acceded, not in over-agreeable tones. 'All I looked for was a distinct and honest acknowledgement that I had recommended, or even suggested, to him to try chloroform.'

'But have you received no recognition at all?' I could not

believe so kindly and generous a Christian as Simpson might show such petty meanness.

'*A footnote.*' Waldie spat the word with contempt. 'A footnote to the pamphlet on chloroform which Dr Simpson published at the end of last year. A mere mention, that I had named chloroform as worthy of a trial. Such parsimony of acknowledgement has been considered by my friends as inadequate – nor is it altogether satisfactory to myself. His reputation cannot suffer by my getting credit for what I am justly entitled to.'

The chemist fell silent, gulping his wine and savouring his indignation. I was most uneasy. I wished to extract myself with no commitment to attack Simpson, for whom I had high regard. 'There is the danger the public might think you were simply picking a quarrel, for its own sake,' I warned him. 'Dr Simpson has been hailed as a great benefactor.'

Waldie made a dismissive gesture. 'Even the world's benefactors have their peccadilloes. Though I do not feel inclined to go a-begging for more credit than those concerned are willing to give spontaneously. A footnote!' he repeated. 'That device was well adapted – if not intended – to lead to my share of the matter being altogether lost sight of.'

His indignation had grown, rather than diminished, with the exercising of his spleen. I shortly made my excuses and left. I was sad, not for Waldie but for Simpson. The dour Liverpool chemist was a man of different stamp from Jackson – or from Wells or Morton, for that matter. I could believe his story, if I could also believe he inflated its significance. But I was sad because even so high-minded a man as Simpson showed a base human inclination to snatch the halo for his own head.

(Many years later, after Simpson's death, Waldie reiterated the complaint he made to me the night before he left to endure the rigours of an outward-bound Indiaman. In 1870 he published in Edinburgh his pamphlet, *The True Story of the Introduction of Chloroform into Anaesthetics.* Indeed John Snow had written earlier that Waldie *had a greater share in the introduction of chloroform than Dr Jackson had in the introduction of ether,* which

I, for one, took as damnably faint praise. Waldie died in Bengal, very rich. I believe they are to raise a plaque to their wronged son in his native Linlithgow, where they take such slights most seriously.)

As it occurred, I could not have puffed Waldie's claims in the newspapers at the time, even had I wished.

I presented myself at Aubery House the next morning as the clock on St James's Church was striking eleven. I was received by a pomaded page, passed to a powdered footman, led across the great chessboard of the hall, and delivered to a stouter and grander functionary, all wig and blue and crimson and gold lace, in his hand something like a beadle's staff. He preceded me up the staircase, very slowly. This was all to indicate that the presence of Lord Aubery was far too solemn an area to be entered with heedless pace.

At the top, we went through the open door of a light, airy anteroom, opposite the reception-room which had seen my humiliation just over a year previously. Sitting behind a desk was a thin young individual dressed severely in black, with long sidewhiskers and a disagreeable look for visitors.

'Mr Romilly, sir,' announced the servant, passing me on like a parcel through a succession of railway companies.

The secretary waved me to a sofa along the wall, and ignored me. He appeared feverishly busy with the papers on his desk, which were augmented or diminished by a succession of boyish messengers. An air of such arrogance is often assumed by the intimate hangers-on of men with a wide circle of friends or enemies, who must be regularly intimidated. The French clock on the elaborate marble mantelpiece struck half past the hour.

It was a quarter to noon before a bell tinkled, and a footman appeared to produce from an inner door a tall grey-bearded gentleman in expensive clothing, who the secretary saw obsequiously right down the staircase. He was clearly an item far too valuable to be trusted to the rough care of beadles. The young satrap returned briskly, and with a 'Mr Romilly' and a jerk of the head passed unstopping across the anteroom into Lord Aubery's study.

This was a large room which might have graced a French *chateau* of moderate grandeur. The *décor* at Aubery House had possibly been introduced by an ancestor who fancied to ape Louis XIV. Lord Aubery himself sat behind a huge desk of uncompromisingly English oak, in black satin waistcoat and black silk cravat, the high points of his collar directing attention to his beef-face and piggy eyes. The secretary withdrew, leaving me standing before the desk, from which position I received no invitation to ease myself.

'Well, Mr Romilly, you would smite me with the handle of the Broad Street pump.' There was no humour in this remark. Or if there was, it was impenetrably disguised behind his usual suspicious, arrogant, and baleful stare. 'You seem to enjoy a fine knack for riding a quill in a following wind. Mark me, this crotchet of etherization — narcotization, anaesthetization, or whatever you call it — will pass like any other airy whims and fads. Like the polka. Must we really believe Englishmen have become so puny they cannot even bear to have a tooth pulled, or a nail avulsed, without sniffing like dogs to obliterate their senses? No, sir. Men will come again to endure pain, as is their duty. Not to flee in its face like cowards.'

'I respect your Lordship's views. But dare I say they will be disproved, and even forgotten, by the time Halley's comet appears in the skies again?'

Lord Aubery took no notice of, nor appeared to hear, this remark.

'Cholera is caused by bad air. Everyone knows as much. That's all there is to it. Yet you impute that I am responsible for the present outbreak at Golden Square.'

'I did not, my Lord. I wrote that you were the landlord of the area afflicted. But if you think the cap fits, you are at liberty to wear it.'

'Don't be so impudent,' he exclaimed, so loudly I wondered if the secretary might appear in alarm. 'Who are you, sir? A nobody, a nothing. A half-Frenchie, whose dam bolted the stable. A cur who deserves a whipping, and who'd have got one a year or two back. Then I'd have been applauded for my trouble. Nowadays people prefer to use soft words for hard meanings, and suit tender actions to strong passions. But don't deceive yourself, Mr Romilly. I could still have the skin off your back one dark night, a few of your bones broken and your nose slit to the root. As easily as inviting you to dine.'

This threat was so vivid, and uttered with such malignancy, that the resolution to square up to the man began to bleed from me. I may have trembled. 'Our fine gentleman is brave only on paper, I think,' he sneered.

'I am afraid of no man,' I said, but falteringly.

'Oh, save your rhetoric to cool your porridge. I need not trouble myself to spill your blood in a London alley.' He continued to stare at me evilly. 'There's hempseed sown for you, my pup.'

This remark brought a singularly uncomfortable feeling round my neck. He tossed a piece of paper at me across the desk. I was startled to see my name on it, and picked it up wondering what letter my tormentor had found. My blood froze. Even feigning bravery was beyond me. It was the draft for £100 on Coutts's Bank, which Lady Aubery had endorsed over to me, and which had been signed first by the man glaring at me across the desk.

'Her Ladyship kindly consented to furnish my expenses to America,' I managed to get out.

Lord Aubery sat back, staring at me, pudgy fingers spread on satin waistcoat. 'A hundred pounds is a tidy sum.'

'It was a kindness of her Ladyship which I greatly appreciate. Of course, I shall repay it. This very day, if you wish.' I wondered how. Perhaps the generosity of Dr Snow must be exploited again.

'I signed this draft for her Ladyship on April 20, 1846, to cover some expense, the nature of which I forget. You stole it from her Ladyship's bureau, the afternoon you called, and forged her signature to an endorsement in your favour.'

I was so appalled by this stark lie that I could bring no word to my mouth in defence.

'Well may you pale and tremble.' Lord Aubery leant more comfortably in his round English chair of leather and horsehair. 'Forgery is a hideous crime, and punished accordingly. D'you know it's a hanging matter? And a dissecting matter, think of that. I could have you dancing the Tyburn jig if I cared to.'

'But I have forged nothing. I have done no wrong,' I burst out, seeing myself the centre of that sickening scene I had so often witnessed in Newgate.

'Why, guilt's written across your face, as plain as a poster on a brick wall. Where should you find a jury to believe you? You, a gentleman of the three outs – out of pocket, out of elbows and out of credit. You needed money badly at the time. You were living in mean circumstances, turning a penny where you could as a scribbler. Your father died, leaving you only debts. You had your crack to pay for.' I wondered miserably how he had come to learn even of Floy. 'My word against yours. Well? Whose would the jury take? You're not the first thoroughgoing rake who's risked his neck for his pleasures.'

'But Lady Aubery signed that draft. Not myself. I swear as much.'

He looked outraged. 'You suggest her Ladyship tells lies? To her husband? Lady Aubery informed me that the draft was stolen. At the time, my secretary made some inquiries, a servant was dismissed. Pray do not mention her Ladyship's name again, Mr Romilly.'

It was a vicious trap. Lady Aubery had given me the money partly through feelings of kinship, partly through some affection, and partly as a spirited gesture of independence. She knew the endorsed draft was too small a matter of domestic business to come before her husband's eyes. But when my name became notorious in the household, the secretary may have remembered it, and laid it as a fine trophy before his master. I doubted whether Lord Aubery had even taxed his wife with the document.

That it *was* a trap, and a transparent one, rallied my courage like the sailor's swig of rum before action. Lord Aubery's bloody threats, his offhand information that I was born to be hanged, had unbalanced me by the vigour of their utterance and by the power of the man himself. But seeing them afresh, as part and parcel of a false accusation, mounted by malice and impelled by a stroke of fortune, restored some of the resolve with which I had entered the room.

'I assure you that it is distasteful to me as to you, my Lord, mentioning Lady Aubery in a quarrel between ourselves. But there is always the possibility of a mistake having been made. Her Ladyship must have many such papers through her hands, in the management of so large an establishment.'

Or she may have told a falsehood, I reflected, when confronted with him, terrifying in his anger. She had to save her skin, if to imperil my neck. But even so mild a protest brought Lord Aubery's fist to the top of his desk. 'You will *not* mention Lady Aubery,' he repeated. 'I am satisfied that no mistake was made, none whatever.'

'Could not her Ladyship be invited to join us? Then my defence might be put to her directly.'

'What? You suggest I summon my wife to my presence, at your behest, like one of my servants?'

'I do not suggest it, my Lord.' I became somewhat startled at my own boldness. 'I demand it. A man who is accused of any crime, whether he committed it or not, is entitled to face the witness against him. This is the basic right of an Englishman. You cannot deny that. Nor would you deny it, if you are the gentleman the world takes you for. And that I take you for, too.'

The effect was gratifying. My red-faced adversary looked almost cowed. However unscrupulous Lord Aubery in achieving his various ends, he dare not appear anything but the bulky embodiment of all that was best in the British Constitution. And to give my tormenting devil his due, there was little pose in such conduct.

'This is not a court of law, sir,' he countered.

'It is worse. You have managed to encompass indictment, trial and sentence into a few minutes.' I was playing a hand of low cards, but the trick I had taken encouraged me to table another. 'If it comes to a court of law, you cannot then demand my silence over Lady Aubery's name. Even you must bow like everyone else to a judge who represents the Queen. I should produce the same defence from the dock as I do in this room. And tongues would wag, as surely as church bells on Sunday mornings.'

He growled. 'What do you mean?' To my elation I saw that he knew well enough. If I did not have the fellow on the run, at least I had fended him from my neck.

'You know the nation, my Lord, and I know the newspapers,' I returned quite cheerfully. 'Men in taverns and at street corners will gossip that I am better looking than yourself, which is admittedly a matter of opinion, and that I am younger than yourself, which is a matter of plain arithmetic. The world would imply an *affaire de coeur* between my humble self and her Ladyship.'

He made no reply. He was a politician far too experienced to become emotionally disturbed at the unexpected end of his course of action. Then he eyed me almost fondly – though as a cat its mouse. 'Well, you are a scoundrel. But I am pleased to see an intelligent scoundrel. You are learning fast. The hangman is an apt teacher.'

'If I have caused your Lordship distress,' I continued with a mixture of generosity and smugness he must have found most vexing, 'I shall be happy to make reasonable amends.'

'You may. Sign that.'

He threw another document at me. It was short. A confession of my guilt.

'But I *cannot*,' I protested, in even greater disarray. 'You cannot expect any man to put his name to a crime which he did not commit.'

'You are raising niceties. I accept that to have her Ladyship's name bandied about in court, is a game not worth your own existence. If you sign that, and repay the money, you shall eat your dinner tonight.'

'And if I don't?'

'You leave this house in the care of a pair of constables. You would not sing so chirpily in court, I think. But nor do I think you would take the risk of finding yourself on so dangerous a perch. Am I not right?'

So it was to be a compromise. Another estimable feature of British public life.

'But why should not that fate still overtake me?' I complained. 'My situation would be the worse in the dock, with a confession waved in the eyes of the jury.'

'You have my word for it it shall be the end of the matter.' I bowed my head in acknowledgment. When Lord Aubery gave his word there would be no slipperiness. 'If I have your word in return,' he added.

'My word for what?'

'That you shall write no more.'

'But words are my business, my only means of livelihood,' I cried.

'A sprig like yourself should shoot as well in any other bed. You do not strike me as a young man with a capacity for starving.'

'I will assuredly promise never to write again about your Lordship, or about cholera, or about etherization.' These words brought shame that they should come impulsively from one who used the same language as Wilkes, or Swift or Defoe. But even the first of these gentlemen never wrote under the threat of the rope.

'You shall write nothing. It is a compliment to your dexterity, that you might continue to poison the minds of others without daring to show your own face. Twist and turn as you like with a dozen *noms de plume*, but be assured I shall find you out in London. Perhaps you had best go back to America, and stay there. It is a more agreeable destination than Botany Bay. Come, Mr Romilly. You are in no position to quibble. And you have stolen too much of my time as it is. Sign, pray. The gentleman in the anteroom will witness.'

He rang the small handbell on his desk. The secretary appeared in an instant. I had a horrible decision before me. Had I not been wearied with the fight, and not still overawed by Lord Aubery's presence, I might have refused and strode from the house, risking that he dare not send the constables after me. The notion he instilled of my return to America was powerful. Personages like Lord Aubery were as rare as dinosaurs in that young land where all men were equal. In the end my surrender was a deed of impulse, and of an agonizing desire to breathe the fresh air of St James's Square. I confessed to a felony I did not commit.

'We shall leave your confession undated for the nonce, Mr Romilly. That may be added, to give it some immediacy, whenever I should choose to make use of the document. You may take the next twelvemonth over repaying the money.' Lord Aubery spoke easily, as the secretary busied himself with the seals. 'And if you go back to Boston, the duns cannot follow you there.'

'Your Lordship would banish me?'

'What colourful language you use.' His tone was mocking, almost amiable. 'Most young gentlemen of slight means would think the road to Plymouth one to riches rather than exile. You should know, as you have trod it once already at my expense. And the Yankees, being revolutionaries, have an appetite for your seditious stews. Pray remember that the sentiments which you addressed to Her Majesty's subjects were, but a few years back, a matter for the pillory, with your ears sliced off, and your cheeks warmed up with a red-hot iron. Good day, sir.'

Another minute and I was crossing the chessboard hall, feeling myself accursed I was ever concerned with the processes of relieving human suffering.

32

IT WAS SENTENCE of death. If a man is given by God the talent to write, to divert the hours, and sometimes the opinions, of others, to deprive him of its use is as cruel as Cornwall's gouging Gloucester's eyes, and as savage as Regan's taunt that the blinded man might smell his way to Dover.

I was just turned twenty-three, and my success over the past year had raised my opinion of myself as hot air raises a balloon. I see now – I saw then, within a year or two – that Lord Aubery's threat was more bombast than buckshot. And Lord Aubery knew as much, I am sure. I could have written under a dozen names, and a dozen editors would have relished ringing his nose when he came sniffing after my identity like a pig after truffles. But I was green in the world. Faced with Lord Aubery in his wrath and magnificence, my resolution was exposed as a *mirage*, the elusive water which deluded the French army marching through the deserts of Egypt.

I prided myself that his antagonism was personal, or that he was jealous of my shining in the eyes of his wife. But I was no more to him than the hundred pounds itself, a midge on an elephant's back. He was concerned only that I might debase the value of his property through my exposure of the cholera, and the value of his opinions through my espousal of etherization. I was a pestiferous and dangerous nuisance, to be eliminated. This disjunction of the passions became confirmed to me a little later.

I am not a writer like Shaw, who is inclined to think of the thunderous steam printing-press as his artillery. If my words helped to stave off human pain, and even death itself, they were written partly for the reward of money and fame. I think this is the same with many whose pen is beflagged with a Crusader's pennant. It is simply the proportion between coveted cash and coveted veneration which varies. I was prepared to let cholera and chloroform equally go hang. But Lord Aubery held a piece of signed paper, which might literally be fatal. And my only escape from the *oubliette* into which he had thrust me was to America. I think now that was the destination of the plot he had concocted against me. He wanted me only across a good stretch of salt water. He was a humaner man than he dared let me imagine.

But I did not relish returning to the rough life of New England after the civilized enjoyments of London. Besides, I had exiled myself before with the enticement not of fortune, but of Charlotte. And she was then doubtless over-providing Mr Tooms with those crowning delights of life which he had mentioned to me on his front doorstep at Hartford.

When I reached my rooms in Cadogan Place I was sick, violently, into the slop-bucket under my washstand. I took this as the physical effect of my mental torment. I staggered back to my front room, wiping my eyes, massaging my stomach against the cramps, wretched and sorry for myself. I had no appetite for a meal. I poured a glass of Madeira and took an Oliver from my biscuit-bag, but a mouthful of each sufficed. Then I noticed that my landlady had placed three letters from the morning post against the chimney glass. Two were addressed in Morton's hand, one postmarked *Boston Jan 27*, the other *Boston Feb 7*, their synchronous arrival the fault of the winter gales. The writing of the third was unknown to me, it being posted in London the day previously. Taking things tidily in order, I opened Morton's earlier letter first.

His pen had dipped even deeper in the well of pessimism. The Congressional Committee's invitation to the public at large, to submit their claims to discovering etherization, had the effect of Our Lord's invitation in the wilderness to the four thousand to eat. But the loaves and fishes of public honour could not be multiplied.

Yet another has taken the field against me, who I must see as a more serious antagonist, Morton wrote from Etherton Cottage. *A Dr Crawford Williamson Long, of Jefferson Ga., has submitted to the Committee a paper of which he (being by all accounts a decent and well respected gentleman) sent me a copy. He states that he excised two small tumours from the back of the neck of a Mr James M. Venable under the influence of ether, in the presence of four witnesses, and with the infliction of no pain whatsoever, on Wednesday, March 30, 1842. That is, the better part of five years before I administered ether for what, heretofore, I and the world accepted as the first surgical operation.*

Dr Long claims that he performed one or more surgical operations annually on patients in a state of etherization since '42 – the extirpation of small tumours, the amputation of fingers from a Negro boy, and the like. It at once entered my mind (and I trust it entered the collective mind of the Committee) that Dr Long's failure to publish his successful cases indicated that he had no confidence in sulphuric ether or its possibilities. When I wrote to him on this score, he replied honestly enough that he had to be absolutely sure of ether's effectiveness, and even more so of its safety, before proclaiming his method. For fear, should fatality occur, he should in such an area of the Union find himself lynched!

But now I hear, within the past week, that Dr Long wrote to a Dr G. L. McCleskey, formerly of Jefferson Ga. (who fortunately took the matter up with me directly) saying that a dentist travelled south from Boston to Jackson County, where Jefferson is situate, for several weeks in 1842, or 3, or 4. And that this dentist obtained knowledge of Dr Long's use of ether in surgical operations. And further, that this dentist was either Dr Wells or myself! That is a stark untruth, and smells of Dr Jackson. But it may cause argument and delay in Washington, of which I have had enough of both. I see no possibility or relief for my pocket or my pride before summer, when all Washington quits its dirty, choking, half-finished streets.

Morton ended by urging me to speed his case in Chancery. I knew no mortal could effect that, more than puffing into the sails of a windmill.

I looked up, as my landlady knocked. She asked why I had not rung for my meal. I managed to inform her, as delicately as possible, that I had the gripes. She agreed, with the sombre enthusiasm of her class, that indeed I looked quite peaked. I knew the victuals would not go to waste, between her and the servant girl and the cat. I reached for Morton's second letter, and as I turned it in my fingers a shaft of ice struck at my heart. The seal was of black wax.

I opened it hastily.

> *Tremont House Hotel*
> *Boston*
> *Mass.*
> *Wednesday, January 26, 1848.*

Mr Romilly, Dear Friend —

I write to tell of awful news. I have just heard from New York that Dr Wells is dead.

I had no information of him for several months, though I heard rumours that his health was poor, and none appeared to know the nature of his affliction. Today, all is too painfully clear. Last Friday evening, Dr Wells was arrested in Broadway for throwing vitriol into the face of a woman of the unfortunate class, who parade there. He had been in New York for some time, lodging in a poor district, and, it would seem, mixing with these depraved females. He gave the police officers a false name, but of course was soon unmasked, being a gentleman of apparent respectability, and he was incarcerated in the Tombs Prison.

That was tragic enough, but it now befalls me to write of worse. Overnight, between Saturday and Sunday last, poor Dr Wells took his life in his cell. He had there his razor, which he had been allowed to obtain from his lodgings in Chamber Street. With this instrument he cut his left thigh to the bone, severing the femoral artery, from which his life must have spurted quickly away.

There was beside the body an empty phial of chloroform. It now appears that this drug had been his constant companion for some weeks, and that it succeeded in these sly affections sulphuric ether. He had taken badly to the habit of 'sniffing', at any time of day and night, and would assuredly have been in a half-narcotized state when committing his outrage upon the Broadway street-walker.

How sad it is, that he who assisted to bring the world such relief of its suffering, should bring so much to himself! The Coroner's Jury recorded a verdict of suicide during mental aberration. Dr Wells left a short letter to his poor wife, which leaves no doubt that this verdict was the correct one. Morton ended characteristically, *And now I suppose the blame for my former partner's strange and painful death will be laid at my own door, like so much else.*

I stood shocked at Wells's death and at its manner, more befitting the end of some vicious criminal than such a gentle soul. But it confirmed what I had always suspected. That he was somewhat touched in the head. Without thinking, I opened my third letter, which was short.

> *The Garrick Club*
> *32, King Street,*
> *Covent Garden.*
> *Tuesday, February 29, 1848.*

G. Romilly, Esqr.
Dear Sir —
  Mr Maddox has passed me your novel. It is excellent. Please meet me here at 7 o'clock p.m. on Thursday next.
  I am, Sir, your faithful servant,
  Charles Dickens.

33

I NEED NOT describe the excitement which boiled inside me. As the small hand of my watch accomplished its next two sweeps of the face I could not eat, nor sleep more than skimpily, and I woke the next morning riven with headache. I had always scorned Dickens's works. It was curious how an hour or two served to convince me that such criticism was presumptive, misguided, ignoble and ignorant. He was the greatest writer on earth, and we Britons should be grateful to God for placing him among us.

The lustre of my summoner, and the electrifying prospects of his favours, drew me to Covent Garden a good half hour early that evening after receiving his letter. It was a muggy, misty, drizzly day, when it was never quite raining and never quite stopped, though I felt it chilly to the point of shivering. I had made acquaintance with Covent Garden during my weeks with the pastrycook, and now found the flickering gaslamps beatified by haloes from the indecisive moisture in the air, while the cobbles shone damp, like the stepping-stones of a brook in moonlight. I stood under my umbrella, dressed in my best, wondering how to kill time, and feeling severely weak at the knees.

There was little to divert me, the market at that time of the evening enjoying its daily hibernation. The granite Tuscan columns were deserted, their stalls shuttered, the flagstones accommodating only a prowling cat and scurrying rat, amid the rubbish of cabbage-stalks, squashed potatoes and trodden onions which made a permanent and noisome silt in the gutters. It was impossible to imagine its animation between five in the morning and noon, when merchants in tall hats and sober clothes were jostled by rough-dressed red-faced country-men from Barnet and Bromley, amid huge-handed women of rough complexion and rough tongue with their laden baskets of daffodils, porters with hard hats under trays like stout cheese-trenchers, a stately Peeler or two, crossing-sweepers with their reeking street-breakfasts, yapping dogs and restless horses, and the inevitable shrill ragged urchins. And every-where great bundles of carrots, beets, cabbages and turnips, in season tomatoes, cucumbers, asparagus and all refreshing furnishings of a gentleman's table, with sacks of potatoes, strings of onions, baskets of beans and bunches of sea-kale, like some extravagant and riotous Harvest Festival.

Becoming damp, I moved my shelter to the deep portico of St Paul's Church, Inigo Jones's 'handsomest barn in England'. I looked sadly at the muddied state of my feet, without a shoeblack in sight. As the church clock struck three-quarters, there rattled past the piazzas a coach, well-lit inside, with a glimpse of fine people making for the Covent Garden Theatre. I shivered again. I shortly left my arbour, and as I passed Evans's Supper Rooms on the corner of King Street a cart drawn by two pair of horses lumbered past, three men in smocks perched on top amid their round wicker baskets, the first of the night's farmers to arrive, and an illustration of the unending, regular performances in the theatre of life itself, which outlast any succession of players.

The Garrick Club seemed a snug tenement, with a double flight of steps from the street. I recalled that the building had previously been Probatt's Family Hotel. It was one of the clubs sprouting on the luxuriant London social pastures around the established oaks in St James's, founded in memory of the actor David Garrick, and patronized by mummers and *literati* of the better class. After some minutes' idling, I stepped boldly inside. The hall was small and gloomy, with a bust of Shakes-peare, staring at me I thought somewhat disagreeably. A clock somewhere struck seven. A tall, stout, square-faced gentleman in cutaway coat and grey worsted trousers, reading some long sheets of paper closely against the gas-lamp, pushed up a pair of small round glasses and exclaimed, 'Ah! The man from *Punch*. Here's my copy.'

'I . . . I am not the man from *Punch*, sir,' I protested, as he thrust the sheets under my nose.

'You're not?' He looked offended. 'Not from *Punch*?'

'No, sir. I have come at the invitation of Mr Charles Dickens.'

The person gave a loud grunt. Then he pulled down his glasses and continued his reading, ignoring me.

I looked round nervously. There was a porter's box, but no porter. The place had the smell of boiled mutton and ink. A padded-leather door flew open, emitting a functionary in bottle-green coat with brass buttons and a red-striped waistcoat, on his heels a page bearing a pair of volumes.

'Give the books to Mr Thackeray,' the porter directed the youth impatiently, nodding towards my companion. 'Sir?' he demanded of me, not over-politely. I repeated my business. 'Tom, the smoking-room,' he directed the page briefly. Another minute, and I was led into a smallish, square room, built over the leads upstairs, and the presence of the most adulated man of English letters.

Dickens looked craggier than I expected, though I knew him only from the painting by Daniel Maclise, reproduced in *Fraser's Magazine* and on a thousand fly-sheets since. That had depicted a Dickens only four years past my own age, smooth-faced, full-lipped and boyish, hair rich, gaze visionary but authoritative, fingers spread across blank writing-paper as imperiously as a royal seal, body sitting in a stunningly costly tapestry chair. But at thirty-six the hair was thinning and somewhat disarrayed, and hard lines round mouth and chin were relieved by a brief moustache and beard. He was rather fat. He was dressed tidily, without flamboyance, or even style. I noticed how small his feet were.

'Ah! Mr Romilly.' He appeared to burst from his chair rather than simply rise, seeming to contain the energy of a fast-spinning whizgig. He shook me by the hand warmly, speaking rapidly and vigorously. 'Good of you to come, very good. I hope not inconvenient? A man with a dozen appointments in Town forgets that a man with few may be sorely put out, fitting into his timetable. I assume you *have* only few appointments, with respect, Mr Romilly? At your age, a gentleman has the great pleasure of owning his own time. Sit down, sit down, we'll have some wine, some claret. Harker! Harker! Where are you? Ah, there . . . a pint of claret, Harker, if you please . . . and biscuits . . . sit down, Mr Romilly, sit down,' he repeated as I stood weathering the conversational waves breaking over me.

Dickens gave me the impression of such vitality, that his soul seemed to be marching on a red-hot treadmill. Certainly, I felt myself in the presence of one utterly exceptional to the general line of human goods. The influence of many authors on our lives is as subtle, distant and cold as of the stars. But Dickens blazed like the sun. He would have made a splendid character for himself. No wonder Thackeray disliked him.

He spoke affably enough, his eyes constantly roaming towards the comings and goings at the smoking-room door. I had already noticed my manuscript on a table at his elbow, my feelings those of a mother discovering her long-lost child, not with the gipsies, but in the family bosom of a rich nobleman. Harker brought the claret. Sitting back in that deep chair in that cosy room, I thought how pleasantly life was ordered in a gentleman's club. (The wildest thought did not enter my head that in a few years I, too, should be sending Harker for claret.)

'May I respectfully express my immense enjoyment of your work, sir,' I said over my glass.

'Kind . . . very kind . . .' replied Dickens, eyes still roaming. I supposed he was so accustomed to praise he accepted it with automatic courtesy, as if bid good-morning by a passer-by. 'I have recently been to Italy, Mr Romilly,' he continued. 'Have you been to Italy? They are an absurd but touchingly childlike people. There is heat, discomfort, flies, and nothing arrives in the mails from England.'

'I have travelled only to America, sir.'

'Ah, America! The slavery is horrifying. Where were you in the Union? North or South?'

'New England, sir, Boston.'

'Boston ... very beautifully situated, and the people so agreeable. Learned, well lettered and religious. In Boston stands the famous oak in which King Charles's charter was hidden.'

'Is not the Wadsworth oak to be found in Hartford, sir?'

I at once thought this remark unwise, but Dickens said, 'Indeed?' and dismissed the mislocation as insignificant between two professional purveyors of fiction like ourselves. 'Tell me about yourself,' he invited.

I gave something of my family circumstances, explaining that my mother had lived abroad for some years, for her health.

'Your schooling?'

'Rugby School, sir. My father was a strong admirer of the late Dr Arnold. Then I became a pensioner at Trinity Hall.'

'Oxford and Cambridge are the two most overrated habitations in the Kingdom,' Dickens said forcefully. 'I wouldn't give a brick of Harvard for both of them.'

I perceived from the outburst that these seats – indeed thrones – of learning regarded Dickens as but an upstart newspaper scribbler, decked out in hard covers and popular acclaim. Indeed, they do today. Dry-nosed dons sniff the taint of popularity like an old horse the knacker's yard.

'Your own book, my dear Romilly. It's most worthily done, most.'

I warmed internally, as though my stomach had received a tumblerful of brandy, neat.

'Though you seem more interested in machines than in people,' Dickens continued. 'In this mechanical age, that attitude could be an advantage. Readers seem concerned with everything new from steamships to Baker's patent mangle. Our modern life is being so swiftly changed by the hands of man ... hands which I pray to be directed by God. I am not interested in machinery in the slightest,' he confessed. I noticed how he was always nodding and moving restlessly in his chair, an indication of his bubbling inner vitality, like the jerking lid of a full boiling kettle. 'Well, you are no stranger to me, Mr Romilly. You have introduced yourself in the most revealing manner of all, with your pen. I have read, I think, everything you have had to tell us about the cholera.'

I made some remark, in a tone of crushed modesty, of my duty towards the sick poor, knowing my companion to be bursting with benevolence towards all fellow men with empty pockets, empty bellies and empty minds.

Dickens asked about Dr Snow, who I explained had a large ether practice.

'It seems quite to have displaced mesmerism,' the novelist reflected. 'I remember ten years ago I went to see mesmerism performed, by Dr Elliotson, the professor at University College. I was accompanied by Mr Cruickshank, the artist. We went into a ward among all the sick people, where the professor gave an exhibition. Most startling! There must have been two hundred persons present. Mesmerism was quite the talk of London in those days. The professor resigned his chair later, I recall. Puzzling, rather.' He had clashed with Liston. 'Did you know that he was the first medical man to grow a beard?'

With this odd information, Dickens drew out his watch. I saw our business must be cut short. He promised to send a note of recommendation to his old publishers, Chapman and Hall, with whom he had quarrelled but was now reconciled. Or to his new ones, Bradbury and Evans, with whom he was on good terms, but was about to quarrel. As I stammered my thanks he gulped his claret, rose, shook me ardently by the hand again, and said that he was pleased to help any young man who showed talent at the age when he himself had written *Pickwick Papers*, that Mr Maddox was the most valued of friends, and that he must be at the office of the *Daily News* directly. A carriage was already at the club door. I was left on the pavement clutching my bundle of manuscript. The horse was clattering off when Dickens pulled down the window and stuck his head out. 'You must rewrite Chapters 18 to 21,' he shouted, and disappeared round the corner towards the Strand.

I started to walk home, my feelings in disarray. The impact

of praise from such a writer as Dickens – and praise with such a practical application – was too powerful for my mind to absorb. I had the stunned feeling that, even should I not become overnight a literary somebody, I should at least cease to be a literary nobody. But there was Lord Aubery. He had silenced me as effectively as the Inquisition had silenced other voices, which they found awkward to hear. I wondered again how I could squirm out of my harsh and forced bargain. But whatever stratagem I devised, the one terrifying fact remained. Lord Aubery possessed a piece of paper which could send me to New South Wales, if not on the shorter journey to the Press Yard at Newgate, and which he could use whenever the whim took him.

I stopped in my tracks. My head was so spinning that I could barely keep my balance. Clutching tightly my precious bundle, I leant against a wall telling myself that the strength of claret served at the Garrick Club paid a compliment to the hardiness of the members. I noticed an old servant-woman in bonnet and shawl staring at me, clearly with the same impression about the cause of my condition. I said, 'I think I am a little ill. I have been out of sorts these last two days.'

She looked concerned. 'Where do you live, sir? Is it near by?'

'Cadogan Place . . . I'll find a hackney-coach.'

I looked round, feeling helpless and afraid. I was in Seven Dials, and a sitting hen for the footpads who roamed that murky area. The old woman volunteered kindly, 'I'll fetch you a coach, sir,' and in a minute or two I heard the welcome clip of hoof and ring of wheels from the end of the street. As she and the coachman helped me inside I rewarded her with a coin, which might have been a threepenny piece or a shilling, I could not bring myself to care. When I reached home I went upstairs and threw myself on my bed, without even lighting my candle, shaking like an aspen.

34

I WOKE TO hear the servant girl in my sitting-room next door, playing her morning *carillon* on the fire-bars as she laid the coals and blacked the grate. I was aware at once of some unpleasantness, like some shadowy hooded figure shaking me awake. I found my nightshirt was so wet with sweat, it might have been plucked directly from the copper. I was undeniably ill.

I lay dozing until a knock on the door of my bedroom announced it was eight o'clock, and the girl had brought up the hot water. I rose from my bed, a little unsteady as I drew the curtains to reveal another misty day, the bare trees in everyone's back garden glistening with moisture unshed by heaven. I took in the can, shaved and dressed. I couldn't eat my rolls and coffee. I sat in my easy chair by the newly-lit fire, with no appetite even for the morning paper.

I stared into nothingness, until ten strokes tinged from the clock on the mantel. My landlady appeared, immediately asking if I was quite well. She was a kind-hearted woman, as brisk as a summer bee, and always in an outfit of unrelieved black, though whether through economy, or choice, or her relations dying at regular intervals, I knew not. I said I suffered only from lassitude. She handed me a card, announcing I had a visitor downstairs.

I read without recognition, and without relish, *Michael Cudmore Furnell.* 'What's the gentleman look like?'

'He's a *young* gentleman, sir. Very respectable. His hat is well brushed.'

I thought I had best receive him, if only to send him

packing. He turned out a spindly fellow with a hawklike nose and close-set eyes, wearing a moustache in the springtime of its crop. He was dressed respectably in a dark cutaway jacket and plaid trousers. Standing but briefly to greet him, I indicated the chair opposite.

'I am a student of medicine, sir.' He eyed me solemnly.

'Well? And what's your business with me?'

'I was the first person in the world to try chloroform.'

Not another pretender! I returned snappishly, 'Sir, you talk nonsense. The world acknowledges that honour is due to Dr Simpson of Edinburgh.'

'No, sir. It was myself.' He looked appalled at what he had said. He must have steeled himself for weeks to lay his claim at my feet. 'May I give you my story, sir?' he asked hesitantly. 'Since '46, when I was seventeen, I have been studying for the examination of the Royal College of Surgeons, which I hope in due course to obtain, and enter the medical service of the Honourable East India Company. I wish to see as much of the world as possible.'

And to make as much money as possible, I reflected.

'I was attending a course of practical pharmacy under Mr Joseph Bell, when I read your account of the late Mr Liston's operation. I afterwards amused myself with inhaling sulphuric ether, until Mr Bell forbade it.' He hesitated. 'Flouting his authority, sir – which I beg you to overlook by reason of my youthfulness – I searched the laboratory for some substitute, and found in a dark storeroom a neglected bottle of chloroform. As it smelt pleasant, I tried it in an inhaler. It produced insensibility,' he ended simply.

'I assure you, sir, you will not make a brass farthing from *that* story,' I said shortly. 'The air of Washington is thick with kites flown by gentlemen with similar hopes to yourself. You took no steps whatever to make your discovery public.'

'But I *did*, sir,' he returned, with a look of innocence. 'I had chloroform used in St Bartholomew's Hospital last spring, a good six months before Dr Simpson. I took the bottle to Mr Holmes Coote, the demonstrator of anatomy at Bartholomew's. He was also etherizer to Mr William Lawrence –

President of the Royal College of Surgeons at that time,' my visitor added, with as much emphasis as he dared. 'On assurance that I had taken the chloroform without ill effect, it was given for Mr Lawrence to remove a cirrhus of the breast. And for several operations in private practice.'

He sat back, with an air of great relief at shedding his burden. I had grown interested in his narrative, expressed with such openness, and capable of confirmation by so eminent a surgeon. If this lowly medical student of eighteen summers had discovered the use of chloroform, and had it used in a great hospital in the City of London, it was a tale worthier than the chemist Waldie's. (It was a tale which came to be told. But not until the issue of the *Lancet* for June 30, 1877, when my youthful visitor was a surgeon in the Indian Army at Madras. By then, of course, nobody cared a fig's end *who* had invented chloroforming.) The tale was never told by myself, through what happened immediately next.

Perhaps I stood up. I never knew. I found myself stretched on the floor, my visitor leaning over me, looking more frightened than ever.

'Sir, you are not well,' he announced, somewhat obviously.

I raised my hand, my head seeming to contain one of Mr John Smith's trip-hammers.

'You must see a medical man, sir.'

'*Sal volatile* . . .' I murmured. 'From that corner cupboard.'

'I must presume, sir, the authority with which my profession will one day invest me,' said Furnell firmly. 'You are a sick man and must be treated. I shall summon a doctor.'

In truth, I was only too glad to accede to the suggestion. 'Then fetch Dr Snow from St George's Hospital . . . please take a carriage . . . some money is on the mantelpiece.'

I crawled back to bed. My landlady came busily with jellies, infusions, compresses, and ice-bags, if no ice. Snow arrived within the hour, as he entered unclipping from the interior of his tall hat his stethoscope, which resembled a hunting-horn. I resigned myself thankfully to his care.

The next two weeks were the most terrifying of my life. Early in my illness I staggered in bravado from my bed, only to see from my front window a man spreading straw across the street, and my landlady in the act of muffling the knocker with a fourpenny white kid glove. Then I knew I was sick nigh unto death.

I have, thanks to God, suffered no illness so severe in my fifty-two years since. I had not the strength to make notes, nor the inclination to log my daily passage towards the estuary of the Styx. Dr Snow was magnificent, both as physician and friend. He brought leeches that morning in a stone jar from the hospital's aquarium, and I recall watching them gorging themselves and dropping off my furnace-red skin. He bled me himself, not delivering me into the hands of the cupper, scarifying my flesh with his lancet. When I became weaker he performed on me 'dry' cupping. I leant forward on my bed, hugging my knees, as he laid out his set of small, domed cupping-glasses, from which he drove the air by igniting spirit, to draw hillocks of flesh on my back, and cause a lesser pain which eased the greater inside my chest. In the mornings I shivered, at night I sweated, death my only companion, and one never distant.

It appeared that I suffered congestion and inflammation of the lungs. The disease today would be termed pneumonia, and by some doctors ascribed to the pneumoniacoccus microbe, though it is still as perilous to men both very old and very young. I saw feverish visions, more frightening than any ghost from Shakespeare's gallery. I fancied Warren, or Simpson, or Morton were chatting to me, my replies alarming my landlady when in earshot. On the evening of Wednesday, March 15, I had a hallucination of Charlotte. I imagined she came in the room with my landlady, that she was standing at the foot of my bed, exactly as I remembered her from Hartford, perhaps prettier, in a dark dress and a shawl of distinctly American style. I fancied her to say in tear-choked tones, 'Guy . . . poor dear Guy . . . you are sick.'

I remarked to the landlady, 'I have had the sweetest of apparitions. I think I am managing to rally a little, and that Dr Snow will be pleased with me.'

'And you are here all alone!' The mirage continued, 'You

must let me come and look after you. I discovered your whereabouts only this morning, from Mr Lloyd, the editor.'

I remarked it was strange so airy a creature should have cognizance of so prosaic a figure as Edward Lloyd. 'But Guy!' cried the phantasmagoric shape. 'I am here. I am real.'

I still doubted my enfeebled senses. 'Then what business brings you to London?' I asked wonderingly.

'I have come back. Two days ago. To live with Mama.'

'But Mr Tooms . . .?'

'He is in Heaven.'

Charlotte looked instantly embarrassed, at referring to this transition in the company of one who might soon be undergoing the same. Producing a small lace-edged handkerchief, she reinforced her grief for me with a sob or two for her husband. For the first time, I found strength to raise my head from the pillow. 'But when did that . . . unhappy event occur?'

'On Christmas Day in 1846. Suddenly. It was the angina pectoris. My poor husband!'

I noticed that my landlady had silently withdrawn.

'I tried to find you in Boston. I was a widow in a foreign land,' Charlotte continued tearfully. 'I so wanted to see another English face. But you'd left the city. You could have been anywhere in the Union. I thought you'd gone looking for gold in California. I had to stay at home in Hartford, with so much of poor Mr Tooms's business to be settled.'

A matter occurred to me. 'And your children?'

'I have none.'

'Oh, I'm sorry. Mr Tooms's last words to me, that summer's day in Hartford, expressed a desire for a large family.'

She gave a half-sob, half-moan. 'Mr Tooms was . . . unable to.'

'Unable to?'

She nodded her head, tearing at the corner of her handkerchief with her lovely white teeth. 'Oh! I should never have said that. It was wrong of me, quite wicked . . . but you and I, Guy, were once on terms which allowed the passage of such intimacies.' She fell into a confused and blushful silence.

'You mean, he was unable to ... not even once?'

She nodded again. 'Not once. Though he tried quite hard. So I am ... a ... a ...'

'As good as new?' I supplied.

She burst into tears again, I doubted if from regret at her cold marriage-bed. She sat on my coverlet, and taking my hand declared, 'What a relief you're not married to some hussy! Now I can stay and nurse you back to health.'

I smiled. 'But even with a *sick* man, Charlotte, your Mama will not care for you to be unaccompanied in his sleeping quarters.'

'Fie to Mama!' she said spiritedly. 'I am a widow-lady, and I can do exactly as I please.'

She leant forward to kiss me solemnly on the forehead. The tears which dropped from her eyes on to my wasted cheeks were the best of physic. I gripped her hand as hard as my strength allowed. My brain, which had been put through the mangle of fever, was scarce able to accept all her news, or that she was in fact no ghost but warm and loving flesh. 'It is getting dark,' I warned her, 'and you have a long journey to Kew.'

'I have a carriage outside waiting.'

'You should have paid him off and taken another,' I chided. 'Such American habits seem extravagant over here.'

'Oh, it is my own carriage.' She looked a little offended. 'Mr Tooms was a wise man in real estate, and I am his sole beneficiary. Dear Guy! You do look so pale.'

The next day Charlotte arrived with a hamper of delicacies. I began to sit up, taking beef tea from her hands. Snow appeared as usual in the early evening, received her introduction in his usual grave manner, set about my chest briskly with his 'hunting horn' and pronounced me immeasurably improved. The congestion was resolved, and the cough which raked my wasted frame but an evacuation of the *débris* in my lungs. He warned me – his glance at Charlotte graver still – that I must not on any account overstrain myself, that my convalescence must be long and where the air was not too stimulating. Bath rather than Brighton, and anyway sea-bathing was strictly contraindicated.

When Snow left, I bade Charlotte fetch my manuscript, and she sat on my bed reading it aloud. What bliss for the author! I was recovering from my physical derangement, but entering the more common one whereby a man sees a woman as a goddess.

But there was still Lord Aubery.

The following day I told Charlotte of the dreadful piece of paper. Like any woman, she was inclined to make light of it, to say he would never put his threat to the test, that he was a blusterer, and that he should anyway be roped to a gun-barrel and shot through. When Snow arrived we were still discussing my plight, and for the first time I acquainted him with it. There had seemed little point before, exhausting myself by explaining the possibility of my dying on the scaffold when there seemed the more immediate one of my dying in bed.

'That terrible man,' said Snow glumly. 'He fills his ennobled body with the prejudices and fears of the common people. That's the cheapest price of popularity, with the multitude not accustomed to think for themselves. If Lord Aubery appears to be moved by their own qualms, and by their own hates, how delighted they are when he bellows in his own loud voice those insults they would never dare utter themselves.'

But he clipped his stethoscope back in his hat, bidding me to take heart. He might be able to achieve something on my behalf. His kindness warmed me, though I doubted that even so respected a practitioner as he could perform anything in those remote regions where Lord Aubery gyrated like a star of ill-omen. He said he would call to sound my chest at the same hour on the morrow, and left us. It was that evening when Charlotte agreed to become my wife. Her only doubts – with sobs which were only perfunctory – were on the propriety of marrying barely a year after her husband's funeral. I suggested that Mr Tooms being an American, in some way it didn't count.

The next day was Saturday, March 18. Charlotte had ridden out to Epsom, where the Reverend and Mrs Conybeare were staying with friends, to acquaint them with our joyous news. There was no question of my asking her father's permission, she repeated. She was perfectly independent, and could have married a chimney-sweep, or Dr Snow, had she cared. I suggested that from politeness I should present myself to him, just as soon as my legs could carry me there. That evening, Snow was late. I was up, sitting by my fire, tucked into my tartan rug, sipping the hot negus brought by my landlady. The clock on the mantel advanced past ten. I was drowsy, and would have made for bed. At half past came a thunderous crack on my door, which flew open to admit Snow, grinning like a Barbary ape and immediately hurling his hat on to the sofa.

'Where have you been?' I asked, almost startled from my tartan cocoon at so uncharacteristic behaviour.

'Buckingham Palace.'

He sat down opposite, leaning forward, hands clutching knees in his familiar way, but eyes gleaming twice as bright. 'My dear Romilly, within the past hour Her Majesty has been delivered of a princess. Tomorrow the guns will be thundering in Hyde Park.'

I still did not grasp the implications of his news.

He grinned the wider. 'Her Majesty was a model patient.'

'*Your* patient . . .?'

He nodded. 'Her Majesty took chloroform when her labour had reached the stage of the grinding pains. The inhalation lasted fifty-three minutes. It was administered on a handkerchief, in fifteen-minim doses. The Queen asked no questions and breathed as directed. She expressed herself as greatly relieved by the administration.' He lay back, folding his hands across his broadcloth waistcoat with an air of overwhelming satisfaction. 'Who dare *now* speak against chloroform, against anaesthesia? What British subject – *however noble* – dare proscribe a method wisely chosen by his Queen? However subtle his knowledge of the Scriptures, what cleric dare contradict the very Defender of the Faith? The big-

300

bellied scholars of Cambridge can hardly deride a process which their own Chancellor the Prince so obviously approves.'

Snow chuckled. For one moment, I thought him in danger of throwing his heels in the air. '*Chloroform à la reine*,' he continued, hardly hearing the congratulations which were as effusive as my strength allowed. 'By Monday morning, every lady in London will know of it, and every mother in childbed will be asking for it. Romilly, have you some Madeira?'

I looked startled. 'Yes, in the cupboard.'

'I declare, I shall indulge in a glass of wine.'

He fetched my decanter and two glasses. Both were raised. 'To Dr Snow, and to chloroform,' I said.

He took the faintest sip. 'No,' he announced, in his usual serious voice. 'All my life, I have wondered whether I should like wine, if I tasted it. Now I find that I don't.'

He set down his glass, and ignored it.

'It was the Prince who directed Dr Clark to send for my services,' Snow revealed. 'His hand is behind much in this Kingdom of which we learn nothing. His Royal Highness received me with great kindness, and spoke most intelligently on the scientific points of the process. He is acquainted with your work, Romilly, on etherization and on the cholera.'

I bowed my head in recognition of the honour. Then I recalled the deaths under chloroform, which had given such encouragement to its opponents. 'Knowing the dangers as you do, you still gave the drug to the Queen?' I asked seriously.

'Why not? I should have given it in childbed to a servant girl, should I not? It is the best drug we have for the purpose.'

'You are a man of great courage.'

'On the contrary, Her Majesty was the one of courage. For myself, Romilly, I may be a total abstainer, but I am a dangerous gambler. Now my enthusiasm has run away with my duty,' he continued, shaking his head. 'Pray keep silent on my news about chloroform, until an announcement from the Palace. There are a few ruffled feathers at court, some of them medical ones. But I have performed one service already for the young princess. I understand that she is to be christened

Louise Caroline Alberta. Until I dissuaded him, the Prince in his enthusiasm was all for naming her "Anaesthesia".'

The bells of the Abbey crashed out. Within minutes their distant chime was taken up like fire by every steeple and belfry in the capital. I even had the wild fancy I caught the joyful thunder rolling from St Paul's. Snow became solemn again. 'Those chimes celebrate the birth of anaesthesia, Romilly,' he said as dourly as ever. 'Which shall never die.'

The next morning, a messenger arrived from Aubery House bearing an envelope containing my signed confession. Attached was a note which said,

Mr Romilly, Sir—

When the Prince commands, loyal subjects must obey. Never accept money from married ladies. When you grow out of such follies, a clever little devil like yourself, with your obnoxious talent for ingratiating yourself with your elders and betters, could be of use to me.

Aubery.

35

MARY KINGSLEY IS dead. I had the news this very midsummer morning as I sit, my book near finished, looking from the study window across my garden in Putney. She died on June 3, 1900, of the enteric fever, contracted while working selflessly as a nurse among the sick Boer prisoners at Simon's Town Palace Hospital. She was buried at sea, as her long expressed wish. She was afforded Naval Honours, as her due. She was thirty-eight.

Mary Kingsley died for her ideals, in this war which is worse than pernicious. It is stupid. For Britain to become sucked into the Irish bog was folly enough. To seek being choked by the dust of the *veldt* was an act of rabid lunacy.

But I must attend my work, as always in my long life of writing, whatever passions blow round my brain like the winter gales rattling the tiles. It is to be read by a young doctor I have invited for lunch this Sunday, Dr William Maugham from St Thomas's Hospital, who is well connected, has literary pretensions himself, and is already the proud author of a 'modern' novel.

The medical men who keep company in these pages now sleep in Heaven. Morton's end was barely less stark than Wells's. After twenty years of struggle to be recognized and rewarded as the prime benefactor of the world, after addressing countless sessions of successive Congressional Committees, after initiating countless law suits, penning countless pamphlets, and spending countless dollars, he found his farm in West Needham, Massachusetts – 'Etherton Cottage' – seized by his creditors, his stock and chattels sold, and himself with

neither roof, nor occupation, nor friends. He provoked a book
– *Trials of a Public Benefactor* – but the public were by then
even more bored with his squabbles than with the long-drawn
impeachment proceedings against President Andrew Johnson.

In that summer of 1868, the infernal Dr Charles Jackson
bedevilled Morton with a pamphlet again claiming etherization as his own discovery. Morton decided he must vindicate
himself with a suit for libel. He travelled for this purpose to
New York on July 15, where he drove on an evening of
stifling heat across Central Park, was taken with an apoplectic
seizure, and died in the open air in the arms of a wife whose
devotion and duty towards him was angelic. Morton had lived
forty-eight years. And in truth, I believe that as a youth
myself in Boston I saw the happiest months of them. As for
Dr Jackson, my suspicions of his mental equilibrium were too
sadly correct. By 1873 he was unequivocally insane, and in
1880 he died mad in a home for madmen.

James Young Simpson passed on in 1870, a baronet. He
lies beneath the rainy breezes from the Firth of Forth, his
widow refusing burial in Westminster Abbey (even with all
expenses paid). On the morning of June 9, 1858, dear, good,
abstemious John Snow was at work finishing his second book,
On Chloroform and Other Anaesthetics, had just written the word
exit, was taken with a paralysis, and on June 17, at 3 o'clock
in the afternoon, he slept the euthanasia.

Nowadays ether is given everywhere. Horace Wells's
nitrous oxide gas is back in favour. And Simpson's chloroform,
of which the student Joseph Clover grew to be the skilful
exponent, lies under a pall of suspicion. It may be the usual
drug to which we are submitted for a surgical operation of
any consequence, yet we know its sweet and subtle vapour can
bring death suddenly and inexplicably, from but a whiff or
two, even to the young and vigorous. I have had sad experience
of this. A young lady who was to marry my grandson Thomas
– himself a doctor – was to have a small external tumour
removed by no less experienced an operator than Frederick
Treves, Surgeon-Extraordinary to Her Majesty. The care
enjoyed by the patient could not have been better in the

Empire. Yet within a minute of the inhalation of the chloroform, she was dead. It was my lot to inform my grandson.

Despite such tragedies, life with no anaesthetics at all is as unthinkable today as walking on the moon. We still cannot say how these strange things work. And we still cannot say who wears the crown of their invention. We can only distribute lesser coronets thankfully among the claimants.

I would not play anatomist to dead controversies, particularly those inclined to stink. Though in truth, I should say the 'onlie begetter' was the man dead with his blood covering the floor of his cell in the Toombs, Horace Wells. Both he and Morton admittedly wanted to make money rather than benefit humanity. But man's highest achievements not uncommonly spring from his basest motives.

Charles Maddox painted my portrait, which hangs in the room where I write. And Floy married a farmer in Dorset. After publication of *The Water Gate* and my marriage to Charlotte I turned my interest towards the wider shores of science, which now wondrously stretch into the distance, the mists of ignorance having cleared away during my own lifetime. I am a gossip more than a historian, and a lightweight of a novelist, I know. But my experience of scientific matters warrants my trumpeting a hopeful note in my old age.

Anaesthesia was the first great scientific advance made in my life. Now these press so closely into the pages of the newspapers that we scarce notice them. But I am convinced that man has at last mastered his environment. And he has mastered the hardest science of all, of living in peace with his fellows, within his own country's borders and without.

Our lunacy in South Africa is so obvious, it must soon shake itself into sanity. Our neighbours in Europe, every year more prosperous and contented, all see the folly of breaking that peace which God gave our glorious Empire the duty of imposing throughout the world. The twentieth century, into which I have ventured, will be one of unparalleled health and happiness for all mankind.

A Pelican Book

AWAKENINGS

OLIVER W. SACKS

Awarded the Hawthornden Prize for 1974

'Have read *Awakenings* and think it a masterpiece' –
W. H. Auden

Between 1916 and 1927 a bizarre disease – sleepy sickness – spread throughout the world, taking or ravaging the lives of nearly five million people. A third died in states of unshakable coma or sleeplessness. Many of those who survived were left as living statues – totally motionless for hours, days, weeks or decades.

Fifty years later, in 1969, it was discovered that the drug L-DOPA had a dramatic effect on these patients – many experienced a sudden 'awakening', moving from frozen standstill or tormented agitation to a zenith of intense well-being and harmony rarely experienced by normal people. Their awakening did not last more than a few weeks or months, but through this experience many patients were able to come to terms with their catastrophe, and gain a deeper understanding of their situation.

The main body of this book tells the stories of twenty patients with whom the author worked for seven years. The account of their 'sleep' and 'awakening' is intensely moving.

'Dr Sacks writes beautifully and with exceptional subtlety and penetration into both the state of mind of his patients and the nature of illness in general . . . compulsively readable . . . a brilliant and humane book' – A. Alvarez

A Peregrine Book

PATTERNS IN NATURE

PETER S. STEVENS

In a stunning synthesis of art and science, Peter Stevens explains the universal patterns in which nature expresses herself. He provides a fresh way of viewing and understanding the physical world.

'When we see how the branching of trees resembles the branching of arteries and the branching of rivers, how crystal grains look like soap bubbles and the plates of a tortoise's shell, how the fiddleheads of ferns, stellar galaxies, and water emptying from the bathtub spiral in a similar manner, then we cannot help but wonder why nature uses only a few kindred forms in so many contexts . . . It turns out that those patterns and forms are peculiarly restricted, that the immense variety that nature creates emerges from the working and reworking of only a few formal themes.'

With his elegant and lucid prose, illuminated by hundreds of photographs and geometrical drawings, the author examines those themes and explains how they evolve according to the laws of stress, flow, turbulence, least effort, surface tension, close packing, and, most important, the constraints of three-dimensional space.

A Peregrine Book

A MODERN HERBAL

MRS M. GRIEVE

'At last a complete herbal, encyclopaedic in form and matter. The botany is good, the recipes good, and the plates pleasing and numerous' – *Observer*

Coltsfoot for coughs, speedwell for skin disease, foxglove for heart trouble: the lore of herbs stretches back for hundreds of years to the days of village 'cunning men' who prescribed their herbal cures with the aid of spells and incantations. Although botanists and chemists made enormous strides in increasing our store of knowledge about plants, herbalists still relied on seventeenth-century herbals to practice their trade until this book was published in 1931.

A Modern Herbal brings our knowledge of herbs up to date, drawing together both scientific and traditional information in a comprehensive encyclopaedia. It describes, in alphabetical order, over one thousand British and American plants, giving details of their cultivation, of their chemical and medicinal properties, and appearance, as well as of their significance in folklore.

'This is a work of real learning and scholarship' – *Listener*

THE BIRD OF NIGHT

SUSAN HILL

Francis Croft, the greatest poet of his age, was mad. His world was a nightmare of internal furies and haunting poetic vision. Harvey Lawson watched and protected him until his final suicide. From his solitary old age Harvey writes this brief account of their twenty years together and then burns all the papers to shut out an inquisitive world.

The tautness and control that characterize Susan Hill's work are abundantly evident in *The Bird of Night* as she magnificently handles the heights and depths, the splendours and miseries of madness and friendship.

Also published in Penguins:

THE ALBATROSS AND OTHER STORIES
A BIT OF SINGING AND DANCING
I'M THE KING OF THE CASTLE
STRANGE MEETING
IN THE SPRINGTIME OF THE YEAR

THE SIEGE OF KRISHNAPUR

J. G. FARRELL

'A new novelist arrives, bursting with vitality, to show us just how superb an explosion of original literary talent can be' – Eric Ambler

In the Spring of 1857, life for the British at Krishnapur. conscious of the benefits civilization has brought to India, confident of the March of Progress embodied in the Great Exhibition, is orderly and genteel. Only Mr Hopkins, the Collector, senses danger.

Then the mutiny, violent and bloody, comes to Krishnapur; the British community retreats into the Residency to fight for its life; and for the first time, European civilization confronts the world it thinks it rules.

'What a book. It has everything you could expect to find in a big old-fashioned novel or several of them – characters, suspense, military action, romantic attachments, satire, wit, tenderness, philosophy. In my family, nobody, from the age of eighteen to over sixty, could put it down' – Mary McCarthy

Winner of the Booker Prize 1973.

Also published in Penguins:

TROUBLES

DOCTOR IN CLOVER

RICHARD GORDON

'You may be surprised to hear,' I announced to my cousin, Mr Miles Grimsdyke, FRCS, 'that I've decided to do the decent thing and settle down in general practice.'

Unlikely, you might surmise, knowing Dr Gaston Grimsdyke as you do. And you'd be right. Despite heroic efforts to maintain at least an outward appearance of respectability in the fog of Porterhampton, under the gaze of the kindly Dr and Mrs Wattle, Grimsdyke gets out, to engage in a series of adventures which lead him from the rural bliss of Little Wotton to the fleshpots of Monte Carlo, and even Brazil. His is the human story of a man who, pursued by busty maidens and regretted by his cousin, achieves fame and fortune as a best-selling author.

As Sir Lancelot Spratt once remarked, 'Nothing is quite so dangerous as the dedicated man.' No possibility of that sort of trouble here.

Also published in Penguins.

DOCTOR AND SON	DOCTOR AT LARGE
DOCTOR AT SEA	DOCTOR IN LOVE
DOCTOR IN THE HOUSE	DOCTOR IN THE NUDE
DOCTOR IN THE SWIM	DOCTOR ON THE BOIL
DOCTOR ON THE BRAIN	DOCTOR ON TOAST